THE

THE

TYPEWRITER

Girl

ALISON ATLEE

GALLERY BOOKS

New York   London   Toronto   Sydney   New Delhi

G

Gallery Books
A Division of Simon & Schuster, Inc.
1230 Avenue of the Americas
New York, NY 10020

First Gallery Books trade paperback edition January 2013

GALLERY BOOKS and colophon are registered trademarks of Simon & Schuster, Inc.

For information about special discounts for bulk purchases, please contact Simon & Schuster Special Sales at 1-866-506-1949 or *business@simonandschuster.com*.

The Simon & Schuster Speakers Bureau can bring authors to your live event. For more information or to book an event contact the Simon & Schuster Speakers Bureau at 1-866-248-3049 or visit our website at *www.simonspeakers.com*.

Designed by Jaime Putorti

Library of Congress Cataloging-in-Publication Data
Atlee, Alison.
 The typewriter girl / Alison Atlee.—1st Gallery Books trade paperback ed.
 p. cm.
1. Young women—England—London—Fiction. 2. London (England)—History—19th century—Fiction. I. Title.
 PS3601.T545T97 2012
 813'.6—dc23
 2012007883

ISBN 978–1–4516–7325–8
ISBN 978–1–4516–7327–2 (ebook)

Manufactured in the United States of America

10 9 8 7 6 5 4 3 2 1

For my family

It is very important that you should learn the key-board
so thoroughly that you can see it with your eyes shut,
and can strike each letter without the least hesitation.
—Mrs. Arthur J. Barnes, *How to Become Expert in Type-writing*

*T*ype-writer girls, they oughtn't think too much.

Betsey knew it was so. She understood the detached and nimble attention required for speed and accuracy; she had learned to sustain such attention for pages and pages at a time. When it faltered, she was able to remind herself: *Concentration, not contemplation.* The words in her mind had the patted-down accent of Miss Slott of the London Working Women's Training Institute.

Miss Slott had been imported from America, just like the Remington Standards her students used in their lessons, and as she chanted over the violent clatter of the typing machines, she might touch her pointing stick to your back, just beneath your shoulder blades, or slip it under your wrists to lift them. Posture worked toward efficiency, just as it did toward attractiveness, another important detail. Miss Slott had ever advised each pupil to consider how she must be like a beautifully made clock, not only functional and constant but also a complement to the sur-roundings—pleasing to the eye, should the eye happen to notice more than the hour.

Betsey understood. She had mastered it all, and she was fast. Fast and accurate, more so than most of the type-writer girls at Baumston & Smythe, Insurers, where she worked now. She'd had to be: Word had gone round not long after her hire at the insurance firm that Betsey Dobson had not finished her course at the Institute. Betsey Dobson had been *dismissed*. Not even a fortnight from the finish, and with no character given her! But truly, what could be done? What sort of character could be written for a girl who'd had a love affair with one of the *instructors*? That was the word that went round.

So she'd had to be good. Impeccable posture. Efficient, accurate.

Truth be told, that affair with Avery Nash had helped her improve at least as much as Miss Slott's instruction, for Avery owned a type-writing machine. He was something vain of this treasure, but certain favors could persuade him to let her practice upon it—half-strikes, to save ribbon.

That she dragged the thing out to the stairwell on a blanket each night she spent in his flat, he never knew. A fuck made him a sound sleeper, and she always brought her own paper.

And while typing in a stairwell wasn't conducive to good posture, those middle-of-the-night drills had served her well otherwise. Except for the expulsion, of course. And the gossip.

Concentration, not contemplation. It was a good motto, and not just for type-writer girls. It could save you from brooding over stale if mostly true gossip.

Or suppose you needed to pull some dodgy deed, right in the open—why, then the advice was wise indeed, for in such a case, you had no business contemplating the shoulds or shouldn'ts, the dodginess of the deed. Such self-consciousness could only draw attention. There was room only for concentration in such a case: Mind your posture. Pay attention. Be efficient. Do the deed.

Dear Mr. Jones,

An image of him flickered in her mind longer than it took to type his name. Mr. Jones, her hero, if he didn't turn out mad, or a liar—

Regarding the character of one Miss Elisabeth Dobson, we at the firm of Baumston & Smythe, Insurers have found her a skilled and valued employee these eight months past.

It might have been tricky, but she had prepared. Avery's type-writing machine was long gone (a card game, just the way he'd come to possess it), but he had helped with the wording of the letter and laughingly encouraged her whenever her conscience had bristled. Three evenings she'd spent with her fingers poised over imaginary keys, committing the words and motions to memory. Now, she pasted her eyes to a fire policy and did not pause once to lift the carriage to check her work. It was finished in moments. She folded the letter without looking at it and slipped it inside her black type-writer's smock, into the waistband of her skirt, doing her best to make the movement appear as no more than a simple shift in weight.

Load more paper. Glance at the dais at the front of the office.

Mr. Wofford was not there.

Hell. And hell twice more, for Mr. Wofford, the least junior of the junior clerks in this office, was nowhere within her range of vision. Had he gone out altogether? Betsey dared not lift her eyes from her work again, not until the bell for the afternoon rest period rang.

The din of hammering words eased away. The words came in shushes now, the type-writer girls softly continuing conversations they'd suspended at the end of the lunch period.

Betsey risked a half-turn toward the three tiers of desks behind her, where the junior clerks perched on their stools. They were not permitted to take their breaks alongside the women, but that did not keep them from pausing in their work to watch the typewriter girls exit. *Finest part of the day,* Betsey had heard them jest more than once. Only Avery, a junior clerk for far briefer a time than he had been a composition instructor at a working women's college, seemed determined not to be distracted. The smart thing, of course. The two of them acted as strangers here in the office, and though Cora Lester had whispered her knowledge of Miss Dobson's expulsion, when she asked Avery to speculate as to which of his fellow teachers had been *in league* with her, Avery obliged, noting how suddenly the elocution tutor had departed. *Oh, but Mr. Hadfield went with the Baptists to the West Indies,* Miss Lester had protested, but it took only a shrug from Avery to make her breath catch and her eyes light. The elocution tutor! No wonder Miss Dobson was so well-spoken!

The smart thing. Betsey might have wished Avery had told Cora Lester to mind her own business, just as she wished now he would meet her eye and give her a fortifying nod, but such wishes were foolish, so she didn't permit her gaze to rest, and made certain it avoided James Chesney, who'd taken to leering at her since Cora Lester had done her whispering. Well, he was not the only one, and not even the boldest. No, that distinction belonged to Mr. Wofford.

Who, she saw now with a swoop in her belly, stood waiting near the wall of coat pegs. Waiting for her, plain enough, waiting at her peg, the one labeled with her name, adorned with her tweed jacket, though whether he'd noticed her, or only wished her to notice him, she couldn't tell.

She'd dodge him, she decided. She would stick herself to the far side of Maude Rudwicke's little group and duck out with them. Laugh at her own absentmindedness when they pointed out she had left the office still in her smock.

But ducking out wasn't easy. Betsey was taller than Maude Rudwicke and every other girl in the office; she was taller than Mr. Wofford himself, though she hardly felt so as he intercepted her at the door and said, "I'll have it, Miss Dobson."

She stared for a moment at his hand outstretched, the squared-off tips of his fingers, bulging pinkly in comparison to the pale line of skin peeking out from his shirt cuff. The bustle around them ceased, the girls suddenly uninterested in taking their break.

Mr. Wofford's two middle fingers twitched, beckoned.

"It is personal, sir, if you please." Useless, her low tone in this tight knot of girls. Mr. Wofford seemed to have no intention of bidding the girls on through the door, nor of prompting the clerks to put their heads back over their work.

No, when she looked up, he was trying not to smile too broadly, as successful at that as he was at growing a beard. She judged the scraggly blond mess had another ten days before he gave up again and shaved. He was young, Mr. Wofford. Old for a junior clerk, true—three junior clerks had been passed ahead of him since Betsey's hire—but still young, and anxious about this condition.

"I cannot see how that's possible," he said. Only his bottom teeth showed when he spoke. "What you have folded away there came straight from a Baumston and Smythe machine."

"Begging your pardon, Mr. Wofford, are you certain?"

"Miss Dobson."

A whisper wormed its way through the knot: *What's she done? Hush,* came the answer, for no one wished to miss a thing by taking time to explain. Plenty of time later to poke it over, plenty of lunches, plenty of breaks, plenty of arm-in-arm walks to the omnibus.

Mr. Wofford's fingers twitched again.

A moment.

Betsey set the letter on his pink fingertips.

After he finished reading the first few lines (aloud, of course), the attentive silence in the office remained. Mr. Wofford asked, "You've composed your own character, Miss Dobson?" and then he got the stir of shock he wanted, slight exchanges of glances, the softest of gasps here and there. Her first months with the firm, she had imagined him shy. But the gossip about her had emboldened him, somehow released him, just as an eager audience did now.

"Efficient, I grant you," he said, "but not likely to be very objective, is it?"

"There's nothing untrue in it."

"Oh? But so often, the deceit is in the omission, is it not?" He looked down at the paper again but, thankfully, read to himself now. "And such is the case here, I see—you've neglected the key portion of the typical character letter, that being the *character*. Though I do suppose that's implicit, considering the blatant fraud of the younger Mr. Smythe's name appearing at the bottom of this letter. As though he himself had dictated it and intended to put his signature upon it."

Another ripple of movement. The younger Mr. Smythe was abroad for the next three months, everyone knew it.

"And look." Mr. Wofford held out the letter. "The paper. The ink and machinery. The very *time* taken to produce this forgery. More dishonesty. Thieving, really. That would be the more precise term, would it not? Theft?"

Theft and forgery. Betsey kept a steady eye on Mr. Wofford but realized with a fresh grip of fear the man could make a lot of trouble for her. He could do more than merely utterly humiliate her, more than get her dismissed on the spot. For those things, she'd tried to prepare herself, though really, she'd believed she could carry this off.

She tried to calculate: What fraction of her weekly wage of eight shillings had she stolen in the five minutes it took to type that letter? How much ink diverted from company business to those few sentences telling her skills and experience? As for the paper— naturally, she'd bought her own.

That added together, plus forgery—no, only *intended* forgery, that was the most Wofford could claim with an unsigned letter—was it enough to interest the law? She didn't know. Certainly Baumston & Smythe was no Covent Garden coster complaining about a filched apple. And there was Richard to consider, toiling in an office on a floor below, still ignorant to this mull of his sister-in-law's making.

"I've but—" Betsey began, but the words were just air, no sound. She swallowed. She did not, would not, look at Avery. "I've but three days left to my notice, Mr. Wofford. Perhaps it would be best if I collected my wages and took my leave today."

His mouth stirred, making her decide seven, not ten days, for the blond whiskers. He liked her offer, just as she'd guessed he would—he hadn't the authority to dismiss her, but now he could feel he did. She elbowed her way past the girls standing next to her, tugging out of her black smock as she went to her coat peg. Someone touched her arm, murmured a sympathetic *Betsey?* Julia Vane, ever kind, one of the girls who still risked being friendly with her.

She heard Mr. Wofford say, "I suppose we ought to see Mr. Hutchens prior to that. He may be of the same opinion as I as to whether you deserve your wages."

Betsey's hands shook over the buttons of her jacket. Only a few minutes ago, the prospect of leaving Baumston & Smythe with less than a full week's pay and the letter of reference had been unthinkable. That letter had been the only thing Mr. Jones had said was a condition of her hire at the pier company. She had to have rail fare to Idensea, a payment for Richard, money for Grace. Now, suddenly, she might leave empty-handed, a possibility only a hair less terrifying than getting turned over to the law.

She fidgeted over her gloves, grabbed her hat. No one said anything, and as she walked out of the office, she supposed it appeared she had some sort of plan, that she knew what she was doing.

The corridor outside the office, with a great arched window at every landing of the staircase, was filled with May, the light like a remembered dream. Two flights to the street, one to the office where each Tuesday she stood in a queue for her wages.

Mr. Wofford called her name and she halted on the second step down, fingertips on the banister, though she didn't turn round to him. "I've been here more than eight months, Mr. Wofford," she said, trying to keep her voice from carrying up and down the staircase. "Never missed a day nor been tardy. I've been one of your best type-writers, and I've earned three days of wages for which I've not been paid. Let me collect them, and I'll be gone."

"Ah. I have stated the difficulty with that solution, have I not?"

With some hope in candor and decency, she turned. Mr. Wofford had left the door open, and every face in the office, including Avery's, was looking out of it. The hope sank, but she told him anyway.

"I cannot go without an entire week's wages, sir."

"I imagine not, a girl like you."

His agreement intended no sympathy. "A girl like you" meant what he knew of her, that she wasn't like the other type-writers, a girl helping out her family till she married. She was older (four-and-twenty now), unmarried, supporting herself: peculiar. And of questionable morals, of course. The story of her expulsion had only confirmed the suspicions.

"It seems peculiar," he continued, "you would not have considered that before. It seems peculiar as well, you taking such a foolhardy chance when I did agree to write your character myself."

"A *qualified* character."

"One must be truthful in such matters."

She sprang back up the two steps. "It's unfair. Everything you would have insinuated had nothing to do with my work here. You couldn't've complained about that; I've been a model employee."

"Until today."

Betsey felt herself flush. She looked at the window, where there were no spectators.

"Ah, Miss Dobson, what I think you, and a great many others of your sex, misunderstand is the risk a business runs simply in taking you on. You're an unknown quantity, so to speak, you young . . . ladies . . . in an establishment like this, or like that pier company you mean to go to. Extracted from your feminine sphere, you create a precarious unnaturalness with your presence which can only be countered with the assurance—"

"Do you mean to let me collect my wages, or don't you?"

His bottom lip wavered as though to respond to this interruption, but he didn't speak until he turned on his audience suddenly and directed them all to return to work. Avery's head, Betsey couldn't help noticing, was already bowed. None of the type-writer girls raised audible protests against the abbreviated rest period.

Cora Lester, apparently the only one to have escaped to the W.C., came bobbing up the steps, hesitating in a kittenish sort of way when she saw Betsey and Mr. Wofford in the corridor.

"Again, Miss Dobson," he said, "I would remind you there is an order to things in business. It isn't for me to decide whether you get your wages. It's for me to take you to Mr. Hutchens so *he* may decide the matter."

"You could let me go down the stairs."

He brushed Cora Lester into the office with a wave. He lifted his brows at Betsey.

"Could I? And overlook the proper procedures? There is call for such a thing, on occasion."

He looked her over. He stood in the open doorway, before everyone and yet unseen by any, and he looked her over. The snaps of the type-writing machines grew muffled as he pushed the door almost shut, one hand curled round its edge. The other hand slipped to the front of his trousers. He gave himself a squeeze. It was a dainty squeeze, and it was the daintiness rather than the squeeze itself that mystified Betsey.

"You should have to convince me the present situation is such an occasion," he said. He pushed back his coat and hooked his thumb on the waist of his trousers. "You see?"

Mr. Wofford looked her all over.

Concentration, not contemplation. It was a good motto, and not just for type-writer girls. So many situations in life called for one to pay attention yet not think overmuch. So many times when the proper posture would promote one's efficiency. Suppose, for example, you wanted to give a bastard his due—why then, it was wise advice indeed.

Betsey nodded once. "I see." She offered a closed-lip smile, a slow blink. She witnessed the shift, when some of the marbles came rolling her way. "Mr. Wofford, you are . . . *entirely* correct."

And her breasts were far from ample, but with the proper posture, she could endow them with a certain significance. She did so now, an efficient way of holding Mr. Wofford's attention as she moved to the doorway and, with an efficient, concentrated motion, kicked the door to its frame, an efficient and concentrated way of telling a bastard to go to hell, especially when the bastard's fingers were still curled round the door.

And then she concentrated on the most efficient exit from Baumston & Smythe, Insurers.

OBSERVE THE BELL.

The bell rings to warn the writer that he is approaching
the end of the line.

—*How to Become Expert in Type-writing*

*S*he had four shillings in her boot, stashed there the previous payday until she could earn five more to purchase
rail fare to Idensea. Above all, there must be the rail fare, Betsey
had thought, and so she had done without the meat the shillings
would have bought. She'd been comforted by the coins' hard presence in her shoe the past few days, but now, having fled the City
and made the long walk to her sister Caroline's house in Brixton,
they had begun to torture the ball of her foot. Single fares to Idensea cost nine shillings, not four.

Reaching Caroline's door, she turned the bell and sank down,
unable to wait a moment longer to loosen her laces and make
adjustments. She cursed softly upon finding the ill-fitting boot had
rubbed a hole in her stocking.

"Elisabeth! Come in, for pity's sake! I'd thought you were
coming Sunday!"

Betsey worked her foot back into her boot, not quite ready to
look up at her sister. "A change to my plans. I shall leave tomorrow
instead of next week, so I've come to say good-bye."

"But why? I thought your notice . . ."

Betsey stood, managing a blithe smile. Caroline noticed nothing but Betsey's hair, however.

"You've got a fringe! And—is your hair cut? Elisabeth!"

Caroline lifted her hand to test the length of Betsey's hair between two fingers. Betsey intercepted the gesture, tucking up into her hat the strands of hair that had fallen during the walk from the wigmaker's to Caroline's house. The strands promptly slipped down again, and she hooked them behind her ear. Ah, God, she would have to buy more hairpins to have any hope of keeping it up. The back almost grazed her shoulders, but the front was shorter, owing to the way the wigmaker's apprentice had bound her hair before sawing through it with scissors Betsey suspected were less sharp than they ought be. The fringe across her forehead had been the lad's conciliatory gesture.

"Why?" Caroline wanted to know. "All these years letting it grow again, how could you bear it?"

Her sister regarded her with great compassion, as though Betsey had been forced to sell her child rather than her hair. It had felt like that the first time, back in Manchester when she'd been but seventeen, with nowhere to go, no idea where the next coins would come once those she'd got for her hair were spent.

This afternoon, however, Betsey had sat on the wigmaker's stool and wished there were some magic potion to drink, some oil or cream to apply that would make her hair grow faster so she might sell it again. She'd wished for hair the color of corn silk, to fetch more coins. "Dull as mud!" the wigmaker had spat, and when he saw the length wasn't what it ought be, he'd turned her over in disgust to his apprentice.

"Needed money," she told Caroline. "Why else?"

"But your wages, you said—"

"Got sacked today."

"No! Why? How could they? What about Richard?"

As if her husband could have, would have helped. Obviously Richard had never told Caroline, as he had Betsey, that helping

Betsey get the position was the extent of his participation in her career. She was to make nothing more of their connection, not even to do more than nod if they met each other at the front doors at the end of the workday.

Richard would be furious when he heard of the spectacle she'd made this afternoon. Thus, she wanted to give her good-byes to Caroline and the children before he came home. It was late already. She'd lost time at the wigmaker's and in the walk to Caroline's house, avoiding the need to turn over any of her few coins to the omnibus company. Richard, she knew, divided his journey from work to home, walking part of the way and then catching the omnibus. No doubt he possessed some formula to calculate the most economical division between the costs of bus fare and shoe leather.

With some vague reassurance to Caroline, Betsey went inside, calling for her niece and two nephews and finding them at games in the back garden. She had sweets for them, not the sugar mice or toffee she'd wanted to bring, only peppermint sticks, and even the penny she'd handed over for those was more than she should spare.

Still, lowly peppermint made the children's eyes grow wide and solemn with wonder. Dick and Emma, the eldest two, cradled theirs in their hands for a moment, then snapped them and held out halves for their mother to store away. Four-year-old Francis watched them, red stripes melting into his fist.

"No," Betsey protested. "I mean for you to have it all, right now. A treat, you see. You don't have to put it away."

Dick and Emma regarded their aunt as though she'd told them Jesus was a fiction. They looked at their mother: Would she confirm this heresy?

Caroline was uneasy with the burden of such a decision, but with a nod, she told them, "I suppose, since Papa isn't here . . . if you wish . . ."

But the training ran deep. The halves were relinquished, and as Caroline put them in her apron pocket, Emma wrenched at Francis's fist, warning, "You'll be sorry if you don't. Me and Dick'll have some when you don't, and you'll be sorry then."

Francis butted his forehead into his sister's chin and fell back on his bum as she let him go. They both went to tears, Emma for her stinging chin, Francis for his sweet, broken upon the brick pathway where he had fallen.

As Betsey brushed off the peppermint and set about trying to convince Francis it would taste just the same, broken or not, Caroline suddenly straightened from Emma's side. "I hear Richard coming in, I think," she murmured, and rushed back inside.

Betsey looked toward the door at the far wall of the garden. Even if she might have seriously considered it as an escape, there was not enough time. Richard's children were weepy and sticky, and she was in the midst of it.

"They're looking for you," he said to her after he'd directed the children into the house.

Behind him in the narrow doorway, her head not quite clearing Richard's shoulder, Caroline asked, "Who? Who is looking for her?"

"Some of the Baumston and Smythe managers. Has she told you what she's done?" When Caroline didn't answer, and Betsey offered no confession, he continued. "She broke a man's fingers today in her temper."

She'd broken Wofford's fingers? No wonder he'd howled like a lost child.

"I was not in a temper," she corrected, because truly, it wouldn't do to smile just now, Richard's censuring brow directed at her, Caroline peeping over his shoulder with dismay.

But dear Caro. What she said was "Elisabeth, what had he done to you? Are you all right?"

Richard swung round to her so fast she fell back a step. "He caught her at theft and forgery, Caroline! And after she'd assaulted him and run away, it's me Mr. Hutchens seeks out to find where she lives." To Betsey, he said, "You might have gotten me dismissed. To be sure, I'll be a laughingstock at best and suspect at worst, now that everyone knows I've the misfortune to be related to you by marriage."

"Richard, I am sorry—I would never want to cause you—"

"What did you tell them?" Caroline interrupted to ask Richard. "When they asked where Elisabeth lived, what did you say?"

Richard cast unwilling looks at Betsey and then his wife. "What do I know of where she lives? I told them it was likely some jerry-built hovel somewhere in the East End, where neither I nor my wife were wont to be found."

"'Tis not a hovel," Betsey said softly.

"Do you think someone will come to see if she's here?" Caroline asked.

"Don't you imagine it's quite possible?"

A moment passed. Betsey tried to smile at her sister, to say, *I suppose I'm off, then,* but the words caught in her throat when she saw Caro's eyes fill. Caroline pushed past her husband to catch Betsey's wrist and draw her back inside the house.

Caroline gave Betsey hairpins for her falling hair; she gave her a length of twine because she knew Betsey's ancient valise had a troublesome latch. She tried to press other things on Betsey as well: a tin of lavender-scented powder, a bottle of ink, a pair of stockings darned but once in one toe. Betsey promised she had no need of any of it, and Caroline led her to the kitchen and took the next day's loaf from the bread box. She ignored Betsey's protests and wrapped it into waxed paper.

"And what will Richard say when you run out of flour too soon?" Betsey asked.

"I shall remind my beloved we might have had to give you an entire plate, meat and all, had you been able to stay to dinner. He'll feel fortunate it was only a bit of bread then."

Richard did not look as if he felt fortunate, however, and even less so when Caroline informed him he would see his sister-in-law to the omnibus and pay her fare, too. Caro's voice sounded as soft and sweet as that lavender powder as she told him this, but her tone was this-is-how-it-will-be. Betsey loved that tone, so rarely used, yet employed on her behalf tonight, despite the fact that she wanted neither Richard's escort nor his money.

She told him so as they started down the lane, saying she would walk to her flat. He pointed out the failing twilight and the descending fog that would make the journey treacherous for a woman alone. She assured him she would be fine, shook her head at the coins he was counting out: "Consider it a payment toward what I owe you if you must, but I shall not be taking it."

He snatched out for her arm, jerking her to a halt. "You'll take it. You'll take it, and get yourself away from here safe enough, and keep your sister from that worry at least." He smashed the pennies into her hand, pressed it closed, and then clamped his fingers so tightly over hers she felt a bit of sympathy for Mr. Wofford. "And as for what you owe, let's leave off pretending about that."

Betsey held still, afraid a struggle would make him angrier. She had never liked him. He had helped her, loaned her money for her courses at the Institute and a new suit of clothes to wear to Baumston & Smythe, but the smallness of his spirit choked the gratitude she wanted to feel. Until now, though, she had never been afraid of him.

So she held still and whispered, "I shall send portions of my wages from my new position, Richard. Twice a month. You know—"

He shook the words from her mouth. "Never mind it! Here is how I want you to repay what you owe: Stay away. Go on wherever it is you're going and don't come back. Write Caroline now and again to save her from worry, but when you've made whatever wreck you'll make of it, don't bring it back to my family. I've had enough, do you hear?"

Betsey nodded, but he held her until a carriage turned into the lane. Released, she walked beside him numbly to a street where the omnibus would pass, and they waited for it in silence. When it came, she dashed up the steps for a seat on the upper level, feeling she would need the air, and the perspective.

The evening was cool, a good explanation for why she trembled the first few minutes of the journey. In the bus's halting progress, fog-blurred streetlamps drew near and fell behind, drew near and fell behind, belying the noisy exertion of real life occurring below their dreamy haze. Her hand throbbed. Turnabout. She wondered at her mute submission to Richard. It was the fear, of course, and the fear because of the surprise—with some humor, she tried to convince herself the surprise came not from how he'd gripped her but from his forgiveness of her debt. It didn't work.

Did he honestly believe he could keep her from Caroline and the children? Why hadn't she simply told him to go to hell?

Because he was right?

She pulled a bit of the waxed paper away from the bread Caroline had given her and stuck her nose near the loaf, a much nicer scent than the ones that grew stronger the closer the omnibus came to her stop. That she had made a—what had Richard said?—a *wreck* of things was unquestionable. That she would do so in Idensea—

She had to believe the matter was not so cut-and-dry as Richard assumed.

She knew Idensea was in Hampshire because Baumston & Smythe insured the Idensea Pier & Seaside Pleasure Building Company's holdings, but she had never been there. Still, something about living beside the sea resonated within her: She had a remembrance of pinching sand from the damp hem of a faded blue frock, only to discover how it stuck to her little-girl fingers, and of her mother kicking salty water into the sunlight, telling her daughters—and son, for Daniel had still been with them then—to look and to look. And behind her mother, laughing, was a man Betsey had believed to be her father, at least until a few years ago, when she had tried to make Caroline remember Blackpool, and Caroline said no, no, it was impossible their father had been there on that occasion.

Then who was he?

I don't know. Some stranger, just someone who caught your fancy, perhaps.

Though the memory of her family all together had already been as frail and jumbled as a ball of dust, Betsey regretted this alteration to it.

She didn't know how she would get there, but she was going to Idensea, and was glad of it, glad to be leaving behind the filth and disappointment of London. She was to be a *manager*—that Mr. Jones used that term rather than *manageress* always made her smile—arranging day excursions for tourist groups, playing hostess to them when they came for their dinner dance at the new hotel, earning commission for every group she booked. Risky seasonal work, to be sure, but Mr. Jones had promised she would have office duties in the winter.

Why had he offered her such a chance? She didn't know. She didn't know why he had followed her from that meeting where she had been summoned to take dictation. He'd asked if she liked being a type-writer, and, suspicious and irate, she had given him some pert response. Worse than pert. Fearful of the resulting assumptions if anyone saw them speaking, she'd intended to put him off entirely with that worse-than-pert response.

But he kept following after her. He mentioned the wages, and it was then she stopped to truly look at him, and listen. Because the wages were good, and so was his face. A good face, open as a summer window.

No one had come looking for her tonight, her flatmate Grace assured her, nor had Avery shown his damn face about, a rather hostile response to Betsey's casual question.

How much effort would Baumston & Smythe put toward finding her? Had they notified the police? Betsey fretted over it, as well as the problems of rail fare and the confiscated letter—*Bring a good character letter or two, for Mr. Seiler and Sir Alton,* Mr. Jones had instructed—while she fed bites of bread to Grace's little son, Sammy, and dropped crumbs into the bottom of the birdcage for Thief, her canary. Why didn't she simply write it by hand herself, Grace wanted to know, or Avery, he was bound to have a right proper hand. But after today's experience, Betsey had no more stomach for forgery.

Avery didn't come. It was not so unusual, even if this afternoon's events made it seem so, and memories of how he'd simply faded from her life after she'd been expelled and he'd been reprimanded were unhelpful at present. She and Grace, who had already arranged for new lodgings, packed. Sammy made it a game, darting about the room and lugging anything he could carry to either Betsey or his mother. Most of his selections belonged to Avery. She hadn't realized how many belongings Avery had, even after selling most of his books and other valuables. Transporting it all to Idensea would be either pricey or awkward.

Of her own things, however, all but her winter cloak fit into the valise, and a few hours later, neighbors had helped Grace and Sammy to their new flat and Betsey lay shivering in her own bed. Her first job in Manchester after being dismissed as a housemaid had been as a laundress, and she'd spent her nights on the floor in a back room with a dozen other women. How many times since then had she wished for her own private room? Yet tonight, she missed the whirring pulse of Grace's rented sewing machine, and the flat seemed very quiet. So quiet she could hear the fragile steps at last approaching the door, the careful grind of the door latch.

His clothes fanned scents into the room as he removed them, tobacco and ale and something else—smoky but more substantial, roasted—and she wondered why she'd not guessed, *the theater*. Avery had friends who had missed him when he'd dropped from their circle, and who, for the past month, had been happy enough to spot him an admission or a supper. They apparently were not the sort of friends to keep you from losing your best chance for a stable income in a card game, nor to care for you during an illness, but Betsey supposed those were rare enough amongst men.

His hands smoothed along the empty space in the bed beside her, then patted more firmly, searching for the blanket, which he wouldn't find because she'd already given it to Grace as a poor substitute for the money she'd wanted to leave. His fingertips brushed the wool of her cloak and paused, but didn't grasp, didn't pull.

He eased into the bed, and after he had lain utterly still for a moment, Betsey rearranged her cloak so both of them had at least some cover. Mostly healed from pneumonia Avery might be, but the night was cool and he wasn't wearing a stitch.

"Damn it all," he said.

"I wasn't sleeping."

They moved closer, huddling rather than embracing. She thought he would speak.

"You saw a show?"

"Only the Alhambra," he answered, the *only* because variety entertainment didn't rate as true theater to Avery, regardless of the opulence of the venue.

He added nothing else; perhaps he believed there was a chance in hell he'd be permitted to drift off to sleep. But the last time he'd seen her, she had been enduring Wofford's jobation. If he didn't wish to discuss that, he at least had to know she was leaving London on the morrow. They had plans to make, the two of them.

"You do realize how I hated it this afternoon," he whispered abruptly. "Having to . . . *sit by*."

He sounded as if he were accusing her of something. She thought of how she had waited, briefly, irrationally, in a doorway where she could see the Baumston & Smythe entrance. Just catching her breath after her run out of the building, that's all that was, she told herself.

"Both of us with no wages for the week would be a fine thing," she said.

"Still, I wish there had been another way. I felt like the lowest sort of cad, watching it all, and once you vanished, it only became worse. Lizzie, the sensation you caused, you cannot—"

"Don't call me 'Lizzie.'"

"You're cross."

"I'm not. I've been waiting, is all."

"I needed respite tonight, you understand, after all that dreadfulness. I brought you a pasty. Shall I fetch it now?"

She nearly said yes. Her stomach felt empty, and suddenly she yearned for the decadent comfort of eating in bed in the middle of the night. They'd done that, she remembered, in the beginning. Picnics in Avery's bed, in that wonderful flat of his near the Institute. She wished he'd come in without a care for waking her and begun hand-feeding her.

"I'd best save it," she said. "Tomorrow's apt to be long. I—I've packed, Avery. I decided to go on to Idensea tomorrow."

"Oh." He sounded confused, caught out. "Well, it makes sense, doesn't it, if you won't be type-writing? And if Wofford's determined to find you. . . . Damn him. But what if that Jones fellow won't take you on without the letter?"

She thought, *I don't know,* and pressed her hand against the lurch in her gut. Avery, inclined to answer his own questions, didn't this time.

Instead, several moments later, he said, "You might let it go," which she didn't understand in the least.

"A bit absurd, isn't it," he said, "going all that way only for a job. How long would it take for you to get another type-writing position?"

"What, here in London?"

"Certainly not more than a few days. Granted, without references, you would have to look a step or two down from Baumston, but if you answered some adverts . . . Or the switchboards. Openings there by the hour, it's said, and your accent isn't at all repulsive, you know. I've always said so."

So she might let it go. She might just stay in London. She

might have just told Mr. Jones *no* and never asked Mr. Wofford for a character and thus never made herself a spectacle and a . . . an *outlaw*. She might still be a type-writer at Baumston & Smythe, Insurers with high hopes of still being a type-writer at Baumston & Smythe, Insurers in five years more, which was the length of time a female type-writer could expect to work before she earned a wage that granted true, livable independence. That had been the extent of her hopes until a few days ago.

She tugged a fraction of her cloak back, blocking the draft on her backside. "You've changed your mind."

"I believed some days remained before I had to tell you."

Tell her what? That he would stay in London, certainly. That he wanted *her* to stay as well? Stay with him? He had been the one to suggest he come to Idensea with her—there was bound to be a school where he could find a position, he'd said, and doctors claimed sea air as a curative.

Last week, he had shrugged, concluding *why not?* and Betsey had caught her breath in surprise, because men didn't come after Betsey Dobson once they'd got what they wanted. To her credit, she never asked them to.

And now she listened to him explain, wondering if she would hear *stay* but hearing mostly *I: I need to be where I can take my opportunities when they arise. This clerking is dreadful, but now that I'm writing again, I need tolerate it only a few months more.*

"Good luck, then," she interrupted.

He fell silent and then coughed, but it didn't go into a fit. "Good luck."

She rolled to her other side. Her cloak came with her. Avery's presence in the bed seemed to expand, his elbow pressing her shoulder blade as he lay on his back and crossed his arms. He twitched, one hard contraction of his entire body.

"Where is our blanket, pray tell?"

"I gave it to Grace."

She supposed he realized his error in using the word *our,* for not even a grunt of displeasure escaped his lips. She added, "She moved to her new place tonight, she and Sammy."

"That explains the quiet."

He shivered again and coughed, and then, in a gesture so sudden and unlike him that it brought tears to her eyes, threw his arm over her waist and pulled her close to him. She had tied what remained of her hair into two sections, and she felt his breath on that bare space of her neck, warm, whispering, "I do believe I shall miss you."

Her eyes shut. She thought of Avery in the lecture hall at the Institute, Avery in his flat, Avery with all the answers and his own type-writing machine and a nymph-shaped lamp with a mother-of-pearl shade, and she wondered if she wanted the wrong thing, this job that could end with the turn of a season, this life in a place she'd never seen. She found his hand, thin yet from his illness, and nestled her fingers between his.

"I haven't enough for rail fare." She whispered this confession even more softly than he had his, for she hadn't intended to speak it at all. Richard would be the last man she would be beholden to, she had determined some time ago. And Avery—well, she had never given him the chance to offer, not really. But with his arm tight around her, the words slipped out.

His chuckle vibrated against her neck. "Is that the going rate?"

The question obliterated all the tenderness of the moment. Betsey curled her hand back inside her sleeve. As swiftly and surreptitiously as possible, she swiped all the dampness from her cheeks, removing the evidence of her weakness from herself as well as Avery.

He massaged her hip. "It isn't unreasonable, I suppose. And, as always, your practical nature beguiles me."

He nuzzled his face against the skin exposed above the neckline of her nightdress, suckled at the side of her neck. And all the while, he pressed her hip, urging her onto her back.

"Be good to me, Lizzie," he said when her resistance could no longer be mistaken for something else. *It makes me feel so wicked, going to bed with a Lizzie,* he had explained once after she had corrected him.

He pushed her cloak off of her, onto the floor, and slipped a hand beneath her nightdress, between her thighs, promising to be good to her in return, promising, "Good Lizzie, every coin in my coat pocket for a wicked farewell."

They have no idea of the possibilities of their writing
machine, of the beauty and variety of the work it is
capable of doing. All they know is what they have 'picked
up' in somebody's office while working for practice with .
little or no pay.

—*How to Become Expert in Type-writing*

The going rate. Her desperation wasn't so deep as that,
no. She turned onto her back and let him settle between
her thighs, keeping her face from his kiss. Her hands skimmed
along his bare back, then slipped between the two of them, and
Avery laughed and groaned as if he quite enjoyed the sensation of
her chilled fingers curling round his cock. Admittedly, his warmth
was better than any pair of mittens she'd ever owned, and she felt
especially cold at the moment.

"My, Avery, not ready yet, are you?"

She could scarcely make out his handsome face in the room's
darkness, and she sensed rather than witnessed his displeasure at
this remark. A brief stillness about him, but a stroke of her hand
had him moaning again. "My *God,* Lizzie. Lizzie, God, there you
are, good Liz—"

His voice broke with a screeching breath in, his eyes widening
as her grip tightened. "Damn it—what—"

"I've said to you half one thousand times not to call me Lizzie."

"Are you mad— *damn*— damn it all, *stop*—"

"And I swear to God, if you put this *bit* near me again tonight I shall twist till it snaps and throw it down the steps for Mrs. Bainwelter's terrier to have for a gnaw."

She let him go. He shoved off of her, cursing her, and she sprang out of the bed, grabbed her cloak from the floor, and took the two steps to what had been Grace's side of the room. The quilt that had divided the space was gone now, but the bed remained, stripped and awaiting the next renter. She lay down on it and huddled under her cloak, her back to Avery.

He was coughing, and it didn't stop. Betsey heard him pulling on his clothes, coughing all the while, and she was glad he'd thought better of trying to sleep without any cover. But then she heard his shoes, the faint squeak of leather as he pulled on his boots.

"Don't be ridiculous," she told him. "We each have a bed, and I shall be going in the morning. Is it worth making yourself ill?"

Her answer, after the coughing subsided, was the creak of the bed as he lay down. What else? He had nowhere else to go, same as when she'd brought him here more than two months ago. Such a shock, seeing him after so much time, though not enough to account for the drastic change in his appearance. Once, he would have clearly been a stranger on this street, but that day, he had the hard-worn look of its residents.

Indeed, at that particular moment, his aspiration had been to *become* one of the residents. He was foolishly attempting to negotiate a lower rent, and all but stumbled into her arms when the slumlord pushed him off the threshold in order to shut the door in his face. *Took up with another of your students, did you?* she asked him when he admitted he'd been dismissed from the Institute not long after she herself had left, and he swore to her, *No.* Likely he would have sworn a good many other things to her, too, except, weak with fever, he nearly collapsed on her, right there in the street. She'd taken him home.

She could tell from his breathing now he didn't fall asleep directly. They lay, parted by a few steps, by darkness, by mutual refusal to speak a few softer words. By her decision to go.

It's good for you, Caroline had told her tonight. *We will miss you, but a new start—and you'll be good, I know it, won't you, Elisabeth? You'll be . . .*

She hadn't finished, but Betsey knew what her sister meant. In all the world, who but Caroline worried for Betsey's soul? Where others condemned, Caroline grieved and hoped for better.

Betsey hoped, too. With the fervor of a saint or a gambler, she hoped.

These tears! If Avery heard her, he would think they were for him, and they weren't, not really. They were because this day had been dreadful and because this night was long, and with sleep eluding her, she had nothing to do but *contemplate*.

Richard could well be right: She could make a great wreck of it all. Again.

Eventually, she slept. In the morning, the only thing she took from Avery's coat pocket was the pasty he'd bought her. The less than a shilling's worth of coins, she left behind.

Which meant she only had money enough for a ticket that would barely see her out of London, to Woking. She pretended her terror was Thief, a bird in a cage, and threw a dark cloth over it as she turned over all but a few pennies to the ticket agent.

Waterloo Station boiled with Londoners eager to quit the city for the Whitsun holiday, tight clusters of families keeping count of one another, wide snaking lines of excursionists bound by their common itineraries, companions oblivious to anything beyond their own circles of laughter. Betsey, smothering under the weight of her winter cloak, navigated the din in deep concentration: *Don't let Thief's cage be knocked. Mind the valise grip, it's delicate. Platform Four. No turning round. Most of all, no turning round.*

The third-class carriage smelled of smoke and straw and some-thing pickled. Betsey felt lucky to find an empty place until she realized that seat was Hadrian's Wall between two warring elderly sisters, and she spent the journey half-listening to two different accounts of a convoluted story involving a potted mignonette, a sticky door, and a headstone inscription. By the time a conductor called, "Woking!" Betsey was being prevailed upon to judge the logic of dividing a set of shirt studs.

The train stopped and waited—*and waited*—at the platform, but Betsey remained in the compartment, suggesting the studs be sold, the money divided.

Finally, movement.

She'd done it. Fare-dodging could now be added to her life's transgressions.

She wondered whether she'd get away with it. Stomach knot-ted, she felt the miles she hadn't paid for adding up, rumbling beneath the carriage. The sisters reconciled, or at least began speak-ing again, and though their conversation over Betsey's bosom felt awkward, she suspected it saved her, disguised her as their com-panion. In any case, no conductor checked her ticket again.

She had to change at Southampton. By the time she maneu-vered the crowds there and found the train, the guard's last whistle was sounding. She hoped to board in this final scuttle, but a con-ductor spied her and waved her toward him.

"On your own, miss? A good carriage for you here."

Betsey braced herself for the end of this escapade. Already, the conductor was shaking his head.

"Didn't they tell you, miss? The bag's of a size for the parcel rack, but there's no animals in the carriages." He nodded toward the birdcage.

"Ohh"—she held that vowel, thinking, revising—"*dear!* What shall I do?"

She sounded dismayed. She sounded helpless. She widened her eyes and put herself into his care. Perhaps he liked that. Perhaps it was the whistle, the slamming doors, the shouts and the escalating rush passing them by. But the result was he waved her toward the carriage door, and Betsey and Thief boarded.

The carriage was a "good" one for her because women and children populated it. A great many children, perhaps double the carriage's intended capacity. Had she been in the position to hold preferences, Betsey might have preferred the supposed indignity of traveling alongside unknown men.

The boys and girls showed instant interest in the birdcage, though it waned when they learned Thief would not sing and, no, Betsey would not let the canary out to fly about the compartment and come to their outstretched fingers. She covered the cage again and set it in a corner, hoping it would escape any additional notice from the conductors.

The children were from an orphanage, one of their chaperones told her, their seaside outing provided by a church benefactor. Betsey was playful with them and chatted with the chaperones, all the while praying a scoundrel's prayer for luck to hold just a little longer.

A conductor looked into the compartment, cursorily. She could only hope he'd taken her as part of the orphans' outing, since church chaperones, to her knowledge, did not dodge fares.

The compartment was stifling, with heat, with competing voices, with questions: She had no family in Idensea? What sort of work? Didn't she have a husband?

After another lengthy wait at a station, a conductor appeared, a different one. He sighed at the overcrowded compartment, and Betsey knew: He was resigned to inspecting every last ticket.

She continued a cat's cradle lesson with two girls, following the conductor's reflection in the window, calculating the distance to the door. She felt ill already; that would not be a lie. She was ill, she needed air, that was true. She'd only need to play it a little bigger.

With the beginning of a moan, she crumpled the yarn in her hand, but the sound caught in her throat as she saw one of the smallest boys take a tumble out of his seat. Betsey knew luck when she saw it. In an instant, she was kneeling on the floor beside the lad, cooing over him, checking his limbs, righting his clothes, offering cheerful encouragement and a moral about holding on. The boy's own mother—that is, supposing he'd had one—could not have demonstrated more tender concern and devotion than did Betsey in those moments as the conductor finished his inspection.

She instructed the children sitting on the bench with him to please have a care, and then she rose.

The conductor stood in the compartment door, next to Thief's cage. He touched his hat.

"Miss, if you're ready now, your ticket."

No, church chaperones did not dodge fares, nor even think of it. That much was evident from the shock expressed as the conductor questioned her.

Down to no options, she told him she had someone in Idensea who would vouch for her, and even pay the difference on the ticket.

"And who's that?"

"Mr. Jones. Mr. John Jones."

"The Welshman with the pier company?" he asked, and Betsey nodded hard, because it was clear the conductor knew Mr. Jones, and because of that, she had a chance.

He let her stay on the train, though he appeared at the door at every stop afterward, to make sure she didn't go anywhere. The chaperones called the children to them, and in that crowded compartment, Betsey sat on the bench alone, her gaze again fixed upon the reflections on the glass, the pale motion of the children as they seemed to forget the whole scene and return to their play and prattling. She wished she and every other adult could move on so easily.

Would Mr. Jones vouch for her? She didn't know. However, she felt rather certain she'd reached her limit for public humiliation.

The call for Idensea went out, and the children's excitement swelled again. A child twisted in the bench ahead of Betsey to ask her, "Do you know what a pier is like? They say we will walk on one today."

Betsey smiled, but the child was distracted by a seatmate and didn't wait for a reply. The train pulled into Idensea, a small station with just two platforms, though they were covered. In the lull between arrival and departure, the station was largely empty, and a shock went through Betsey when she realized Mr. Jones was there, waiting on the platform. The distance was significant, and his light-colored clothes were nothing like the serious black suit he'd worn at the Baumston & Smythe offices, but she recognized how he stood: a favored prince, or new angel, or—for heaven's sake—a contented dog, solid and easy, confident of his master's goodwill. A straw boater sat far back on his head, revealing a shock of his black hair.

Basic logic deserted her, and Betsey thought, *He's come to meet me*. The very comfort in the notion was what made her distrust it, and in the next moment, she realized it was impossible. She'd arrived four days ahead of schedule, and he'd given her directions to make her own way to the Swan Park Hotel, where the pier company had its offices. Then, with the train reaching its full stop, she saw him adjust his hat to a more level and appropriate position. She noticed the flowers in his hand. She understood his tan-colored Norfolk jacket was for leisure, not business.

He headed toward the first-class carriages. Betsey remained in her seat as the children and their chaperones filed from the compartment, then followed the conductor. He bade her wait on a bench on the platform; he gave her Thief's cage but kept her valise to make certain she wouldn't run off. Run. Where? Mr. Jones, with whom she'd had a single ten-minute conversation, was her sole resource.

Now he greeted a group from the train, a mother and her daughters, Betsey guessed, all of them dressed as prettily as cakes in a baker's window; the mother and the eldest, a young woman,

wore high-crowned hats made higher with a profusion of trim-
mings. The two younger girls, somewhere between ten and fifteen,
had yellow hair spilling down their backs, lit by the skylights over
the platform. Mr. Jones crouched on his heels before the youngest,
to all appearances in a most earnest conversation with the child
before he presented a handful of posies and let her choose. He rose
and let the middle daughter make her choice, then the mother,
whose neck took on a girlish slant as she accepted the gift. His
hands were empty when finally he turned to the young woman.

But no, a surprise, another flower, a white blossom distinct
from the others, somehow produced a moment after the tease. The
mother turned, stooping to help the girls affix their flowers to their
sailor blouses. Mr. Jones and the young woman drew together. She
tilted her head over her shoulder, and her hat hid Mr. Jones's face
as he stooped to pin the posy to her bodice. Briefly, he drew even
closer. And then his laughter was ringing down the platform, and
he stepped back just as the mother finished with the younger girls.

The young lady adjusted her posy, moving it from where Mr.
Jones had pinned it and refastening it at her waist. The mother
chatted with Mr. Jones as they waited, her hand slipping down
her youngest daughter's hair again and again. Betsey watched the
absent gesture, hypnotized, until a pang of something like home-
sickness (silly!) struck so hard she had to look away, bending down
to lift the cloth covering Thief's cage.

She looked up when she heard the train lurching out of the
station. Down the platform, the stationmaster spoke with Mr.
Jones. All of them, Mr. Jones and his women, were looking at her.
And Betsey could well imagine the course of the conversation: *Mr.
Jones, we've a fare-dodger, claims you promised to pay once she arrived
in Idensea. Easy enough to write her a fine or turn her over to the constable if you don't want her.*

Mr. Jones seemed to squint in her direction. His eyes were
green. Betsey couldn't see them from here, of course, but she suddenly remembered his green eyes. She remembered he'd put on
spectacles to read, and that his right eye drooped a touch because

of a pink scar at its outside corner. Below that, another knot of scar tissue made his bottom lip puff slightly. The top lip? Only a brisk and graceful scrawl. Betsey remembered all that, so surely, surely he would recognize her, too, and claim her.

She stood.

Mr. Jones nodded at the stationmaster and turned away, ushering the mother and daughters from the platform.

Betsey needed a new plan.

If you form a careless habit in the beginning, you will probably always keep it.

—How to Become Expert in Type-writing

*L*illian Gilbey was peeved when John told her he would meet them at the Swan in half an hour. John discerned this from how amiably she agreed to the delay and how she chastised her mother and sisters for expressing disappointment. "By all means," she said as he handed her into the carriage he'd hired, "take all the time you like. We will find plenty of diversion and not suffer a bit for your delay."

He pressed her hand before letting it go. "Thirty minutes or less, I swear it."

"Thirty minutes or *fewer*, thirty minutes or more, you really needn't swear over so trifling a thing, I'm sure!"

She smiled like the first dawn. Peeved, all right. John laughed to himself as the carriage pulled away. Well, what was he to do? He could hardly leave his new manager to the mercy of the stationmaster, and he knew he could persuade Lillian back round to a good humor later. If the weather held, he'd planned for a stroll down the pier and along the Esplanade, where he would be able to show off the building sites for the pleasure railway and the Kursaal, the indoor amusement pavilion due open by the time the Gilbeys returned for their August holiday. Then to the hotel for a tour and a specially ordered tea, with six kinds of sandwiches and at least as many desserts by the Swan Park's new pastry chef.

At some interval in the midst of all that, he needed to get Lillian alone and Say Something. It had been niggling in his brain for months, though he'd kept putting it by since his mother's death this spring past—Say Something. The sticky portion of it was that what he truly wished to say amounted to *Save my place, Lillian*.

Which wouldn't do. Not for Miss Gilbey, who was buttercup-pretty, fresh and soft, for all her feints of sophistication; who was clever, even in the ways she played it down with her beaux; who had a father usefully connected, nearly as rich as John himself intended to become. Such a girl as that could be a man's best asset, and she was not a common commodity for the likes of John Jones, born Iefan Rhys-Jones in a Pembrokeshire slate town. To such a girl as that, no man could say, *Save my place, and I'll come back for you*.

That was the trouble with Lillian Gilbey. She'd come along too soon. He would be finishing his work here in Idensea in a few months; he couldn't ask for Lillian's hand until he had another job secured. A fine thing it would be if he could put her up for a season, the way his mother had done with the blackberry conserve each summer. Lillian would sweeten up that way, and one frost-bright Christmas morning, he'd take her down and lick her up with his toast.

He was hungry. He'd taken time only for a leftover apple tart this morning.

Back inside the railway station, he found the stationmaster's office, where Stationmaster Carey had said he would have Miss Dobson wait. However, he discovered the door locked, and he thought the room empty until a shadow of movement caught the corner of his eye. He removed his hat and put his forehead to the door's glass pane, turning his head so he could see the far end of the office. There, Miss Dobson was opening the window, engaged in effecting her escape.

Trying to, rather. Perhaps the thing had been painted shut. Perhaps she'd forgotten to unlock it. John could see she'd shoved Carey's desk to the wall, and now she was in a wide-kneed squat atop it, apparently seeking better leverage. Her bum bobbed with each renewed heave against the stubborn sash.

Bless God. Bless the bleeding Christ, what did she think she was doing? He would have liked to see what would come of this caper, but instead, he knocked on the glass, two decorous taps.

She whirled about, tipping dangerously before she managed to stand. Her skirts sent a number of items on Carey's desk flying. John saluted her with two fingers to his brow. Then he ducked down to the keyhole.

"Warm, are you, Miss Dobson?" he called through it, then peeked at her over the wooden portion of the door. Still on the desk, hair falling, twin cherries for cheeks. Wildly, he wondered, was this the right girl, the one he'd promised to hire? Because she did not at the moment seem the same to him as she had in London.

Through the keyhole: "I'm going to see the stationmaster and fetch the key, you see. You ought come down from there. See if you can't restore Stationmaster Carey's belongings, and I'll return shortly to collect you."

He dashed off. He knew Carey because he'd come to be acquainted with nearly everyone in Idensea at least a little in the past four years he'd lived there. Carey was a stockholder in the Idensea Pier & Seaside Pleasure Building Company—a respectable few dozen shares, if he was not mistaken.

The man scolded John, said he ought to fine him and the girl both, and John expressed the proper regret and appreciation, pulling the price of Miss Dobson's fare from his pocket as he did. He bit from his tongue a question about the necessity of locking the girl up and letting her think he wasn't coming back. Instead, he suggested Mrs. Carey might well enjoy a dinner at the Swan this week: Why didn't they stop by Thursday as special guests? All was forgiven by the time the lock unhitched.

"Wondrous convenient things, doors are," John said in a low

voice as Miss Dobson exited the office, a free woman. Her frown became more severe. She had brows like a demon's, even when she wasn't frowning, he remembered that.

She was also just his height. John had noted that the first time they'd spoken, at Baumston & Smythe, and he remembered it now as she kept an equal pace beside him on the walk from the rail station. This lane, known as the Compass Walk, shaded by pines and wending through tiny parks, was meant to offer the pedestrian from the station or town center a leisurely amble to the Esplanade, but John had a deadline, so they hurried until he saw they would be waiting for the tram anyway. Horse-drawn trams, alas—Sir Alton had convinced the county council an electric one would be an eyesore.

He watched Miss Dobson take in her first sight of Idensea's seafront. Steam cranes and scaffolding still blocked much of the Kursaal, a three-acre site on the cliff above, but just west they had a good prospect of the pier, eight hundred and one feet toward the horizon, the concert pavilion a white jewel at its head, a paddle steamer now departing its landing stage. More than a thousand tons of iron and steel beneath the wooden promenade; seventy-two cast-iron screw piles, some of which took more than a week to secure into the seafloor. One man's life lost before it was finished, another man maimed. The reason he'd come to Idensea four years ago, to build that pier.

Miss Dobson gave it a silent, restless glance which soon moved on, out, to the sea and sky, perhaps to discern the Needles parading away from the Isle of Wight, certainly to avoid meeting his eyes. Even in her cloak, too dark and heavy for May, and incongruous with her little straw hat, she was all angles and points. Every part of her profile threatened to make a straight line and then, at the last possible moment, tipped up. Her lips, for example: straight and pink until they thinned into tiny curled-up lines. The same sort of tilt for her pointed nose and chin, her demonic eyebrows, and a hint of it at the corners of her eyes (color?—he hadn't a notion, even though at her height she could look him straight in the eye). Even the fringe across her forehead was severely straight but for a rebellious curve kicking out from the temple.

She glanced over at him, then away. Brown eyes. Brown, brown. Teary, too, and the tip of her nose red. John crouched beside the birdcage she clasped before her and turned up the cloth to find its occupant, a yellow canary shifting in response to the burst of daylight. Its willow-twig cage had been mended with string and newspaper.

"There's pretty." The words came out laden with his Welsh accent. It happened sometimes, now because he intended some comfort. "What's his name?"

"Thief." Her voice was thick; she'd not recovered herself yet.

"Thief! Poor creature there, such a name to overcome."

"I didn't choose it."

"Will he sing?"

"Female. That's why she was given to me. A neighbor of mine. Didn't want her."

She sounded steadier now. John thought it safe to rise. Finding her swiping an eye with the hood of her cloak, he offered his handkerchief. She took it the way she'd accepted the job he'd offered her: warily, like Jack's mother regarding the magic beans just before she chucked them out the window.

What would he do with her? And why wouldn't the tram come? John tapped his thumb against the twine-wrapped handle of Miss Dobson's valise and tried to estimate the size of the crowds strolling along the Esplanade and the pier. Certainly greater than at last year's Whitsun holiday, but it pained him to think what they might have been if only the Sultan's Road had been ready to open. He'd pushed as much as he could, but Sir Alton's initial opposition to the construction of the pleasure railway had troubled the project throughout.

"Am I sacked, then?" he heard her ask.

Trepidation filled her voice. John reminded himself that, yes, she was entirely justified in her fear of being dismissed, but still, he struggled to reconcile this timid, teary girl with the one he'd met in London. Where was she? That girl had moved like a lissome general, Joan of Arc in a shirtwaist. That girl had quirked up a curious eye to see who else had caught Gerald Baumston's offhand reference to a deleted rider and furtively slid Cornelius Fuller's inkhorn out of range a full minute before he began flailing. That girl permitted herself to share—or begin to share—an across-the-room smile with John, seeing he knew what she had done.

That's what I need, John had known that day, and so there had been nothing for it but to follow after her when she was dismissed from the meeting and see if he could get her.

She'd wanted nothing to do with him. When he observed she'd actually been enjoying that meeting, she only replied (in better English than he'd expected, a touch of Lancashire in it) that she supposed it was something different from the usual, that's-all-if-you-please-sir, and tried to mince away, a docile little type-writer girl.

She hadn't been able to keep that sham up. "You're right, of course," she'd said, when he continued to follow her, suggesting type-writing must be dull work for someone like her. "It is dull, and it will be years before the pay is enough to keep me under a decent roof. But did you know it is almost the best job in London a girl could hope for? No, why should you? So you can't understand how grateful I am to have it, at least until the day I get a fine suit"—her eyes had swept from his shoes to his face with that—"and sprout a prick between my legs"—another, more pointed glance—"at which time I'm certain I can secure any sort of work I wish."

It was then John realized he could look her in the eye straight. Which was more wicked, her tongue or those eyes? He'd not witnessed such coarseness in a woman since his days working on the Severn Tunnel, and the women who followed the navvies were much rougher sorts than Miss Dobson. It had made him grin and blush, bless God, and know that if he wished Betsey Dobson as the pier company's excursions manager, he ought to speak straight, and of money.

How certain he'd been of her that day. *That's what I need.*

He wouldn't dismiss her, not when he'd persuaded her to leave the best job in London a girl could hope for, but he was experiencing an unfamiliar mistrust of his instincts.

"You're not sacked," he said. "I don't know that you will be the excursions manager, but we will find a place for you."

"Oh." Then, "What—what sort of place?"

"I'm not certain." He didn't have time to think of it now. He would take her to the hotel and pass her off to someone who could show her about, and then speak about her to Tobias Seiler, the hotel manager, after Lillian and her family left this evening.

"Hotel laundress?" she said. "Taking toll at the pier? Or does your company permit a woman to have such an exalted position as that?"

The bitterness in her voice took him aback. He asked, "What about window washing? Is that what you had in mind back in the stationmaster's?"

Her fist flew to her lips, and she cursed into it. "I know. I haven't any right! It is only—I'd begun to believe I could do this job. I thought you were mad, offering it to me, but then . . . I began to think I could do it, that is all. I do still."

"Girl," he began. She turned wary at the familiarity, and probably the Welsh brogue rolling in the word. John checked it, as well as the question he'd been about to ask about why she had refused the money he'd offered for her travel. A few shillings, they could have avoided this. She wanted the position; she *thought* she could do it. John had *known* she could, during that brief meeting in London. He wanted that certainty back.

The tram was drawing up.

"Miss Dobson, you brought your character letter?" he asked.

Her eyes darted to the tram. John gestured, waving ahead those waiting to board. He pulled Miss Dobson aside, and her eyes came back to him, a hard shine to them. He wanted, suddenly and very much, to press one or two of his fingers to her lips.

"Don't lie," he advised instead.

5

There is no excuse for a misdirected envelope.

—How to Become Expert in Type-writing

*B*etsey Dobson bit her bottom lip. The curls at each corner of her mouth tightened. Titus Rew, the tram conductor, called John's name.

John waved Rew on. He pushed back his hat. He and Miss Dobson stood waiting to hear what she would say. She didn't have the letter any more than she'd had a ticket for the train. He knew it. Would a good reference have reassured him? He'd told her to bring it for the benefit of Tobias Seiler more than for his own, but Tobias would trust his recommendation, character letter or none.

"I haven't got it."

"Because?" *Don't lie.*

"I—I left on bad terms, at the very end. My supervisor refused to write a fair reference—the reference I deserved—and . . . it was a bad scene, rather."

"Why should he refuse?"

"He is a pri— He didn't like me." Her eyes dropped. "Or perhaps he did. So to speak. In either case, it was bad."

Again, John recalled that meeting at Baumston & Smythe, this time how every eye in the room had followed Miss Dobson's entrance and her exit. A great beauty she was not. On the street, in an emporium or church services, she mightn't get such notice (though with her height, and her . . . *something* . . . she could scarce be overlooked), but in that room of men at their business, Betsey Dobson was a wrapped package, novelty and mystery and possibility.

What was it for her to work in that building each day? No wonder she'd aborted their exchange of smiles, or that she recoiled when she had discovered him following her.

"That is why I hadn't all the fare for the train," she was saying. "I didn't get any of my wages. I hadn't enough money, either to stay or to come, so I came, because I had nowhere else to go. And I wanted to."

The breeze blew wisps of hair across her mouth, where they stuck. She used her little finger to try to remove them, discovering in the process the rest of the fallen locks. With a puff, she set down her birdcage, took off her gloves, and went to the task of pushing the hair back under her hat.

She removed her cloak when she finished and draped it over her arm. She wriggled her shoulders, put them back, then faced him as though to re-present herself, her chin tucked slightly down, giving the effect that she was looking up at him. A disarming ruse there.

"You know Baumston and Smythe has a company outing here in a few months?" he asked, and she nodded. "How will that be for you, meeting up with them, that supervisor, again?"

Miss Dobson's demonic brows rose. "If I am a manager, Mr. Jones, I imagine it will be very sweet."

John turned to smile broadly at the seafront. It would be raining in ten minutes. He'd start with the hotel tour, then, when he rejoined the Gilbeys. He said, "Here it is, Miss Dobson. Sir Alton, who owns much of the land you'll walk upon in Idensea and who sits in the director's place at the company board meetings, doesn't want this excursions scheme. He wants to keep Idensea very posh, and day-trippers don't suit his idea of it, especially company outings such as you would be managing. He'll be seeking any reason to persuade the board of directors to call it off. So we need it to go well, you see. So well it's irresistible, to the board if not to Sir Alton himself."

"I see."

Perhaps she did. No doubt she understood there would be no need for an excursions manager if there were no excursions scheme. Here came a tram in the opposite, wrong direction. John considered it. He and Miss Dobson could cross the Esplanade and take it, and he could see her to Sarah Elliot's, where he had arranged a room for her. That would take longer than to drop her at the hotel, but he could still make his half-hour deadline with Lillian. He'd told her thirty minutes so he could easily exceed her expectations.

Taking this tram would be a decision, however. A manager could afford room and board at Sarah Elliot's. A hotel laundress, say, much less so.

"Did you try the lock?" he said. "Back there in the stationmaster's, on the window?"

"Did I . . . ?" Miss Dobson lifted her chin a touch, insulted. "Just what do you take me for?"

Eye to eye, they both made grabs for their hats in defense against a sudden, violent gust from the sea. John was laughing. He touched Miss Dobson's back, urging her to hurry across the Esplanade. They needed to catch this tram.

Such a sky. The widest she'd ever seen. Even more than the long bow of the shoreline and the eternal spread of the sea, it was the sky Betsey could not fold into her understanding, the cliffs and hillocks of the land overturned, sculpted into the stony clouds and softened with the promise of light. She almost laughed with the exhilaration of it, how something so unfamiliar could feel like a part of her, call to her from a place deep inside. Had it been like this at Blackpool, all those years ago? If she couldn't recall that, no wonder she'd conflated her father's hazy figure with that stranger's.

Her gawking caused a gap in the tram queue; Mr. Jones touched her arm to move her forward.

Thief's cage got her dubious inspection from the tram conductor, but with Mr. Jones at her side, nothing came of it but a mild directive to "take it up top." Resigned to Mr. Jones's guardianship for now, she added the fare he paid to the list of debts she would settle this summer, provided she had a job. Despite his burst of good humor, she wasn't taking that for granted, especially since she believed she'd glimpsed the Swan Park Hotel opposite the tram's current direction.

She felt like a pebble under a pillow, a hair in an iced cake, her worry a bit of nastiness at odds with all the holiday-making around her, day-trippers debating whether the German band played rain or shine, a young couple with their heads together, shuffling through a set of postcards. Mr. Jones beside her, in his Norfolk, impatient to return to his sweetheart.

Through music-laden wind, the tram broke the sea of promenaders. Betsey folded back the cage cover. Could Thief smell the change, the absence of London's dense and practical air, sense the wideness of the sky? She fingered the latch of the cage, tempted.

She, Thief, and Mr. Jones rode with the sea at their backs. Below, along the Esplanade, a row of shops and eateries nestled against the cliffs, and terraced above was Idensea itself, the weathered brick of the original village a frayed strand amongst furrows of dark gables and fresh, deep reds. Mr. Jones pointed ahead. "The Sultan's Road is there. Open next month."

Betsey squinted. The Sultan's Road was plain and clear, being enormous, but she could not make sense of it immediately, a Sphinx of a structure, part fanciful palace and stage-scenery mountain range, part utilitarian tracks—impossible to follow, given the peculiar fashion in which it emerged and disappeared.

"A switchback?" But she knew the guess was wrong.

"Pleasure railway. Not a thing its like in Britain."

As they passed, everyone on the tram turned to look at the

facade, where colorful arabesques embellished an arcade between two towers with tops like sugar kisses.

"You built this?"

"Not alone," he replied with a smile, but she sensed his pride, how he enjoyed the stir of excitement and speculation amongst the passengers. She begrudged him none of it. A mountain range rising up from the English sand, that dainty pier holding against the sea—she would have called it magic if the word did not seem to discount the work.

The yawning central arch of the pleasure railway echoed the shape of the towers, four or five stories at its kissed peak. It appeared to be the entrance, but the view was hidden by a painted canvas curtain with lettering that promised ADVENTUROUS & EXOTIC SCENES OF THE EAST! ALL-MODERN LIGHTING & MUSICAL EFFECTS! A THRILLING COAST OVER THE GRAVITY TRACK!

And: "6d Admission."

Betsey multiplied that number by her rough estimate of the crowd at hand. "What a shame it could not open for Whitsuntide."

He laughed as though this pleased him. She took the opportunity to ask, "Are you taking me to the hotel?"

"The Bows, you'll stay there. Tobias—Mr. Seiler—hasn't time to see you today."

She disliked both nuggets of information. "The Bows" sounded like a lodging house, and she'd expected to live in the cheap staff quarters at the hotel. Nor would she be at ease until the hotel manager himself assured her of her position. She held her tongue, however; she'd left her power to argue along with her wages at Baumston & Smythe.

She felt a raindrop on the brim of her hat and had begun to unfold her cloak when Mr. Jones sprang from his seat with fingers in his mouth to deliver a piercing whistle over the side of the tram. He shouted to someone, then urged her off the tram, and they ran to an empty dray headed away from the Esplanade. Before taking a place on the dray's end, Mr. Jones handed her up to the driver, who took one look at her and said, "You ain't his London girl, not you."

The sprinkles ended, and the rain began. They drove up into the yellow heath, a mile or two from the Esplanade, and Betsey's spirit turned as soggy as her cloak. These were homes along the lanes, real ones with property, tended gardens inside cast-iron fences, places where families grew, not make-do housing for transient holidaymakers, or anyone else who might be moving on soon.

And The Bows, indeed, was one of these homes, its name true to the matching pairs of broad bow windows on each side of the house, both the first and second stories. Mr. Jones seemed to notice her sluggishness in climbing down from the dray, the trouble it was to keep her under his umbrella as they walked to the door, but aside from assuring her this was a fine house, he ignored it.

A discreet plaque at the door stated "The Bows, Mrs. Elliot, Proprietress." The maid let them in and promptly harangued Mr. Jones as to his purpose here—how could he bring Miss Gilbey without notice, or was that Miss Gilbey, couldn't be, and did Mrs. Elliot know what scandals he was up to now? Through it all, it was plain no better treat existed than to have Mr. Jones turn up at the door of The Bows.

Betsey half-listened as Mr. Jones explained his errand and her identity. With increasing panic, she looked into the parlor at her left, which, with the dull light from the overcast day and the absence of any occupant, should have seemed forlorn. It didn't. It looked inviting, and . . . pretty. Pretty green wallpaper and hooked rugs and gilded picture frames, groupings of pretty chairs for conversation, a pretty bowl of peonies sitting on a cottage piano.

Pretty. Far, far too pretty.

"Dora Pink," Mr. Jones offered to Betsey as explanation for the maid, now off to find her mistress.

Betsey coughed to clear her throat of the thick and mortifying rise of tears. "I won't—I cannot stay here."

"Sarah's held a room. You're lucky to—"

"I want to stay at the hotel, in the staff quarters."

He was shaking his head as she spoke.

"Why not?"

"Tobias would never approve, not if you're a manager. And it isn't right—we've people leaving their families, counting on those quarters so they can have wages to take home at the end of the season."

"It's too far—I'll have to pay for the tram every day, to say nothing of the price of the room—it's just too dear, I'm sure, too—it's too good."

Her voice cracked over that last word. Mr. Jones's impatience fell away, as palpably as if he'd dropped her valise, picked up a book, and begun leafing through the pages to the one he wanted. Her composure would be a damn bloody stump by the end of the day, the way she'd sunk her teeth into it and held, but she wouldn't let go now. She would not be the object of this curious, perceptive sympathy. She met his eye.

"It won't do, Mr. Jones."

He didn't stop it, that reading. After a moment, Betsey realized the proprietress had come.

"Sarah," he greeted her, "Here's Miss Dobson. She may stay, I don't know. I do know where she'll *not* stay, but the rest I leave to her. You and Charlie still for tea?"

She would not miss it, the proprietress said, and swore to be quite prompt. Mr. Jones put on his hat and took his leave, his guardianship concluded.

"Well." Mrs. Elliot smiled and nervously passed both hands down the blond hair over her shoulder, a thick, rough braid of curls threatening to explode. She wore widow's blacks but could not have been much more than forty. "You don't have to stay on, naturally you don't. But the holiday, you see. You may find it difficult just now to find something else. As for . . . Well, I don't think my rates are— Mr. Jones helped me set them, and no one's complained . . ."

Landlords and landladies, in Betsey's experience, never shied of speaking of money, but Mrs. Elliot's embarrassment prompted Betsey to be blunt. "I haven't a thing to pay you, Mrs. Elliot."

"Oh!" She laughed with relief. "That! *That* is quite all right. I mean, you must have wages first, mustn't you? You'll be paid soon enough, and then we will—ah! May I see your bird? He must need water, and you? An easy journey, I hope. But your cloak all wet . . ."

Hot tea, a bite to eat, a look around the house, introductions to other boarders along the way. Betsey treated it all as she would a pretty flowerbed marked off with round stones.

She was shown a room on the third story. Mrs. Elliot's son, Charlie, had already brought up Thief and the valise. Betsey turned the mended part of Thief's cage to the wall. The valise, sitting on the white coverlet of the bed, looked dark and shabby, and when she unwound the twine and opened it, London and Avery and the tiny flat rushed out to her in scent. Betsey moved it to the floor.

The picture rails were intact. They'd been stripped in her other place, used for fuel by some previous tenant. Botanical prints hung from these, and the room held other superfluous items, a wool rug beside the bed, a rocking chair with a needle-point pillow. As she walked to the windows, she dragged a fingertip along the curve of the iron bed frame. Cool, smooth, never chipped and repainted.

The windows looked down on the front garden and hedgerow lane before the house. Below, left and right, were the wide canopies of the bow windows, connected by the roof of an upper-story porch—almost a private balcony, if one was willing to brave climbing out the windows. The rain had stopped, and over rooftops and hills knobby with yellow furze, she had a view of the pleasure pier and sea. From here, the waves were only long rents in the water's fabric, and it all looked . . . yes, majestic and grand and all that, but *manageable* was what Betsey thought. Manageable, comprehensible.

A flowerbed, this house, this room. Not for her to cut from or wallow in or even sniff at too deeply. Still, she was here till tomorrow, perhaps even Monday. If she used a drawer or two, she could hide that ugly valise under the bed until she needed it again.

She unpacked. Three or four minutes that took.

Now what?

6

None but clean fingers should ever touch even the margin
of the paper. (Alas! that it is necessary to say this.)

—*How to Become Expert in Type-writing*

*L*illian Gilbey was no longer a committed diarist; dia-
ries, she'd concluded, were the province of little girls
and middle-aged men, and in any case, her life as a young lady
who was Out provided far more riveting material than it did time
to actually record or reflect upon it.

Therefore, her current diary, when it was filled, would be her
last. It had been languishing since she'd left finishing school, and
as much as Lillian Gilbey loved beginning projects, she abhorred
languishing, incomplete ones. She conceived a plan to finish it off,
dividing the blank pages by the two years until she planned to
marry, with a dozen or so pages reserved at the end for wedding
details. *No more by thee my steps shall be,* she would write her final
night in her parents' home, and thus would she close the literal
covers of her girlhood.

Just now, however, she mentally composed a more prosaic
notation for the half-completed volume. *John Jones,* she would
write this evening, *inattentive at the worst possible moments.*

Here he idled, one foot propped on the balustrade that fronted
Idensea's Esplanade, his elbows at rest on the top rail. His gaze had

been fixed upon the gray sea and foreshore longer than the view really merited. Did he not realize here lay the opportunity he'd been awaiting the day through—her mother and sisters gone for another stroll down the pier, his final chance to be alone with her today? After all these months, did he not wish to say *something* to indicate his intentions toward her?

He'd been about to. At least, Lillian had thought so for a moment, and she'd dropped her eyes, as she believed she ought in such a situation, and reminded herself how far she would allow him to proceed. Not all the way to a proposal, certainly—there were too many diary pages yet to fill before that event could occur—but she needed some sort of *something* to help her decide whether his name should progress from Candidate to Contender.

She'd surprised herself the night she'd added his name to the Candidates, crossing off Patrick Markwell to make room in her list of ten. *John Jones,* she'd written, *potential.*

Not that you'd know it now, the way he was slouched over the railing, practically with his back to her, leaving her with nothing to do but twirl her parasol.

But then—

Then he looked over his shoulder and smiled at her, and she could not regret the lines through Patrick Markwell's name. Lillian did not think John's face very refined. It was too full and boyish for that, but when he smiled, it almost completely disguised the scar that made his eye droop and she could admit him good-looking, if somewhat raw. She scarcely registered what he was saying to her, something he'd noticed down on the shore.

She nodded as if she'd been joining him in his contemplation all along. For herself, even as a child, what she had found most remarkable in her seaside visits was how people lolled on the beach, quite as if they were home in their beds rather than in public. Idensea did not permit mixed bathing, and today's weather gave the sea a foreboding appearance, so most of the bathing machines and their horses stood unused on the beach, but all along the shore, men and women cozied right alongside each other.

Lillian found it difficult not to stare. Because it was so vulgar. Many of them were only laboring types, come on cheap rail fares for Whitsuntide, so such unfortunate vulgarities must be expected. From *them*.

"They are having a fine time, aren't they?" John said, just as Lillian had caught sight of three full-grown women sitting in the sand, not a one of them in a proper bathing costume, their bare toes pointing to the water. Each time a wave thrashed them, they squealed with the thrill of the cold and the rush, careless (or perhaps perfectly mindful) that the water had thrown their skirts well above their knees, putting all that flesh on display to whomever cared to look.

But John, as it happened, meant a circle of two dozen or more children sitting on blankets just below, their heads bowed. They were a ragged bunch—some charity outing, no doubt— but perfectly precious nestled on their blankets, chattering as the prayer concluded and they tucked into the sandwiches one of their chaperones was distributing from a wicker hamper. And wasn't it rather adorable of John to note it? *John Jones, amenable to children.*

He suddenly straightened from the balustrade and touched her shoulders. "Wait here."

And he left her. She turned to the sea to pretend she found it mesmerizing and whatnot, impatient, wretchedly aware of her singularity in the promenading crowd.

He returned with a brown paper bundle in his hands, filled with rock, bright sticks of candy with the word "Idensea" molded in the center. She gaped at the quantity until he said, "Help me pass it round," and then she understood he meant to give the sweets to the charity children.

She had already refused one walk in the sand and felt annoyed that he was forcing her to say *no* again—one of her most effective tactics in man-management was to say *yes* as often as possible—but her new shoes and the chenille-embroidered hem of her walking costume were no more appropriate for trekking unpaved ground than they had been an hour ago, and so she bade him toward the children with the assurance she was quite happy to wait.

He vaulted over the balustrade and, rather than distribute a sweet to each child, put the bundle in care of one of the chaperones, whose bless-you-kind-sir was not audible to Lillian but evident all the same. He strode back, shoes and trousers collecting filth. Lillian sighed, fully aware of her ambivalence. She liked the impulse behind the stunt better than its execution; she found him exasperating, and she found him compelling.

John Jones, such a great deal of work.

Yet the notion of polishing the diamond in the rough, of being the power behind the power, appealed mightily to Lillian. A woman had her place, she believed; it was on a throne, and not merely an ornamental piece.

"You might have saved yourself the trouble and paid the vendor to take it for you," she told him.

"The trouble was the fun of it."

Impulsively, he stroked her cheek. His thumb was enormous, hard and rough against her skin. Her throat felt tight, her knees fluid. The sensations, being involuntary on her part, were not wholly agreeable to her.

He had kissed her once, the only man who'd ever done so. When he had started kissing her *entire* mouth, she'd pushed him away in shock and . . . something else. He'd apologized, and she had not written a word about it in her diary, unsure how to phrase such a thing. And if she did record it, did it do John credit as a suitor, or count against him? Had it been appalling, or something else? Ever since, she'd been trying to decide.

As they strolled arm in arm toward the hotel to meet her mother and sisters for tea, she listened to his talk of the little railway he'd helped design. She said *oh* in all the appropriate places and with all the appropriate inflections, as appearing anything less than enthralled with a man's interests profited a woman only on certain rare occasions. If she married him, she would have to listen with more attention to be of any use to his career. A shame his ambitions weren't more toward poet laureate.

She found them rather silly, these seaside buildings of his, insubstantial, like drawing-room ballads compared with a Bach cantata. But neither were they nothing, especially for a career as young as John's. Someday, he and she could be walking toward something that truly mattered—a grand concert hall, an important museum, a cathedral. Someday, John Jones and his wife could be the toast of society.

"You never showed us your office when you toured us round the hotel," she said after John had greeted the doorman and they'd come inside.

"It seemed best to get you out of doors whilst the rain held. And you were bored."

She bristled. He dared her to deny it, enjoying her embarrassment. That he'd noticed her boredom all but insulted her femininity, but what did the man expect, dragging her round to boiler houses and underground kitchens and sprawling laundries?

He warned her his office was of the same practical character but granted she could have a look on their way to the tearoom. She sighed when she saw how accurate he'd been. Land surveys tacked to the wall, a bookcase of engineering journals and reference manuals, a frightfully muddy pair of workman's gloves on the desk. She approved, in general, of the industrious feel of the room, but the utter lack of a personal aesthetic distressed her. Indeed, she had such a great deal of work to do, if she picked him.

She ran her forefinger along the spines of a row of journals. "Where is the Tennyson?"

With his head, he motioned toward a door behind his desk. "My rooms."

Lillian swallowed. She'd known he lived here at the hotel, but not precisely *here*. Being alone with him in his office stretched the boundaries of propriety to their limit. To be a door away from his private quarters was quite, *quite*—

"Do you read it?"

He joined her beside the bookcase. "Times." He smiled down at her. "When I want to sleep."

"You're a beast."

Perhaps it was only a nod, but his head moved, and her eyelids fell shut. She felt his lips on hers, and when he did not kiss her entire mouth the way he had last time, she parted her lips a little more. Had it been appalling, or something else? A credit in his favor, or not? It was necessary to know, so she parted her lips.

Yes, appalling. She was certain of it now. Appalling, how it conjured up the maddest thoughts, of shedding her gloves, of indiscreet day-trippers lolling in the sand, how it took her quite from her *self*.

She pushed him away, informed him again he was a beast, and immediately regretted breaking the kiss. A little longer would have done no harm, but now she couldn't possibly close her eyes again and offer her mouth, not with John standing there not apologizing like he had last time, looking like she'd surrendered a secret to him.

"I ought to be done with you this moment," she said.

"Before tea? I've ordered a fine one for you. And your mother invited me for your musical society in June—"

"Why did you accept? I'm sure you've never had a lesson. You'll only embarrass us both."

"And then you're here again in August for your holiday. You might as well wait till autumn, Lils, when you can make a clean finish of me, hadn't you?"

He wasn't worried. She didn't know when she'd allowed that to happen. The moment she'd parted her lips?

"Mother and everyone else will be waiting."

She swept out of the office ahead of him. The presence of someone in the corridor emphasized how reckless she'd been, how easily she might have been caught kissing John in his office. She halted only when she realized John had stopped to speak to the person she'd almost run down, a young woman.

Lillian could hardly enter the tearoom alone. She waited and busied herself with adjusting the wilting camellia John had given her. The woman was unnecessarily tall and apparently worked for the hotel in some capacity, though Lillian could not imagine what. She wasn't dressed as a chambermaid or as kitchen staff. Switchboard operator? Or some sort of assistant to Mr. Seiler—she was asking John about him.

John shook his head. "That is why I took you to Sarah's. Tobias is meeting us"—he indicated Lillian—"right now for tea, and he'll be too busy this evening; he makes a point to socialize with the guests on Saturday evenings."

"I see."

It was clearly the end of the conversation. But neither of them moved. Then they both murmured, "I'm sorry."

John added, "I thought Sarah understood. She oughtn't have brought you."

"No, it wasn't her fault."

Lillian said, "Mr. Jones." She made it lilt.

John put out his arm for her, but she had to move a few steps to take it, and she could sense his uneasiness over the hotel girl, even though her predicament was of her own making.

"Come with us," he said.

Both Lillian and the hotel girl laughed.

Lillian saw her own panic reflected in the other girl's eyes.

7

The exercise of taste and good judgment are as necessary
to success in type-writing as in any other occupation.
—*How to Become Expert in Type-writing*

*T*obias will be happy to meet you," John went on. "You'll
be able to get acquainted before—"

"Mr. Jones," Lillian said, no lilt.

Of all the mad notions, inviting an employee to dine with a
superior. From age twelve, Lillian had navigated more garden
parties, soirees, socials, holiday meals, and balls, both masquer-
ade and otherwise, than she could count, but the thought of the
awkwardness this situation would bring—and just as she was
meeting for the first time John's dearest friends in Idensea—was
more than she could stomach. And did he have no feelings for
the hotel girl herself, how humiliated she'd be in the tearoom
dressed as she was? *John Jones, oblivious to the most basic social
mores.*

"You already invited Mr. Dunning earlier today," she reminded
him. "Let me go ahead of the two of you, and give the tearoom
staff a bit of notice of these last-moment changes, hmm?"

She released John's arm as if already en route. But if she were
forced to enter that tearoom without an escort, and all to ensure a
switchboard operator or whatever she was had a chair—

But no, she was safe. The hotel girl was begging off, walking off, cutting off any chance for John to argue or persuade. She and the hotel girl had rescued each other, good feminine sense prevailing in the onslaught of male idiocy.

John, however, was too quiet on the way to tea.

But she knew what to do. Here at the table were his friends: The Seilers each came from old hotelier families in Switzerland; Mr. Seiler was the Swan Park's chief manager, while his wife headed housekeeping. Then, Mrs. Elliot, a widow for several years, sitting with her son, a lad of twelve or so. John had lived with the Elliots his first months in Idensea, before Dr. Elliot's death.

Lillian would dazzle them.

And best of all, there was that last-moment addition to the party, Mr. Dunning, Sir Alton's only son.

"How best to punish our tardy host, Miss Gilbey?" he asked as she and John were seated.

She smiled at him. They'd become acquainted in London, when he'd been tagging along once with John. Wasn't that a funny way to think of it, a baronet's son tagging along with John Jones? Yet the reverse hadn't been the case.

"Hide the sweets, of course," she replied.

"How awfully cunning of you. But you wouldn't be very comfortable huddling beneath the table, I fear."

The jest was not the wittiest she'd heard, but she laughed all the same, because she found something appealing in its delivery, and because it suited her to let John hear her laugh with another man, let him hear her speak with another man about the upcoming Albert Hall season. Invite another man to her music society party in June.

Mr. Dunning was young, fresh from Cambridge, but he made her think of her parents' eighteenth birthday gift to her, gleaming pearls nestled in black velvet. Immediately, effortlessly attractive, inspiring a dozen ready visions about how and where they would be worn. Noel Dunning was easy to like; he didn't discomfit her with ambivalence.

John Jones, a great deal of work. Worth it? With Mr. Dunning at the table, it was impossible not to think of Sir Alton, who'd come by his title through his music, a composition memorializing Prince Albert. Could not a builder who served the Public Good hope for some similar honor?

These things, too: Whom else did she permit to call her Lils, or to kiss her entire mouth? Things like that surely meant Something, even if neither of them said so.

In her determination to extract herself from Mr. Jones's invitation as rapidly as possible, Betsey went the wrong way, deeper into the hotel rather than where she wanted to go, out. Out, for God's sake. She halted when she realized the light had changed and found herself in an airy space with ferns and palm trees—entire trees, indoors! On the furniture, on the islands of carpet atop the parquet, on Betsey's own sleeve and glove as she started to touch her forehead, dapples of light glowed blue and turquoise, and she could only look up.

The source was a dome of colored glass, white feathers and yellow scrolls strewn over a patchwork of watery hues. Betsey allowed herself to stare, to wonder at the imagination behind it, one unfettered by practicality or moderation. She followed the repetition of the scrolls and plumage in the plasterwork as it ringed the dome and cascaded down to the pilasters with the easy profusion of cake icing flowing from a piping bag. Each archway surrounding her framed its own ideal view of some other architectural feature, like the stairway directly across from her, itself an exhibition for the ladies gliding down the steps, the misty fabrics of their gowns wafting behind them.

No one here rushed.

The carpet beneath her boot soles felt like it had been rolled out over sponges.

Cream-colored upholstery covered the settees and chairs. People actually sat upon them, extending their arms along the backs in utter ease. At least one held a cup and saucer.

Behind her hand, to herself, Betsey whispered, "Hell and hell." As she retraced her steps to find her way out, she wished she'd stayed put at the lodging house and delayed this misery.

How could she work here? The parlor at The Bows had nearly done her in. How could she ever even enter here and not feel like a playactor or a foreigner whose very name was unpronounceable to the natives?

"Miss Dobson?" An apple-cheeked page stopping her.

"Yes?"

He looked relieved. As the hair on the iced cake, Betsey reckoned she'd been easy enough to pick out, but the boy had not been certain. "Ma'am, Mr. Seiler sent me. He's eager to meet you, he says, and wonders if you'd be so kind as to await him in his office."

Mr. Seiler, at last! "Certainly—"

But the boy had memorized the entire message; he would relay it. "However, as it may be some time before he is able to join you, he does not wish you to feel obliged. If the wait is an imposition, he is pleased to see you Monday morning."

These were the most courteous words she'd ever received from a supervisor, but Betsey didn't fool herself that they were anything but an order to stay. The page showed her to the anteroom of Mr. Seiler's office, very near the hotel's main entrance. Tea arrived minutes after she'd taken a seat, white china with a leafy gold border, a harp imprinted on the saucer—no, a lyre, the head and neck of two swans creating the curved sides of the instrument.

She took her time preparing her cup. She expected to wait a good piece, knowing Mr. Seiler was at tea with Mr. Jones and his London girl—Miss Gilbey, Sarah Elliot had told her during the ride to the hotel.

Mr. Jones, asking her to join them. As if her fare-dodging and arguing were quite forgotten. As if she, in her tweed and falling-down hair, could be just another guest at the table. He was mad, he must be. What else could explain such impulsive, reckless kindness?

She'd stirred tea with a silver spoon twice today. Before that, the last time she'd held silver, she'd been polishing it, in service at the Dellaforde household in Manchester. This spoon was plainer yet more substantial, and she watched her hand rotate it within the cup. *Well then,* she thought, *if I don't belong here, where better?* If she'd not disgraced herself with the Dellafordes' son, might she be there still? And would it suit her better?

No. She knew that as truly as she knew anything. And knowing it made something else clear: She had better stop letting everything cow her, or Tobias Seiler would never see a place for her here.

Mr. Seiler was as polished and graceful as a silver candlestick, his form slight and trim, his presence weighty. He bowed as he gestured her into his private office, expressed gratitude for her patience, doing him the favor of waiting. Betsey could almost believe Mr. Jones had revealed nothing of her disastrous arrival in Idensea. Her propped-up courage firmed a bit more.

She matched his dance of courtesy, apologizing for interrupting his leisure time. "Mr. Jones mentioned you mingle with the hotel guests on Saturday evenings."

His brows rose with amusement. "I am an hotelier, Miss Dobson," he said, his European accent giving the proper slide to *hotelier*. "Only well away from the Swan Park am I at my leisure. Mingling, any day of the week, is perhaps the most serious work I do."

With an incline of her neck, she admitted her mistake. "Though to the guests, it must not seem so."

"You understand." Against the whiteness of his hair and trim whiskers, his pale blue eyes assessed her. She rather thought her response had pleased him. "Much we share in our duties in that regard, no?"

He drew prayer-poised hands to his chin, waiting. Betsey faltered, unsure how her work as a type-writer could be likened to having charge of a palace such as the Swan Park. But she was more than a type-writer girl now.

"You mean we mustn't allow our guests to see the effort we put in, that we're hosts as much as managers. I suppose I've known since I was a girl in service that few care to know the work behind the pleasure. It's like that, wouldn't you say?"

Mr. Seiler did not say. But his waxed mustache lifted a fraction. A smile. "There is more to the position than hospitality."

"Yes. I must promote, and make bookings and travel arrangements. Entertainments and tours must be organized, and each group is served a dinner here at the hotel. An enormous number of details to tidy up in all that. Quite frankly"—she smiled at him without reserve—"it seems you ought have hired me before now, Mr. Seiler. It is nearly June."

A laugh rumbled in his throat, even as his lips remained pressed together. "*Wie schade.* A pity Baumston and Smythe had you hidden away. Which brings us to the matter of your character. Mr. Jones instructed you to bring it, and I understand you have failed to do so."

Her stomach dropped. What had Mr. Jones told him already? Relating Wofford's vileness in the vaguest terms to Mr. Jones had been awkward; detailing it to the refined Mr. Seiler in his gleaming office would surely take her down to ashes. The unfairness of it bolted through her again, that she had to sit here and admit to failure before she'd even begun, that she'd reduced herself to fare-dodging and asking Avery for money, and nearly let tears fall in public, Mr. Jones looking on. A better woman would feel rueful for inflicting harm on another, but God help her, she could only wish for Wofford's fingers under her boot heel right now.

"Yes. I have failed to do so." She braced for the inevitable question. Mr. Seiler's silence did not so much surprise her as induce her to add, "I am sorry."

"*Merci.*" He put on half-rimmed spectacles, opened a leather portfolio, and thumbed the pages inside. "It is not my wish to frighten you, Miss Dobson, but I must speak as your supervisor."

"Of course."

He found the sheet of paper he sought, notes she supposed he'd taken from Mr. Jones. "Type-writing, dictation, composition, bookkeeping, elocution—cookery?"

"It was a female institute. They were duty-bound to make at least a portion of the education practical. What's shorthand worth once a girl's married, after all? But a nice fish cake . . ."

She left off, letting the lifelong value of a fish cake recipe speak for itself. Mr. Seiler gazed at her over his half-rims for several uncomfortable moments. But then he chuckled down in his throat again, and having gained that, Betsey thought better of expounding on the practical nature of the other courses, how bookkeeping was called "Domestic Accounts" and that elocution had consisted mainly of reciting moral verse which seemed to have been written for children.

"I did well in all my courses, Mr. Seiler. My instructors said I learned quickly. The headmaster chose me to assist the reading room supervisor—that was an honor he awarded, you see—"

"But no letter from the school, either."

"No, sir." She could not blame Wofford for that.

"Mr. Jones still believes we should, as he says, try you on."

"And what do you think, sir?"

"Ah!" He threw up his hands, finding her question facile. "I find you delightful, and I should normally be pleased to give you a trial. However, as you yourself have noted, June is upon us, and our season to profit is fleeting. I have not time for trials. Nor failures. You understand."

Betsey flexed the hand resting in her lap, remembering the pressure of Richard's grip. *When you've made whatever wreck you'll make of it, don't bring it back to my family.*

"Mr. Seiler, I understand you perfectly."

After providing her with a small notebook and pencil, Mr. Seiler escorted Betsey to the basements via his private stairway, hidden behind one of the panels in his office.

These basements were a city, the reverse of the leisurely and upholstered world above. The maze of stores and kitchens, of lifts and laundries and staircases could be mastered only with time and familiarity; Betsey reserved her concentration for Mr. Seiler's directions, furiously jotting notes as he explained his expectations, suggested methods of organization, provided names of staff with whom she'd be working.

Selectively, he paused to introduce her or take a question, but otherwise, they moved quickly, in a river of pricked attention rippling with curtsies and nods and *Mr. Seiler, sir*.

In the lift back up, Betsey confessed she had no idea where in the hotel they would be when the operator opened the door.

"To be expected," Mr. Seiler replied. "Do spend time learning your way, *avec discrétion*—my staff is to be always at hand, never on display. I trust you understand."

She did. Moreover, she vowed to remember.

The rear of the hotel's main floor opened onto a wide veranda with a lattice roof; from there spread acres of parkland, nothing she would have believed had she seen it in a painting, what she suddenly understood people meant when they used the word *idyllic*. Every sandy path beckoned with some promised bliss, to shelter in a tunnel of ivy and blossoms, descend between the slopes of a chine for a shaded and fragrant walk to the shore, be soothed by the swans' effortless passage over the green pond. The more sporting could head for the tennis court or bicycle shelter, or croquet and bowl on a carpet of trimmed grass.

"Oh, good God."

"Miss Dobson." Mr. Seiler nodded meaningfully toward the guests on the veranda.

"Such a sweet little garden." She scanned the property again, this time to find the open-air pavilion where her excursion groups would have their dinner dance. She did nothing so gross as point when she spied a glass-and-iron cupola through a copse of fir trees, but Mr. Seiler confirmed it was her pavilion.

She wanted to go to it right away, but Mr. Seiler ushered her back inside to a familiar corridor, the one where she'd found Mr. Jones's office. The hotel and pier company offices were here as well. He unlocked a pair of wide doors, and Betsey felt silly when she realized she had expected to see rows of type-writing machines and tiers of clerking stands. This was a much smaller space, divided by three broad arches, the twilight filtering through a bank of windows and a skylight. A glass partition with narrow doors indicated a few private offices, and the longest solid wall was filled up with cabinets and shelving, two telephones, and a single type-writing machine.

Mr. Seiler apologized for her desk, clearly a recent addition, squeezed in beside the doorway and stacked with record books and loose papers.

"You see we have been collecting things in anticipation of your arrival," he said. "Monday, your first task shall be to . . . ah, consolidate these matters. The excursion scheme has suffered from too many overseers, I fear—we had thought to distribute the responsibilities amongst the staff, but all too soon it became clear that was inadequate. You have here the records and invoices and such from the various departments of the hotel. Once you have sorted them out, let us meet again to discuss what you've learned—a quarter past five?"

"Yes, sir."

"Let me amend. This is your second task. Your first—" He pulled a silver case from inside his coat and gave her his card. "Prevett's, King's Lane. Let them fit you for a suit of clothes to wear Saturdays, something to show you as part of the staff here. Mr. Hamble"—he gestured toward one of the desks—"shall arrange to have half the cost taken from your wages in installments."

While the disarray on her desk made Betsey's fingers itch to be busy, she balked inwardly at this command. She had her gray tweed and her brown tweed; they were decent and had served her well, not to mention that the cost of them was included in the sum she *would* pay to Richard, regardless of his "forgiveness." An entire new uniform for a single day of the week!

"Would not a ribbon or badge of some sort do as well, sir?"

Perhaps she hid her gall too well. "Not at all," he responded without a trace of concern. "Mr. Creacy is two shops down from Prevett's. He will fit you for gloves."

She expected him next to tell her where to buy hairpins, but with a check of his pocket watch, he escorted her to the main entrance and arranged a carriage and a staffer to wait with her before she had the chance to refuse. Amidst ladies and gentlemen dressed for the evening, a glowing fountain, and the melody of some unseen violin player, Betsey was handed into a carriage as though she too wore silk and pearls.

She stripped off her gloves as soon as the door shut. She was diligent about keeping them clean, but they were two years old, and damn it, what a long way she'd come since rifling Avery's pockets for a pasty this morning.

Still, Mr. Seiler was right. She needed new gloves.

And God, she could buy some. He had not sacked her.

The carriage avoided the Esplanade, taking the road on the cliffs and through the town center. Betsey happened to be looking out when the lights on the pleasure pier below flickered and lit. How strange and lovely, those burning points over the water. She would never find the sight ordinary.

She could see them from her windows at the lodging house, she remembered. *The* windows, not hers. She hadn't found the right time to ask Mr. Seiler about the staff lodgings, however.

Perhaps she wouldn't. If Mr. Seiler was right about the gloves, then perhaps Mr. Jones was right about this lodging house. Alone in the carriage, Betsey relieved her exhaustion with a wild, delicious stretch and drummed her fingertips against the carriage walls, thinking perhaps she would just stay put.

8

All ordinary work should be without an error.

—*How to Become Expert in Type-writing*

Almost a fortnight since ordering the damn uniform, Betsey was thinking Mr. Seiler might have been right about it, too. For frugality's sake, she took it from the seamstress to do the finishing work herself, and with her first excursion group arriving in the morning, she stood on an ottoman while Sarah Elliot helped her prepare the hem.

They worked in the room that had been the office of Mrs. Elliot's late husband, a physician. Dora Pink, one of the few servants in the household, made her way about the perimeter of the room, needlessly repositioning objects with a dramatic bustle. Betsey recognized this as the tactic of a maid who wanted attention, but Mrs. Elliot, fully absorbed in her task and inclined to be dreamy in any case, failed to notice until the light in the room fell by one lamp.

Mrs. Elliot sat back on her heels, mystified. Then she caught sight of the maid reaching toward another lamp. "Dora Pink!" she exclaimed, but the lamp was out before the name.

Dora jerked back her hand, all the way to her mouth, a fair simulation of innocence. "Begging your pardon, ma'am! It's just they's lights on all over the house, and somebody's got to keep on

to it, you know. See if the pendant lamp ain't enough—I'll wager
it is."

"My servants think I am a fool, Betsey," Mrs. Elliot said upon
Dora's departure, and then sighed. "I fear I'm still not terribly
clever about treating my home as a business, am I? Turn again,
now."

Betsey obeyed. She already had noted how the lodging house
staff, with amiable stealth, either supervised or ignored Mrs. Elliot,
but hadn't been certain if Mrs. Elliot herself had. She was a distracted mistress and incautious giver, protected by an affectionate
collusion between staff and lodgers. At suppers, she insisted plates
be refilled, and no one complained when Dora Pink apportioned
the extra servings as though they were lifeboat rations. For new-
comers, she demonstrated the lighting fixtures in the house, and
Dora Pink issued three candles per week per lodger, and it was
clear whose lead was to be followed.

Charlie, Mrs. Elliot's only child still at home, came to the door,
stopping short at the threshold to consider Betsey standing on the
ottoman. Betsey gestured at the new skirt. "Will it do, Charlie, do
you think?"

His eyebrows, normally so fair as to be invisible above his deep-
set eyes, took on a glow as the skin around them darkened. He
shrugged a shoulder. "It's not that bad. Mum, John's come for his
piano lesson, but don't hurry, because I've got that annual to show
him."

He was off. He was thirteen.

Mrs. Elliot finished the pinning, then bade Betsey to make use
of all the lamps she needed to finish up. "I know I've said you must
call me Sarah!" she interrupted as Betsey tried to thank her for her
help. She clutched both of Betsey's hands and squeezed them as
she put a quick kiss on her cheek. "You will be wonderful tomorrow, I know it!"

Betsey would be hosting a hundred employees of Pollit & Company Glassworks. Nervous enough, she could have melted in Mrs.
Elliot's burst of warm encouragement. In her surprise, she faltered

for some way to return it and finally managed to say, "I am so glad Mr. Jones made me live here, Sarah."

Mrs. Elliot laughed, but Betsey cursed herself for how awkward the comment sounded, how shallowly it reflected her gratitude.

Mrs. Elliot gone, Betsey changed out of the skirt and finished the hem on the sewing machine, then started for her room, where she would sew the buttons on to the vest. Most of the lodgers were in the parlor, the purr of comfortable chat broken by Mr. Jones's intermittent plinking on the piano. He'd begun lessons, of all things, coming to The Bows nearly every evening so Sarah Elliot could teach him to play the piano. Or one particular tune, rather. He worked at the same piece, over and over, something he was preparing for a party in London, Mrs. Elliot had told her. Miss Gilbey's party.

He sat watching Mrs. Elliot's hands now, his elbow propped on the piano, his head on his fist. His gaze flicked up as Betsey passed on her way to the staircase, and his smile for her was ready and lavish, and no less stunning for its brevity. By the time she'd returned it, he was looking down again, telling Mrs. Elliot, "Now the difference I hear. Let me go at it once more."

Who could learn in such a way? More evidence of his madness, Betsey thought, though all she knew of music lessons came from overhearing the Dellaforde children practice their scales. Mrs. Elliot had tutted upon realizing Mr. Jones had no intention of learning to read the music, that he was certain he could mimic the process of this one piece if she only showed him how enough times.

Betsey suspected he'd found it trickier than that. Unseen on the steps, she paused with her uniform draped in her arms and listened to him play, stumble, correct; play, stumble, correct. A growled expression of frustration. A jeer from Charlie Elliot. A threat about moving out from one of the lodgers. Mr. Jones, laughing, pleading for mercy; Mrs. Elliot laughing, too, demanding more diligence.

Half-afraid of her happiness in the moment, she rushed upstairs to her room. *Her* room, shared with no one but Thief. That she woke with astonishment morning after morning had nothing to do with the unfamiliarity of it all. She knew where she was. She just couldn't believe it.

Betsey turned up a lamp and opened the small windows in the dormer, admitting the voices and piano lesson inside. She readied her needle and spilled seventeen buttons from an envelope onto the coverlet of her bed, then grabbed them up and let them sift through her fingers. It felt luscious. A miser with his gold. Her brother-in-law, Richard, with his full bins of flour, or whatever he most adored. For a moment, Betsey understood him.

A small extravagance, these buttons, only brass-dipped tin, to be sure, but still a dearer choice than she might have made. Adding each one to the vest, however, she couldn't regret it.

A final fitting. She tilted the small looking glass on the dressing table, and, alternately ducking and standing on tiptoe, she tried to get a sense of the whole effect. She couldn't see it, quite. She could feel it, though. She knew how she felt behind the buttons, inside the thin Coburg wool.

No, indeed, Mr. Seiler. A ribbon or badge would not have done as well, not at all. In this uniform, she could believe the cheery reassurances she'd written to Caroline were more than wishful thinking. She could believe things would go as they ought tomorrow, that she could move past Mr. Seiler's warning about trials and failures. Tomorrow, in this uniform, with all her preparations in place, she could impress him. Mr. Jones, too. Mad, kind Mr. Jones who'd chosen to be her ally for some reason. Tomorrow, she wanted him to be glad of his choice.

The excursionists' train was punctual. However, the char-à-banc Betsey had hired was not. It irritated her, but she held her "Pollit & Co." sign aloft with a smile and greeted the arrivals as they filtered out of the rail station and gathered round her. She gave her

welcome speech, distributed the handbills printed with the schedule and a simple map, and concluded with the assurance that, for
those who cared to wait, the char-à-banc for the tour to Castle Hill
would arrive shortly.

Most ambled off toward the Compass Walk, but the fifteen or
so who remained would nearly fill the conveyance. She waited with
them, waited with small talk, waited as the small talk grew halting.
However fondly she had regarded Mr. Jones last night, she had a
few ill thoughts for him now, for he had recommended this particular driver as a knowledgeable guide for the tours to Castle Hill.

The watch Sarah had loaned her ("I *never* use it," she'd sworn)
weighted Betsey's pocket as she refused to check it every minute.
In any case, the clock outside the rail station was within view, so
she knew very well the fellow was twenty-six minutes past due
when he at last arrived.

The excursionists streamed for the char-à-banc before it
had even stopped. Betsey let them go ahead and begin boarding, intending to have a private word with the driver before they
departed. The vehicle and its team of horses appeared impressively
maintained, the harness and wheels clean, green paint glossy, and
six rows of bench seats polished. On the char-à-banc's side, in red
and gold letters, "The Sundial" was scripted.

As she noted this irony, she realized her excursionists were
finding something else amusing: their driver, welcoming them
aboard with extravagant bows, lurching each time his head went
near his knees. "Good Lord, he's soused," she heard someone say.

Suddenly, the horses moved, jerking the char-à-banc and causing a man boarding to fall and all the twittering and guffawing
to swoop up in a collective gasp. Betsey rushed toward the fallen
man, but someone nearer helped him up. He seemed unhurt.

Betsey spun on her heel and marched to the driver, who'd
taken the bridle of the nearest horse. "*Mr. Noonan.*"

She watched his flushed cheeks drain. Squirming beneath her
gaze, he drew his coat sleeve over his mouth. "Must've something
bit. No harm."

Her silent response to that made him shrink further. His red-rimmed eyes shifted away, and though he was certainly above forty, he looked like a child about to weep.

Betsey turned to the excursionists. She already had their attention. "It seems we'll not get to the castle ruins today, ladies and gentlemen. I'm so sorry—"

"Here, now, what's the need—"

"Mr. Noonan. *Mind your horses.*"

To the excursionists, she continued, "You've been good to wait such a long time, I know it's a disappointment, but I must ask you to leave the char-à-banc now." She reminded them of the amusements awaiting them on the Esplanade and about the photographer who would give them a special price if they came before noon. She heard complaints and regrets and jokes as they filed away, and all of it felt wretched.

"You won't need to call off the afternoon tour, ma'am," Mr. Noonan said in a low voice. "By then I'll be—"

"Less drunk? Never mind. You needn't come back this afternoon. I'll not be requiring your services at all this season, so pickle yourself at any rate you desire, it's no more my concern. Good day."

"But I come today." He tore his cap from his head and gestured toward the char-à-banc. "Took days gettin' it ready for you. Painted the gig and all."

She understood him suddenly. "You want to be paid! For what, a performance? If you think you'll do a bit of good—"

Something made her stop. His jaw jutting forward, a deflation under his coat. Something stung her with guilt, and she felt stupid and weak for it, because she was doing what was required, what was black-and-white right, for God's sake.

"There's nothing I can do about it, Mr. Noonan."

He knew she was right, too. He was giving up as she spoke. Betsey moved from him quickly, only to realize one of the excursionists had been waiting for her.

Or no, not an excursionist.

Avery Nash. With baggage.

He smiled. "At last, the little manageress notes my presence."

Betsey could only stare, overcome with the confused pleasure of seeing the familiar in a foreign place, with the thought, incredulous but not yet skeptical: *He's come after me?*

With a laugh, he took her elbow and kissed her cheek. "My darling Lizzie."

"What in hell . . ."

Avery, for all his admiration of theater that held an unblinking mirror to an imperfect audience, now proceeded to spin an awfully sweet tale, beginning with his missing her—"You always woke me in time for work, you know"—and raveling its way to a happy conclusion that hinted a return to London at summer's end: "Once everything shutters here for the season, you'll be ready to go back, and I'll certainly have my play finished, perhaps even another one started. You were right, I've realized . . ." He paused to lift his face toward the sky and take in a deep breath. "I can heal here. I can *work* here."

Certain details remained ambiguous. He'd left Baumston & Smythe—what good could clerking do him?—and exactly how, or whose idea that had been, was unclear, though it seemed to have originated with Betsey herself, who had failed to wake him for work, she being, of course, gone.

"And when Mrs. Bainwelter came round for the rent sometime after that, I was still gone," Betsey pointed out.

He wondered what he should do with his bags. Betsey offered no suggestions. "I'm working, Avery, and I shall be working until late this evening. Tomorrow, perhaps, we may meet, but I cannot be distracted today."

He called after her, told her to be fair. He'd come all this way to declare his affections.

Over her shoulder, she remarked, "Is that what you're doing?"

Both of the morning's encounters left her more rattled than she hoped she'd shown. As she had planned to accompany the tour to Castle Hill, the cancellation left her with some open time; she might have spared Avery a half hour or at least directed him to

an inn. But it was too shocking. She didn't know what to do with
him.

She headed for the hotel, darting past holidaymakers leisurely
admiring the tall pines and small parks along the Compass Walk,
until she brushed by Mr. Pollit, the owner of the glassworks. He
recognized her. He and his wife had already heard about the char-
à-banc incident.

"I was thinking of everyone's safety," she explained. Channel-
ing Mr. Seiler's calm demeanor, the way he never let people believe
they'd interrupted something important, she walked alongside the
Pollits to the Esplanade, turning the conversation to the private
tour of the Swan Park that she'd arranged for him and his managers that afternoon. "I can scarcely think of anyone who will appreciate the stained-glass dome more than you, Mr. Pollit."

She found them shady seats by the bandstand where they
could enjoy the forthcoming performance. Mr. Pollit and his wife
seemed content enough when she left them, but Betsey disliked
the blemish on the day. She spent the remainder of the morning at
the pavilion and in the kitchen and stores of the hotel, making certain all was in place for the dinner dance. In the afternoon, when
she went to the office, she was cheered to find letters on her desk.
More bookings, she hoped.

But no, they were bills, one she'd been anticipating, from an
advert she'd placed in a weekly magazine, and the other already
opened. Flowers.

She glanced about the office. It was a half-day for nearly everyone but her. Most of the workers were leaving, but Arland Hamble, the bookkeeper, was still at his desk.

She went to him. "I don't understand why this has come to
me."

He flipped a glance over the bill. "Your accounts. See. *For.
Pavilion.*" He pointed at each word as he slowly pronounced them.

"I'd meant to make use of the old bouquets from the dining
rooms." She felt queasy. She'd just come from putting arrangements on the tables at the pavilion, where she and her assistant

had remarked to each other how fresh they were. "I didn't order flowers. Why, it's dated before I arrived."

"Someone did it. See. *For. Pavilion.*" Again, he pointed at the words. "Your accounts."

She gave the moonfaced prick credit: He condescended to everyone alike, not just to her because she was new or a woman.

"It will put me over budget! There must be something to do about it."

"I suppose I can ask Mr. Seiler—"

"No." *No time for failure.* With Ethan Noonan and his char-à-banc hanging over her head, she felt desperate to find some alternative.

Unfortunately, she needed the cooperation of a moonfaced prick.

Never allow yourself to strike a wrong letter . . . Criticise, correct, and rewrite until you get a perfect copy of each exercise.

—*How to Become Expert in Type-writing*

ere, between *emaciation* and *emanate,* ought to be something like *emaculate*. Or so it seemed to John.

A few pages over, perhaps? *E-m . . . m?* Two *m*'s was not entirely outside the range of possibilities.

"Good Lord, why don't you simply ask me?" Noel Dunning, all but horizontal in one of the visitors' chairs, stretched up a leg to give John's desktop a kick. "Do you know what torture it is to watch you wade through that dictionary?"

"Never mind, I've got it." John scribbled in his best guess for the company secretary to sort out. The poor fellow was used to it, God knew. "As for whatever torture you experience whilst watching me work . . ." Over his spectacles, John looked at Dunning, shrugged, and returned to his letter.

"Fair enough," Dunning said. "But it would be all to your benefit, you know—imagine the time you would save. You might even find yourself able to take advantage of what is, in theory, your half-day."

"And 'take advantage' means a round of golf with you," John said, since that had seemed to be Dunning's original purpose in dropping by. More than half an hour had passed since John had told him he couldn't go.

"We could take the *Scherzando* out if you'd rather."

Sir Alton's racing yacht. John's pen hovered over the paper, a moment of *someday*. Dunning saw the hesitation and stood, coming to ease a hip on the corner of the desk. He picked up a seashell kept in service as a paperweight and put it to John's ear. "The *Scherzando*, Jones. The wind wants her."

"Sunday, eh? I'm promised to tour Rolly Brues round the Sultan's Road this afternoon."

"Ah. That is why I can't tempt you. Such a penchant you have for magnates, Jones. Too many readings of Samuel Smiles, or is it their daughters you find so fascinating?"

What John liked about men like Rolly Brues was learning how they'd made their fortunes, and since he hadn't heard a story yet that included spending a fine Saturday afternoon on a golf course or a racing yacht, he kept his head down over his work.

Dunning failed to notice he was being ignored. "Horace Gilbey, for example. Is it his carpet empire or his daughter's fair face?"

At this, John glanced up, but Dunning appeared intent on the seashell, holding it aloft as he studied its clean spiral. "This ought to be the inspiration for every building that goes up in Idensea," he mused. "Not all this tired Neo-Renaissance rubbish."

John valued the shell as a gift from young Charlie Elliot, and because it fulfilled its function as well as any other heavier-than-paper object might have. There had even been moments when he had paused to pick it up, admire it, and marvel a little at nature's design. But as architectural inspiration? Dunning probably had something.

"You ought to have met the plasterer with your father and me this morning," he told Dunning. "He would have appreciated the artistic advice on the moldings."

"Father? I think not. Though . . ." Dunning's lifted hand dropped and curled around the shell, his thumb pressing on the narrow point. "He didn't always used to play so careful, you know. I remember more than he'd like about Alton before his *Sir,* and he never appreciates it when I remind him of it. Anyway, he caught me at the piano with his whiskey last night and didn't seem to appreciate that at all, either. Thus, I'm little inclined to trot along after him as he sees to all his projects." Dunning put down the shell and reached inside his coat. "Mind?"

"No. But off my desk now, won't you?"

Dunning made a perfunctory offer of the cigarette case. He remained on the desk, tapping an unlit cigarette against the case. John slipped back into his work and forgot him until Dunning said, "I heard *you've* been on the piano some yourself lately. Preparing for Miss Gilbey's soiree?"

John grunted. Noted the second reference to Lillian.

"I'd have helped you, you know."

"Have I hurt your feelings, young Noel?"

"Bugger yourself."

"Off my desk."

Dunning went to one of the wall sconces to light his cigarette. He had been John's first thought for a cram-course music teacher. Dunning might be oblivious to many of life's realities, but in music, he was gifted. But then, at the tea, Lillian had invited him to the party as well, and John had immediately revised his strategy. Too much information in the hands of the competition.

Whether Noel Dunning intended to *be* competition, or even if Lillian's intention went no further than to make him jealous, hardly rated. The cultured, educated son of a first baronet was competition for Iefan Rhys-Jones.

A knock sounded at the office door. The papers that would have been under the seashell, had Dunning returned it to its proper place, took flight in the crosscurrent created by the open window and opening door. John grabbed for as many as he could as he greeted Tobias Seiler, come to tell him that Rolly Brues wanted John to join the dinner party he was holding in the hotel's dining room tonight.

"Rolly Brues," Dunning said from where he was crouched on the floor, collecting papers. "Unlikely name for a millionaire."

"Those damn Americans," John agreed drily. "Let anyone who can make money, they will." More than one of the volumes of *The Building News* and *The Engineer* stored in the bookcases opposite his desk referenced Brues's work in the States. Being asked to show him around Idensea was one kind of honor; an invitation to eat with him and meet the hotel's wealthiest guests was something else altogether.

He caught Tobias's pleased expression as he removed his spectacles. Likely, the invitation was the result of some deft finagling on Tobias's part, done in such a way that Brues thought it his own fine idea.

"Marta says I must order you to send her at least two of your neckties for the laundry to prepare," Tobias said. "Brues has two daughters of marriageable age."

The Seilers—much interested in seeing John marry well, and soon—kept him apprised of this sort of information, though this reminder of the Brues daughters was likely habit, as they had both spoken highly of Lillian after her visit. John started to tell Tobias to remind his wife he had but the one neck, but raised voices drew Tobias out into the corridor. John stood up to gain a better vantage point past Dunning, who had also moved in order to see what was happening.

"Bless God," John murmured.

"Quite," answered Dunning.

A thrill kicked through him. It was wrong. The sight of Betsey Dobson standing next to one of the pier company's bookkeepers, her jaw set like a cornerstone and her brows pulled together more fiendishly than usual, could mean only trouble, but there it was anyway: a tug of anticipation, as though a stage curtain had begun to part.

And on the topic of parts—Miss Dobson's. Hips, waist. A bosom that seemed like it should have been more thoroughly noticed before now. And where had all that neck come from?

"Nothing would do her but to sit over my arm and tell me how to go about my job," the bookkeeper was saying to Tobias. His name was Arland Hamble. Married not long ago. Whenever John remembered that fact, he experienced a general sympathy for Mrs. Hamble and any future Hamble offspring, as well as anyone they happened to marry when they grew up.

"Mr. Seiler, I was not trying to meddle," Miss Dobson said. "I only wanted—"

She hesitated, drawing her bottom lip into her mouth as she glanced into John's office, obviously discomfited by his and Dunning's observation of the scene. Yet enough authority rested in that glance to prompt Dunning to make haste in removing his cigarette from his lips. "Forgive me," murmured the baronet's son to the type-writer girl.

Her bottom lip escaped, a symptom of her unease. "I wanted his help in working out payments. So there would be a—"

Again, she glanced into the office, a pensive aspect about her eyes. Which were brown. He'd noted that before. But they were *quite* brown, weren't they? Brown looked well with blue—gorgeous, really, with the sort of blue Betsey Dobson wore just now, the same rich blue found in the Swan Park's carpets and wallpapers and glass dome.

"A solution in place before we came to you," she finished.

Solution. Required only in the presence of a problem.

"I see," Tobias said. His tone was mild and confident, assuring all involved he truly did see, even if he hadn't yet made up his mind on anything. He pulled out his pocket watch and interrupted Hamble's protests with concern for the bookkeeper's loss of his half-day, and while his sacrifice was appreciated, what a shame, for surely Miss Dobson and he himself could sort it through in a matter of minutes, and it so happened he had a few right now. "No more, no more!" he insisted when Hamble tried to go on, and he sounded at once like Hamble's superior and his guest, unable to accept such excessive hospitality.

John would have smiled to witness such grace, but Tobias's

expression turned grave as Hamble departed for the day and he and Miss Dobson started for the company offices, located farther down the corridor. John rubbed his thumb along the side of his forefinger. He smelled a fresh waft of tobacco as Dunning returned to his cigarette.

"Who," Dunning said on a subsequent exhalation, "is your she-general there, Jones?"

Miss Dobson. He began rifling through the papers on his desk, the ones that had gone flying when Tobias had opened the door. He went through them twice before he noticed Dunning's arm extended, the papers he'd collected from the floor still in hand. There it was. He saw it before he snatched it from Dunning, a letter from some clerk at Baumston & Smythe, making the most outlandish claims against one Miss "Elizabeth" Dobson. *Assault?* John had said, skeptical, to the company secretary who'd brought the letter to his attention, and the secretary had replied, *I can hardly credit it, either, sir.*

Well, John could credit it now. By God, he could give it all degrees of credit, having seen that creature who'd come ripping down the corridor after Hamble.

He headed for the company offices, the letter tucked in his coat.

He hoped to make a quiet entrance, but he had forgotten Miss Dobson's desk, squeezed into the office last week, exactly where the door would strike it if one opened it too far.

Which John did. With the rest of the staff gone for the day, the noise seemed tremendous. Tobias and Miss Dobson, standing at Hamble's desk, looked up from the ledger they were studying.

She-general. The aptness of Dunning's word registered suddenly. This was Betsey Dobson in her uniform, the one Tobias had told her to get.

It fit. It fit so well he'd scarcely noticed it earlier. It was a feminine nod to military wear, with an open bodice jacket that revealed a sort of waistcoat whose banded collar stood stiff and high. Yet, somehow, a column of milky flesh still showed above it. A procession of brass buttons traveled down from there and braved the swell of her breasts, and where other women's skirts surrendered to surges of flounces and gathers, only stripes of dark ribbon and razor-sharp pleats were permitted on hers. The entire getup was frill-less and direct, nothing but proper, and it beckoned, decorously, to be rumpled up.

Tobias was saying something about Miss Dobson's budget, how something was wrong with it, and he was saying it to John, who, despite his determination to rid Miss Dobson of any more of these surprises that kept popping up around her, hadn't been paying the strictest attention.

"I'd understood her—" He checked himself. It felt ungracious to talk about Miss Dobson when she was so fully present. "I'd understood you to have a bookkeeping course at that institute of yours."

It rather hurt him, the way she narrowed her eyes at him, as if trying to make out whether he was trying to aid or to sabotage.

"The course was—well, it had a strong domestic bent," she said. "The instructor seemed unable to imagine that we'd ever account for much more than the pantry stores in a modest household."

Tobias shook his head. "*Viele köche,* that is the cause of this predicament, more so than your training, Miss Dobson. One broth and too many cooks, do you agree?"

She looked as if she'd like to. Tobias added gently, "A mistake corrected is not a failure. Let us see what might be done."

John stood aside as Miss Dobson and Tobias went back to the ledger. They huddled at Hamble's desk, and John took the opportunity to study her more closely than he had since freeing her from the stationmaster's office. He now had trouble imagining her assaulting her supervisor. At Tobias's side, she seemed as disciplined and alert as a field commander taking in battle strategy.

Two baskets sat on Miss Dobson's desk just to his right. One held dozens of inexpensive clay pipes, each tied to a small packet of tobacco with a blue ribbon; the other held painted picture frames of heavy molded paper. Favors for the excursionists, he guessed, taking a frame from the basket to examine it. He recognized it as the work of a local cottage industry, an inexpensive trinket but pretty enough that John could imagine women like his sisters pleased to display it in their homes.

He returned the frame to the basket and considered the rest of the desktop, which took but a moment. A pen stand, its occupant poised for use. An inkwell. He lifted the hinged lid and found the porcelain lip of the well as clean as a teacup waiting in a sideboard. He picked up the one other item on the desk, a record book.

Ah, he'd distracted her. He gestured with the book as he caught her watching him. A shake of her head, and he would set back the book. But she looked down again, so he put on his spectacles and opened it.

Lists. Reminders. Names, dates. He'd caught a look of that tight, neat handwriting of hers when he'd met her at Baumston & Smythe. Seeing it again, he believed it had surely been one of the factors prodding him to offer her the job.

Tobias had mentioned she'd already made a number of new bookings. Other letters were tucked near the back of the notebook.

"Tobias," he interrupted, straightening suddenly from where he'd been leaning on the desk, "did you see what she's getting from this brewers' association?"

He carried the notebook to Tobias, but before Tobias could look it over, Miss Dobson said, "You told me I might try to raise the charges for the height of the season—that's all I did, Mr. Seiler. I suppose it may be a trifle early, but if they're willing to pay? All the entertainments will be open, and the new pleasure railway—it is supposed to be finished before then."

She fixed John with an accusing look, as if his current absence from the railway's building site would keep it from opening on time.

Though she couldn't have the least notion about the state of the railway, her doubt nettled him anyway. "It'll be finished, Dobs."

Tobias said, "Miss Dobson, you cannot think Mr. Jones or me disappointed that you're making a tidier profit? I admit my reservations as to how much we could get our first season in such a scheme, but you have proved me wrong." He closed the notebook and the ledger and presented them to her. "Do it again."

If she felt any relief or pride in Tobias's words, she didn't show it. She nodded and spoke her thanks, and Tobias excused himself. She hugged her ledger like a chastened school miss once he was gone.

Why did I follow her here? John wondered, because he was certain he must have had some reason. He took his time removing his spectacles, trying to recall it.

"He has been so kind to me," she said at last. "You've kept my—my trouble from him, it's obvious."

Which trouble? No letter? No train ticket? The attempt to flee custody? Or—he touched his coat pocket, remembering his purpose here—that supervisor she'd allegedly assaulted?

"Tobias trusts me, Dobs," he said. "I had to tell him all of it your first day here. He let you stay on because he trusts me, but he wants you to do well."

"I know. This hotel is everything to him, I see that."

Not his point, but he let it pass. A more pressing matter awaited.

"Now tell me. Who is Joseph Wofford?"

*W*offord. Betsey would take an office stacked with Arland Hambles if it would save her hearing that name again.

"You must know, if you have his name," she replied. "He finally sent my character, then?"

"Something to do with that, he did."

Which seemed to bring them to an impasse. She felt she held her life, this new one in Idensea, between her forefinger and thumb, a tiny clod of earth liable to crumble and scatter in a dusty rain if she altered her hold. She didn't know what answer she could give Mr. Jones that would maintain the just-so pressure.

She carried her books to her desk and felt glad for the taps of her boot heels, the shush of her skirts, the silence broken.

"Prevett's finished your frock, I see."

"This is not a *frock*," she said, then bit her lip. How foolish to correct him. She grasped the handle of the single drawer on the desk and jiggled it, the most successful method she'd found of working it past its sticky place. "I took it from them and finished it, to save a bit of money. It will do, I hope?"

She glanced over her shoulder at him as she slipped her books into the drawer, expecting that discerning gaze of his. Instead . . .

Instead.

She looked away. She pressed down on a growing smile. Mr. Jones needn't say what he thought. She knew. She liked it, too. She liked what he was thinking. In the same instant, with a disillusionment as sharp as her pleasure, she thought, *Is that what he's after?* and she knew she could use it; Mr. Jones hadn't all the power anymore. Like the electric lights on the pier, she could turn on, be bright and warm. She could beckon, just enough to make Mr. Jones feel fine, fine about giving her a second-or-so chance.

How lucky to have this stubborn drawer, the extra moment it gave her as she coaxed it shut. The entire desk trembled with the effort.

Then she turned to him, leading with a smile, one less spontaneous than its predecessor.

He never saw it. He was yanking things from his pockets—handkerchief! spectacles!—and then set about an intense polishing of his lenses, so plainly and uncharacteristically flustered that Betsey was swallowed up in a wave of guilt.

He tucked away his spectacles without even putting them on. Inside her, a stupid, girlish adoration squeezed like a handclasp at the close of a prayer.

She turned back to her desk and righted the artful arrangement she'd made of the frames in the basket. Mr. Jones hadn't disturbed it *so* much, but it seemed prudent to find a reason to be annoyed with him just now.

"I ought to have haggled a better deal," she said of the guest favors. "Or just left them altogether. They didn't help my budget any."

"They were thoughtful touches. Tobias liked them, I think." He came to her desk and picked up one of the pipes and tobacco packets. "Perhaps leave off with the tobacco—no doubt Tisling's would appreciate the business—and next time, for the ladies, nosegays might be more economical."

Next time. She wasn't about to get the sack, then. Trying to hide her deep relief, she leaned toward him to reach one of the pipe-and-tobacco packets whose ribbon was askew.

"Or soap," he added suddenly. "The hotel has its own, local-made. Wrapped in blue paper, with a picture of the hotel on the label. It . . . it has lavender in it."

Betsey knew about the soap. Mr. Seiler's wife, who oversaw the housekeeping staff, had given her some. She'd washed her hair with it just last night. But she didn't like the idea, nor the one about nosegays. What was wrong with him, that he could think flowers more economical? Besides, people had their photographs taken when they came to the seaside. The frames were perfect, if only she could pay a little less for them. She finished tying off the blue ribbon, answering, "Perhaps."

Another fall of silence. How to speak to him? Mr. Jones had always crossed those distances of station, but now he said nothing, and with her heart racing, she could only tie up another slipped bow and feel his eyes upon her. Did he want her to say more about Mr. Wofford? Or did that gaze feel so heavy because of something else?

"Miss Dobson," he said, and she replied "Mm?" quickly, too quickly, though she kept her attention trained on the blue ribbons in the basket, and he said, "I've things to do." From the corner of her eye, she watched him exit.

Seconds later, out in the corridor, in a voice that was probably meant to be hushed: "Bless God—*damn*."

And then the door struck her desk again. Both of them winced. Mr. Jones apologized; Betsey lied that she had grown used to it.

"I'd meant to ask," he said. "Ethan Noonan. I saw him in town today. You'll need to pay him something."

Betsey stared. Her unease fell lank. "If you saw him, Mr. Jones, then you know good and well why he won't get a penny from me."

"Well." His hands went to his pockets, a posture which might have seemed passive but for that perceptive gaze of his. "Well, there's sorry for the trouble you've had, Dobs. I ought have warned you. But you will pay Ethan Noonan for his trouble, I am thinking."

"Warned me?" The morning's aggravation swelled again. "Why should you have thought to warn me of a steady man like Mr. Noonan? I waited there till half-ten, making promises to the guests; I let them board only to tell them to come off a moment later, and you knew all the time!"

She stopped herself. Or truly, a whip crack in his eyes stopped her, alerted her to her toe upon the line. He'd been giving her an order. It had come out tuned with his sweet Welsh brogue, and he called her "Dobs" and stood with his hands in his pockets as though she and he were two old chums, but an order, that's what that had been. He had every right, of course. The only good response here was *Yes, Mr. Jones*.

Her jaw locked.

"So, when you send him his money, Miss Dobson," he continued, the only change in his voice being the resumption of the good English he more generally employed, "write him a message, too, to bring his char-à-banc to the hotel Saturday next, and early, before the train. Then, if he isn't in fit condition, have one of the grooms drive instead, and pay Mr. Noonan for the use of the char-à-banc."

"Why?" she demanded, *Yes, Mr. Jones* having dissolved like sugar on her tongue. "He didn't just humiliate *me*; he was representing the company. Why should I?"

"Because Ethan Noonan—" he began, and stopped. "Because I have said so, and so would Mr. Seiler if he knew. Enough of an explanation there."

And wasn't it, though? Nothing like the simple truth to hack a discussion off at the knees. How refreshing to have a man admit it, none of that prosing like Wofford would do, pretending to be just, pretending to think. Nothing but sheer authority, and why should she be surprised he would use it?

Still. She could wobble that pedestal of his, she knew it now, he'd let her see. She tipped her chin down so she could look up at him. "I see," she said sweetly. "Mr. Jones, you are . . . *entirely* correct."

A closed-lip smile, a slow blink: It was due compliance or coy invitation, and she wondered which he would see.

A test for him, a game. If he chose the invitation, she couldn't slam the door on his fingers. She wouldn't even want to, she admitted, despite the fact that, of the two of them, she was the only one who could fail, the only one who could lose the game.

She sensed a wariness coiling up in him, but he remained quite still. He thanked her for her cooperation; he had an appointment to keep, he told her, and then was gone, and Betsey knew she was lucky.

He'd decided not to play.

John couldn't think what he'd been about, standing round discussing paper frames and tobacco. Lavender soap, bless God. He had a building weeks behind schedule to oversee and an American millionaire with two daughters of marriageable age to meet.

Betsey Dobson, she was mad, one moment daring him to sack her, the next to—

What had that smile been daring him to do?

He ducked the mystery of it, or tried to, by setting his mind to showing Rolly Brues the Sultan's Road, the pleasure railway due to open in little more than a week's time. John was proud of it. He'd been the one to bring the idea to the board, the one to keep pressing when Sir Alton had opposed it, and he felt honored to have the chance to show it to Brues, the owner of a prime streetcar company in America. But the madness of Miss Dobson chewed at him like he was wearing all his clothes wrong-way out.

Because I have said so. Of all the stupid—

He quelled his distraction well enough as he and Brues inspected the railway and Brues told him of California and the expansion of his interests along the coast, but when they returned to the hotel grounds and found Mrs. Brues and her daughters having tea in the shade of an oak, John lurched without grace through the introductions, his attention diverted by a glimpse of deep blue against the grass.

It was Miss Dobson, crossing the grounds toward the hotel pavilion where her day-trippers would have their dinner and dance tonight. She was not alone. She carried her baskets of pipes and frames, and some fellow was doing his best to slow her progress, trotting into her path, nearly walking backward at times. Certainly not a staffer. One of the trippers? He did have that brushed-up-for-a-day-out air to him, an attempt to look smart that fell short of fitting into the elegant surrounds. It took money, not just soap, to rub out the marks of working-class life, and even then, secrets remained which neither this fellow nor John himself would ever master.

Mrs. Brues was insisting he join them at the table, John realized, and he accepted the invitation. It was as he was taking his seat that he saw Miss Dobson halt. She and the fellow held one basket in tug-of-war fashion.

John bolted up. The man didn't fit. He didn't fit there next to Miss Dobson; he didn't fit here at the hotel. "Pardon me," he murmured, and turned in Miss Dobson's direction.

But then it was over. Miss Dobson resumed her pace, baskets in tow, and the fellow, trotting backward, stumbled and fell back on the ground. He got himself up quick enough and strode off in another direction, while Betsey Dobson marched onward to the pavilion without a backward glance.

The man had taken the sharp side of that wicked tongue of hers, John had no doubt, and he would have given a great deal to have been close enough to hear. *Go after her,* said the voice he trusted.

Here was the millionaire, though. His two daughters of marriageable age. And a most delectable-looking tea. He sat down, a nagging unease curling in his shoulders.

Perhaps that unease was what made him play such ferocious croquet with the American girls once tea was done. The younger— just sixteen, John discovered, and thus not of marriageable age—only laughed at his cutthroat play and served it back to him in a way he couldn't help but admire, but when he knocked the older daughter's ball nearly to the tennis courts a second time and she looked to be on the verge of tears, he was appalled at himself. He'd trade colors with her, and it would please him very much if she would take his next two turns, he said, exchanging his blue mallet for her red one.

He trotted off to see where the ball had got to, found it under an azalea, got the devil stung out of his hand by a bee when he reached in to retrieve it, and there the afternoon's recreation hobbled to a halt.

He'd be disinvited from the dinner party, John was certain as he delivered the young ladies back to their parents, the younger with her hair fallen and her white frock sullied with grass stains, the elder silent and sulky over being forced to quit the match once it had begun to go in her favor. Rolly Brues, however, only recommended his elder daughter "buck up," while Mrs. Brues undramatically instructed the younger to follow the maid back to their rooms to change. *Again?* girl and maid complained.

Thus, some hours later, there John sat in one of the hotel's private dining rooms, sharing a meal with several of the hotel's wealthiest guests along with Sir Alton Dunning, recently returned from a trip. Sir Alton gave him a wry smile to hide his surprise at John's inclusion in the party. John's connection with the pier company and hotel had provided such opportunities before, but with his work in Idensea coming to a close, they mattered more than ever now. A single conversation with the right person could lead him to his next position.

His earlier unease had almost gone. Still, he was not much surprised when a staff member spoke low into his ear: "Mr. Seiler asks you to come, Mr. Jones. Trouble at the pavilion with the trippers."

Pushing the keys blurs the printing. Strike them squarely, with a light, springing blow of sufficient force to make a clear impression, and no more.

—*How to Become Expert in Type-writing*

*J*ohn followed Tobias Seiler's cool example as the two of them traversed the great hall and the Palm Lounge, but he broke into a run as soon as he cleared the hotel's rear terrace, which was crowded with nattering, speculating guests, all their faces turned toward the electric glow of the pavilion. Thankfully, the distance between the buildings ensured the glow was all they'd be able to make out. A few people hurried along the path leading to the pavilion, intending to get a first-class view of it all; John sprinted ahead and trusted Tobias to tactfully herd them back to the hotel.

But the pavilion was bedlam anyway, shouts and cries where there ought to have been music, writhing knots of people who seemed uncertain as to whether they witnessed horror or entertainment. John recognized hotel guests and Idensea locals, and knew the crowd to be much larger than it ought.

He looked over his shoulder to make certain Ian and Frederick, the most brawny of the staffers who'd followed him from the hotel, were still on his heels, then plowed through the throng, now hearing one voice above the rest of the confusion. "Avery Nash, you goddamned fool," Miss Dobson was crying, and she sounded not the least confused.

It blinked in his mind then, the certainty that in the midst of this chaos, he'd find that jack he'd seen her with this afternoon. John didn't bother to consult her, or to think whether Ian and Frederick were close behind as he broke through the crowd. He saw the men grappling on the floor and went for the one currently on top, grabbing collar and coat and yanking with all his strength.

He nearly fell back with the weight, then pitched forward as the man he'd grabbed tried to pull from his grasp. The man reared, flailing, and his elbow cracked into John's mouth. John lost his grip, then regained it as the man's balance faltered. Again, the man flailed wildly. John heard a sharp cry accompanied by a gasp from the crowd, and when he risked a quick look, he saw Miss Dobson, her face bloodied.

John spun the man around, served a quick punch to his gut, another to his already bloody face. The second dropped him. John came down with him, planting his knee in his chest and gathering his coat in his fists. The fellow was gasping, a barking cough at the end of each hard breath. It was the man from this afternoon, John was certain.

"Finished here, you." To make sure the fool understood, he repeated, "Finished. You don't belong here, and you're finished."

Frederick had taken care of the other fighter and now held him back. Apparently, there'd been quite a brawl—John noted several others standing about, disheveled and gulping air while their subduers kept wary hands upon them. Miss Dobson crouched down beside him, saying, "Mr. Jones, John. John, he isn't well," and when John saw the red smearing her mouth, he jerked on the lapels balled in his fists and gave his captive another good shove into the brick floor of the pavilion. "Mr. Jones!" he heard her say again. The man had struck her in his heedless flailing, not intentionally, but John couldn't convince himself that this mattered.

"Get the constable. See to Miss Dobson." He spoke to no one in particular, but feet scurried around him nevertheless. Miss Dobson rose, and John heard her instruct someone, "Tell the musicians to play a galop."

Then she was at his ear again. "Must the constable come?"

He stared at her. She touched a finger to her bleeding lip, catching the gist of his dark thoughts.

"He isn't well. And the constable, on the hotel grounds? It won't look good."

Beneath him, John's captive—Avery Nash, Miss Dobson had called him—reached the conclusion of his coughing fit and groaned, "Lizzie."

"Shut your face, you," Miss Dobson hissed. "Every damn bit of this is your doing."

The music started up with fierce cheer. Miss Dobson swiped at her mouth, stood, and joined the crowd shuffling its way back to merriment. John's consternation waylaid him only a moment before he hauled Nash to his feet. Nash was a mess, and John felt rather disturbed to realize he didn't know how much of the damage he'd done himself. Nash's teeth showed pink when he smiled at John.

"The picture of refinement, is she not?" Nash said. "Fortunately, she's apt to forget her manners 'in the middle of her favors.'"

Still clutching the man's coat, John drove Nash back to the low balustrade of the pavilion with such violence that they both nearly flipped over it. John couldn't have even articulated the reason for his rage but for the vague feeling he'd had some filth forced upon him. He was relieved to hear Ian at his side, suggesting Nash and the fellow he'd fought with be taken to the stables until the constable arrived. He let Nash go, and had a hard time not planting his boot in Nash's backside as Ian and Frederick led him off the pavilion.

Miss Dobson. He finally caught sight of her in conversation with one of the hotel's watchmen. Approaching, he found her doing what he himself should have thought to do earlier—asking the watchman's aid in politely but efficiently removing the locals from the hotel grounds. The watchman glanced up at John: He wanted approval. John didn't even nod. The watchman did, though, and made his way to a group of young men making a poor job of blending in.

Miss Dobson started to move. John caught her arm. "Come, you."

She obeyed until she realized he meant to lead her off the pavilion. "I can't leave—the dance is nearly through, they'll be going to their train soon."

"You're hurt." He urged her forward.

"It's nothing."

He stopped. Her top lip was puffy, tender-looking, jutting over the bottom one. It gave her an appearance a touch comical and fully infuriating, and his fists itched again for Nash's flesh. He wanted to lick his thumb and dab at the traces of red she'd missed.

She touched her mouth, not that tender upper lip but its mate, at the place where his own mouth had begun to smart a right bit. "Oh," she said. "Do I look half a fright as you?"

They left the pavilion. The path leading back to the hotel was still lively with to-ing and fro-ing, so John steered her off into the grass. "You know him," he said.

She continued to match his pace across the shadowed lawn but said nothing.

"A good man, our constable. He'll have the doctor if it's needed. A crowd like that, there cannot pass such a scene without having the law, not if the hotel hopes to keep a good name." But doubt needled him even as he spoke. Loosed from whatever had possessed him up at the pavilion, he wondered if he should have heeded Miss Dobson and revoked the call for the constable.

"Hell. Hell and hell. What have I done?"

It was hard to say. He understood the dread in her voice; he felt it himself. A damn sorry mess, this, the excursionist scheme blown to bits on its first try, Sir Alton and Rolly Brues and every guest in the hotel to witness it. His chance to dine with Brues and his wealthy friends gone as well. And the worst of it was how simply it all might have been prevented. He'd seen Miss Dobson with Nash and persuaded himself out of following them.

"Best you tell me who he is, Dobs. He's not a local."

"No. From London."

"And all this way he's come for you? Your—your husband?"

She laughed. "No, Mr. Jones. Avery wouldn't marry me, and I—I'll not marry anyone. I don't know what he means coming here, for he could hardly answer himself when I asked him. I only know he seemed very put out when I told him Sarah Elliot would not be so lenient as our former landlady."

Landlady? For some moments, he didn't understand her meaning, and then the chill of realization left him without words. Nash's insinuations had some truth to them, then. He felt shocked, as though he should have known such a dramatic fact from the beginning, just by looking at her.

"And now you know how it was," she said softly.

The grass whispered the count of their steps. Louder than that was the rustle of her underskirts. He couldn't unhear it, suddenly couldn't keep himself from imagining what they looked like.

"A way of going along, it is." He still didn't know what to say.

She halted, laughing again, but she'd clapped a hand over her eyes. "That's right. Going along. Managing. A roof over the head, some bit of warmth."

"Dobs. Miss Dobson." He regretted shaming her, and his tongue felt heavy with questions and comfort, but he struggled with them and too much time passed. At last, he simply said, "Betsey, I know what it is to want a roof, a meal."

"'Twas more than that."

"Loved him, then?" For John had already made up a story for her: She loved Nash, thought she'd marry him. Probably he was capable of all sorts of rascality and she too naïve to realize it. He'd lured her into his house, told her they'd go for the marriage license within the week, when what he planned all along was a free maid and convenient nick for as long as he'd have her. A story like that, an innocent duped by the wolf, was easy to understand. A story like that allowed pity.

But Betsey Dobson, her eyes still covered, razed his story with a shake of her head. She dropped her hand, picked up her skirts, and strode away toward the rear terrace of the hotel.

John didn't know what to make of it; it was like being informed he'd been looking at a building plan upside down. He was inclined to let her go. But a glance at the terrace told him more trouble waited ahead.

He ran to catch up with her. He thought how long her legs must be under those rustling skirts, to have taken her so far so quickly. He touched her back to slow her down and said into her ear, "You are about to meet Sir Alton Dunning."

Her tension, already palpable in the tips of his fingers, ratcheted like an overwound music box.

"I am with you," he said.

Sir Alton stood on the terrace, his bland smile masking his intent examination of the grounds. He put his glass of port to his lips upon catching sight of John and Betsey emerging from the shadows, then made his way down the steps. No matter how leisurely he took them, John did not miss the fact Sir Alton was too agitated to wait for John to reach him. Noel Dunning straggled behind his father, nothing about his indifference contrived.

"Well, well, well! Such excitement, and now we reach the conclusion of that little experiment, don't we!"

Sir Alton's tone rarely varied. He could have been reciting "A Visit from St. Nicholas," he might have been delivering a death sentence to a condemned man; it all swung to the same serene, cheery inflection, relentless as that metronome Sarah kept telling John to mind during his piano lessons.

"Who should have guessed my hypothesis to be confirmed in such a stirring fashion?" Sir Alton said. "Excepting myself, I admit. I trust you'll pardon some gloating on my part—I cannot seem to help myself."

He settled his gaze on Betsey. No one would have described his smile as anything but pleasant and civil.

John wished he had prepared her. "You've not met Miss Dobson," he said. "She is the young lady we hired to oversee the excursions scheme. Miss Dobson, Sir Alton Dunning. And," he added, noting Noel Dunning's languid arrival at his father's side, "you've met his son, Mr. Dunning, already."

Sir Alton's bow was courteous, if subtle. If Betsey offered her hand, she'd be required to reach out an awkward distance. Sir Alton generally made limited efforts in that regard. Dunning had once said he remembered his father being one of the most effusive conductors he'd ever watched, but John could only ever imagine him directing his orchestra with shifting gazes and nose twitches.

Betsey didn't so much as nod.

"Miss Dobson," Sir Alton said. "Delighted. Though I regret a young lady has been forced to witness such boorish behavior from our—heavens, I was about to say *guests,* but that isn't quite accurate, is it? How dismaying for you, finding yourself supposedly in charge of such a frightful group of ruffians."

The first strike. John checked Betsey in a sidelong glance to see how it landed. Pale as a cloud she'd gone, her fine straight back as rigid as Sir Alton's, though with terror rather than self-restraint. Picturing the demon-soldier he'd seen this afternoon, John thought it a sorry comedown for her. Their moments alone would have been better used to bolster her confidence rather than crosshackling her about Avery Nash.

"Noel." Sir Alton addressed his son without turning to him. "How sly you've been, keeping your good fortune in meeting Miss Dobson all to yourself."

Dunning fumbled with his cigarette case. "I suppose—well— it slipped my mind, Father, I suppose. It didn't seem terribly relevant, so I suppose—"

"No, no, it doesn't matter at all." Sir Alton reached back to draw his son beside him, giving him a clap on his back. "My asking you to pay attention whilst your stepmother and I were away was mere habit. I hardly expected you in fact to do so."

Another clap on the back, and cigarettes rained to the ground. Dunning jerked awkwardly, as though he would stoop to pick them up, but then did not and instead curled the case into his hand, his face brilliant with heat, his eyes fixed to the darkness beyond the terrace. Betsey Dobson made a tiny sound in her throat. Her hand clutched the placket of her vest, half those brave brass buttons of hers crumpled up in her palm.

John touched her elbow. "Miss Dobson, you ought to go on to the kitchen, get some ice on that wound so you can finish your duties for the night."

She gave him her wary, magic-beans look. She would be only too happy to escape this confrontation, John could see, but she didn't trust what might happen once she was gone. His smile made his injured lip smart, and he received naught but a scowl in return. He squeezed her elbow. "Yes, Mr. Jones," she muttered, and took a wide path around Sir Alton on her way to the terrace.

"She came from Baumston and Smythe, sir," John said as he stooped, picking up the cigarettes and passing them in one smooth motion to Dunning. "You know they take on the top people."

"Indeed I do. If you don't mind, what duties, precisely, did she perform at Baumston and Smythe?"

"She . . . she was a type-writer girl, as it happens."

> If the paper does not run in straight but one side feeds
> faster than the other, one of the rubber bands may have
> slipped off one of the pulleys. . . . This is generally the
> cause of the paper's feeding crooked.
>
> —*How to Become Expert in Type-writing*

*I*t was not that Sir Alton's face went untouched by whatever he thought or felt. All of it showed, all of it—but fleetingly, palely, the fluid meeting of warm and cool.

After a moment, Sir Alton said, "My ignorance of typewriting must be profound indeed, to be unable to imagine—but of course, the girl's character must have detailed a great many qualifications."

"Mr. Seiler and I have been pleased," John answered, hoping to skirt the issue of Betsey's character letter. If Sir Alton pressed it, he'd not be able to explain, far less justify, his recommendation to hire Miss Dobson. *I saw her, and I just knew,* he couldn't say. Neither: *She came with a perfectly fine character, except for stealing rail rides and living with a man not her husband.*

"Never think I meant to question you, Jones. Whatever is in the girl's reference, whether she is a type-writer or a chair caner or Thomas Cook's own twin, as long as she's capable of canceling the remainder of these day-tripper bookings, it satisfies me."

Having seen Betsey Dobson's accounts this afternoon, John felt nothing less than ill—and goddamned furious—at the thought of all that revenue lost, money turned away as if it weren't just as good as any other money, and when the hotel had yet to make a profit.

John grinned at Sir Alton, grinned though it sent pain streaking from his smashed lip. "Monday, perhaps, we can discuss how to present that to the board? As soon as we have their approval, we will put an end to the entire scheme."

Sir Alton, who was never pleased to be reminded he had a board of directors to whom he must answer, said, "Excellent, then. Come to Iden Hall. By Monday, I should have a good sampling of newspapers—we'll read all the accounts of what went on here tonight over a pot of tea. Won't it be fascinating to see Idensea's reputation transform right before our eyes?"

You'd better learn to give Father's sarcasm back to him, Noel Dunning had advised John soon after he'd arrived in Idensea. *Otherwise, he'll think you a stupe.*

John had altered certain things about himself over the years for the sake of inspiring confidence in the Englishmen for whom he'd worked, chipping away for any advantage because everything about his background seemed to work against him. He'd learned to speak with hardly a trace of his Welsh accent. He'd changed his name, for God's sake. Dunning's advice, however, he'd rejected outright, so contrary it felt to his soul.

Dunning had been wrong, as it turned out. Sir Alton didn't think him a stupe; Sir Alton had come to rely on him. So when John simply replied, "Monday afternoon, then," Sir Alton put his port glass to his lips and, over the rim, considered John with respectful suspicion.

"Very well," he said. "Noel and I shall go to the smoking room and talk the entire debacle down to a minor inconvenience. Noel, it's a task to suit you, shrugging it all away as though it were of no consequence. And you—"

"Smooth things out amongst the excursionists," John guessed.

"Precisely." For a moment, Sir Alton's smirking mask seemed wistful. He glanced at his son, but though Dunning stood beside his father with the steadiness of a sculpture, he was otherwise quite gone. "But don't be long about it. Brues asked particularly after you, and wants you to rejoin us as soon as you might."

Rolly Brues! There might be some salvaging of the night, after all.

"And"—with a gesture of his eyes, Sir Alton indicated John's bloodied mouth—"you'd better do something with that."

Betsey obtained ice from the restaurant kitchen, where the hectic atmosphere forestalled most curiosity, then fled to the offices and used a small looking glass on the wall to check her appearance. The convex mirror was a comfort; the injury to her mouth could not be nearly as grotesque as reflected there. She snatched some hairpins from her desk drawer and left the office, trying to put her hair to rights.

She expected and dreaded Mr. Seiler at any moment. This was a mistake uncorrectable; this was a failure; this was her disaster, and she did not expect to survive it.

But it was Mr. Jones, not Mr. Seiler, she encountered in the empty corridor. They both stopped dead. In the shadows, his hair appeared like a cut-paper silhouette of fire, wildly mussed from the fight. The sight filled her with caution and anticipation, held her in place with her hands in her hair as she pictured him driving Avery to the floor.

She fixed the last pin, lowered her arms, and braced herself for immediate dismissal. But at the base of her spine, she felt, too, the press of his hand, how he'd spoken strength and alliance through the tips of his fingers.

She liked him to a terrible degree. A staffer had told her Ethan Noonan suffered a crippling injury during the construction of the pier, and all her frustration over Mr. Jones's obstinacy in the matter dissolved upon the discovery—dissolved, and wore another tender place for him inside her.

"I was about to return to the pavilion," she said. "If I'm not sacked?"

"Not this night."

She sought hope in this, found little.

He nodded toward the door of his office. "I must clean up. Wait, you, and we'll walk together."

Once inside, he turned on a lamp for her, then went alone into his private rooms. Betsey surveyed the desk and bookcases from where she stood until she noted, with some dismay, that he had tacked a number of diagrams to the wall, right into the pretty wallpaper. One depicted a railroad track, peculiar because all the hills and curves it followed were not those of the land but of a sinuous trestle. The pleasure railway, she decided, but stripped of its tunnels and scenery. She had moved closer and was tracing a fingertip along the track when she heard Mr. Jones return.

She turned from the diagram. His hair was damp and neat now, his bottom lip cleaned of most of the clotted blood. In empathy, she rolled her own bottom lip in and out of her mouth, waiting for him to speak.

He did not. She perceived his interest in her, fresh and keen and tangible, needles of sleet and ribbons of wind.

"Sir Alton is very angry?" she asked, too softly, for it seemed he did not hear her at first. "What did he mean, 'the conclusion of that experiment'?"

His expression cleared; this was a simple question. "He's fearful."

"Is that what you call it, how he was back there?"

"Trust me. The board forced him to accept the excursions scheme to begin with. Now, with what happened tonight, he sees a good reason to call it off."

Her hope shrank, hearing this, picturing that ruthless embrace Sir Alton had given his son, while he smiled and singsonged his scorn.

"You've got to show him we cannot do without it."

She hadn't the least idea in hell how she was to do that. She had the sense not to say so.

"Get you your books together, girl. Do the figures on those bookings you've made. Show what those higher rates you're asking will do by summer's end, and come Monday, tea at Iden Hall we will have, you and I and Sir Alton Dunning."

It struck her as a bad, bad idea. While she could do the figures he asked for, surely he or Mr. Seiler should be the one to speak to Sir Alton. Why did he think she could? But he did, so she answered, "Very well, damn it."

A grin broke his face, halted as he winced and put his knuckles to his mouth. Above his fist, his eyes still laughed, enjoying her nominal bravado. "I knew what you would be for, Betsey Dobson. That day at Baumston and Smythe, I knew it. I'm not wrong."

Her cheeks burned with pleasure. She could not have said the last time a compliment had made that happen.

If you keep your hands in the proper place over the keyboard, you will find it easier to finger correctly. . . .
—*How to Become Expert in Type-writing*

Both Mr. Jones and Betsey were eager to speak with the excursionists and prove no real harm had been done, but the pavilion was hushed when they reached it, Mr. Pollit delivering a speech to close the day's festivities. Sensing Mr. Jones's frustration with the delay, she told him she didn't need him to play diplomat. He'd promised Sir Alton, he said in hushed reply.

With another staffer, she distributed the pipes and paper frames as everyone left the pavilion. Amazing how far a simple gift went toward restoring goodwill and cheer. The tram, when she squeezed aboard, was loud with happy chatter. Near the rear of the car, she caught sight of Mr. Jones in conversation with Mr. Pollit, and hoped it was going well.

The car emptied at the stop for the Compass Walk to the rail station. When she saw Mr. Jones preparing to reboard after bidding Mr. Pollit and the others good night, she called, "It's the last run—you'd best not ride to the end."

He hopped on anyway and joined her, though he remained standing. He tugged at his tie and braced himself as the car lurched forward.

"I am sure Sir Alton did not order you to see me home."

"Someone must."

"I made my way about London quite alone as a regular event."

"No doubt, if that jack Nash was what you depended upon."

She bowed her head to hide a smile. More amusing than the idea of depending on Avery was Mr. Jones's peevish tone. She knew she had shocked him, admitting how it had been with Avery. How extraordinary that he did not condemn her for it.

A streetlamp threw light into the car as they passed. The high polish of Mr. Jones's boots caught her eye, as well a heel that betrayed he'd worn these shoes for more seasons than a gentleman's magazine would approve. No one would notice but she, hiding a smile at his feet, tender as a marshmallow over this incongruity.

"You're dressed awfully smart tonight."

"I was in a dinner party. The Brues family, and some others."

That explained his earlier impatience. He would be in the private smoking room by now if not for the trouble on the pavilion. "Mr. Brues is very rich, isn't he?"

"Like a sultan. Western Car Company—streetcars, for the greatest part, but it's become the custom in America for streetcar companies to have a pleasure park at the end of the line to keep up business on Saturdays and Sundays, and he's begun developing amusements for them."

"Like the Sultan's Road?"

"Some. Rolly Brues's cars run up and down streets from Chicago to San Francisco."

Betsey assumed this an impressive distance. "And he invited you to dine with him."

Her mock awe made him smile. "And but a dozen or so places from his right-hand side, too."

"I've seen his daughters. Perhaps he'll invite you to be his son-in-law after another week."

"Spare you some pity for me, Dobs. Girls like that, shopping for titles, and there I sit with Sir Alton's Cambridge-educated heir."

But no mention of Miss Gilbey. "You could persuade them round, if you wished."

Another streetlamp. Their gazes touched in the pool of light. Betsey made a prim cross of her hands over her lap, holding her gloves, but indulged in a slow, raking account of his person, back down to the heels of his boots.

Mr. Jones spoke not one more word the remainder of the journey.

At the stop, she tried to dissuade him from walking her all the way to The Bows, reminding him it would only delay his return to the hotel.

"You oughtn't walk back alone, and it so late."

"You intend to see me home each week? Provided I'm not sacked?"

"Hush of getting sacked. I will see you home, I or someone. Tobias, perhaps. He'll see to you."

"Mr. Seiler, leave the hotel on a Saturday night?"

"Charlie, then."

Charlie Elliot was starting as a page at the hotel this summer. "Charlie! Won't his mother like that!"

"It won't be often, whatever."

"Saturday comes every week. You ought to have given me a room in the staff quarters, as I said in the first place."

"Girl!"

She could not help laughing at his exasperation, which evaporated the moment he heard her.

"Needling, is it?" he said good-naturedly. "I'm thinking you wouldn't take one of those staff beds now if you could."

"No—too far from The Bows."

A half step ahead of her, he looked back to grin and offer his hand. When she took it, he tugged her into a run, and she knew it was highly questionable, if not out-and-out mad, to run and feel such banking joy after this botch of a day, when she teetered on the edge of losing it all, but run she did, Mr. Jones's kite on a string, bobbing, dancing, about to soar.

An alley of stone steps provided a shortcut to the roads over the cliffs, if one had the stamina for it. One of the oldest constructions in Idensea, the passage was too narrow, the steps too ragged and steep to take in bounds. Breathless, they slowed, Mr. Jones leading her up the steps by the hand.

"I sent Mr. Noonan three shillings."

He stopped to look down at her. A high window spilled feeble light into the alley and made dark pools beneath his brows. How fine the night breeze felt here, funneled into the space, cooling the back of her neck, whipping a lock of hair against her cheek.

"There's generous."

She shook her head. He was the generous one, the one thinking of Ethan Noonan all this time after the accident during the pier construction. She had not even noticed Noonan's limp.

"What a kind man you are." She stroked the hard pillow where her thumb rested against his hand, remembering his swollen knuckles. "Your hand all right? You should have had ice, too."

"Bee sting, that."

She laughed, softly, briefly, saying *ohh*, considering for the first time that perhaps Mr. Jones's day had been as trying as her own. A step up, another—he made room for her on his step so readily.

She splayed her hand beneath his, stroked the swollen sting with a brush of her fingertips. "Poor Mr. Jones." She bent over his hand and pressed a kiss onto his knuckles.

The contact stung, just enough to recall her warped reflection in the convex glass and make her laugh again, a bit spoony. "Ouch." She looked up, touching her lip. "Still hurts."

"Dobs." His friendly name for her, but his voice was a husk that revealed him, encouraged her to carry on.

"What about yours?" She turned her fingers over on her lips, offering him a testing place, her hand or any other nearby spot.

She was Mr. Jones's kite on a string, a taut and pulling string.

Her breath snapped in surprise when he grasped her hand; it was so sudden, his hold so firm, his thumb filling the hollow of her palm, stroking her there. She went slack against the wall behind her, knees slushy, and he came with her, keeping their hands by their mouths, nothing but a feather of vibrant air twisting between them.

"See if it hurts." A gnat at his ear would have been louder.

At last, he chose, moved his thumb, set the kiss in her palm. Everything alive in her rushed to that hollow, making her fingers tremble against the yielding cushion of his eyelid, the protective ridges beyond. "It does," he whispered. "It hurts."

But John pressed his mouth to the heel of her palm again anyway, pressed hard so the tender soreness would strike him deeper. He pressed until his wound broke and his blood changed the taste of her flesh, and when he finally heeded the fresh pinch of pain, he crumpled her hand inside his and rested against her, tilted and slipping.

Brass buttons prodded his chest. Wool tickled his lips. He clenched the gritty, pocked stone of the wall while against her neck, his ear filled with a tidal roar of blood and want.

Distant, sweet, a whisper: "I think you're rather wonderful, Mr. Jones."

She thought him rather wonderful. *Lie down with me,* he thought. *Here, anywhere—now.*

"Betsey." His whisper was caught by the wool of her collar and the skin at her jawline; it returned to him, hot and damp. "I am not for you."

For a long space, there was nothing but breathing.

"Miss Gilbey?"

"It is." Or *is not,* he meant to say. Right: "Not. That is—"

"You are engaged then?"

"What I mean. She isn't—"

"Mrs. Elliot mentioned—"

"We're not. Not engaged, whatever."

"You weren't—"

"Not yet."

"Yet."

"But if not her . . ."

They both fell silent.

"Someone like her," she finished, and he was relieved, though it felt like the devil to hurt her. But he couldn't see how it might have been avoided. She having been the one to start it all.

"Perhaps you'd best step back, then."

Amusement touched her voice. John pulled away, the swiftness of the action betraying his embarrassment. But she didn't look as if she were trying not to laugh at him, at how he was lost and floundering and goddamn couldn't breathe. He released her hand, and she left it crumpled and aloft as she remained shrugged up against the wall. She didn't look amused; she looked weak, she looked sated, but—but *not,* not either of those things, certainly not with her cheek wearing the weals of his collar and her buttons straining to keep their places on every breath.

He imagined the whole lot of them skittering down the steps, ripped from their tidy long row and showering down in clattering, bouncing pops of light.

Up. Climb. He moved, each step an act of will, his fingers digging into the stone on either side of him.

He reached the top and realized she wasn't behind him, but still propped against the wall more than halfway down, making her top button wink in the dim light as she twisted it. With a sigh, she pushed herself off the wall and started up the steps.

"You—you should have a different frock," he said, a sort of friendly suggestion.

She halted. Passed a hand down her jacket. "I'd thought— What is the matter with the uniform?"

Besides reducing him to a hard-cocked gawpus, "Nothing. For the evenings, I mean. For the dancing, you should have a gown and be on the pavilion with the guests."

Her eyes winked up at him like the buttons had done, only softer, the gloss of water, not metal.

"You'll be asked to dance. And perhaps find a good husband that way."

Ass-handed, mud-headed stupidity. He'd intended consolation, some way to move them forward, but the words now out, it sank into him what stupidity he'd spoken, albeit at a slower rate than it took Betsey herself to puzzle over it, apprehend it, and discard it for the rubbish it was. And somehow, despite her location a number of steps below him, the look she gave him seemed quite level. John had to fight an urge to step back, retreat.

"I see, Mr. Jones. That way we'd both marry up, wouldn't we?"

On the higher ground, he should have had the advantage, but to see Betsey Dobson ascend the dark steps with her hellion eyebrows, in her blue uniform and its winking buttons, was to feel woefully outnumbered. She reached the top step and stood before him, just his height. Another rush of blood swelled his temples, made his cock plain *hurt*.

"My, Mr. Jones," she said. "I little expected you to be as great a snob as Sir Alton. Certainly not whilst a stander like that's on you."

She brushed past him, left him speechless, demolished, razed and burned, not a thing intact except bless God, his *stander,* all the prouder from Betsey Dobson's notice, pointing him to the back view of Betsey Dobson's swaying skirts.

"It's ridiculous, you walking me," she said when she realized he was following her. "You'd best go after your cigar."

Cigar?

He didn't even smoke, not unless—not unless—*some rich man offered it.*

Brues, all the rest, back at the hotel, growing very chummy, no doubt, while he cindered away the chance to be with them, dallying with the excursions manager.

"Tell Charlie I will return his cycle tomorrow," he said at Sarah's house, the first and only words either of them spoke during the remainder of the walk.

His urgency to get back to the hotel was such that he didn't even trouble to adjust Charlie's bicycle; thus, a few minutes out from Sarah's house, with his legs already cramping and no tools with which to make the adjustments, he left the bicycle inside a neighbor's gate and began walking.

It didn't matter; it was already too late for cigars and conversation. He'd find a piano, then, rehearse the tune for Lillian's party, rehearse until either he got it right or his fingers crumbled over the keys. But he could think only of the pianos in the Swan Park's music room and ballroom, certain to be still in service this time on a Saturday night.

The Esplanade, however, was largely deserted, suspended in a state of eerie peace in which the roar of wind and water dwarfed the structures that seemed so solid and significant when people filled them. Except for the Sultan's Road. As he stood before it, having to sway his back to view the top of the main arch and the domes, the Sultan's Road felt significant to John. He'd risked his position to bring the proposal for the pleasure railway to a board member after Sir Alton had rejected the idea outright. It was something for Blackpool or Southend, Sir Alton had told him, a tawdry working-class amusement that didn't belong in Idensea.

Here it was nonetheless, flanked by stone leopards and palms transplanted from the Isles of Scilly. A week, that canvas curtain would fall and reveal the ziggurat of hanging gardens, and the pleasure railway would be open to the public. John walked the arcade, pausing to pass his hand over one of the mosaics. Not so long ago, he'd never seen anything like the intricacies and colors of the arabesques the designer had shown him, and now the tiles warmed under his touch.

He crossed the Esplanade and walked backward for a distance, scrutinizing the approach to the pleasure railway. Then he about-turned, earnest about reaching the hotel now.

Why hadn't he said *something* to Lillian? They'd stood here along this railing, and he'd felt grateful for the distraction of the children and their picnic, glad to dash after the rock vendor rather than have that moment with her.

The wife mattered. She didn't have to; he knew it was possible, provided she were a certain sort of female, to keep her under glass and do little more than tend her. But she could matter, and it was better when she did. He'd learned that much in his life from his mentors, even from Sir Alton and his own father.

One week to the opening of the Sultan's Road. It would be ready. A day shy of that week, he would see Lillian. He would practice; he would go to Lillian's party and not embarrass either of them; he would speak to her and not change his mind about what he needed to say.

In her room at The Bows, Betsey cut the buttons off her vest, letting each one fall to the floor. They landed with tawdry-sounding clicks, lacking the weight of real brass, and she went to bed, leaving them where they had scattered.

A little later, she was on the floor, gathering them up, not crying. She put them with her mending notions, in a dented biscuit tin that featured an image of the house where supposedly the biscuits had been made with care by a Mrs. Knight of Derbyshire. She pushed the lid shut, then lingered over it, tracing the embossed details of the house. She used a single fingertip, the way she had ventured to touch the furnishings in Miss Elizabeth Dellaforde's doll's house when she first went to work—almost twelve years old, and tall enough for her and Caroline to safely lie about her age. That toy had looked so true Betsey had imagined it something like a seed: Planted streetside, it would sprout a real-sized house occupied by a complete family a few weeks later.

Later, she'd sought solace before that seed of a home, even though she'd grown too old for such fancies. After Caroline married Richard and moved away to London, she would slip to the nursery, long empty of Dellaforde children young enough to inhabit it, to sit on a low stool before the doll's house. She came there to cry one night, holding a letter from Caroline, a letter too similar to its predecessors: *Only another few months, dearest, and we'll send for you. Richard tells me the household expenses are simply too close now, but soon . . .*

But the nursery had not been empty that night. Thomas Dellaforde, home from university, was there hiding his smoking from his father.

Stay and have one. It will distract you from whatever's made you cry.

On a tiny stool, she'd sat and pretended this was her first cigarette, shocked to discover Thomas Gregory Dellaforde already knew her name.

"But it's not a very nice name, anyway, is it?" he'd said. "Lizzie? You'd be better with Liza, or Beth."

"My mum always called me Elisabeth. Elisabeth with an *s*. Mrs. Filgage called me Lizzie when I come here, though, and I was too timid to say different, so everyone else says it, too, now."

But his sister was Elizabeth. "Let it be Betsey between us. Awfully pretty, I've always thought. Very—"

He had said a word she'd not known back then, and couldn't remember now, but she'd liked the sound of it. She forgot her desolation over Caroline's letter. She forgot the doll's house, only a few feet behind her. She didn't think of it again for a long time after that, even when she and Thomas went back to the nursery sometimes.

Still, as the tin house on the biscuit container warmed beneath the tip of her finger, she remembered it clearly, more clearly than she remembered Thomas's face.

Sit in an erect and comfortable position close to the machine.
—*How to Become Expert in Type-writing*

*Y*ou are aware, Miss Gilbey, Lord Tennyson has a poem named for you."

Lillian continued leafing through Mr. Dunning's sheet music, pleased to think of him brushing up his Tennyson just for her. They were using this Sunday afternoon to rehearse their duet for her music society party, though on a break for tea at the moment.

"Yes. Papa used it to scold me when I was a very little girl, if he thought I was sulking."

Mr. Dunning turned from the table to speak to Mama and Aunt Constance, chaperoning from a distant corner of the drawing room. "Ladies, you must tell me the greater fiction, that little Miss Gilbey sulked or that her father ever had need to scold her?"

"Horace Gilbey cajoles his daughters into obedience," Aunt Constance said. "I'd be surprised if he knows the meaning of the word *scold*."

Mama smiled. "Little enough reason for him to."

"As I suspected." Mr. Dunning rapped Lillian's knuckle with a single finger. How exquisite, his musician's hand. "You fabulist. Poetic justice is one thing, but whoever heard of poetic scolding?"

"'Airy, fairy Lilian' is hardly a pleasant girl. I should have to change my name if I truly had inspired such a deplorable depiction."

"Deplorable!"

Lillian laughed, supposing him surprised that she could find fault in her beloved Lord Tennyson. But genius was not infallible. Witness Mr. Dunning's music collection, whose only standard for inclusion appeared to be notes on a staff. Hymns and drawing-room ballads and operettas were as likely to appear as Schumann or Handel. At a chance meeting at Albert Hall last week, he had confessed a penchant for the music hall, and just now, she had come to a piece titled "Oh! Angelina Was Always Fond of Soldiers." The lack of boundaries perplexed her.

"Mr. Dunning, your indiscriminate assortment of music here worries me enough. Please don't say you admire that poem."

"I found it . . . well, lovely, rather. I suppose."

They had often sparred like this, debates that enlivened them both, but he was giving up now—his single fault, to Lillian's observation, this diffidence to which he surrendered occasionally. He must learn to manage it if he hoped to get anywhere; it only required the right sort of discipline.

Thus, she pressed, "But so trivial and obvious! No theme but a coy and guileful female, do you not agree?"

The tips of his ears turned pink. He pulled his portfolio of music from her, thumbed to the back, and removed a manuscript.

"I suppose I don't—that is, I set it to music, you see."

Lillian froze, envisioning herself having to strike Noel Dunning from her List tonight, and not because she wanted to. If he learned something of the perils of beating round the bush, fine, but that good lesson was no use to *her* now. How was she to repair this insult?

She began by sniffing at the manuscript, a skeptic. "Well, I certainly must hear it. If you can make something bearable of those verses, Mr. Dunning, I shall avow your genius far and wide."

With an air of challenge, she directed him toward the piano, prepared to rhapsodize over any old thing he mashed out. But within the first measures, she knew no playacting would be required. Under the spell of his melody, doggerel became achingly beautiful, and "cruel little Lilian" seemed worthy of the heartache the speaker lavished on her. Lillian halted the maid entering with tea with an upraised hand and went like a sleepwalker to the piano, where she leaned, transfixed, until the final note faded.

Mama and Aunt Constance applauded, but Lillian could only sigh, "Oh, Mr. Dunning, oh. *Mr. Dunning.*"

After a bashful glance, he started to fold the manuscript. Lillian snatched it from him.

"No, no, no, Mr. Dunning! It is . . . exquisite, extraordinarily exquisite. Did you hear it, Mama?" Her skirts swished as she twirled to her mother, then again to the piano. "You must play it at the party. Tell me you will, you must."

"But our piece . . ."

"Yes, yes, the duet—you'd have two pieces in the program, if you're willing. You are, aren't you?"

"I'm grateful to possess the means to grant any of your wishes, Miss Gilbey, but I shouldn't impose—you were remarking upon how crowded the program is already."

Mama brought Mr. Dunning a cup of tea. "Dearest, it's true. You spent the whole of yesterday afternoon putting the performances in an order that suited you—it is all ready for the printer's. You'd undo all that?"

Lillian waved away this question. She had slaved over the program not to suit herself but to create sensations and transitions and moods, not to mention balance politics and protocol. Mama little understood the complexities.

Nor how they signified nothing. The very theme of this gathering was new pieces: a composition never yet published nor played in public, performed by the dashing son of a famous composer who happened to be a baronet . . .

Coup was the word. Sydenham Music Society would get a notice in the papers, which would open the door to who-knew-what-number of new invitations.

And it was a gorgeous, gorgeous piece of music.

She would have too many performances, though. But someone might develop laryngitis, or stage fright, or magnanimously step aside to make room for Mr. Dunning—

John. Surely by now he was regretting the task he'd set for himself. He would be positively relieved for a way out. Not to mention how it would ease her own mind. She'd already had a nightmare of John taking the stage with something appalling, even worse than "Oh! Angelina Was Always Fond of Soldiers."

She didn't voice her idea. Mama was partial to John and wouldn't like it. And Lillian and Mr. Dunning no longer used John as a topic of conversation. It was uncomfortable, and besides, they'd found so many other things to discuss.

She offered Mr. Dunning the plate of biscuits. "It will work itself out. Nothing to bother over now."

She persuaded him to play his song again before he left for the afternoon. She declared it perfect, absolutely perfect.

"Except . . ."

She hesitated, certain Lord Tennyson would condemn this request. But with phrasing like "love-sighs" and "crimson-threaded lips," and John, not Tennyson, in company, did she have a choice?

"Might you use another name, Mr. Dunning? Marian? Gwendolyn?" To protect him from insult, she dropped her gaze sideward—her modesty could not bear such attention, he must understand.

A true gentleman, he did. "Marian it is. But will you grant me a similar favor? A change of name?" Into her ear, he whispered, "Noel. If only now and then, Noel."

Success. Desperately, she wished for privacy, having hypothesized lately that John's kisses were not as singular as she'd thought, that other men might like to kiss like that. Perhaps the son of a baronet?

Revising the program after Mr. Dunning departed took only a moment. She could hardly cut the regular society members, and John, he could not care so much. And if he did—well, he would forgive her. He'd just have to forgive her.

"He must be mad for you," concluded Sarah as she and Betsey gathered herbs from the kitchen garden Sunday afternoon. "To come from London, to fight for you. One could almost pity the man"—she smiled self-consciously as she reached up to place her cuttings in the basket Betsey held—"if you would let one."

Betsey put a sprig of rosemary to her nose. She couldn't join Sarah in fantasies of Avery's unrequited love for her. Nor could she begin to explain the prosaic arrangements of her life to someone like Sarah. *A way of going along.*

More than that, she'd told Mr. Jones last night, and what had she meant? A type-writing machine to practice upon? Extra writing lessons? A reminder of Thomas Dellaforde, with those lines of literature Avery carried about in his head and the books stacked up in his flat once upon a time?

She wouldn't risk an alteration of Sarah's soft warmth toward her, and thus, she spoke of last night's events in the most general terms possible.

Laughing, Sarah stood and tucked a flower behind Betsey's ear. Sarah's haze of curls was already strewn with tiny blossoms and leaves. "All right, then, he is the lowest sort of cad, and I shan't waste my pity on him."

"He could have—he still might—cost me my position, Sarah."

"I meant to say 'villain,' of course. The seedy variety, without a trace of romance." She frowned with renewed concern as she considered Betsey. "Your poor mouth. How did you ever—"

She interrupted her own question to cock an ear at the house, and Betsey was glad, for Sarah's curiosity about Avery had been driving toward increasingly difficult-to-dodge questions.

"I shall absolutely wring his neck." Sarah dropped her shears into the basket and started to pull off her gloves. "A thousand and one times I've warned him about his noise in the house, especially when there are boarders at home."

But when her son burst through the door that led to the back garden, he got no more than "Darling, hadn't you best stay out of doors if you want to make such a racket?" The fist planted on her hip was very stern, however.

Charlie, who appeared ready to take flight, such was his excitement, failed to notice it. "John's come back with me—he's waiting out front."

"I'll take these cuttings to the kitchen," Betsey said. She had managed to avoid Mr. Jones at church this morning, keeping Charlie and Sarah as a buffer between them, distancing herself from the groups of chatting congregants after the service. With luck, she could escape to her room without seeing him now.

Charlie said, "Let 'em rot. It's you he's waiting for, come on."

She glanced at Sarah, and regretted it. Sarah looked so curious and . . . alert. All that had passed between herself and Mr. Jones last night had been communicated to Sarah as "he's disappointed in me," a broad umbrella of a phrase that covered everything from her mistake with the budget to the fact that she wasn't an heiress, or a virgin.

She didn't want to be forced into civility after he'd insulted and condescended to her. She didn't care to spend another jot of time remembering how foolishly she'd allowed her feelings to run away from her.

But Charlie, impatient, said, "He told me to fetch you," and she understood she'd been *sent for*. She pulled Sarah's flower from her hair and permitted Charlie to tug her through the house to the front door, where she followed his order to cover her eyes before he opened it.

A bicycle. Mr. Jones had brought her a bicycle. It and he stood in the road before the house, waiting for her.

"John and me picked it," Charlie said. "It's from the hotel— they got new ones for the guests, and you get an old one, just to borrow, but it's not old, really, it's good as new—we fixed it for you, John and me."

He ran down the walk and hopped the fence at the edge of the front garden, then squeezed the front tire of the safety bicycle. "Pneumatics!"

Betsey came to the gate, but she didn't go through. She stared at the bicycle.

"I asked Tobias," Mr. Jones said. He added, "A solution to getting you home when you are late at the hotel," as if that predicament had been the extent of their interaction last night.

As Charlie swung a leg over the cycle, she murmured, "Keep us safe from dillydallying, won't it?"

Mr. Jones colored. He looked like a boy, blushing, standing there in his Norfolk, his soft cap pushed back on his head. Very different from Mr. Jones in his dinner suit, but both versions produced the same impossible longing in her, and she was glad she could make him uncomfortable, glad she could rattle John Jones's easy confidence.

"I don't know how to cycle, Charlie."

"Why, John'll show you—he taught me, and you see how I do." Charlie pedaled away, suddenly looking gawky as he turned his elbows out and made laborious shoves down on the pedals, causing the bicycle to list to and fro. He wobbled up the road in an awkward hunch with elbows and knees poking out, putting on an act of incompetence only an expert could manage.

Betsey glanced sidelong at Mr. Jones. He was smiling. "There's cheek," he said.

"You see, a fine teacher!" Charlie called as he turned around. Then he was graceful again, releasing the handlebar and holding his arms out at his sides as he came coasting back toward them.

"A peacock." Mr. Jones raised an eyebrow at her. "Taken him out of my pocket, have you?"

"I don't know what you mean."

"I mean you're a witch, Dobs."

The comment dropped mildly enough, but she bristled anyway. She hadn't tried to influence Charlie, enchant him away from his devotion to Mr. Jones. He was lucky Charlie pulled up just then, or perhaps she was the lucky one. In any case, she checked her tongue.

"You see?" Charlie said, dismounting. "It's ever so easy."

"I don't need a bicycle," she said. She reached across the gate to draw a single fingertip along the curve of the handlebar. "The tram's good enough for me."

"But cycling's much more fun than an old horse-tram," Charlie said.

"And no fare to pay," Mr. Jones pointed out. "Not that you worry much for paying fares, but—" He put a hand on Charlie's shoulder and leaned over the boy. "You see that look, Charlie? Like we've sold her cow for beans instead of gold. Forgot, she has, that the beans did turn out to be magic."

"They did," Charlie said, as if this were a completely logical point that didn't overlook the facts of the ruined garden, a missing son, and an ill-tempered giant. Also, that it was a fairy tale.

"I haven't a cycling costume."

Mr. Jones *phh*-ed, knowing this excuse to be even more preposterous than the magic beans argument. Ladies had specific costumes for every public activity in which they engaged, and probably for their private activities as well, but she was just Betsey Dobson.

"You'll manage fine. Mind your skirts is what there is to that." He gestured as if to demonstrate how she ought to lift her skirts. But as their eyes met, the motion turned awkward and charged, and he left off, blushing again.

He used both hands to pull his cap down, then held open the gate. "Come along then, Miss Dobson," he said, so Englishly, so supervisorously. "The afternoon is about to get away from us."

She wanted to refuse, remind him this was *Sunday* afternoon, and that even given the because-I-have-said-so factor, he hadn't any right to demand she learn how to ride a bicycle, nor to send

Charlie to fetch her at his convenience. It didn't matter that cycling seemed a rather glorious activity, and that she'd long wanted to try it. Just now, she wanted to be difficult.

A small bit of torture. Just to even things up.

"Very well, damn it," she said, and came through the gate.

Well, fairness was a luxury, after all, and one made dearer by her actions last night. If she became more difficult than he cared to abide, what would happen to her?

Sarah called Charlie back to the house. Mr. Jones adjusted the saddle for Betsey, then straddled the steering wheel to hold the cycle steady while she mounted to test the height of the saddle. He made a clumsy inquiry regarding the angles of her knees, and she lifted her skirts so he could judge for himself.

"Off," he ordered. "More height, you need. Go put on some low shoes whilst I fix it."

"I'll make do with my boots."

He raised his brows. He clearly did not care to repeat the command, thus compelling her to explain, "I haven't any others."

"They'll do, then," he admitted. "'Tis but a matter of comfort." A few moments later, his focus trained on the saddle, he murmured, "You made yourself scarce after church."

He didn't ask why or where she had gone, so she let the comment hang. The second adjustment was perfect, and they walked, pushing their bicycles, toward a neighbor's open field where Mr. Jones said she should have her first lesson, and she promptly questioned why she couldn't practice on the road before he shoved her into oblivion down a hill, and he said it was a slight downward grade, not a hill, and it would help her learn more quickly. Also, he'd be right beside her, not shoving her anywhere. It was a hill, she insisted, and she was sure she would do better on the road. He explained about motion and friction and balance, and how the grade—"the *hill*"—would make gravity work for her, and she explained how she'd seen bicycles on roads many a time, and in fields exactly never.

"The grass makes a nicer landing place when you fall."

"I have decided not to fall."

"Then no difference it makes, and my way we will have it."

Betsey said nothing, not with her mouth.

"Since I'm the one what's done it, you see," he said, his voice low with victory, his Welsh brogue tapping along the tops of the words, vowels like a boot heel cutting into loose dirt.

"I do see. Mr. Jones, you are . . . *entirely* correct." She smiled at him, closed-lip.

"Ow—*damn*," he grunted, the poor thing having rammed his shin into his pedal as he walked. "Learn to balance, you will, but when you feel yourself going over, you must try to remember to put the steering wheel in the direction of the fall. To turn it away will mean a fall for certain. Keep hold of the handlebar, no throwing your arms out to catch yourself. Break your wrist or worse that way."

She had no wish for broken bones. She put aside her contrariness and gave him her attention. He was, as Charlie had promised, a fine teacher, especially after he became so engrossed in her progress that he forgot the self-consciousness with which he drew close to her to help her balance, an arm before and behind. By the time she completed her first lengthy run, unassisted and fairly steady, he was jubilant, running to her as she came to a sloppy halt and shouting that he'd known she would take to it.

How could he have known? She hadn't. But she, too, was rising in a bubble of elation, amazed at herself, reveling in his approval, as nourished by his confidence in her as by any meal she'd ever eaten.

He let her practice on the road next, and she readily agreed to his suggestion for a longer ride. They rode toward Castle Hill, where the ruins of Iden Tower overlooked the sea.

He didn't stop as the incline steepened. Behind him, Betsey struggled, straining to propel the bicycle, her thighs afire and her previous pleasure waning. When Mr. Jones looked back, she muttered a curse between gritted teeth. He was pedaling more slowly now as well but didn't appear to be suffering. She pushed on longer than she thought she could, but when her pedaling grew too sluggish to keep the bicycle upright, she surrendered.

"I'm done!" she gasped, coming off the cycle with none of the technique he'd taught her, scarcely able to keep the heavy machine upright.

"Bless God!" he shouted, and hopped off. "What is it you're made of, Dobs?"

Betsey did not have the breath to answer. She pushed the bicycle to him and then asked, her words coming in gulps, "Why . . . didn't . . . you stop . . . then?"

"Determined to go so far as you, there's sure. Bless God!" He took off his cap to run a hand over his brow, then into his hair. "I didn't guess you carried a racehorse's heart in you."

She balked when he asked whether she was ready to resume their journey up the hill.

"We can have a look at the ruins. It isn't far now," he said.

"I can see them from here. I can see them from the hotel. I can see them from nearly anywhere in Idensea, for God's sake. There's no reason to send ourselves into apoplexy pedaling up this hill. And I can't. I simply cannot."

"We will have to walk it, but Dobs, if we don't go up, there's no coasting down." He leaned over his handlebar toward her, tilting up a frankly cajoling smile. "You of everyone shouldn't wish to miss that ride."

Betsey contemplated it, losing her breath all over again. A glorious downhill coast on a bicycle, a flight into the green shine of his eyes—she contemplated them both for a moment too long, a moment that allowed the two separate things to become fused into one thing she wanted. Looking away over her shoulder at the road declining away behind her, she worked at unfusing them.

"I know you're not afraid," Mr. Jones said. "Or if you are, it'll not master you." He touched her jaw, two fingers that set her face back to the road ahead.

The touch fired through her, too akin to what he'd done last night, too much like he had the right. Too little of everything else.

Something she didn't know how to refuse, because of her own feelings and because he could finish an argument with *because I have said so*.

She moved from the touch diplomatically, by bowing her head and beginning the plod up the hill. "Very well, damn it."

Never fail to use Mr., Esq., or some other title when addressing a gentleman.

—*How to Become Expert in Type-writing*

*J*den Hall you can see now," he said as they neared the crest, and Betsey paused. Sir Alton's home nestled on a distant hillside, a gray, symmetrical arrangement of chimneys and columns and rows of windows.

"I'll go alone tomorrow," she said. "You needn't come." She had decided this last night as the two of them finished their silent walk to Sarah's. She'd liked being rescued by Mr. Jones far too much.

She was prepared to defend her decision. But he didn't tell her *no*. He asked, "Why do you want it so?"

"It's my responsibility. My position at stake, my bookings. My fault." She sighed. "I might have placated Avery when he turned up at the pavilion. He wanted to tell me how he'd already spoken to the headmaster at Parkhurst about a job. I might have taken two minutes to listen."

"Had time for a chat, did you?"

The irritation in his voice surprised her. But he meant it for Avery, didn't he? And yes, Avery's timing had been wretched. She was absorbed in her duties, dozens of details to keep straight, a hundred mistakes to avoid. She hadn't time to listen and sort out his intentions, her feelings. He wasn't supposed to be there in the first place. He'd been drinking; his eyes had burned with it.

"No," she answered, "I didn't."

"So I thought."

He leaned his cycle into a hedgerow of field roses, took hers to do the same, then walked beside her to the ruins, still another steep rise away. No wonder the picnickers and holidaymakers up here appeared so languorous, worn out from the climb, lulled by the nuzzling breeze. You could count shades of green like stars up here, from the glow of the tender shoots at your feet to the earthy burr of the heath far below. *Put out your hand for mine again,* Betsey thought. She'd take it and tell him her gratitude for putting the world at her feet this afternoon.

The stones of the tower were so ragged that the broken circle looked like a wreck hauled from the sea, covered in barnacles, frayed scraps of sky showing through vaguely arch-shaped openings in the walls. Out from the tower, foundations and walls breached the ground cover of daisies and grasses, but irregularly, and not by more than a few feet. As they passed one of the taller remnants, Mr. Jones put his hand to it, making such purposeful contact that she felt compelled to do the same. The initial warmth was deceptive; beneath it, inside, the chill and damp of springtime held.

He reached into his coat pocket. The folded paper he held out to her read "Betsey Dobson" in Avery's handwriting. "This came to the Swan this morning. Meant to give it to you at services . . ."

But she'd made certain there was no good time for that. "He'll be wanting money," she predicted, managing to sound careless, though her hand rolled into a fist as she took the note. She hurried ahead, lifting her skirts as she climbed the sharp rise where the tower ruins sat. Mr. Jones didn't try to catch up with her. She wandered alone amongst the ruins—which, thanks to Ethan Noonan, she'd glimpsed only from a distance until now—found a seat on a stone that had once been something grander, and unfolded Avery's note.

Twenty-one shillings. He suggested an advance on her wages,

or surely she knew someone who would make her a loan. He'd sacrificed everything to follow her to this damned carnival; if she could leave him to rot in a ten-day sentence when it had all been a mistake, an accident anyway, then she was a witch, an icy, vengeful Morgan le Fay.

So be it. She tore the note in half, then again. She sensed his desperation; she knew that with some alterations to her careful budget, her modest plans, she could, in marked contrast to her situation a fortnight ago, help him. But paper squares collected on her lap in a heap.

Two children raced past her, chattering of pirates; a third tripped and would have fallen headfirst into stone if not for Betsey sitting there. The tiny girl bounced off Betsy's skirts; paper flurries swirled into the breeze.

"Oh, ma'am, won't you fix it?"

"It" meant a rapier fashioned from two sticks the child held, along with a bedraggled white hair ribbon intended to hold them together. Betsey took the articles and made a neat job of it, with the child at her knee, breathing heavily.

"That's got it," she said, presenting her handiwork. "Now take care for pirates."

"Me, I'm the pirate, ma'am," she was informed.

"Oh! Good luck to you, then."

The girl ran away. Bits of white paper trailed over grass and stone, rolled over the tips of Mr. Jones's shoes. She hadn't noticed him till now, standing a few steps away, framed in a broken arch.

"Have you brothers or sisters?" he asked as she stood and joined him. They walked out from the ruins, to the grass where a few holidaymakers were lingering over the remains of afternoon picnics.

"A sister in London. A brother somewhere. Alive, we hope, possibly at sea, but it's been years and years. You?"

"Seven sisters," he said, smiling. "A brother, Owen, to be four soon, and two others passed, though I knew but one: Davey—Daf-fyd—in heaven since I was twelve."

Before she had a chance to express her sympathy, he added, "I am starved! Do you think Sarah will put by some of tea for me, to have before my lesson?"

His music lesson, he meant, the piece he was learning for Miss Gilbey's party. Betsey often listened from her third-floor window or climbed out and sat on the roof, especially when he rehearsed the lyrics. His voice, low, lush, and serrated, betrayed no effort of concentration, unlike his playing. But he'd been tenacious these past weeks, apparently determined Miss Gilbey must not suspect what trouble he was taking to please her.

Betsey could have told him, *You're all wrong about that.* All those evenings, listening to him doggedly correct each mistake, hearing him trying to erase the evidence of effort—ah, she could have told him: Had Miss Gilbey been there on the roof, too, each mistaken note could only have made him more and more dear to her.

"I'm certain Sarah will see to it you have whatever you wish," she said.

"And there Dora Pink will be to take back half of it."

"Not while you keep leaving a few coins behind. She blesses you frequently for that."

"Not before Sarah, I hope." He settled into the grass, stretching out on a hip and looking down to the harbor. "Someday, I'll be rich, and I will go to my house, in the middle of Wednesday, to a grand spread of a tea—three, four sorts of jam, and a tower of sandwiches, and boys and dogs tussling on the rugs for the last biscuits."

"Boys and dogs," Betsey repeated, and laughed to chase back a sigh. "Having sisters ruined you for daughters, did it?"

"Ah, the daughters. They are on my knees with all the sweets they can hold." He looked up at her, blocking the sun with his arm. "Well you would do to take you a rest, Dobs," he said, and when she hesitated in joining him on the grass, he added, "You needn't worry for your frock. The sort that hides the dirt, it is."

"A gracious invitation."

"Pardons. Thought that was what you must be thinking of."

Betsey sat down beside him, and—because a small bit of torture seemed only fair—instead of smoothing out her sensible and perfectly clean brown tweed skirt, she left it rumpled and stretched out her legs, putting her ankles within his view.

He rolled onto his back. Pulled his cap down to cover his eyes. Betsey counted it on her side of the tally.

"My mam used to fret over it," he said. "'Twas how she picked all the fabric for the clothes we had, and my poor sisters despaired of it, always wanting something prettier." With a soft chuckle, he tucked his hands behind his head. "One Christmas after I'd gone away—I left home young—money enough I had to send back a present or two, and I found a bolt of cloth—only muslin, you know, but pretty. Blue, but the sort that's in snow of a morning, see?"

Betsey didn't think she'd ever seen snow like that. But far below her, the sea was winking white and yellow and lavender at her, so she answered, "Yes."

"Thinking of my mother in a new dress, I buy it and send it off to her. In the years after, I go back, and what do you think I find?"

"She'd used it to make curtains."

He jerked, turning on his stomach to look up at her. "Right, you witch. Snow-blue curtains, everywhere in that little house."

Betsey laughed. "I'm certain she enjoyed them as much as she would have a new dress. Perhaps more, since they were in constant use."

"No, you're not understanding. All over, they were. Even windows not there had curtains. I paid a call to our reverend and I saw blue curtains. I went to collect the eggs in the henhouse . . . snow-blue curtains."

"You exaggerate!" Betsey said, laughing hard now.

"Do I! No woman in the village had blue thread for six months! 'Mam,' I said to her, 'a dress I was meaning for you, not curtains here to the Bristol Channel.'"

"And what did she say?"

"She looked like I'd gone soft. 'Think how the dirt would show, Iefan-my-boy! Think of the dirt!'" He rolled to his back again, and Betsey watched as one hand, resting on his stomach, moved up and down with the rhythm of his laughter.

"Bless God!" The rhythm slowed, ending in a deep exhalation. "Bless God, my mother," he said, in an undertone.

She plucked a long blade of grass and wove it between her fingers, distracting herself from the impulse she felt to comb them through the black hair touching the grass beside her, shining like silk against the green blades.

"Did you send her brown tweed next time, then?" she asked, though she believed she knew that answer already, too.

"No, never any cloth then, but a frock ready-made, for her to wear for my sister Mair's wedding, and yellow it was, but only a touch, not even as much as is butter."

"And did she wear it?"

"I think so, once and again. I know she had her picture made in it, her and my dad and the little ones. And they buried her in it, just this March that has gone."

Betsey started, letting the blade of grass fall into her lap. She pulled her feet up under her skirts. "Oh, I am sorry. I didn't know."

"They, my sisters, told me what they'd done when I came for the funeral, and I just laughed, and good and furious they grew, but I was laughing because all I could hear was my mother railing from her grave, 'Think how the dirt will show, Iefan-my-boy!' Then I wept hard, for no one else had thought of it, and I'd come too late."

He made a sound as though he would continue, but he didn't. Again, she resisted the desire to touch his hair, though it sprang from a different source now. If she touched him, it would be for his need, not her own. Only along his temples, only to smooth, simply to say, *I understand your loss*.

Voices fluttered from the ruins. A train knocked along in the distance. Over the grass a bee buzzed, rested, and buzzed again.

"I expect your mother felt like a duchess, the day she had her picture made in that dress."

The train continued on, became too faint to hear.

"Do you think so, girl?"

"Oh, yes."

After a moment, he turned over again, propping himself on his elbow to look up at her. An expansive craving destroyed her moment of altruism, laid it flat under a greediness to answer every wondering question in his eyes. Men looked at her, they looked in all sorts of ways, but this sensation of being *seen* . . .

She wanted more. She wanted to be known by this man, this one. She couldn't help biting her lip, but otherwise, she held still and let him see.

"Thanks. For the bicycle. The lesson."

"Most need more than a single lesson."

"I like it."

"I know. Good, I mean. I mean, I knew you would. Believed so, whatever."

Yes, he'd said that during the lesson: *I knew you would.* And last night: *I knew what you would be for.* The downy, tickling joy in her chest threatened to carry her away.

"Iefan is your Welsh name?"

"Iefan Rhys-Jones. Iefan's John in Welsh."

"Iefan." She hugged her knees and rested her cheek on them, feeling the slubs of tweed against her skin, something like the roughness of his cheek last night. "Iefan?"

"What is it?" he answered, but really, she had nothing she'd intended to say to him. She only wished to say his name. And kiss him. That was all. Say his name, kiss him, and touch his hair again, that was all.

She reached out. Her fingers tugged gently at a piece of black hair kicking out from under his cap.

"Grass," she explained, and flicked her fingers as if returning some dried blades to the ground.

He didn't move. But he asked, "Any more?" and she lied, "Mm-hmm," and touched his hair again, and then his shoulder, brushing away imaginary bits of grass.

"You've some," he said, and Betsey didn't remind him that she'd not been lolling in the grass. He sat up, captured a fallen lock of her hair, tossed away whatever he'd pretended was there, and tucked the lock behind her ear. It fell, and he did it again, taking more time, tucking more firmly.

"Any more?"

He seemed to need to think about it. She had never had a man take so long to decide whether he would kiss her, to make such a to-do over the business, and it felt like a loss. Maybe it was an insult, this indecision, but all she felt was that she had been cheated before now; all she wanted to say was the same foolishness she'd whispered last night: *I think you're rather wonderful.*

"How is your—" His finger hovered over her lip.

"Better."

"A bit of sun you've got. Here." He touched her then, his finger grazing the bridge of her nose. She held her breath, she held herself still as he said, "And here," and pressed each apple of her cheek.

"Come without my hat, haven't I?"

He was not for her. He'd said so. But maybe he was. It seemed they both were thinking maybe he was, and so she took his cap from his head and set it on her own. It promptly slipped down to her eyes. Laughing, she peeked out from underneath, idling her fingers along the brim.

To her horror, this ounce of flirtation crashed the scales. Mr. Jones turned from her, back to the sea. For some time, he said nothing, only studied his laced fingers while she wilted under his cap.

"Sir Alton is a composer, did you know?"

Betsey supposed this to be some effort to rub out the past few minutes, put the scales to rights. It showed him a fast learner, since it was a better tack than telling her to get a dancing frock.

"No."

"Well, no more, but he was. 'Twas how he came into his title, his music."

"And he gave it up to open a hotel?"

"Not because he wanted to become a man of business. Hates that part of it, from what I can tell. No, he was bankrupt, or close to it. The Idensea estate he had, and that was all. Lady Dunning's his second wife—she was the one with the money."

"Always an answer to a prayer, the rich wife."

Probably he glanced at her during the following beat of silence. She was watching her fingers comb the grass, her face still shielded by his cap.

"Sir Alton's, sure," he admitted evenly. "But not only because of her money. Lady Dunning has sense, all sorts of it. All the best touches in the hotel, the ones that delight people and make them want to come again—Lady Dunning, that is. 'Twas she who saw what Idensea could be, convinced him it was worth the risk. He dreads it, risk. And that's what I'm saying to you, Betsey."

The sound of her name lifted her head with the sense that she should've been paying better attention, that this accounting of Sir Alton's history had not been mere distraction.

Mr. Jones pushed the bill of the cap up off her face. "I learned quick his decisions come from fear, and that he portions out his trust the way Dora Pink does her lamb stew. Lady Dunning he trusts, and Tobias, and certain of the board members. Me, too."

So she would be foolish to go to Sir Alton alone. That's what he was saying. Without calling her foolish, without forbidding her to do it, that's what he was saying.

She took off his cap, set it on the grass between them. Promptly, his hand covered it and rested there.

"Something else I know. A heart-knocking thing it can be, coming alone to a place like Iden Hall and wondering whether you should go to the front or use a service door."

She had no trouble guessing what his decision had been. She knew he was right, about how it would feel to go alone, how anything she said would be useless if Mr. Jones wasn't there to validate it.

She might as well go to a duel with a piece of straw. If she hoped to keep her job, she had better say, *Yes, I need you with me*.

"I understand." She stood and started for the hedgerow where they'd left the cycles. "You'd better come tomorrow then, I suppose," she added over her shoulder.

How stupid. She couldn't say it to his face. She'd thought she'd held steel, not straw. She'd put his cap on her head. How stupid.

She heard him close behind her as she took hold of her cycle, telling her not to mount yet, that they would walk partway down.

Now she turned to him. "You said we'd coast."

"I'd forgot how steep it is. Too steep, and you new at this. You don't know how it can get away from you."

Arguing was pointless. Neither of them could question his greater experience, and only Betsey could trust her deep knowledge that she was ready to take on the hill. She didn't know if she did trust it, but she was ready to try it, do something out of his reach.

"I understand. Very well."

He released the cycle to her and turned to retrieve his own.

She'd mounted and was careering down the hill before he had a chance to remind her about how to steer if she began to fall. She was a witch, streaking away on her broomstick.

The bicycle had no brake. A brake was an unnecessary weight, Mr. Jones had said, damaging to the tires, too, and he had demonstrated backpedaling as a way to slow the cycle. Betsey was hardly proficient at it, but with the bottom of the hill still so far off, she didn't care and was glad no brake weighted her down. Her sleeves snapping against her skin, her shins exposed, and her hair escaping its pins, she flew and knew glory. In her arms, in her pelvis and spine, the machinery vibrated, and she understood perfectly that the control she felt was an illusion, a thread easily snipped.

Well, wasn't it always? Just rarely in so thrilling a fashion. This flight had death or disemployment at its conclusion, she felt sure, but she kept her feet on the coasting pegs all the same.

The ground leveled. She heard Mr. Jones pedaling up behind her, demanding to know whether she had any idea what a lucky fool she was.

"Indeed I do, Mr. Jones." She glanced over to him, but for the life of her, could not mask her rapture behind anything suggesting contrition. She saw his irritation, but she also saw it giving way to . . .

She had to watch where she was going. Whatever displaced his anger, she missed it. But he played poorly that evening. In her room, trying to describe cycling in a letter to Caroline, Betsey shut the windows on him.

16

Your employer will prize you more highly and will pay you
better if he sees that you are careful about his property.

—*How to Become Expert in Type-writing*

*M*r. Seiler would accompany her and Mr. Jones to
Iden Hall, Betsey learned Monday morning. He
summoned her to his office to see what she had prepared and made
her a gift of a simple but pretty hair comb. "My wife often presents
these to her staff," he said, and did not suggest she make use of
it immediately, though the Swan Park's chambermaids appeared
starched and impeccable at all times.

Later that afternoon, they stopped by the Kursaal construction site to collect Mr. Jones. Mr. Seiler had to put more than
one of the workers to the task of finding him—it was a sprawling property which, when it opened in August, would hold a
recital hall, winter garden, and skating rink, amongst other
amusements. Betsey wished it were open now so she could be
charging more for the excursions. Though the Kursaal presently
was surrounded by an expanse of rutted mud, it was a beautiful
structure, a fanciful tribute to a Greek temple, all pale stone and
pediments and columns. Iron and glass wrapped the lowest floor,
winging out from the entrance and ascending to a high barrel
vault in the rear.

Betsey liked seeing Mr. Jones come out from under some scaffolding, carrying his coat and beating dust out of it as he spoke to a laborer. The Kursaal was situated east of the pier, closer to the Swan Park, upon the cliff overlooking the Esplanade, and Betsey had never been so near before. All this under Mr. Jones's care and direction, and Sir Alton was pulling him from it for that scuffle of Avery's. Some of her fear of Sir Alton subsided with this realization, diluted by simple irritation on Mr. Jones's behalf.

He swung into the carriage with a somewhat absent greeting and something about electrical wiring. He gestured at Mr. Seiler. *Am I presentable?* Betsey was amused to interpret. As far as she could discern, Mr. Seiler did no more than nod, but the next moment, Mr. Jones swiped his pocket handkerchief over the tops of his boots.

And then he frowned at her. "Where is your uniform?"

"It needs mending," she replied, taken aback. "And it is for Saturdays, anyway. And anyway, what is the difference to you?"

"Miss Dobson," Mr. Seiler murmured.

She'd been too sharp. Her nerves. However, what *was* the difference to him? "Forgive me."

Mr. Seiler regarded her kindly. "Your attire is appropriate and you look well."

"I didn't mean"—Mr. Jones yanked at his shirt cuffs—"that she didn't . . . that you don't . . . well, it is only that the uniform . . ." With a guttural sigh, he stretched an arm across the back of his empty seat and looked out the side of the barouche. "It does you something."

Betsey almost wished she had worn it. Today might have been her last chance. What if she were dismissed before it had been paid for?

Too, she could have used the boost of confidence the uniform gave her as the footman admitted them inside Iden Hall. Though the manor house lacked the Swan Park's magnificence, she felt the same intimidation she'd experienced her first day at the hotel.

Worse, rather, knowing everything was for the use of one man and his family.

Add to that the fact she was evidently not expected. Indeed, Mr. Seiler had to introduce her as though she and Sir Alton had not met two nights ago. But it was a pleasure, Sir Alton assured her, and ordered a chair for Miss . . . *Dobson*, and himself pointed where it should be placed, right beside his desk, subtly beyond the boundary of easy conversation and conferral.

Considerately, he had folded the newspapers to the pages reporting the "incident," or "brawl," or "disorder," or "rioting," as it was variously labeled. No London papers thus far; they were all provincial, the first page of the *Gazetteer* and less sensational mentions in the others, a few lines amongst the resort notices. Mr. Jones passed them her way once he and Mr. Seiler had skimmed them. They stacked up on her lap, and she could not stop herself from reading and rereading. Preparing for the meeting, gaining distance from the event itself, had dulled the disastrous edge it had held for her. The printed accounts brought it all back.

"It is not what we would hope," conceded Mr. Seiler. "But let us consider also the good to come from Idensea this summer. The Sultan's Road, for example, opening within the week."

Betsey winced. She knew from Mr. Jones that Sir Alton hated the pleasure railway from the first suggestion, and had grown no fonder of it during construction. Quickly, Mr. Jones added, "And after that, the Kursaal opening and the visit from the Duke. People will think of those things when they think of Idensea."

"If only you'd mentioned this earlier," Sir Alton said. He sat sideways of his desk, and she could not see much of his face, but he sounded so very amenable. "I should have slept like a newborn these past nights, having heard such charming tales. What do you think, Miss Dobson?"

She needed the expectant glances of Mr. Jones and Mr. Seiler to fully realize he'd spoken to her. He'd neither looked her way nor varied the low, rhythmic cadence of his voice.

"Is my anxiety for Idensea's reputation excessive?" he went on, now exerting himself to speak over his arm to her. "Am I mistaken in assuming persons of Class will find a horde of brawling bricklayers an undesirable addition to their seaside holiday?"

They weren't bricklayers; they were from a glassworks, craftsmen with their wives, the booking approved by Mr. Seiler himself before she'd been hired. And who was to say a party of bricklayers would not have been better behaved?

And what in hell did she know of persons of Class?

Which was why he'd asked her. He'd not been addressing her at all, only making a point to Mr. Jones and Mr. Seiler.

She peeked at those two men for some guidance as to how she should respond or an indication that one of them would intervene, but Mr. Seiler's expression was inscrutable, while Mr. Jones merely appeared interested, as though she were about to take the stage.

Well, maybe she would. Playact. Sir Alton could play a man, and she could play like she wanted him to like her.

"A brawling horde of anything would spoil my holiday, I'm quite certain," she agreed. At last, Sir Alton turned in her direction. She took the opportunity to catch his eye and smile at him warmly. "The couple above my old London flat is proof enough of that, and they only spoilt my tea once or twice a month. Now then." She passed the newspapers that had collected in her lap to Mr. Jones. "You'll let me show you these figures? I've waited to see what you think of them."

At Sir Alton's raised brow, Mr. Jones said, "You'll want to know the financial consequences of suspending the excursions scheme before you ask the board's approval."

A mild threat. Sir Alton took it with apparent grace. "It sounds very informative. Do proceed, Miss Dobson."

She opened her ledger, no staging in the fumbling she did with the pages. "A bit keyed up," she confided in a playful hush and took an unhurried moment to remove her gloves.

"You wouldn't mind if I . . . ?" From the awkwardly positioned chair, she moved behind his desk and placed the ledger before him. "Won't this be better?"

"You are my guest."

One could find satin and velvet at the rag shop, but one would do well to check for mites. Sir Alton sounded disconcertingly sincere, and Betsey found she simply could not judge the hazard. Her heart thumping, she leaned over his arm, created a space for only the two of them, and began at the end, what the earnings could be by September with every Saturday booked, how she had asked and received more for the summer's later bookings. She grazed her fingertips prettily over the pages of her notebook, guiding his inspection of her correspondence lists and advertising copy, proof she was not offering the hotel grounds willy-nilly to dustmen and navvies. Her budget error—easy enough to tuck that behind all the promise of what was to come.

She suspected she might have done rather well. Straightening from Sir Alton's side, she looked first to Mr. Jones.

His expression was grim, pinched. He might have had a stray pin in his coat.

Mr. Seiler's "Thank you, Miss Dobson" brimmed with approval. But without validation from Mr. Jones, she felt it less.

Sir Alton said "Thank you," too, shutting the covers of her books and sliding them to her. "It's enchanting, hearing you speak of numbers. Please make yourself comfortable again—I confess myself too seasoned by etiquette to let you stand whilst we gentlemen take our ease."

She took her books. Mr. Jones rose to pull her chair closer to his, in front of the desk, but it was too late. She was hot with dismay.

"Pray tell, Mr. Jones," Sir Alton said, "are you as clever with dogs, or monkeys, say, as you are with type-writer girls?"

"Depends on the heart of the beast, I find."

She wanted to crack her ledger over one of their heads—it was only a question of which one.

"Mr. Seiler, you've seen these plans?" asked Sir Alton.

"Certainly. You know I shared your concerns, but the scheme makes good use of the resources the hotel has already, and putting Swan Park in the black a full season sooner than expected is no small consideration."

"Forgive me, I must disagree. Compared to the hotel's good name, the difference of a season is a small consideration, especially when we've had a clear warning of how wrong this pavilion venture could go. You're very kind to remind me, Jones, that we must carry on with this nonsense until the next board meeting, but you'll understand I would be shirking my duty if I did not include the matter on the next agenda. Until then, we shall suspend any future bookings—"

"Suspend bookings!" Betsey broke in. "The summer is brief enough, I could be filling Fridays and Sundays, as many—"

"Sun. Days." Sir Alton's interruption, quiet and swinging with cheer and amusement, stopped her protest. "What an extraordinary notion, Miss Dobson."

Betsey bit down on her lip, exchanged a quick, communicative glance with Mr. Jones. It was not an extraordinary notion; it was a damn good, logical next step. But she ought have kept it to herself a little longer.

"Speaking as a shareholder, I assure you a season makes a difference to me," Mr. Jones said. "And clearly, it makes a difference to the board. It may make a further difference when they learn none of the excursionists were involved Saturday."

"Innocent bystanders, all of them? Extraordinary."

"Unless they were helping to break it up. It was provoked mainly by one fellow, as I understand it to have gone, and he's a— an incorrigible blackguard, obviously, but the constable's dealing with him, and he won't be back."

Betsey smiled to hear Mr. Jones use a priggish word like *blackguard* to describe Avery. It was surely for Sir Alton's benefit, though that promise, *he won't be back,* held more conviction than she felt. She added, "The rest were locals or others who had no call to be there. Mr. Seiler and I have already decided to post more staffers to make certain the gathering remains private."

"A fine idea. I shall recommend the suspension of the scheme at the next board meeting, so our manageress here needn't trouble herself with making new bookings." He stood and extended his hand to Betsey, who in her confusion over this gesture, could only reciprocate. Patting her hand, he lilted cheerfully, "In fact, I absolutely forbid it."

"Manager*ess*," Betsey said, as though substituting the word for a good hard spit over the side of Tobias's rig.

John could swear his eyes ached from all the darting they'd done, watching that duel of amity and good manners between her and Sir Alton. She couldn't appreciate how well she'd come out.

"You were flirting with him."

Her eyes widened in surprise, then it seemed a denial was forthcoming, but finally, she settled her hellion brows in a mutinous angle.

John said to Tobias, "You saw it, didn't you?"

"Flirting? A small amount, perhaps." Tobias considered Betsey, his affection evident. "A pleasant amount. Not an improper amount, I would say, but then, I am not British. Did it seem so to you?"

John shifted under their expectant gazes. Any answer seemed dangerous and he was sorry he'd said anything.

"A great deal of good it did me," Betsey said. "He called me a trained monkey. *Your* trained monkey."

"A compliment, it was."

"To you!"

She turned her face aside, watching the trees clip by. She'd been roundly licked, she believed, but John knew better. That trained monkey remark revealed fear on Sir Alton's part, some acknowledgement that his position was not as sound as he'd believed. Somehow, Betsey had made him listen. Those slim fingers of hers sliding over the paper, for one. But not all. A good mind, too, the tongue to share it.

The rig swayed, and with it, Betsey Dobson's knees, more defined beneath her skirts than other women's. The plainness of her gray tweed, perhaps, or what she wore under it. In her lap, her books slipped back and forth across her skirts. John watched her agitation play out in her thumb, tracing back and forth over the top corner of her ledger. Beneath her glove, her knuckles rippled.

"How long must I wait to make new bookings?" she asked.

"A little more than a fortnight until the next board meeting."

Her thumb and knuckles stilled. She splayed her hand across the book cover and pulled the volumes close. Her face was still turned aside, watching the sea now that it had come into view. He wondered, suddenly, about her canary, whether the mending she had done to the cage with string and newspaper had held.

She was calculating, he guessed. How many bookings could she have made in a fortnight? The weeks left to the season. Commissions lost. The wages of other jobs she might get in Idensea. The cost of a move back to London.

His chest felt peculiar. Blown to smithereens. Was she sorry she'd come? Had he been wrong, persuading her to leave everything behind? *Y ferch a wnaeth wayw yn f'ais,* an old Welsh lyric began. *Girl who struck this pang in my side.* He remembered it now, remembered his young brother Owen, too, for trying to say goodbye to that child was the last time he'd felt his chest blow apart.

To both himself and Tobias, Betsey said, "I was awaiting a few confirmations. If they come, they wouldn't really be new bookings, would they?"

"No reasonable person, in my opinion, could consider them so," Tobias answered.

John nodded his agreement. Neither of them would promise Sir Alton to be reasonable, but they would back her if necessary. "And you need to plan on that board meeting, prepare yourself to speak as you did today."

"I? Address the board?"

Tobias asked, "Would you prefer the question framed to the members by Sir Alton alone?"

She exhaled. The word *hell* might have escaped. "Certainly not. But won't they—I'm only—"

"Speak as you did today, girl. I know it's in you."

Her blushes. When they rose, he wondered if he'd ever seen a girl truly wear one before.

Here was the Kursaal already. But in a few hours, when he went for his music lesson, he would see her.

He needed to practice; he needed to settle things with Lillian. His impatience for proficiency, for the days before Friday to pass, was on him again, a burst like a breaking balloon.

"He works hard. A great many ambitions." Mr. Seiler spoke quietly. "The right steps, he may realize them."

Betsey was watching Mr. Jones stride back to work, thinking, *He will come for his lesson tonight.* "I expect so."

"Miss Gilbey has much girlishness in her yet, but she will mature into her natural gifts. But you have not met her, I think?"

She suspected he meant to protect her as much as John. The wound was the same. "I have met Miss Gilbey, actually," she replied, and because his reminder had served its purpose, and her ability to feed and house herself was a more pressing concern, she changed the topic.

"I shall begin preparing my address to the board right away. But what else? Sir Alton has stripped me of a good portion of my duties for the next fortnight, but I cannot sit in the office and twiddle my thumbs."

"It may be for more than a fortnight. *Die Schlägerei* . . ." He shook his head. "What happened at the pavilion Saturday could sway the directors to Sir Alton's side. Even if it does not, what they decide for this season may not hold true for the next, or the next. Are you prepared for those possibilities, Miss Dobson?"

The mere words planted a choking vine of panic in her throat. But that was not for Mr. Seiler to know. She smiled at him. "Not in the least. I am only prepared to do whatever necessary to keep those possibilities from coming to pass."

"I little doubt that, my dear Miss Dobson." He discreetly consulted his pocket watch. "Until then, the submanagers and I examine the complaint books each afternoon at half-two. As we rarely have enough hands to carry out the resolutions, join us when your duties permit, and let the others in the office know you are available to assist them with correspondence and such. You will find yourself relieved of vacant time soon enough, and shall find it valuable education, in any event."

In any event. One such being the permanent suspension of the excursions scheme.

She couldn't let it happen, that was all. And why couldn't she persuade the board? It was the simple difference of less money or more, after all, and she didn't know a more persuasive argument than that.

Sir Alton notwithstanding.

As in music so in type-writing; it is the repeated practice
of the same thing that brings improvement.

—*How to Become Expert in Type-writing*

*T*ruly, Lillian disliked bullying her mother. The lady was so reticent and sweet that during parties like this, Lillian was resigned to allowing her to inhabit some far corner and have extended, sincere, and thoroughly unpartylike conversations with those who cared to seek her out. Lillian's father had recognized early his daughter possessed the talent for circulation his wife lacked, and since then, Lillian had served as the auxiliary hostess for the Gilbeys' functions, removing the burdens of warm wit and innocuous gossip from her mother.

So Mama owed her, didn't she? And it was not as if she'd been asked to give a speech before everyone or to be the belle of the ball. One conversation with one person she liked anyway, merely the communication of one piece—a *snippet,* really—of bad, or more accurately, just *somewhat* unfortunate and otherwise *insignificant* news.

It had to be done, that was all, and her mother was the only one who could do it.

From her place alongside one of the columns in the salon, Lillian watched for some sign her mother had delivered the message. Mrs.

Gilbey had already been successful in drawing aside John Jones for a tête-à-tête, but that was no surprise. She and John had ever got on well; John always able to put her at ease. They occupied the same settee and appeared quite as cordial as they had a few minutes ago, when Lillian had turned away to speak to some of her guests.

Bother. If her mother failed in her duty, Lillian would be forced to tell John herself, which wouldn't do. She couldn't have John associating her with unpleasantness.

"Pray tell, who's the quarry?"

The voice was low, playful, and next to her ear. Noel Dunning. "Quarry, sir?"

"This is obviously a spy mission. Now who—ah! Mister—"

Their faces nearly brushed together as she turned to him. He straightened quickly, but it flustered her, almost as much as his accusation. "Spying! Don't be absurd, Mr. Dunning."

But Mr. Dunning was too good to question her. "A thousand pardons, then." He lifted a cup of lemonade, offering it. "It's hot," he cautioned as she sipped. "I asked that it be warmed for you."

Lillian licked the inside of her lips. "Honey?"

"For your voice."

Their duet would close the festivities tonight. The lemonade might have been best offered nearer that performance, but she didn't mind. "How very thoughtful you are, Noel." She smiled at him, sincerely pleased, though she itched to steal another glance at her mother and John. "You appear quite untouched by nerves. You don't mind, then, that I put you first on the program? I meant it as a compliment."

"Honored, of course. Though I admit, surprised."

"What better way to introduce you?"

"And John—" Mr. Dunning held up between two fingers the printed program, on which John's name did not appear. "Is he not to be introduced?"

"Mm." She sipped her lemonade to suppress the urge to look over her shoulder. "He changed his mind. I suppose he thought it best to give way to . . . trained performers."

Mr. Dunning looked baffled, and Lillian could tell by the way his gaze shifted that John was still on the settee with her mother.

She wished she could snatch back her lie. It would be found out as soon as Mr. Dunning and John spoke.

"But I thought he'd been practicing, at least here and there, a bit."

"Well, perhaps," she murmured, now fearing Mr. Dunning's disapproval as much as John's.

"May I say, Miss Gilbey . . ."

"Lillian." She'd been thinking of this all week. "Once in a while. It could do no harm."

"How especially lovely you are tonight, Lillian. It's provoked this phrase in my head . . ." He hummed. The shine in his eyes shimmered along with a smooth, pretty ribbon of notes.

"A recent composition?"

"Exceedingly so."

"And the next part?"

"I've no idea, I'm afraid."

"I cannot but think it would be worth finishing."

Across the room from them, the piano bounced out "Syd, Syd, Sydenham," a preposterous tune one of the society members had composed as a call-to-order for their meetings. Lillian took Mr. Dunning's arm and felt a swell of satisfaction as they moved toward the performance area. Everyone looked so merry, gathering around the low platform she'd had installed for the evening, chatting and joking. Behind the platform, all five pairs of French doors were flung open to the terrace, and Chinese lanterns bobbed on lines of wire from the garden right into the salon as though the difference between indoors and out bore no significance.

She had gone to a great deal of trouble to achieve a careless, unfussy effect, eschewing the usual rows of straight-backed chairs and instead instructing the servants to bring a thoughtfully mismatched assortment of furniture from all corners of the house and directing the placement of each piece into a spontaneous-looking arrangement. Even the rugs were askew and overlapping. Some of the more bohemian amongst the guests might be enticed to sit right on the floor, and wouldn't that be a thrilling effect?

The sight of John coming in from the drawing room with her mother disrupted her happy appraisal of the scene. It was no effort to smile at John. He looked dashing in his evening clothes, though she recognized his coat and saw her hint about having the lapels freshened had been too subtle. She disengaged from Mr. Dunning and claimed John from her mother.

Chatting, a bright, tumbling stream of chatting. Was John so quiet because she could not stop? She settled him in a prime seat—not beside her, nor within whispering distance, but where they could share sight lines, to facilitate the furtive flirtation of exchanging glances.

Clark Winters, the current society president, made his opening comments, relying heavily on the notes Lillian had provided him. He introduced Lillian as tonight's hostess, who in turn introduced Noel Dunning, a bright young talent certain to exceed the accomplishments of his famous father.

She'd promised Mr. Dunning not to mention Sir Alton. But how could she not? She ought have prepared him for it, though; the audible interest that rippled through the crowd as he approached the piano seemed to rattle him, and he fumbled the opening.

He came to a full stop, jested about the strain of performing in front of so esteemed a group as the Sydenham Music Society, and began again. The audience forgave him; they wanted him to do well.

Lillian tried to enjoy the piece as she had Sunday, but she could not help worrying that John had finally perused that volume of Tennyson. Her friend Roberta elbowed her throughout; she knew "Marian's" proper name.

But the song's sensational effect on the audience could not be denied. As she applauded, she remembered to glance in John's direction. She couldn't catch his eye just then and knew precisely why: John couldn't possibly feel anything but relieved that she had rescued him—and herself—from certain humiliation.

During the interlude, Lillian let John walk her out to the terrace. When she realized he was watching her twist a finger into the pearls circling her neck, she dropped her hand immediately. It was bad for the pearls.

"I'm turning to nerves," she sighed brightly, "this performance waiting for me at the end of the night."

His brow crooked.

"I am! Mr. Dunning's quite accomplished, and I—I don't know that I am equal to the challenge."

His gaze took a leisurely survey of the salon, where, as groups gathered to chat, the liveliness of the party was returning. Clark Winters, who *would* sing German lieder no matter the theme that had been set, had been the final performer before the interlude and had rather depressed the mood despite all her strategizing.

John turned his back on the scene. "I'll eat my tie and your fan if there was ever a thing you didn't believe yourself at least equal to, Lillian Gilbey."

Leave it to John to deliver the most inelegant, bordering-on-insulting, yet truly wonderful compliment. Then he touched her, trailing his fingers along the inside of her arm, the bare space above her elbow-length glove, making the beads suspended from her narrow sleeve tickle her skin.

"Let's go to Idensea, Lillian."

She was holding her breath, reminding herself he would not kiss her tonight. They stood somewhat catercorner to each other, she looking into the light and bustle of the salon, he to the dark garden. This touch of her arm was discreet enough, and all she would allow tonight. No more kissing.

His fingers drifted down to twine within hers. He leaned toward her ear. "Pack up the whole party, right now, put them on a train to Idensea."

The warmth of his breath. She felt dazed. No kissing. Inside, Mr. Dunning, who had been moving toward the terrace, was persuaded to the piano. Roberta shared the bench with him; that flirt Lynette Ramsey stood on his other side.

"There's half the program yet. There's supper—"

"Pack it up. A picnic on the train. Finish the program in the Swan's music salon. And in the wee hours of the morning, I'll rouse one of the engineers and take everyone on the Sultan's Road before it opens to the public."

Ah. His little railway project. "You are quite mad," she said, though taken in by something in his voice. She could see the romance and gaiety in the scheme. It might have been a fine idea if only he had thought of it sooner. February, say.

At the piano, Mr. Dunning punctuated a comment with a playful run of notes that elicited whoops of delight.

"See me to my seat?" she asked.

But he did not offer his arm. He forced her to say, "Absolutely not. I'm sorry, John, but no, it won't do," and she had to return to her own party ruffled and disconcerted and still feeling guilty for having scratched him from the program.

So upsetting she found it, she was of a mind to make him wait until August to apologize to her. Especially since he left early, before her duet with Mr. Dunning.

Which was a triumph, thank you.

Betsey's buttons had waited inside the biscuit tin since the night she'd snipped them off in her pique, but as she needed her uniform tomorrow, they had to be put on again. Even so, it was late on Friday before she began—Sarah Elliot had declared a covert sweet-making session after Dora Pink had gone to bed and couldn't scold her for her sugar consumption, and Betsey and Charlie joined her, which left Charlie wide awake past midnight. He begged to use her window to get out to the roof while she did her mending— John had the same room when he had stayed here and took him out there, oh, all the time, as Charlie told it. At last, with a warning it would not become a habit, Betsey consented.

It was here, as she was finishing off the first button, chatting in hushed tones of tomorrow's opening of the pleasure railway, that Charlie leaned over and kissed her.

The kiss landed on her jaw, almost on her earlobe. A miscalculation, a swift peck that made tears, instant and mysterious tears, bite at her lower eyelids and alongside her nose. She worked hard at the needle between her thumb and forefinger, wiggling it to bring it through the wool before she spoke.

"Now, Charlie, what's that for, eh?"

In the night, the thread made several noisy passes through the fabric, too many for a single button, a waste of thread.

"Because I think you're nice, Betsey."

She almost dismissed him, almost said *pooh* and set him straight, but fresh stings beneath her eyes kept her from speaking right away. "You're so awfully nice to think so, did you know that?"

He didn't answer right away. Then, "I don't know."

"Well, you are. So thanks, Charlie." She tied off the thread, wrapped her fingers in the surplus, and yanked. The thread didn't break.

"You're—you're welcome, then."

Betsey, button and thread at her teeth, glanced at him.

"I s'pose," he added, and shrugged.

They both smothered laughter then, Betsey for his poor confusion and Charlie, she guessed, with relief to have the moment done. He lifted his shoulder and scratched his cheek against it, hiding his face from her. A mistake, giving in to him. But to send him away now would only add salt to his wound.

Another moment of determined gnawing, and the thread came loose. "This will take all night if I don't fetch my scissors."

She felt Charlie watching as she tied a knot and readied another button, but he didn't take her hint about going inside. "Ain't those the same buttons from before? And you're sewin' 'em all over again?"

"They are. I—" Having to recount her own foolishness, she sighed. "I cut them off."

"What for?"

"I don't know. They were too extravagant. I thought to sell them, perhaps, and put on plainer ones, and put the money to a gown of some sort, because Mr. Jones thought I should have one."

"What's John care?"

"He doesn't." *Wishes he didn't, anyway.* "Just ordering me about is all. Likes that, doesn't he, ordering people about?"

She spoke teasingly, but Charlie was too loyal to admit Mr. Jones short of perfect. "On the job, I s'pose."

"In any case, I decided he was wrong. No gown. So back go the buttons, and there they will stay until I need to sell them for bread. And perhaps, when that day comes, I shall eat them instead."

Charlie laughed, but she didn't. The notion of having to sell her buttons seemed all too possible since the meeting at Iden Hall. She shifted carefully, trying to catch more of the lamplight spilling from the window. Hardly ideal conditions for sewing. The moon was little more than a bright slit that would succumb to shadow in a few nights' time, and whenever the breeze stirred itself into a proper wind, she thought perhaps she oughtn't be barefoot.

She was about to suggest they go inside when Charlie said, "Someone's coming." His face was turned to the road, watching a single bead of light joggle toward the house. "John, I bet."

Betsey frowned at the light. "He's in London, at Miss Gilbey's party." And it was far beyond a reasonable hour for a call, even if he weren't. But something in Betsey surged anyway, and she knew then why Charlie's light kiss had stung her eyes with tears. To know Charlie's hopeless hopes was to know her own.

The light was certainly a bicycle lamp. It stilled, and remained still, for quite some time. Betsey imagined the cyclist—imagined Mr. Jones—pausing there, looking at the windows where light still glowed. Looking at her windows? Was that what he was doing?

"Why doesn't he come on then?" Charlie put his fingers in his mouth and whistled.

"Oh, Charlie. Miss Everson always has her window open."

"He'd've stood there all night. See? It *is* him, just as I told you."

So it was. At the front gate, Mr. Jones dismounted, looking up at them. Then, a gesture—a beckoning one, she believed.

"He wants me to come down, I think," she said, rising with less caution than she ought have. The remaining loose buttons she'd been holding in her lap clattered down the slope of the roof and bounced into the night, toy stars lit by the sliver of moonlight.

"Oh, hell." She eased down with a guilty glance at Charlie. "That is . . ." She looked again at the black garden where the buttons had disappeared, more provoked by her eagerness to answer Mr. Jones's gesture than the loss of the buttons. "Hell. Hell and hell." With Charlie snickering, she tossed her vest back through the window, a single boot and stocking, too. Charlie had knocked their mates off the roof when he'd come out the window.

She climbed inside, then heard Charlie say, "I'm coming down with you."

"No." She turned round to the window, where he sat with one leg over the sill, halted by her refusal. "It's too late, and your mum thinks you're in bed already. Besides"—*I want to be alone with him,* she thought with a sweep of shame—"I'm certain it's just some business to do with the excursionists. You'd best just go to bed, then, please?"

He nodded, and she felt like a Judas.

"But I'm seeing you home tomorrow night, ain't I? John asked, and Mum said I might."

It was ridiculous that she must have anyone see her home at all, but she agreed as she put out the light. She tugged off her apron and smoothed a hand over her hair. She'd already fixed it into the two very short plaits she wore to bed and considered taking the time to put it up properly.

"Betsey," Charlie said from the window, "was it . . . was it any good?"

She stilled, her hand falling. Her heart, it flooded. "Oh, Charlie. I suppose it was the dearest sort of kiss there is."

He looked back out at the night. The pale glow of his hair drew her, and she went to him and stroked his head, just once. *Save it for someone who deserves it,* she wanted to tell him.

It came out like this: "And you know, you try any such thing again, I shall be obliged to push you off the roof, don't you?"

Mr. Jones offered her boot to her when she slipped out the front door.

"Didn't find the stocking, I suppose?" she asked.

"Inside your shoe, there."

How bashful he sounded, and over having touched her stocking? She didn't understand.

"Here." He opened his hand. Her buttons seemed small, piled in his palm, and she couldn't help but think how light and cheap they must feel to him. He himself was dressed in his best suit, and even though he'd cuffed his trousers for cycling, and his hair was blown nine ways from riding hatless, Betsey felt the plainness of her own appearance—sleeves of her shirtwaist rolled to her elbows, her skirt the same faded print she'd been wearing when she'd been turned out from the Dellaforde house more than seven years ago, a contrasting border of fabric at the hem to lengthen it. She had been overzealous with the egg whites for the sugar kisses this evening, and only now felt the sticky results on her arms and face.

"Hold them, won't you," she said of the buttons. "My feet are cold." She sat down on the porch step and began to pull on her stocking. "Late for a call, isn't it?"

He didn't answer. She felt for her suspenders and asked him why he was not in London, but he didn't answer that question, either. Too engrossed in watching her sort her stocking, she realized when she glanced up at him, though there was little for him to see besides the shift of her skirts as her hands moved beneath them, attaching the stocking to her suspenders. She made a better show of the second stocking: a hint of naked knee, syrup in her wrists. She could have embarrassed him, forced eye contact, coughed the merest *ahem*. But she was careful to make it seem the task absorbed her as it did him.

They'd barely spoken since Monday. Betsey had tucked away her tangle of feelings for him the way she'd stored her buttons in that tin. At least the buttons had some purpose, and fastened to her vest or strewn in the grass, they wouldn't cost her anything more than she'd already given.

One beckoning gesture, and it was done, she was flying to him. One gesture that could have been a trick of the night shadows would have her lifting her skirts as though she believed lighting his lust could give her the warmth she yearned for.

She pressed her knees together and tucked her skirt around her ankles. To flirt, to tease him because he occasionally noticed she was a woman with all the parts and he found the parts good— that was one thing. To hope he would act on his attraction was to wish for her own destruction.

"Your performance went well, I trust," she said, because they both needed to be reminded of Miss Gilbey. "Sarah will want to hear all about it. But . . . she's long abed, you know." She glanced up.

"Right. I wasn't coming to see her."

"I . . . I sent Charlie to bed."

"Doesn't matter."

Betsey picked up one of her boots and put it her lap. She worked at the laces, fingering them into tidy, evenly crisscrossed lines. *Go in, go back upstairs,* she warned herself, and herself promised she would, as soon as her bootlaces were tidied.

"Did you hear me?"

"You said it didn't matter, Charlie not coming down." Hearing, fine. Comprehension, lacking. Hope, damn it, living. She used her skirt hem to polish off the toe of her boot, then took up the other boot to tend to it.

"I was cycling. Thinking of the Sultan's Road. It opens tomorrow."

"I know." Everyone knew; it was the greatest event Idensea

would see until the Duke of Winchester came to open the Kursaal in August.

She heard him laugh softly above her. "Of course you do, girl. Of course."

And then he crouched beside her, so abruptly it startled her, so close she could see how his smile sat on his face like a drop of clear water, blurring the surface beneath it.

"You'd come with me to see it, wouldn't you, Betsey? Right now?"

She tried to make out the blurry thing beneath his smile. Whatever it was, it made her answer, "Of course."

> Remember that taking a type-writer apart is a dangerous experiment and that any meddling with the screws generally makes a machine worse instead of better.
>
> —*How to Become Expert in Type-writing*

Of course. As though no other option existed and no other questions needed to be asked. She readied herself while he fetched her bicycle, and she went with him.

Tomorrow night, the pleasure railway's loading pavilion would be dazzling with light and full of people eager to ride. Tonight, with the pier closed and the Esplanade empty, the wind ruled, bumping the canvas curtain in the archway and filling the air with the snap of pennant flags and the rustle of palm leaves. Mr. Jones cycled past the arcade and its sentinel pair of leopards to the high board fence that hid the less attractive but more necessary parts of the railway from public view. He had keys for the padlocks, and they wheeled their cycles through the gate and leaned them against the fence.

He took a moment to detach his bicycle lamp, then offered a hand to her. Taking no lesson at all from that other walk in the dark with Mr. Jones, she abandoned herself to the hard shelter of his hand, at once and with kite-like joy.

They walked between the trestle of the track and the cliff that overlooked the bay, a deeply shadowed passage not even as wide as the lane in front of The Bows. The highest ascension of the undulating track she'd traced with her fingertip now towered over her.

She held the lamp while he found the key to a door built into the trestle. Inside, he passed the light over a monstrous configuration of pipes and other hunks of metal she had no names for.

"Engine and boiler," he stated simply, but Betsey suspected that with the least encouragement, he'd be pleased to lecture on every part and its function. She suppressed her minimal curiosity and asked what the passenger carriages were like instead.

Was there another thing in the world he knew better than this railway? He had the lamp, but it was not the reason for the confidence with which he led her. A maze of metal stairs and narrow black passages smelling of paint and fresh lumber and oil, and then she heard a thumping sound, the wind hitting the canvas curtain. And then . . .

A garden. The bicycle lamp was sorely inadequate for the cavernous space where they had emerged, but there was a garden, flowers and greenery rising, rising, even as they draped the balconies of a tall, terraced palace. Any expectations she'd held were forgotten as she tried to reconcile this marvel with something familiar.

"Is it—it's like the theater, isn't it?" Avery had taken her to the Empire once; this was the sensation of being onstage, in a tableau vivant of the Hanging Gardens of Babylon. "I didn't guess—I hardly know what to say, it's so astonishing."

"Wait until the waterfalls run, and when you see it by day from the Esplanade. Or at night, with the lighting." He gestured toward the expansive wall opposite the garden palace. But that was no wall, of course, but the curtain in the wide Moorish arch, hiding the scenery until show time.

She laughed. "Waterfalls." One wasn't fantastic enough? "And the panorama tunnels are similar?"

"*Adventurous and exotic scenes of the East,*" he said, his voice the embodiment of the bloated lettering on the street side of the curtain. "Though not so elaborate, as there's quick you pass through it."

"And you have my six pennies by then, too."

"Come, you cynic. Sit in the carriage."

The lamp directed her to the loading deck, between the arch and the palace, where boarding passengers would create an enticing spectacle for passersby. The conveyances lined up on the track were nothing like carriages she associated with railways; they had no tops, were hardly more than park benches, church pews on a platform. Or small golden thrones, she thought, drawing a single fingertip over the tiny flaming suns carved into the wood.

She sat on the first bench, and though there was room for two, Mr. Jones took the one behind. The track lay ahead, just invisible in the thorough darkness beyond the lamp's weak glow. The wind moaning past the curtain gave her a shiver, amplified the vastness of the space and Mr. Jones's silent presence at her back.

"One final look. Is that it?"

"I suppose." A moment later, he added, "None too fine of me to drag you along."

"You wanted company." *Mine.* But he did not say so, nor did she admit how little she minded being dragged along. She just told him, "It's wonderful, you know. You don't doubt that, I hope."

"You'd like a ride?"

"Oh, yes. I'm bringing my excursionists—"

"What about now?"

"This minute?" She didn't see how it was possible without the operators.

She felt him stirring, leaning forward with his arms on her backrest.

"A fellow at Lillian's party, he hadn't any neck, and he was singing something without any English in it, so a moment it gave me to think, and I thought, why not gather up the whole party and bring it on a train to Idensea? Ride the Sultan's Road a dozen times over, sing and play in the hotel's music room till dawn, and there a tale they'd have for their old age, to prove the passion of their youth."

Betsey smiled. "It sounds like the sort of whimsy the rich enjoy. Why didn't you do it?"

A moment passed before he answered. "Lils—Miss Gilbey—wouldn't hear of it."

He sat back then, and Betsey was glad, for it meant she could look ahead, keep her face concealed from him as she sorted out the meaning of this revelation. It didn't take long.

"Bless God, but there's a stubborn girl!" he muttered, and again, it was good he couldn't see her face, or he would have seen how she wanted to laugh at him, laugh at the both of them sitting here, so disappointed in their hopes when they both should have known better.

"You couldn't have expected her to upend her party," she said. "Disrupt everything to come to Idensea upon the spur of the moment?"

"You did."

"I live here."

"'Tis London I mean. London you left of a sudden to come here."

"It isn't the same. Miss Gilbey has more to think about, more to lose, than someone like me."

He grunted. "One topsy-turvy party in a life crammed with them? While you . . . if I'd left you to the mercy of the stationmaster, say. What would you have left if that had happened?"

Left her to the mercy of the stationmaster. She nearly scoffed, reminded him who he was. But that day at the rail station she hadn't been so sure, had she? That day, she'd been prepared to drop out of a window and see where her wits landed her.

And now look. It pealed through her brain. *Look how you've come to rely on him.*

He awaited an answer. "Nothing but a tale for my old age," she admitted, and swiped at her arms, pushing her rolled-up sleeves to her wrists. Time to go. She had achieved some kind of distance and dignity after the meeting with Sir Alton, but now she'd mucked it up all over again, coming out here with him, unwittingly volunteering to be Miss Gilbey's substitute. Not even a substitute. An alternative. A last resort.

This seesaw would never balance. Time to go.

"I wanted her to say, 'Of course.' Like you, girl."

No doubt. She fastened her cuffs and thought of her uniform buttons, warm in his pocket. She must remember to get them before they parted ways. "I can't think what you hope to gain from comparing us. Miss Gilbey disliked the spontaneity, that's all. It doesn't mean she doesn't care. I came with you—it doesn't mean . . . anything in particular but that I was awake and restless."

And now I'm tired and ready to go, she was about to add as she turned round in her seat. She found him sitting with his elbows on his knees, his black hair windblown, falling over his forehead. A dot of white flashed between his fingers, and for a moment, she mistook it for one of her buttons.

"Iefan," she whispered when she saw what it was. "You were going to ask her to marry you tonight?"

"I don't know. I only—I'm not where I meant to be when I married, is the trouble of it." He glanced up, his brows rueful and crooked. "Is there such a thing as a save-my-place ring?"

"Very convenient for you men if there were."

"I don't imagine she'd wait, whatever. A schedule she has, so her young sister tells me."

"What, with a wedding slated in for this time next year, will you or nil you?"

He laughed. "Something like that."

Betsey shook her head in disbelief. But she remembered what it was like to have such confidence in the future. Perhaps for Miss Gilbey, it was not so outlandish an attitude. Lizzie, the housemaid in love with the master's son, ought've known better.

She reached over the backrest of her seat and plucked the ring from between his fingers. Within a lacy band of gold filigree sat a dark stone, a ruby perhaps, although the low light kept her from being certain.

"Was it your mother's?" she asked.

"My mother's! A silver locket she had from her girlhood, and that was all her jewelry that I know of. No, in London I found it."

"I had a locket once." From Thomas Dellaforde. She'd sold her hair and all the clothing she could spare before she'd finally parted with it. She tilted the ring forward and back, watching the facets appear and vanish, then squinted inside the band. "Faery's child" had been the engraving on her locket, Keats being Thomas's favorite, and Betsey had liked it well enough until she'd looked up the poem and read it for herself. *La Belle Dame sans Merci hath thee in thrall,* indeed. She'd come back to the bookcases multiple times to reread the poem to make certain she had understood it, and finally decided to pretend the inscription wasn't there.

"What is it you're looking for?" Mr. Jones asked.

"The inscription—it's too dark, though."

"Inscription?"

"Isn't there one?"

"Ought there be?"

Betsey pressed back a smile at his alarm.

He shook his head. "For all I know, some other girl's name there is on it. Bless God, I haggled it from a pawnbroker this afternoon, then took ten steps and realized she'd expect some wrapping, like a proper jeweler would have. Where my head was, there's no saying."

"It's beautiful, wherever it came from. You oughtn't let that keep you from giving it to her." She held out the ring to him.

He didn't reach for it. His gaze funneled into the yellow circle as though it were a far-off porthole or a gap in the boards of a fence.

"What ought, then?"

His voice was low, the question flat. Betsey let her thumb and finger relax, and the ring sank into her palm, but the hard focus of his gaze did not alter.

"What if I am sick to the death, girl?" he asked, and his address to her, that he tagged *girl* on the end of the question, surprised her. He'd seemed to be speaking to himself. Even now, he bowed his head as though in private prayer. "Picking out my words before I say them, thinking a worn place on my lapel settles my fate? And goddamned music lessons."

What else had happened at that party? It seemed impossible that he could have bungled his performance; at his final rehearsal at Sarah's house, he had flown through the piece perfectly a half dozen times, working up to such a wild tempo that everyone in the parlor was laughing by the end.

She was about to ask, but he spoke, added something else to his list.

"And not kissing you."

Pardon, she wanted to say in response, but it would have been disingenuous. She'd heard him; each hair on her arm and at the back of her neck now brushed the fabric of her shirtwaist.

And not kissing you.

Pardon?

He lifted his head. "Ought that keep me from giving her the ring, that I'm sick to the death of not kissing you?"

And so. It came to her then, something in how he'd raised his head. He'd brought her here to fuck her. She wondered if he realized it. That she herself, up to this moment, had not, that she'd believed he'd wanted comfort, company, *her* company—that she could have been so wide-eyed—that kind, honorable Mr. Jones could be less than so—

His regard of her wavered only in that the flame in the bicycle lamp did. It was heavy; it held her; it pressed upon her, and she imagined herself in bed, taking his weight. Deep, low, her body approved. But where was the bed? And what new burden would be waiting to be taken up once Mr. Jones had relieved both her and the bed of his weight?

"Perhaps not," she answered, and shrugged. One-shouldered, halfhearted, but she carried it off. No matter, no consequence. Nothing between them lost or changed at all. "Life can be rather a shit in that regard."

At last, his deep concentration broke. His fingers and thumb stretching his eyelids, he massaged his temples and laughed.

"Right. Don't go a-wandering from the path, is that it?"

She could take him wandering. His eyes would permanently cross, she could turn him in another direction so fast. A good lesson if he discovered what a fine leading string his cock made, if he learned his very fine railway couldn't be used to lure one girl to the altar and to fuck another.

"Here."

The light had fallen noticeably, and the ring caught barely a glint as it passed between them. He fit the tip of his finger into it and smoothed his thumb over the band a few times before dropping it into his pocket.

"Let's go," she said. *For God's sake, before I strangle you . . .*

"Do you want me to send for Mil Chester to come give us a ride?"

. . . or fuck you and then strangle you . . .

"Do I want you to rouse from bed a man who has a full day's work coming so that he can indulge a passing fancy of mine? No thank y—"

He touched her head. The firm pillow at the base of his thumb pressed her cheek, his fingers braced against her skull, extending nearly to her crown. On the back of her neck, just at her hairline, she felt the pad of his little finger, rough, like raw lumber or dried-out leather. She was not as safe as she felt, and neither was he, she knew this. But her eyelids fell closed as his hand slid down and took hold of the short braid behind her ear. A gentle, gentle tug.

His lips brushed her jaw. "Sweet. Like sugar you smell."

Before I do something that leaves me with nothing but a tale for my old age, for God's sake, let us go.

The ways she could yield. In trust, her tomorrows swaddled and waiting on some stranger's doorstep. This, she had done before. Or on pretense, weapons hidden but ready. Or under contract—negotiation, give and take, tit for tat. These, too, she had done.

The ways she could yield. None of them so difficult, any of them offering the thing she wanted, some version of it, like the strands of glazed clay pearls the vendors hawked down on the shore, or those dipped buttons of hers, still in his pockets. How bright and real it would feel.

"Elisabeth."

Their lips were touching. Not a kiss, not yet. Just a toy top, poised between finger and floor, string wound and taut. His whisper rushed over her mouth, and his Welsh accent made the *s* softly precise, though he couldn't have known it was the spelling her mother had put to the name. Virtually no one since her mother had called her Elisabeth, and now he whispered it like he uttered a secret, urgent prayer to a saint. *Betsey* for those times he pretended they were equals, *Dobs* when he found her amusing or frustrating, *Miss Dobson* for orders and reprimands. Now *Elisabeth* because—

Just persuasion. She felt his breath warm her skin, the give of everything inside her, and she remembered. She remembered the very place they sat existed because of his talent for persuasion, and that he'd had to employ precious little of it to get her out here. She remembered that only the most malicious of children made a seesaw into a game with a winner and loser.

She didn't have to be malicious, not with him. "You wouldn't use me like this," she reminded him. She pulled away, turned, shielded her lips. She opened her eyes to darkness and thought something terribly significant had happened to her. But no, it was only the bicycle lamp; the fuel had run out while they hadn't kissed.

Cavernous as the space was, their breathing seemed to fill it up, louder than the wind-battered curtain.

"I know what it is," she said. "Using, being used. Kiss me because she hurt you. Kiss me, think of her." She remembered his hand on her back as they'd approached Sir Alton the night of Avery's brawl. "You wouldn't."

There was no light for her eyes to adjust to. She waited in vain, then stretched her arms, feeling her way to the edge of the seat cushion.

"I wouldn't," Mr. Jones said, as though he'd spent all his past silence formulating this response. "I wasn't."

She wanted to argue. However, for a change, she wanted something else more than to be right, so she agreed, "Well then." Rising, holding the sides of the carriage, she thrust out a foot and pointed her toe until it found the platform.

And then she went blind all over again. She squinted and brought her hand to her eyes, her foot back inside the car. Through her fingers she saw his face, golden and shadowed above a flame.

"Wait, you, and you'll not have to harm yourself getting out."

But he made no move to lead, nor to find the lamp. He was letting the flame burn to his fingers. She hated the waste of a match. She worried for the tips of his fingers.

"You told me once you'd never marry." The match died. "Did you mean it?"

"Light the lamp. I want to go."

"Did you?"

In the darkness, she floundered, not even certain why she didn't want to answer him. She fell back on her standard response to prying questions: "Why should you wish to know that?" Uttered with puzzled cheer, it was a magic spell against any inquisitor.

Except him. "I cannot help my curiosity about you, girl."

"No," she agreed. "Not since Avery."

The words took on a presence, growing with the silence, spreading between them, thick and combustible. Well, he wasn't the first. Plenty of others had expressed the same curiosity: whether, as she'd slept with some fellow they knew, she'd sleep with them, too. To his credit, he didn't claim not to understand.

"I'm not going to bed with you, Mr. Jones," she said softly, in case he wondered still.

Beginners sometimes throw the carriage back so violently as to bend the rack down upon the dogs and thus throw the machine out of order.

—*How to Become Expert in Type-writing*

He muttered, "Bless God," and she heard in it how he didn't like it, her barefaced words, even though she'd cleaned them up from what they might have been. And then, more honestly, he asked, "Why not?"

"I want more than a tale. That's all. Don't— You wouldn't punish me for it."

The cars moved suddenly, jarred by the force with which he stood. As though he'd memorized her stance while the match had burned, he found her forearm without a fumble and latched on.

"*Punish* you?"

"Whether I did, or whether I didn't, you could make things . . . difficult for me."

"Bless the bleeding *Christ*. Elisabeth."

He could be offended if he wished. Such a long fall probably hurt. But surely he knew it needed saying.

"I choose, you see," she said. "I need to choose. That's what I learned after Thomas."

"Thomas."

"The Dellafordes' eldest. The house where I was in service. He chose me, but what did I know of the difference? I thought it was more important to work on my accent so I'd sound like a Mrs. Dellaforde ought to sound when the day came."

Mr. Jones, who had done the same with his own speech for a not-so-dissimilar reason, loosened his hold on her arm. He let her go.

"Ah," she said. "You'd assumed Avery the first. The only. No. First there was Thomas, and then I learned to choose."

The darkness offered nothing. She imagined his lip curling toward his nose, his brows coming together, and she hated him sneering at her, even if she'd only imagined it, and couldn't stop herself: "Marbie. Elias. Ned. John—a different John. Even Avery I chose, and you think you know what made that a damn poor choice, but you don't. I lost my chance to finish at the Institute— that's what made it idiotic. Not again, do you see? Not here. I've chosen, and it's not you."

Once more, with grace and accuracy, he found her in the blackness. The tender swipe of his thumb over the back of her hand made her eyes burn wetly.

"Don't imagine me as a woman without consequences, Mr. Jones. Just because you cannot ruin me, just because I'll never get with child and demand that you marry me—"

She felt him react to that. Of course, he hadn't known she couldn't bear children. She felt the change in the pressure of his touch on her hand, she felt the words of sympathy about to fall, and she drew away her hand.

"You want to imagine me as a woman without consequences, speak to Avery Nash. When they let him out of gaol, ask him where he was a year ago."

"I suppose I shall need my buttons?" Betsey asked as John locked the gate on the Esplanade. He recognized the question as a meandering way to determine whether there would be consequences to her refusal.

She'd said Lillian had hurt him. But Lillian's neglect of his pride was like sad old news from an unseen country compared with this question from Betsey. Here was a hurt new and near.

He poured the buttons into her hands. She had no pocket. He opened his handkerchief, and she made a bundle and dropped it into the basket on her cycle.

"Oh, no," she said when she saw he intended to see her back to The Bows, and he yielded because she sounded so certain. She'd sounded sure of everything, sure of all those names she'd listed, sure he'd brought her here to—to lay with her. Sure he would not.

Was it so? Had he brought her to the railway for that?

He wanted to forget the whole episode, of that he was sure. But in his rooms at the hotel, he found one more button in his pocket. Only a moment it would take to place it on her desk in the offices.

His fingers rolled it like a coin. He put it on the mantelshelf. In bed, he turned his face from it and tried to think of tomorrow, when his railway would open.

For six and three-quarter hours, Idensea's newest amusement measured up to its fanfare. Day-trippers and Idensea residents alike formed eager but proper British queues to pay their six pennies and board the cars of the Sultan's Road pleasure railway. For six and three-quarter hours, they agreed the dreary weather did not spoil the views of the Esplanade and sea, nor dampen the excitement of the downhill coasts. They stole kisses when the tunnels were dark, and exclaimed when those tunnels suddenly, mysteriously lit to reveal some grotesque or panorama. Where the journey was exotic, they marveled, and where it was thrilling, they shrieked.

For six and three-quarter hours, the Sultan's Road was a triumph. And then the cable system failed.

A group of John's day laborers at the Kursaal alerted him to the fact the carriages were no longer running. This implied the fellows were spending more time gazing off into the distance than an employer might have liked, but John's concern for the railway took precedence. He left instructions with his foremen, then cycled to the railway, where he found a damn mess.

Two sets of passenger carriages sat out on the tracks, one halted early in the ride, presumably in response to the warning whistle issued by the brakeman on the other set. Those carriages sat a dozen or so feet above the ground near the bottom of the final ascent—*near* the bottom rather than *at* the bottom because the brakeman had seen fit to enlist the male passengers in pushing the carriages up the hill. At the crest, the brakeman would give them the all clear to hop aboard, and the coast would continue from there, whether everyone made it safely aboard or not.

That was the brakeman's plan. He'd voiced it multiple times in protest of the proper procedures the operators had practiced during training.

"Bless the bleeding Christ," he muttered. A damn heartbreak was what it was, to see so much work come to this. Another damn, baffling, out-of-the-blue heartbreak.

"Stop!" John bellowed up to the brakeman with all his strength. "Ease it back! Vernon Crabbe, I'm ordering you! *Ease that carriage down immediately!* Get those passengers boarded!"

"Told 'im he'd best not," said the mechanic at John's side.

"Is it the carriage grip?"

The mechanic looked skeptical. "Could be. But it weren't having no trouble on the other hill. Second time it's happened here."

John covered his mouth, looking up at the track. A faulty carriage was the simpler fix, and it wouldn't force the railway to close entirely. "We've got to get those passengers down. Tell them down front to hold off the ticket selling, then Eady and yourself come up. The service steps at the market tunnel, we'll lead them down two at a time, then go to Chester's carriages."

The mechanic nodded and jogged off to carry out the orders. Vernon Crabbe was recalcitrant, however, when John made his way up onto the track.

"All this fuss," he told John. "My way had 'em all back to the loading deck now. Already done so once today. Change your mind, you would, if you'd been round then to see it."

John wanted to rage, wanted to throttle Crabbe right here on the track. However, he needed the man calm and cooperative, so he offered him terse congratulations and bit back the news that Crabbe was less than an hour from collecting his last wages from the pier company.

John explained to the passengers that they'd be led along the track back to the panorama tunnel they'd just exited, down the service steps just inside, and be right back on the Esplanade shortly afterward. Several expressed dismay upon learning they wouldn't all go at once; they'd be sitting in the rain in a matter of minutes. Better that than to lose toes under a runaway carriage, noted one of the fellows who'd been pushing when John arrived.

Within half an hour, all had been safely, if damply, delivered to the Esplanade, their fares refunded. Sir Alton's coach had been waiting for at least ten minutes. John signaled that he was done, and Sir Alton exited the carriage, a footman with an umbrella at the ready.

"Bit of a setback, Jones? Most unexpected."

Today the mockery took its cut. John shoved his sopping hair off his forehead—his hat had been knocked over the trestle by a woman who'd been terrified to walk the mechanic's gallery on the side of the track—and caught sight of Rolly Brues, the American, stepping down from Sir Alton's carriage. Perfect. It was a stranger claiming the seat of his soul, this feeling that he wanted to say damn to Sir Alton and damn to Brues and damn to every damned thing in Idensea, and sit down in the mud until somebody brought his damn hat back to him.

Sick to the death, as he'd told Betsey last night. Did it matter? *Perhaps not. Life can be rather a shit in that regard.*

Her words didn't rally his humor as they had last night. He told Sir Alton, "That's all the passengers now, safely out. I'm sending them on to Pimlott's for an ice cream."

"An excellent gesture. I do hope you told them it was all at the pier company's expense."

"I knew that was exactly what you'd have me do," John said. Sir Alton's mouth twisted at this sarcasm, not necessarily in disapproval. John felt rather . . . *gritty* for having said it. He looked away to bid good afternoon to Mr. Brues, who had joined them.

Brues cut his ebullient greeting short when he realized he was treading over whatever Sir Alton was murmuring to John. Sir Alton denied he spoke of anything of consequence; they both insisted the other continue; each did, at once. A pause. They both looked at John, weariness about their eyes.

"Repairs," John suggested as a topic. Sir Alton's footman, either drowsy or distracted, let the umbrella list and clip John on the head, sending a stream of water down his back. He edged back. "The carriage isn't gripping the cable on the second hill. Tonight, tomorrow morning at worst, I'd reckon for when we'll be running again."

Brues grunted, the corners of his eyes crinkling. "Haven't the least idea, though, really, have you?"

John couldn't help grinning. "I've been seeing to the passengers," he admitted, "but I'll be speaking with the mechanic next."

His mood lifted a little more as Brues offered to go along and lend his expertise. Brues clapped Sir Alton on the back and invited him to join them.

Sir Alton appeared, fleetingly, as if he'd like to rub his temples, but then recovered his smile enough to decline politely. Brues went ahead to the railway.

"How is my son?" Sir Alton said. "I understand you saw him at the carpet maker's last evening?"

"I did." The "carpet maker" was Mr. Gilbey, who'd manufactured and sold many times Sir Alton's worth in carpets, including the ones in the hotel right now. "Noel turned in a fine performance, a piece he'd composed himself, I believe." Plus that duet with Lillian, but John, of course, had not stayed for that portion of the program. No, John had watched that girl with the confidence of a queen twist a finger into her pearls and fret over being good enough to sing with Noel Dunning, and that feeling he'd been brushing away, that word *done*, was suddenly crawling all over him.

"Delightful," said Sir Alton. "I feared your presence there might distract him, you see, remind him of his responsibilities here, but I'm cheered to know he managed to rise above it. He didn't, I hope, give you any notion he planned to spoil his fun any time in the near future?"

"He didn't tell me when he planned to come home, if that's what you ask."

Sir Alton's voice lost its cheery rhythm. "You could have persuaded him. He listens to you."

"It is not my place, between the two of you."

After a moment, Sir Alton regained his smile. "Very true. It is unmannerly of me to keep forcing you there, isn't it? Especially when Noel knows precisely what's expected of him. Quite recently, I reminded him that it will be you, not him, I shall look to if he continues to misunderstand his priorities. And I do believe I meant it."

It was the most direct Sir Alton had ever been regarding John's prospects with the company. As the property owner, Sir Alton had been in the position to demand the position of managing director when the company was formed, but he craved control of the aesthetics of the development, not the daily operations of it. John had earned some respectable raises, taking on duties beyond his role as contractor, allowing Sir Alton to distance himself from the grime of business.

Managing director. Overseeing what was built already, administer of another man's vision—John felt no more tempted than Noel Dunning would have been. He glanced up to the tracks of the pleasure railway, his one original mark on this place, and he knew what he wanted hadn't changed. His time in Idensea was drawing to a close.

The thing was broken, though, wasn't it? Abruptly, he turned from Sir Alton and called to Rolly Brues, his desire to *fix it* as ardent as first love.

To-day study the ribbon movement, and learn how to reverse it.

—How to Become Expert in Type-writing

Darkness had fallen when John and the other men finally left the railway. Weary, discouraged, he cycled to the Kursaal to judge the progress made in his absence, then headed toward the hotel, unable to decide what he wanted most: food, bath, or bed.

All those wants subsided when his ears caught music, spirited and inviting, as he stored his bicycle in the shelter on the hotel grounds. It came from the pavilion, where a coach maker's employees were dancing away the last hours of their excursion day. Where Betsey Dobson likely managed the entire affair with complete efficiency. Still, given last Saturday's events, he thought it prudent to go by—just to stroll by, that was all—to ensure all was well.

At the pavilion, he leaned against a tree where the electric lights didn't quite reach, pleased to observe that Betsey had seen to posting more staffers about, even though he'd failed to remind her to do so. With less pleasure, he noted Sir Alton's secretary on the fringes of the crowd, no doubt taking detailed mental notes to pass on to Sir Alton in the morning. He wondered if

Betsey had noticed. She was amongst the dancers and in great demand, apparently, because there were more men than women tonight. Or because of the way she looked in that uniform. Or just because.

He'd missed tea, he'd missed supper, and every muscle in his body demanded rest, but he remained shrugged up against the tree trunk, watching Betsey Dobson pass from partner to partner.

It shocked him, really. Not the dancing partners, but the others, the men she'd listed to him last night. A great many, it had seemed. Still did. And no intention to marry any of them?

No, one: Thomas Dellaforde she'd thought to marry. Who was he, besides the eldest son? Why him, and none of the others?

And why all those others, and not him, John Jones?

He sank down on his heels beside the tree. She'd answered that question. He told himself he understood, and in a way no one else in her life did. He understood how you sifted, how you let some things run between your fingers while for others you made a cradle of your palms.

Absently, he ripped up tendrils of grass, threw them away. Betsey thought last night a puzzle easily solved, a choice of this-not-that, *kiss me because she hurt you*, but here was his secret: The reason he'd noticed that ring at all was because the pawnbroker had slipped it on a ribbon and hung it inside an empty birdcage. The birdcage, made of scrolling brass that would never need to be repaired with newspaper and string, had arrested his attention in the dingy London window. The ring, he could admit now, had been a guilty, impulsive afterthought.

He would not, however, admit to seeking Betsey out for . . . for *that*. He hadn't even expected to see her. But as he disembarked the train from London, his spirit had felt as hungry and bruised as did his body tonight, and wind and speed and exertion seemed the remedy. Sarah's house was incidental, not a destination.

It didn't matter, though. Betsey believed he had done so. And he would have taken her. Right there in the passenger car, Betsey saying *please* instead of *no,* he would have taken her.

No pretty thing to know about himself, that. No pretty thing to look at a woman and think, *No consequences*.

Yet it was in him still, and in a mighty sulk over the missed opportunity. Just watching Betsey move about the pavilion, the feel of her still fresh on his fingertips and mouth, that ugly, sulking thing he'd thought he'd mastered long ago was roused and hungry, and it brought him to his feet.

The pavilion was open-air, set up on a base of a half dozen low steps. Betsey, watchful of everything even as she danced, saw him the moment he ascended the first step. She broke from her partner, a frown of confusion gathering on her face as she neared him. Abruptly, John remembered how he must look, coming from his work on the railway. He knew his hands and clothes were streaked with oil and dirt. His collar and necktie were crammed into his pockets. He passed a hasty hand over his hair in an attempt to smooth it down.

"You needn't have come," she informed him as she drew near. "Your spy is a most attentive fellow."

Of course she had noticed. "Sir Alton's spy, not mine, Betsey."

"Who is he, then?"

"Walbrook. Sir Alton's secretary."

She cursed softly. "What will he say? It's all gone well tonight, not a peep of trouble."

"Then that is what he will say, I would guess. I don't know him for the malicious sort."

"No? Then you ought to warn him about me, I suppose."

"Girl," he chided at this self-slander, but she continued to glare in Walbrook's direction, her arms crossed, her fingers twiddling the topmost button of her waistcoat. It should have been the second button, but the one above it was missing. No, not missing. Still on the mantelshelf in his bedchamber it was, by accident kept and on purpose not returned.

Caught fidgeting, she dropped her hand from the button. "I didn't want a new gown."

John, having no idea what she meant, thought it wise to say nothing.

"Scold me if you must, but I haven't the money for it, and in any case, I didn't like how you said it. I don't need a gown to snare a husband."

Ah. *That.*

"So, if it is all one to you, I shall just wear my uniform. Unless you meant it as an order."

Uncertainty marked her last words. Seeing some stocky, red-bearded fellow heading in their direction, John touched her arm to persuade her off the pavilion, just a step or two down, enough to put her out of consideration.

"You do as you like with your clothing. Wear your uniform every day if you like," he told her. "Rule the world and any man in it, you could, wearing that frock."

For this, a concession to what she wanted, and what he believed a rather dashing compliment besides, he got her no-such-thing-as-magic-beans stare, followed by an abrupt, "Good night, then."

"I'll come back," he hurried to say before she could turn away to the pavilion. "Wash up, and come back to see you home."

"Charlie's coming. You arranged it. Good night."

"You heard of the breakdown?"

"Yes." She was about to say good night again, he believed, but then he sensed a sort of general softening about her, which turned up in her voice. "It is too bad. I know you're disappointed. But it can be repaired?"

He nodded. "In a day or two. With luck, there will be some still willing to risk a ride upon it."

"Of course there will be. We'd all go again this minute." She gestured toward her excursionists. She did not try to say good night. She watched the dancers, and he watched her, and he saw before she made a sound that she was going to laugh.

Her laughter was for an idea: "You ought to have Sir Alton and Lady Dunning ride it when the repairs are done, to show their confidence in it. And when the Duke comes for the Kursaal opening, put him in it, too, and have his photograph taken. That would make it famous."

The suggestion blossomed immediately into a vision: the Duke, his Duchess, and whatever number of children they had, all the hangers-on those types invariably trailed with them—an entire railway car, perhaps two, crammed full of aristos having a grand time, documented in London's society pages.

"There is brilliant you are, Betsey," he said, grinning, and she pinked with pleasure, though her mouth remained set. "There's brilliant, girl. You'll do it?"

This compliment pinched her cheeks, but she decided he was in jest. "Yes, if Ethan Noonan's not too drunk that day, we'll meet the Duke when he arrives and drive him right over."

"I expect His Grace will have his own carriage for the tour, but Walbrook over there will have details of his itinerary." As she glanced at Sir Alton's secretary, he added, "And the ability to contact the Duke's secretary, supposing any of those details needed adjustment."

She sucked her bottom lip into her mouth.

"That's your specialty, Dobs. Everyone in the proper place at the proper time, feeling merry and not noticing any of the work that's gone into it. My hands are full with the Kursaal, but the Sultan's Road needs this."

"I'll try," she said, her doubt evident. "You should introduce me to Mr. Walbrook, I suppose."

He stayed her with a touch. "I will, but—"

She waited.

"I was curious," he began, but he'd spoken in too much haste this time and did not know how to finish his sentence.

"Curious? As to . . . ?"

As to all your other fellows, Betsey Dobson. Why you chose them.

She would tease, *Why should you wish to know that?*

And he would have to answer, *Because I want—*

The unspoken thoughts stuck, just as they would if he tried to say them. She stood waiting for him to finish, and the dawning realization that he had no confidence in how he might proceed, how to express what he wanted, was as alien as anything he'd ever experienced in his life. He thought of himself at twelve, alone and lost in Swansea, which had seemed such a great city to him then, unable to find work, hungry and homesick, out of plans and hope and prospects. That was something akin to how he felt now, discovering that when it came to Elisabeth Dobson, he had no instincts.

Bless God, that was a lie. He did indeed have instincts, or rather a single instinct driving him like a whip snapping smart and fierce on some dumb beast's back.

He was the dumb beast. The whip struck, and he strained, wanting to move forward but too stupid to know how to extricate his load from the muck that held it. Before he knew it, he was blurting, "What—what if we dance, Miss Dobson?"

Which proved the desertion of his finer instincts. His dancing, as Lillian had once informed him, put him to no advantage. But the bandmaster was calling for a country dance, and though it had been years, he expected he could playact his way through it well enough, rather as he'd practiced pretending to read the sheet music for Lillian's party.

Betsey's gaze swept over him, and he remembered, again, his appearance, that he wasn't fit to be seen in public, that his dirty clothes and rudimentary dancing could serve only to embarrass her. He undoubtedly stank, too, of sweat and oil, earth and rain. But that sweeping, knowing gaze of hers spoke nothing of distaste or embarrassment. It was, in fact, very much like the one she'd given him on the tram last week, when he'd been wearing his very best evening dress. It restored a portion of his confidence, that sweep of Betsey's brown eyes.

"What if we dance?" she repeated. "If we dance, Mr. Jones, then a dance is all. Nothing else."

"Of course, Miss Dobson," he said, and he offered his arm to her.

He was filthy. Filthier than his clothes were his thoughts, filled up with the blistering desire to *have this girl,* and a sudden, cool determination to reckon out what he must do to be one of the fellows she chose.

They took their places amongst the dancers. John kept an eye to the other men dancing, watching for cues, and believed himself to be making a fair act of competence. Betsey avoided his eyes, so perhaps she didn't notice when he was a half step or more behind. Each time they clasped hands, the sensation of soiling her with his dirt-roughed hand pained him. They moved through the figures, and he was at a loss, trying to match steps and find what to say.

It had been more straightforward with Lillian and the other girls like her. The flirtation, the courtship—they had marriage as their object. With Betsey—

It was different. To say to himself exactly how was not presently convenient.

"You came downstairs last night," he said into her ear as they turned in a chaste embrace, because it seemed she had forgotten this fact, and it was a fact worth keeping in mind, not least because the memory of the front door opening still made him happy. Seeing her climb inside the window, he had thought she meant to stay inside.

"You bade me to," she answered, which rather spoiled the memory.

"Didn't," he managed to retort before the turn was completed. He released her and promptly smashed into a couple who had strayed into his path.

"What is the matter with you?" Betsey hissed, yanking him from what was, apparently, *not* his path.

"I'd forgot that step, I suppose."

He fumbled his way back into the dance, watching, counting. When he felt reasonably secure, he said, "You came down, whatever."

"What is the difference? Nothing."

"Not nothing."

They parted. John turned in a circle with someone else. It might have been another man, for all the notice he paid.

Together again: "Here it is. Before you refused, you came."

She stepped on his toes. They were in the wrong place.

"And—you think me rather wonderful."

Another turn with another partner. Betsey smashed into him and it was his fault.

"No more," she said, and she stepped back and left him holding out hands to empty air. By the time he removed himself from
the dancers, she was extending her hand to Sir Alton's secretary, an
introduction from John evidently unnecessary.

He thought about the word *ruined*. How, in one bad season, a
man's crops could be ruined; in a succession of them, his wealth. A
fever, a fall, an excess of drink or rich food, and he met the ruin of
his health. A secret uncovered, an arrival delayed, a lamp knocked
down, and there might be the ruin of reputation, opportunity,
property. In the wrong passion lay the potential for ruin, both
instantaneous and so gradual that a man mightn't realize until he
found himself revolving over the flame that all along he'd been
impaling himself on the devil's spit.

Back at the hotel, he cut through the kitchen that served the
staff dining hall, where all the sounds came from empty pots, the
whisk of brooms and scrubbing brushes, and the scullery girls
being loud and easy with one another. The one who saw him first
was surely a new hire for the season; John didn't know her name,
and her laugh froze on her lips when she spotted him.

"That's Mr. Jones, Iva. Give 'im whatever he wants, time a' day
don't matter," called Meggie Wright with a wink for John, and Iva
filled a dish for him to take to his rooms. *Are you ruined, little Iva?*
he thought as he took it. *You, Meggie Wright?*

For it had struck him as a curious fact: In all the ways a man
could meet ruin, there was one way in which he could not, one
especial way reserved only for women.

When Betsey said, *You cannot ruin me, Mr. Jones,* it was in that
sense reserved for women. But in the other way, the way men
spoke of ruin, not something they *were* but something they *met,*
she certainly thought it was possible.

He bathed, then took his cold supper. His oafishness at the
pavilion clung to him, not his poor dancing but his clumsy arguing.
Hungry as he was, he chewed slowly, thinking he could change

her mind, make her see he was not the risk to her livelihood that she believed him to be. He could do that. There was enough trust between them to engender more. At least there had been, before he cycled to Sarah's house in the middle of the night.

He could change her mind. And then what? This time next year, he would be gone from Idensea, working somewhere else, some greater project, God willing, that would grow his reputation as a contractor, bring him nearer his own company. Marriage he could put off, but not that. He could not end up managing Sir Alton's interests for him.

Change her mind. And then . . .

It would have to be a secret.

He set his dish away on the small table beside him, though the food was but half-finished. He sank back in his chair, stared at the empty grate of the fireplace. Out of sight, out of reach, up on the mantelshelf sat the brass button he'd stolen, but he thought about it all the same.

A secret. Because he could ruin her. To offer her anything but courtship was to ask her to take a risk she'd already refused, and he did not want to court Miss Dobson. He wanted to bed her. Every desire he'd ever thwarted or stalled was straining toward Elisabeth Dobson, ferocious, slavering, and intolerant.

In his bed, he put his hand under the sheet as though he were no better than a boy. Then, for a long while, he lay in the dark.

You cannot ruin me.

Because she was already ruined. No one would dispute it. And what was that like, to be ruined, to live *in* ruin rather than *with* it? To know it couldn't be overcome because forever it was part of you?

So she believed of herself. And though it was fact, there in the dark, John felt he would like to change her mind about that. There in the dark, his need and his lust unsated, it felt like the noblest thing he could attempt, to show Elisabeth Dobson that ruined was not what she *was*.

Learn how to make wide or narrow space between lines.

—*How to Become Expert in Type-writing*

So Mr. Jones was a maddening, uncomprehending block. As Betsey had told him on the pavilion, *No more.*

And yet.

Monday morning found the hotel office full of sweaty men heaving furniture and grunting. Even Arland Hamble, the book-keeper, was flushed. John's suggestion, Mr. Seiler informed her, showing her a drawing of the new furniture arrangement, rendered with neat precision and labeled with wretched scrawling. Things would be a sight more fit and tidy this way, everyone seemed to agree.

"And here is a pleasant change for you." Mr. Seiler pointed to a rectangle within which was scribbled, "Miss D." "No more of your desk being abused by the door when anyone comes into the office."

It was not the shabbiest gesture a man had ever extended toward her. Mr. Jones had even positioned her as far from Mr. Hamble as the space allowed.

Same for the small card of buttons she found in the desk drawer later, exact matches for her uniform.

Not the shabbiest gesture at all.

•   •   •

Avery vanished. She'd kept track of the days of his sentence, expecting him to turn up once it was done. He didn't. She would have felt relieved if she could have known he was truly gone.

She suspected Mr. Jones in the matter.

"I asked if he wanted to go again to London," he admitted when she interrogated him one afternoon in the staff dining hall at the Swan Park. He was only passing through and had greeted her in the same manner he had the rest of the employees, but she had pulled him aside.

"He said of course, so I arranged for him to ride with Noel Dunning."

"I can imagine how you *arranged* things."

"It was not how you are thinking, girl. Civil, every bit of it, and nothing to pity him for."

She believed him. She always would, it seemed. He was a maddening, uncomprehending block, and probably he had helped Avery in order to serve his own selfish designs; probably he thought her a silly, duped female. But somehow he seemed to know what she felt, learning Avery was gone for good now, and it was not the pure relief she'd anticipated. She was biting the inside of her lip to keep her face from breaking, but somehow he knew, and he put aside his own opinions.

"He's not allowed at the hotel," he said. "Perhaps that is why he didn't give you a proper farewell."

If nothing else, Avery Nash had left her with the skill to compose a graceful business letter. Sir Alton's secretary complimented her style when he read the request to photograph the Duke of Winchester on the Sultan's Road. Though Mr. Walbrook seemed reasonable and even kind, since he worked for Sir Alton, Betsey held private doubts as to whether he would actually forward the request to the Duke's secretary. However, a reply soon arrived:

His Grace would be pleased to oblige, provided his grandchildren might be included.

As for Sir Alton's suspension on new bookings, Betsey did not violate it, but neither did she deny the confirmations which arrived after his decree, and so she was able to fill a number of Saturdays despite the moratorium. It could only help her case when she addressed the board. For the same reason, she kept a record of the other inquiries that reached her desk. But how to respond to the inquirers so they would not think the entire scheme was defunct? She finally hit upon saying the requested dates were not available; should something come open, she would write. Two true statements that would buy her time until the board meeting.

The unintentional result seemed to be that denial created demand. More than one telegram urged her to name a date; it would be accepted. It excited and frustrated her, and Betsey's hopes were swift, unruly children, scrambling out of bounds the moment she relaxed her supervision. She pictured three or more excursions a week, a season at Christmastime, figured commissions in her head before she remembered her hands were bound until the meeting, and possibly afterward, too.

Following Mr. Seiler's direction, she made herself useful in the offices, frequently assisting with correspondence and, of course, type-writing. The complaint-book meetings became a favorite part of her workday. Each department of the hotel maintained a record of the complaints it received, submitting it daily to Mr. Seiler, who came to his office at half-two for the purpose of reading the latest entries and having two cups of the blackest coffee Betsey had ever seen.

Between sips, Mr. Seiler read the complaints aloud and considered suggestions from the submanagers. Betsey remained an observer to this process, alert and studious, anticipating how the complaints might be resolved. Inviting a dissatisfied guest to pack more thoughtfully in the future or to stay at home next summer was never the proper response, no matter how frivolous the complaint sounded to her, but with each meeting, she learned some useful method of appeasement. It might be sending to London for a particular blend of tea, shifting a chambermaid from one set of rooms to another for a few weeks, directing a stern word to a surly stable hand.

Sometimes Mr. Seiler's voice would dwindle down to a rough purr as he read the complaint aloud, and then he would take a sip of coffee and say, "*Für mich.*" This generally meant a personal word with the complainant. He made it seem effortless, even spontaneous, meeting guests as they passed through the vestibule or as he offered to secure them a special table in the tearoom. A simple, sympathetic inquiry from Tobias Seiler generated more forgiveness and goodwill than any size bouquet might.

If he did not see to the resolution himself, Mr. Seiler assigned it to one of the submanagers. Or, increasingly, he said, "Miss Dobson?" and passed the task to her. Small things, jobs that could hardly be bungled even if one tried, but they were chances to prove herself, and Betsey welcomed every one.

As the board meeting drew closer, she practiced her address in the evenings, speaking to Thief or out to the night, perched on the roof. She was there two nights before the meeting when she heard Dora Pink's firm rap at her door.

"Mr. Jones says for you to come down."

The lordliness of this demand could have been Dora Pink's as easily as Mr. Jones's. Either way, she let a defiant ten minutes pass before she presented herself in the parlor. Mr. Jones, at a game of dominoes with Charlie, at first appeared to be waiting patiently enough, but as soon as he saw her, he stood.

"Let me hear your speech."

Sarah and the boarders smiled at her, their evening's entertainment.

"Mr. Seiler has approved it already."

He nodded. He found this interesting or perhaps as he expected, but no reason not to hear her all the same.

"It's not even a speech, really, it is only going over numbers, and why should I bore everyone here with that?"

Because the practice was good for her, he said. Because Sarah and the others were curious. Because she wouldn't wish to disappoint Charlie. Because, in short, he wanted her to, and she saw he was dug in until she appeased him. She retrieved her notes from her room, eager to have it done.

Whatever disappointment Charlie experienced resided in his interrupted game, for he was absorbed in stacking domino pyramids before the third sentence was out of her mouth. Sarah and the boarders listened as though she sang music they appreciated but could not love, and their applause at the close was both affectionate and dutiful.

It didn't matter. Mr. Jones mattered; just like the day at Iden Hall, it was to him she looked for approval and truth. His brows remained crooked in concentration. Charlie knocked down his pyramids and shuffled, inviting her to a game. Betsey accepted but mainly for the opportunity to murmur to Mr. Jones, "Well, what was the matter with it?"

His brows crooked deeper. After a moment, he sprang up, snatched Miss Everson's mending scissors from her, and returned, making Betsey gasp as he jerked her chair into a position to face his own.

He snicked the scissors. "Come, you. I will give you a trim."

Laughter filled the parlor. Mr. Jones ignored it. Sarah cautioned, "John, if you should make a mistake—why, she must stand before all those men in a few days!"

Only then did his intention seem to waver. His grin, both lush and abrupt, already forgave her if she refused.

Miss Everson warned her to keep her distance, but in Betsey's mind hovered Mr. Jones's drawing of the new office arrangement, all those precise lines. From the table, she took a newspaper page, spread it over her lap, and edged forward, her knees between his.

His grin fell away, and she closed her eyes, felt the cool slide of metal against her forehead, needles of hair on her nose and cheeks. His breath touching her lips.

He went slowly. The conversations in the room recommenced. His thumb passed over her skin, brushing away hair.

"There's good," he said.

Betsey tested the edge of the fringe with her fingertips, then opened her eyes to see his throat contract with a swallow, a ripple of flesh at his collar.

"Your brows show again," he added.

"Is that what was wanting?"

"Cannot hurt." To Charlie, he instructed, "Get Animal Grab."

"I don't play that anymore." But Charlie was fetching the cards even as he protested.

Mr. Jones lined the cards faceup on the table. "Here, girl. Your board of directors."

Betsey held up the donkey card. "Sir Alton?"

Charlie hooted, and Mr. Jones laughed, too, but placed the card back in line. His broad finger touched a different card. "Sir Alton."

The brown tabby rested a composed gaze on the viewer, one paw poised above a ball of blue yarn, the same blue yarn tied in a bow around its neck, a depiction so ideal it lacked any sense of vitality. "I see," she said, and he sorted the cards into groups, alliances, giving her names and motivations and histories. He brought the dominoes in as shareholders, explaining the structure of a joint-stock company.

Bored, Charlie wandered off. Betsey scarcely noticed, her mind engaged with the puzzle of making use of this information, her heart puzzling over Mr. Jones. He was uncommonly bad at seduction if he thought talk of common capital and incorporation would do the trick, but she could think of no other reason he would lavish her with such time and care.

Except the impossible one: No motive but to help her. Such purity didn't exist, though. If it did . . .

If it did, he'd be a dangerously good seducer.

He paused thoughtfully. "Your address is clear, convincing. Nothing wrong in it." He swept the cards into a stack and looked up, his eyes grave. "Only you have made it all about money."

Betsey repressed a laugh at this unexpected criticism, repressed the sarcastic suggestion that she might also share her fish cake recipe with the board. There was something so potent in his earnestness; she did not want to sully it.

She said, "The company may earn more money or less—what is there beyond that?"

"Any of us would be richer if money was all there was to it. Still type-writing in London, you'd be, if money was all. A man doesn't choose a business venture for profit and nothing else. These shareholders—" He caged his hand over the dominoes on the table. "We invested in something past dividend promises. If it were all for money, a man would never buy a ring he happened upon in a shop window, do you see?"

She saw. She did not believe. Wasn't he the one with grand ambitions, the one who'd sat on Castle Hill and told her how he dreamed of wealth? She wanted only to be safe and not owe anyone anything. Where he'd come by the notion she'd come to Idensea for anything but money, she had no idea.

"Sir Alton will not be speaking of money, girl. You think that is your advantage, and it is, no mistaking, but he does not go empty-handed. He has a vision to give them."

Sir Alton's dining room was not the most orthodox location for a meeting, but in season, the board members preferred to move the meetings from London to Idensea in order to have the opportunity to see their investment at work. Betsey arrived with Mr. Seiler a few minutes early, edgy as a pocketknife, and nearly snapped under Sir Alton's gaze, it was so unusually expressive. A full brow-rumpling frown, and all for her.

His secretary, Mr. Walbrook, was soon at his side with a whisper that ironed his brow. Her name, Betsey realized, allowing a strangled, nervous laugh to escape at the idea that Sir Alton hadn't given her a single thought in the fortnight since she'd stood by his arm and shown her books to him. The excursion scheme might have concerned him, but she personally—no.

Mr. Seiler murmured something. It was in German and it sounded to her like stones settling together; either he meant to brace her or warn her off giggling. He'd not noticed Sir Alton so much as the general shift in the room, a room filled with men, a little world experiencing a disturbance. The meeting had not yet begun, and many of the board members carried on with their conversations, oblivious to her and Mr. Seiler's arrival, but enough had paused, looked, and tried to make sense of a woman without a tray that the energy in the room had changed.

One man approached, a greeting for Mr. Seiler in his upraised hand, but Mr. Walbrook reached them first. He was apologetic; the board intended to begin privately, the drawing room would be a comfortable place to wait until it was time . . .

He stopped when he realized Mr. Seiler meant to accompany her to the drawing room. He believed—he was fairly certain, in fact—that Mr. Seiler was to remain, that he was wanted for the report on the hotel . . .

"I shall send when the time comes," Mr. Seiler promised, and Betsey thought it was probably for the best, that she would have someone in the meeting to make sure she was not forgotten.

Mr. Walbrook escorted her to the drawing room, an unnecessary courtesy, for she and Mr. Seiler had scarcely crossed the threshold into the dining room. In his diffident manner, he encouraged her to ring for tea if she wished, as he feared it might be a bit of a wait, and invited her to sit anywhere, just anywhere at all she liked, but he looked toward a padded bench along the wall next to the doors as he did, and when he returned to the dining room, he pulled the pocket doors only partway together.

The meeting began. Betsey moved to the very edge of the bench and turned toward the doorway, leaning forward as far as her corset would allow. Everything except Sir Alton's voice she could hear well, even though the room went pin-still whenever he spoke. He could shush a room, draw people toward him with the soft sway of his voice, just as if he'd lifted a baton before an orchestra.

A half hour or so later, voices from the opposite end of the drawing room prompted her to straighten and sit properly. It was Mr. Jones, ushered in by Lady Dunning, whom Betsey recognized but had never yet met. The two paused inside the doorway as Lady Dunning insisted he was due for dinner again soon, or perhaps when the season was over, as she imagined him frightfully busy now. And if it were possible to do so discreetly, could he let Sir Alton know she would send Noel in the moment he arrived?

Then she sighed, resigned. "He was due from London last night. I fear he has forgotten he promised to come."

Betsey ought to have made her presence known. Instead, she watched them exchange farewells, and then Mr. Jones fished his necktie from his pocket and hurried it into position in motions too quick to follow.

She had remembered their conversation on Castle Hill imperfectly the other night. Children and dogs and the freedom to come home in the middle of the day and have sandwiches, if he so desired. That was what he'd dreamed of, not just money.

He paused before a mirror between two enormous vases and passed his hands over his hair, to little effect. Then he started for the dining room and discovered her sitting there.

Too lovely, the pleasure in his surprise, as though she were a coin in the pocket of a coat he'd not worn for a year. She nodded at him.

Closer to her, he frowned and inclined his head toward the dining room.

"I was instructed to wait here until I was wanted," she explained, keeping her voice low.

His lips parted, then met again in a line of grim understanding. He looked at the empty space on the bench beside her, then selected a chair from a separate grouping of furniture, moving it so they would face each other. Very appropriate.

"I'm sure *you* are meant to go right in."

He sat down, defiant, needlessly loyal, faintly ridiculous, for the chair was dainty and he was not. Betsey bit the inside of her cheek.

Inside the dining room, the topic had turned to ordinances and the county council's hesitation in limiting the number of licenses issued to entertainers.

"Why does it matter?" she whispered to Mr. Jones.

He leaned forward, bracing his elbows on his knees, the distance he'd put between them unwieldy for a hushed conversation.

"'Twill be competition for the Kursaal, when it finally opens, so some think. And atmosphere, too. Sir Alton will take that pulpit in a moment, how it lowers the tone of the entire town to allow a license to any jack with three pounds and an instrument or a trained animal."

And indeed, in another moment, all the other voices died away and the room took on that stillness Betsey recognized as Sir Alton speaking. She couldn't make out a single word, but she knew Mr. Jones had predicted aright and stifled a snicker. Mr. Jones chuckled aloud.

A number of voices started all at once, and the discussion seemed to fragment. Mr. Jones's gaze shifted, and following it, Betsey saw that Sir Alton stood in the doorway. He returned Mr. Jones's greeting, but his gaze scanned the drawing room. Her bench next to the doorway behind him was the last place he looked, and again, Betsey felt his confusion: *Who in the hell is that?*

The answer came to him more quickly than it had before. He bade her good day, most cordially, then turned his back on her to address Mr. Jones.

"Noel is not with you? I thought . . ." Another quick inspection of the corners and settees.

"Lady Dunning will send him when he arrives, she said."

The pop of a pocket watch shutting. "Poor Noel has such ill luck with the London trains. Always one running behind the concert schedule, or derailed by a late round at one club or another. And you're out here awaiting a personal invitation, I suppose?"

"As seemed to be the procedure for today."

Past Sir Alton's arm, she saw Mr. Jones nod his head ever so slightly toward her. Sir Alton's smile, when he turned it on her, was the same bland thing it always was, but it chilled her.

"By all means, see our manageress into the board meeting, Jones."

When addressing a young unmarried lady, the salutation is often omitted.

—*How to Become Expert in Type-writing*

*B*oard members filled the table. Chairs along the wall provided seating for everyone else. A few men noticed her entrance and stood; the action eventually rippled across the room. Mr. Jones found her a place next to Mr. Seiler, then took a chair on the wall opposite. One of the directors telegraphed a subtle greeting to him as he passed. Matthew Munsell, she guessed, the tom turkey from Animal Grab, who had given Mr. Jones his first contracting charge years ago and recommended him to the pier company.

As she followed the discussion, Betsey found it calming to try to match the directors with the cards—the toad, the crow, the rooting hog. The sharp-clawed pussycat at the head of the table.

Across the room, Mr. Jones gave her a fine, wry smile. It was how they'd met, wasn't it, a business meeting like this, him smiling, seeming to know her thoughts. She'd found it alarming to be observed so astutely, to feel noticed and known in the same gaze. This time, though, she was not so skittish. She touched the paper frame inside her engagement book, thinking again of Animal Grab and dominoes.

Sir Alton called Mr. Seiler to the table for the hotel summary, and then Mr. Seiler introduced Betsey. Awkwardness ensued as some judged the etiquette to be to stand, others the opposite, leaving those inclined to take cues completely flummoxed. Betsey remained calm. The first part of the address was easy; she had delivered it to Sir Alton already, and the board members had printed copies of her figures.

However, she'd just begun when the Crow interrupted. "Miss . . . Dobson, correct? Why *in the name of heaven* is this bagatelle on our agenda?"

His irritation, so ready and undisguised, staggered Betsey and rendered her mute, a condition more problematic to her present task than the fact she didn't know what the hell *bagatelle* meant.

But had Crow spoken rhetorically? He dashed a glance up and down the table. "The excursion scheme was settled months ago. A one-season *trial*. Do I mistake my calendar? Have I gone to sleep in *May* and waked in *September*?"

Betsey had never heard such diction. The table would be under a shower if not for the fellow's mustache. She found it so dramatic she thought, *Yes, rhetorical questions.*

Except Crow appeared expectant, cocking his head thus and so, most crowish.

He thumped two fingers on Sir Alton's side of the table. "I ask you."

Sir Alton's lips thinned by a fraction.

Someone said, "The riot has added some urgency to the matter."

"Riot, my eye."

"A riot is what the papers say it is." Sir Alton sounded like a Sunday school teacher, gently reminding a child of the Golden Rule. "If the public reads 'riot,' then that is what happened."

"*Riot-my-eye*. The *Times* gave it a line, 'riot' appearing nowhere within. Mischance and false steps are to be expected as part of the *trial period*, and may be reviewed in context once the agreed period is *concluded*. Until such a time, I cannot but be affronted, seeing this girl dragged here before us to waste this board's time, answering objections we have already heard and—*do you not recall?*—overruled."

Whoever at the table might have agreed with him, none comfortably witnessed this challenge to Sir Alton, at least by Betsey's accounting with breath held and eyes darting. She herself might have enjoyed seeing Sir Alton put to the screws if not for her confidence that she'd be the one to suffer for it. She stood there, well aware her sanction to speak had been usurped but lost as to what she could, or should, do about it.

Sir Alton gave Crow nothing. "I'm grateful for the reminder and hope it comforts you to know I do recall, with admitted disappointment, being outvoted. It pains me to think my concern for the Swan Park affronts you, but on one point we agree. Dragging this girl into our discussions is a shameful waste of our time."

"Upon this topic, there is not one damn thing—"

"Mr. Herries, a female is present—"

How touching, Sir Alton's care for her feminine sensitivity. Betsey feared she was about to be dismissed with no opportunity to speak.

"Gentlemen, my goodness." She smiled up and down the table so neither Sir Alton nor Crow would feel reproached. "I can only hope I don't appear as though I've been dragged anywhere."

She lifted her hands, proving the absence of shackles, posing, inviting them to a good look, praying her hair was in place. Mr. Jones could accuse her of flirting later. Behind her, she heard dear Mr. Seiler's low chuckle. One or two others joined him, thank God.

"Let me assure you I'm pleased for the opportunity to address this board, though I must agree with Mr. Herries that the excursion scheme has hardly been given the opportunity to prove its value. The figures I provided you show our expectations. Worth bearing out, I think. Indeed, I confess my belief that the board's time would be better used discussing not the suspension of the scheme but its expansion."

Murmurs. Matthew Munsell, the tom turkey, spoke for the table and asked her to explain.

"Saturday is but one of a week. Some organizations have already expressed a willingness to book on Fridays when a Saturday is not available. Also, our concentration for the excursions has been the London catchment, but a more local trade could be developed through a Sunday scheme, social groups and private gatherings. Sabbatarian criticism might be avoided by engaging clergymen and orators rather than musicians—"

"Do we see the slippery way this wends?" Sir Alton's soft voice hushed her and stole all the eyes from her. "I had thought we built the pier for the public, and the pavilion for guests of the hotel. By 'guests,' I mean those with the means to stay there, not day-trippers."

Several heads nodded, but some had done so while she spoke, too. None voiced his opinion yet. Betsey seized this as permission to continue.

"Christmastime offers another opportunity to make the most of the hotel's resources, and at a time when they are not utilized enough. One of the two ballrooms is closed at the end of the season. Converting wasted space to profitable space is but a matter of promotion—everything else is already there and awaiting use."

Down the table, Sir Alton emitted the merest purr of a laugh and seemed almost to whisper to himself, "*In* the hotel now."

A board member began a question. Crow interrupted. "The *trial* period, gentlemen. Miss Dobson. Why is that thrown wayside? Did we not have the wisdom to conceive it? Then why not the fortitude *to stick by it*? I ask for sober, rational decisions based upon indifferent facts, obtained quite simply—*not instantly*—by honoring our original plan. It was a good one. It will protect us from rash, imprudent action, if only we let it."

Another board member said, "Still, Herries, to look down the road a bit, get an idea of what's possible. Cannot hurt to be mulling it over in the meantime."

"Assuming that is both useful and possible, let us consider that road *looked down* and move to pressing matters. Miss Dobson, please conclude in due expediency."

"Certainly." Her sharp disappointment tempted her to let that be her final word, to sit down and have done with it, her whole purpose here thwarted by Herries the Crow. But there was no one here, from Sir Alton to Mr. Jones, she could stand to witness her surrender.

"If there is one thing I'd have you mull over, perhaps it's the picture of that dark ballroom, sitting there like—" She directed an especial smile to Mr. Herries. "I was about to say a locked treasure chest, but that's too fanciful for you, isn't it? I'm the same." She fingered the frame peeking out from her engagement book, debating still whether she should use it. "But you don't pack your cash into your mattress, do you? You have it out earning more for you."

Mr. Herries gave her a shrewd look. If they met again, he would remember her. With the same feeling she'd had boarding that southbound train from London, she took out the frame. How far could she go on this ticket?

"We give each excursionist a favor at the end of the night. The ladies in the party receive these frames—I picked them, I think, because my mother had one something like it."

She had to stop, paralyzed by the unexpected terror of self-revelation before these men. Better to have hopped upon the table with a cancan. What would it matter to these men, anyway? Below the tabletop, needles of fear pricked her calves and the backs of her knees.

"It held a photograph of us, her three children, from a day out at Blackpool. I was small, too small to remember much of it. I know it was a singular occasion—we never went again."

A restless movement came from Sir Alton's end of the table just as Mr. Herries spoke her name. The needles now worked at the soles of her feet, and heat engulfed her as though she stood tied to a stake. She shot a glance at Mr. Jones, part anguish, part accusation, for it was his fault she stood here in the first place, talking of her mother. She wanted to murder him, or take shelter under his arm.

He met her eye, prepared for either event. He sat casually, ankle crossed over knee, but he was there, with her, for her; she felt it palpably and thought one bright, wistful thing better suited to starry nights than board meetings.

A more grounded thought was that having begun this, she had to get through it. She could. She gestured for Mr. Herries's patience, then drew her hand back to her side, hoping the trembling she felt was imperceptible to the rest of the table.

"That singular day meant something to my mother, though—that's why she kept that picture above the hearth. Sir Alton, pardon me, but you are mistaken to assume the excursionists haven't the means for the Swan Park."

Sir Alton would know her, too, next time their paths crossed. That was evident.

She spoke to the table. "Some of them do. Some will. Not a great many, of course. But whatever their means, their employers have seen fit to dignify them with a singular day. It dignifies this company to help them do it. Gentlemen, will you let me tell you what your business is?"

A dangerous question, she knew, dangerous to leave the door wide for either Sir Alton's sarcasm or Mr. Herries's rabid enunciation. But Mr. Munsell answered her, and if he sounded a trifle amused, at least he'd been good enough to repress it some.

"I for one would be most intrigued to hear your perspective, Miss Dobson."

"Thank you, sir. Perhaps it isn't so different from your own. Simply that this company dignifies leisure. Declares it worthy of a family's wages and the trouble they go to enjoy it. I don't fancy I'm telling you something new, only perhaps that you didn't realize—my mother valued it as much as any lady in the Swan Park's best rooms."

She nodded her conclusion. Another stir ensued as they decided whether Miss Dobson leaving the table called for standing or remaining seated. It made her feel her defeat more keenly. Before she and Mr. Seiler had reached the door, the next agenda item was under discussion.

*   *   *

She waited to cry. At the hotel, she immediately posted the stack of inquiries she'd prepared and held in hopes the board would approve them, but the task was done without the sense of victory she'd anticipated. She conferred with the chef on the upcoming menu, answered telegrams, sent payment for an advert in the *Times*. She got herself through the afternoon, accomplishing all that was expected of her and a few things more no one would have suspected as part of her duties, rode the bicycle-that-wasn't-quite-hers to the lodging house, felt grateful that Sarah was always busy with supper preparations this time of day and that Charlie was out and that she met no one on the stairs as she went up to her room, and then she closed her door, stripped off her jacket, and permitted herself a few tears with Thief as the only witness.

She'd thought she'd kept her expectations reasonable, her hopes grounded. But her disappointment exposed the fact that on some level, she'd been wanting too much, spinning fairy tales for herself.

The water in her washbasin was nearly as warm as her tears, but it provided some refreshment as she splashed it over her face. *No more of that,* she told herself, and self obeyed, even when she spied the letter Dora Pink had left on her bed. The letter would be from her sister, and full of tender reminders of a household that had fallen short of home and refuge for her, despite Caroline's best hopes. And her brother-in-law intended even that to be denied her, she thought. He'd forbidden her from the house that was his, even if he was only one of its residents.

Neither she nor Caroline would allow that to stand, but Betsey wanted more than brazen defiance on her side. She put away the gray tweed jacket she'd worn today next to the brown one she would wear tomorrow. Both suits of clothing had come from Richard, same as the money to pay her course fees at the Institute. As long as that debt was riding her, she wouldn't be able to stand up to him.

And what if, come the end of the season, it was as Richard and Avery had predicted, she in the same desperate, jobless state as in May? It frightened her more now than before. In May, she had not loved her work.

The clock in the corridor chimed. To come late to the supper table would be to put Dora Pink in a mood that would punish everyone in the house, and to not come at all would bring knocks at her door, worried demands to know what was wrong.

That, at least, was a change from a few months ago, Betsey reflected as she started down the stairs. Not a bankable one but worth something, and another reason for her fears.

But while she'd been having her cry, pandemonium had overtaken the household. Lodgers, servants, dishes, furniture—all were heading out the door to the back garden, supper shanghaied, Dora Pink's schedule flouted, Mr. Jones at the center of it all.

He stood behind a tub of ice, coat discarded and sleeves rolled. Laughter filled the air, and when Sarah announced Betsey's appearance in the doorway, applause erupted, and Betsey passed through a gauntlet of congratulations, at the end of which waited a dish heaped with more ice cream than she would have seen in her lifetime had she never come to Idensea. Mr. and Mrs. Seiler were there, too, and when everyone, servants and all, had been served, Mr. Seiler raised a bowl and toasted "Miss Dobson, *l'astucieuse, la douée, la belle.*"

In any language, she knew it for nonsense. But she ate the entire bowl, and when Charlie came to her and claimed he could not finish his second serving, she ate that as well.

Someone pushed the piano near an open window. Out to the garden came the supper dishes, and all order and convention remained suspended for the evening, servants and guests dancing together, dessert before dinner.

Mr. Seiler brought her lemonade and joined her on the ground under a tree. To him, she confessed, "I was not the resounding success everyone wants to say."

"I dozed off, then, when they suspended the scheme?"

"Yes, it could be much worse. But they would not even discuss the expansion."

With a sigh, Mr. Seiler rolled his eyes to the evening sky.

"You warned me not to count on that. I tried not to." She watched Mr. Jones and Charlie tend the fire they'd built and added softly, "I want to stay."

"*Tu veux toutes les fleurs dans le jardin à fleurir au même moment.* You want every flower to bloom at once."

Mr. Seiler's departure with his wife left Betsey sitting alone beneath the tree, but she felt too comfortable to stir. Mr. Jones joined her. He stretched out on the ground much as he had the day on Castle Hill.

"What a terrible expense, all that ice cream," she finally said. She was thanking him.

"Enjoyed it, you did."

"More than anything."

"Then."

A starry night, better than a board meeting for wistful thoughts. The music had halted. Sarah and the others were starting to gather things into their arms, as what belonged indoors must be returned there. Betsey threw a handful of cloverleaves at him.

"You want me to go to bed with you."

She meant to tease, to be playful, but he turned his face out of the firelight, and she knew she'd been cruel. Challenged, demeaned his gift. Offered an invitation she was not sure of. She wished he would not answer.

"I do. Just about mad with it, I am thinking."

Low in her body, something pulsed like a tide. She had not expected him to be so direct.

The fire popped, sending up sparks like skylarks startled out of their ground nests.

"But make you no mistake what this was for," he added, then rose to help carry furniture.

Polish your type-writer with a soft cotton cloth and cover it.
—*How to Become Expert at Type-writing*

*S*ummer deepened. It seemed intent on erasing the memory of all other seasons, and sometimes, coasting down the last hill between the hotel and Sarah's house or in the midst of a long, long Sunday afternoon, Betsey indulged in the fancy that summer was patient, and offered all the time she needed to prepare for the frost.

In truth, there was little she could do but act as though that were true. Her best chance of saving the excursion scheme and her position was to make this season as successful as possible, so when Arland Hamble, the bookkeeper, informed her that her budget had been reduced, she bit the inside of her cheek and nodded. Mr. Hamble might have smirked as he told her, but she knew he merely was passing on Sir Alton's orders. She reworked her expenditures and smirked a little herself as she realized that, with every Saturday to the middle of September booked, her advertising funds could be redirected.

The board had denied her request to host groups on Sundays, but on Saturdays the pavilion sat empty until the dinner dance in the evenings. With Mr. Seiler's approval, she began booking Sunday schools and women's groups for refreshments or light teas during the day. The commissions would be small, and the mad busyness of her Saturdays would increase, but it was money coming her way, and she anticipated making her final payment to her brother-in-law at the end of the summer.

Betsey hoped this would happen when Baumston & Smythe came to Idensea for the company outing, but Caroline's letters continued to report that she'd had no luck in persuading Richard to attend. As the company was covering the costs for transportation and the dinner dance, Betsey knew, even if Caroline would never say so, that Richard must have no wish to witness the reunion of Betsey Dobson and Baumston & Smythe, Insurers. She could not blame him. Wofford's pink fingers wiggled at her each time she imagined meeting the train, and whether she'd broken them or not, the image never failed to make her queasy.

She willed such weakness away. Sometimes she saw it, how tightly she clung, how she fretted to keep all the parts together, the way she'd tried to keep her butchered hair contained with one penny's worth of pins at the beginning of the season. These moments of clarity came not at work as she managed dozens of loose threads, but after she'd edged out Charlie in a cycling race, or on Tuesday evenings, when there would be a stack of fresh linens on her dresser, or at supper as she slipped into her chair, her place at the table in the house she increasingly called home.

One evening, on her way from work to one of those suppers, she slowed her pedaling as she noticed more and more visitors on the Esplanade looking in the same direction, up to the Kursaal.

The lamp was lit, she realized as she came to a stop. The centerpiece of the Kursaal was a hexagonal tower topped by a light, an artistic interpretation of a lighthouse. The long summer day drained the brightness, but it glowed, and for the first time.

She cycled up to the site and found the same expanse of chaotic activity as the first time she'd come here, men shouting over the thumping hiss of steam engines, horses straining at loaded drays, the black smoke of waste fires and mountain ranges of gravel and sand. The work would carry on till dark, she guessed. Mr. Jones arrived at The Bows later and later these days, if he came at all.

She spied him huddled over the back end of a delivery wagon, scribbling across a stack of papers and handing them off to a man in a fresh-looking suit, who kept trying to find a tidy way to balance in the deep ruts of crusted mud.

Unable to summon any excuse to interrupt him, she was about to depart when a laborer elbowed Mr. Jones and gestured toward her. Mr. Jones removed his spectacles, then strode her way. She might have met him halfway. But he looked like a king traversing his ramparts, or a commander the battlefield, dust billowing at his boot heel with each sure and purposeful step, and it would've been a shame to spoil her viewpoint.

But his expression, as he drew nearer, was sober. "Something happen, is it?"

"No. Only . . ." She gestured over the cliff to the Esplanade, feeling foolish for alarming him. "People are noticing the light."

The transformation of his face banished her embarrassment. He grinned up at the tower. "Quite a cheer up here when it knocked on. A view it is, Betsey, up in the lantern room. You'll go up?"

"May I?"

He steered her to the portico, avoiding the busiest areas of construction. "We're readying for the landscaping and the installations in the winter gardens—paths to wander, footbridges, all the greenery and flowers, of course. And statuary, Sir Alton has said."

"And how many waterfalls?"

"Only the one in the dome round back. The glass rises thirty feet there."

Inside, a forest of scaffolding presently occupied the entrance hall, which soared over a grand double staircase and several gallery floors. The space reverberated with the rumbling voices of the laborers and the plinks and scrapes of their tools. "The faience going up," Mr. Jones explained, indicating the colorful glazed tiles. He sounded satisfied, as though the ratio of tiled walls and columns to blank ones was not as dismal as Betsey herself reckoned.

"A refreshment lounge and reading room that way," he said as they approached the staircase. "Below us is the skating rink. I can't take you round everywhere just now, but I'll teach you and Charlie skating when we open, shall I?"

She agreed, and did not say that Thomas Dellaforde had taught her already, one stolen Sunday afternoon.

Though the lantern room was their destination, he could not resist showing her the recital hall, where, aside from eight hundred missing seats, work had been completed. Their place in the rear balcony offered a complete view of the stage, its proscenium ruffled and rounded like an oyster shell. Indeed, the entire hall seemed shell-inspired, a cool and dreamy composition of pinks and whites.

Though he'd meant to be showing off the space, his inspection turned critical. He frowned at the empty floor below. "A call on the factory is in order, I am thinking, or else the Duke and Duchess will sit upon milking stools opening night."

"The speeches best be brief if that happens." She knew he would take the stage as an orator on opening night and imagined the hall filled with seats, those seats occupied. A dining table full of board members had been enough for her. To speak to hundreds, nobility amongst them . . .

Her stomach shuddered on his behalf. "It will be quite a moment for you, won't it? Will any of your family come?"

Mr. Jones locked his elbows against the balcony's low wall. The open doors permitted the noise of the workmen to bounce around them faintly.

Betsey guessed, "Too much of a journey for them?"

"Never taken a train, my dad. I asked him. Said to bring the little ones and my sister Dilys." A soft grunt nearly passed for amusement at himself. "My mother two days in the ground, and I'm asking a man who's never taken a train to leave work and cross the country with three little children to see a nob cut a ribbon. Owen was weeping so, though."

Something raw crouched in the last remark. Owen was his youngest brother, not more than three or four, if she remembered correctly. Betsey didn't follow the connection, but she knew, "It wasn't wrong to ask him."

"There's dense it sounded, and I knew it soon as it was out. But I needed something to say to Owen, some promise for when I'd see him again."

"Ah. He didn't want you to leave."

"That's it." He paused, and above the echoing sounds of the workmen, she heard something new, a peculiar, rasping sound between his body and her own.

His thumb. That broad, hard pad taking a meditative path along the callused side of his forefinger.

He said, "What I did, I missed my train. So he'd hush at last, I stayed another night and left the next morning. Early, him still sleeping." The rasping stopped. He pushed off the wall, taken from his story by someone appearing on the main floor. He called, "You wanting me, young Clayton?"

The boy twisted, finding Mr. Jones above. "Sir, Mr. Jones, it's Sir Alton's carriage coming."

"I'll meet him, thanks." As the boy ducked out, Mr. Jones told Betsey, "Sir Alton's here for the lantern room as well. Make it a group?"

Involuntarily, Betsey's nose wrinkled.

"I'll bring you another time, then," he promised, but the laughter that accompanied the promise halted in a correction. "You and Sarah. Charlie, too."

"Fine," she answered, before he could invite the whole damn lodging house and make it thoroughly proper and well within the limits she herself had imposed.

She had hoped to get away without Sir Alton seeing her, but he and Lady Dunning were alighting the barouche as she and Mr. Jones exited the Kursaal. Mr. Jones made her even more conspicuous by walking her to her bicycle. Just like she was having her first lesson again, he held the handlebar while she mounted. She touched her foot to the pedal, poised for motion.

Still he held on.

"What do you think, girl? Was it the right thing?"

Betsey glanced over her shoulder, trying to make out where his gaze had fixed. Nothing in sight helped her make sense of the question.

She turned back. He looked down to the handlebar as though he knew he should release it, but he didn't. "How I left Owen," he said. He lifted his gaze again, his need for an answer so naked it jarred her. "Was it the right thing?"

Tears scalded her eyes without warning, the only ready answer that she possessed. What would she ever know of children? She suspected Owen woke to distractions of food and play and family routines, that his brother was the only one yet haunted by that day, but was that comfort? He came to her with the question that undid all his confidence, and she didn't know what to tell him.

"That child loves you, John." She had at least that truth to share. "How could he help it? No matter how you had to leave, that is what he'll remember, that he loves you."

"Lady Morey—she finds the reading material in the ladies' lounge is too much of the edifying strain and not enough of the entertaining."

Mr. Seiler reached for the cup of coffee sitting on the corner of his desk, and his glance over the top of the complaint book fell upon Betsey. No longer just an observer, she was expected to supply an idea now and then.

She knew she had the space of a single sip to offer a remedy for Lady Morey's dissatisfaction, and after attending these complaint book meetings regularly over the past few weeks, that should not have been so great a challenge.

But before today, Sir Alton had never been present. He hadn't seemed surprised to find her there, only greeted her with the comment that he'd heard she was making herself useful round the hotel in any number of ways.

The rim of the cup lingered at Mr. Seiler's lips. He graced her with another sip, forgoing his customary practice.

One submanager suggested, "It will be a simple matter to ask the lady what she prefers. A porter may bring it from town, or if it is very extraordinary, we may send to London."

Mr. Seiler nodded. "Very well. For you."

The submanager made a note. Proceeding to the next item, Mr. Seiler turned a page in the complaint book.

"She has a companion," Betsey said in the pause. She was not certain Mr. Seiler would appreciate this addition. Going to the companion would be more discreet, and he preferred complaints to be resolved with minimum fuss, but once the "for you" order had been pronounced, the matter was considered finished, and Mr. Seiler did not revisit it. But having begun, there was nothing to do but finish. "Lady Morey has a companion with her, Miss Thee. She would know Lady Morey's reading preferences."

Mr. Seiler's *hmm* was brief but thoughtful. "For you, then, Miss Dobson."

The submanager struck the task from his list, Betsey recorded it in her notebook, and Mr. Seiler went to the next item, all as if Mr. Seiler asked her to resolve guest complaints every day. What did Sir Alton think of it? There had been none of his previous failure to recognize her when he'd joined the meeting this afternoon.

Mr. Seiler's ritualistic precision meant his two cups of coffee were drained and the complaint books shut by five to three—that was, unless Sir Alton attended, a submanager had once warned Betsey. He had come often in the early days of the hotel, and still was likely to drop in now and again, and his questions and concerns could lengthen the meeting considerably.

Betsey saw no sign of that today. Indeed, at ten of, Sir Alton took his leave, having said very little. Betsey noted the glances exchanged amongst the remaining men after the secretary closed the door. Mr. Seiler shook off his puzzlement and returned to the groundskeeper's complaint book. It was still possible to finish on schedule. "Mrs. Guy—roast pheasant with plum jelly served on a chipped plate, sans jelly."

Betsey left the meeting with an armload of complaint books to return and a plot to chance upon Lady Morey's companion. Mr. Seiler was preparing her, she thought to herself as she turned into the corridor of offices. Once the season was over, if the excursion scheme were canceled, he could still find a place for her here at the hotel, something besides a chambermaid or laundress. If she could learn enough and prove herself—

Had she heard her name? She stopped, looked about.

It was Sir Alton.

If a machine has been properly cared for but the carriage
sticks, the trouble almost always is with the dogs.
—*How to Become Expert in Type-writing*

*H*e stood beside one of the half-columns protruding
from the corridor walls, gloves draped over his hand
in a way that reminded her of a portrait, impossible to miss if she'd
been outside her own head a little more. Startled, disconcerted,
Betsey reverted to her years as a housemaid at the Dellafordes' and
curtsied.

Two of the complaint books she was carrying slipped from
under her arm as she did so. She hesitated awkwardly. Was he
greeting her in passing, or did he mean for them to converse?
About what? And oughtn't he offer to collect the books for her?

Involuntarily, her eyes turned to John's closed door.

"I startled you," Sir Alton said. "Such absorption. Head full of
business, Miss Dobson?"

Betsey forced herself to meet his eyes, then glanced down to the
fallen books. And then at Sir Alton again.

This seemed to amuse him. "Allow me, do."

He stooped at her feet. Betsey put out her hands for the books
when he rose, but he held onto them, inspecting the spines.

"Seiler entrusted these to you."

Betsey remained at a loss. The books were not especially confidential; any page in the hotel might have been given the task of returning them to their respective departments. The advantage was Betsey's, that she had the opportunity to move about the hotel and interact with the heads of each department.

"He likes you. Decided to groom you, as it were. He's done so before—he is an excellent judge of potential, generally."

She did not feel safe to thank him for this oblique praise. His smile held as he offered the books. John claimed the ability to interpret the subtleties of Sir Alton's expressions, but she saw nothing in his face to help her deduce his purpose or feelings. She took hold of the books, and was not much surprised when he did not release them. He nodded in the direction of John's door, and a warmth grew in her, as though she'd been caught doing something she oughtn't.

"Jones, for example. He learned well under Seiler's guidance. I've noticed . . . he likes you, too."

A pair of staffers passed on their way down the corridor, assiduously restraining any show of curiosity.

"Rather more than Seiler, even," he added, so very softly.

She guessed he was having a bad time of it, trying to identify what John might find attractive in her. She thought of helping him, thought of dipping her chin and looking out from beneath her lashes, of letting her lips curl, sounding biddable as she spoke his name.

Instead, she pulled the books into her possession, which surprised him. Still, he made the sparest gesture with his arm, and her intention to continue to the office died. She was not dismissed.

"Yes, Jones learned well. And, in turn, has done well for the company, all things considered. I know Web Fawcett thinks so."

Betsey couldn't help it. She frowned at the name, unable to place it with either a face or a reason for Sir Alton to mention it.

"Surely you've heard Mr. Jones mention Web Fawcett? Of Reading? A rather substantial property there he's preparing to develop."

Fawcett was staying at the hotel at present, she remembered. She could have heard the name from John, but also from Mr. Seiler or any of the staff if he were an impressive enough guest.

"He'll need a contractor."

Understanding at last what Sir Alton was after relieved her to some degree, though it provoked her more than anything. She wished she *did* know John's interests regarding Web Fawcett just so she could keep the information from Sir Alton.

Yet she did know something, didn't she? Sarah sometimes sighed over the thought of how Charlie would miss John once he moved on from Idensea. And Betsey witnessed almost daily how he drove himself, his vision relentlessly future-fixed, except for that night on the Sultan's Road. *What if I am sick to the death?*

She knew John—Mr. Jones—had ambitions that would take him from Idensea. She hadn't thought when. She hadn't thought soon. Sir Alton's questions, the mention of a specific position, made it seem *very* soon.

"I suspect you would be as pleased as I," Sir Alton said, "seeing an opportunity like that come to our Mr. Jones. Although, really, he is not quite ready for such a position—"

He stopped as her lips parted, ready to defend John. His eager accommodation made her change her mind and close her mouth.

He sighed. "I confess, I'd come to think of our Mr. Jones as part of Idensea—many of us imagined he was here for a good long while, working for the pier company. It would be good for him. He could marry. . . ."

The lightest pause.

"The company would help him to a house. . . . Perhaps you know Tinfell Cottage? A good house, some property with it. Fine start for a young family . . . should our Mr. Jones decide to stay on."

She could have laughed. If it didn't ache so, if it didn't feel like such a vicious violation that he had guessed her simple, secret dream, she could have laughed, knowing she, of all people, had become useful to Sir Alton.

Perhaps you know Tinfell Cottage?

She didn't give Sir Alton even a nod, but yes, she knew it. Later that afternoon, she went out of her way in order to pass it. The house was let for the season, and the family in residence appeared to be expecting guests for the evening, so standing here before it, she needed no imagination at all to see it occupied, humming with life. She imagined anyway. She dreamed in a way she had not since Thomas Dellaforde had allowed his mother to strike her a second time; she dreamed wildly and without boundaries.

John had taught her about such things. Mr. Jones and his mad railway tacked up on a wall, Mr. Jones and his fanciful notion that a type-writer girl was something else altogether.

She was in love with him. Soon he would be gone, off after his *someday*, and she was in love with him.

"My God, what a mess."

Noel Dunning picked his way through a stack of building materials, pausing beside a tall crate of terra-cotta tiles. He lifted one tile out and studied it briefly before casting a glance up to the Kursaal, where the tile would soon become part of the frieze over the main entrance. "And you still entertain illusions of having it all done by August?"

John finished his count of pallets and signed the receipt before he answered. "You'll see." The tiles had arrived a week early, the skating rink floor would be finished tomorrow, and all things seemed possible today.

"I won't, actually." Dunning shrugged as John frowned at him. "That's why I'm here, to trade farewells."

He sounded so wistful, John knew at once he meant something more than another one of his jaunts to London or house parties in the countryside.

"I'm being sent away. That is, I'm being given a wonderful opportunity I've done nothing to deserve, so I'm given to understand. Father got a story, remarkably accurate given the roundabout fashion it came to him, but—ah, he didn't mention it, I suppose? That I'd been playing a music hall?"

John gestured toward the Kursaal. "I would have recommended he book you here if he had."

"Dreadful little dive. In Hoxton. We were there as spectators, just larking, you know. Some fellow—obviously a devoted patron of the arts—expressed his dissatisfaction with the show by chucking a chair over the pianist's head. Knocked him cold, and, well, what could be done?"

"The show must go on," John agreed.

"It was a lark. Penny—Lord Penderson—all but carried me down to the stage. No harm done, naught but a foolish lark that first night."

"First."

"It was near a week before the pianist was fit enough to return. What could be done?" Dunning attempted a careless smile. "The reek of the place is still in my suits. Can you imagine what it's like to play somewhere like that, knowing you might be clubbed in the skull should they take a disliking to you?"

"You weren't clubbed, by the looks of you."

"No. I was not." He reached inside his coat and repeated, "I was not."

Dunning offered his cigarette case, but John nodded toward the crates surrounding them, all of them packed with sawdust.

"Right. Sorry." Dunning snapped the case shut. "So I am bound for the Continent, it seems. Stepmother has convinced Father to let me study with a master in Vienna. Father studied under him, back when he cared about such things. I'm to be given a half year to study, a half to do something respectable with whatever I learn, and I'm to be very happy and grateful."

He didn't say why he was not. John supposed there was a world of difference between playing an East End music hall and studying with a European master, but still, it seemed a concession on Sir Alton's part, one that once would have pleased Dunning.

"And you'll miss the opening of the Kursaal?"

"You mean the one aspect of Father's business that mildly interests me? Yes. I'm leaving within the week. Sir Alton wishes to have the twelvemonth done as soon as possible, I think. It will bring me back to Idensea all the earlier, you see, and I shall have all this nonsense behind me."

"Surprised he may find himself, a year gone."

Dunning accepted the encouragement with bleak graciousness. "You're kind, Jones. Better than I deserve from you." He broke off with an uneasy hesitation, and John wondered if he meant to bring up Lillian Gilbey's musicale.

But Dunning blinked rapidly and seemed to change course, brightening with a suggestion. "What about a drive?"

John looked over his shoulder to where Dunning's conveyance awaited, a high, fast stanhope hitched to Alouette, possibly the finest filly in Idensea, neither like anything commonly at John's disposal. Even if John had carried any grudge against Dunning, it was not a bad peace offering. And though paperwork awaited him at the hotel, his day here was nearly done. Dunning waited while John tied off a few loose ends, and soon they were clipping along the lane, John at the reins, anticipating Hawkshaw Road.

"Do you know," Dunning said, "we'd started working on the most horrid little operetta, Nash and I—you remember that fellow, the one I carried to London for you?"

With a response that was not quite human language, John indicated that he did indeed remember Avery Nash.

"I know, he isn't a favorite with you, nor with Father, provided Father ever knew his name. But what a dull ride it would have been, all the way to London without a word passing between us. And as it happens, the man has a knack for the sentimental lyric and witty rhyme."

"He's well, then? In health?"

"Oh, I believe so." Dunning seemed surprised by this inquiry, as was John himself. But if Betsey had one lingering concern for Avery Nash, it was whether her choices had left him in danger of sickening again. "From my observation, quite so. Hiring himself out to a number of theaters, I think, type-writing scripts . . ."

He trailed off as John turned on to Hawkshaw Road. Ahead lay a clean stretch and not so much as a pony cart in sight. John slapped the reins and let them slack, and felt the glory of Alouette's freedom. Over the wind and the noise of the stanhope's wheels, both he and Dunning whooped.

Someone walking a cycle had the greater wisdom or courtesy or outright fear, and moved off the lane well before they passed. "Let Alouette take it!" Dunning shouted, as though worried John would pull the reins. John didn't need the encouragement. They flashed past the waiting cyclist, John realizing in the moment that it was Betsey standing there.

He brought Alouette to a stop more gently than was his impulse, Dunning cursing him all the while. Up at Tinfell Cottage, four children stared, and at the door, a housekeeper was glaring her disapproval. John touched his hat in apology, then dropped the reins in Dunning's lap as he stood in the gig, turned round, and called to Betsey.

She had already continued on her way, walking her bicycle. She turned when she heard her name.

"Anything the matter?"

She looked about, and John could feel her distaste for shouting back at him on a public road, at least with witnesses. How he wanted her tire to be flat. But she waved that she was fine and moved on.

"I'd better see to her," John said. He shook his head when Dunning offered the carriage—one of the three of them would be without a seat, and there was the bicycle, too.

"The operetta Nash and I were working on . . ." Dunning said as John hopped down. "We'd been speaking with that music hall owner about it. It seemed . . . well, I couldn't help thinking all the while how it should make you laugh, Jones."

John didn't know whether Dunning meant the operetta itself or his choice of collaborator, which would surely have caused his father to implode and didn't bring John's heart any great warmth, either. John decided to err on the side of generosity, assuring Dunning, "Traveled to any reeking music hall in Britain, I would have, to hear it."

Dunning accepted John's hand. "It is more than I deserve," he said, repeating himself.

Nothing was the matter with her bicycle, Betsey insisted; she'd only felt like walking for a bit. "Walking seemed safer," she added while he was sitting on his heels, inspecting her tires and chain. "Lunatics drive this road, I've heard."

"And a lonely stretch it has, too." He gave her an eye as he rose off his heels. "It's not your way home."

"I can get there this way."

There was a brief tussle over custody of the bicycle. She gave in too easily, he sensed, was avoiding looking at him. As they walked along, she admitted she was not yet headed to Sarah's but had to place an order at the bookshop for Mr. Seiler and pay a call on the photographer who would be taking the picture of the Duke on the Sultan's Road, two errands which made her route by Hawkshaw Road a more puzzling detour.

Her determination to look nowhere but ahead made it easier to steal glances. He might have become a master pickpocket by now, had he applied all this practice of slyness to purses rather than Betsey's person. Then again, just this week Charlie Elliot had walloped him with the football and crossly asked whether he intended to play or watch Betsey hang her laundry.

The Esplanade, he promised himself. At the Esplanade, he would leave her to her errands; he would go to his office and do his paperwork.

Beneath the brim of her straw hat, her cheeks were pink. She was too hot in her tweed suit. He was too hot in his own suit. It was a hot day, very hot.

At the Esplanade, he suggested a water ice and waited for her outside the photographer's studio. The ices were sold at the refreshment stand all the way at the head of the pleasure pier, and when she pointed out, "We'd have to pay the pier toll in order to be able to buy the ice," he laughed, though it might have been wiser to hide how she delighted him, ever surprising him by being precisely herself. He convinced her that as it had been his idea in the first place, the fair thing was for him to pay the toll.

"I shall buy my own ice," she warned.

"Mine will you buy. And I yours."

Her eyes rolled, and he saw the start of her smile before she ducked her head. They left her bicycle with the photographer. John walked with his hands clasped behind him.

Really, it made no difference whether his paperwork was done now or a few hours from now, and this walk with Elisabeth Dobson seemed even more urgent when he discovered that in all the time she'd lived in Idensea, she'd never strolled the pier before. "The view from the Esplanade doesn't cost a cent," she explained as he fished his pockets at the tollhouse, but he heard the doubt in her voice, as though his shock that she'd never done this made her wonder what she had missed. He wanted to kiss her forehead. He himself had come onto the pier only for work or the sake of someone else's entertainment, but how shameful that Betsey had passed by nearly every day and denied herself the fun of it.

"Show me what coins you have," he said, and received a sort of suspicious, magic-beans compliance in return. He held her open hand and used a finger to sort the coins on her palm, pushing all of the ha'pennies and a few pennies together. The others he scooped up and placed in her other hand.

"Back in your pocket, these. And these"—he moved four ha'pennies into the valley of her palm—"you owe to me for an ice."

"Owe you!" But her eyes danced.

"And the rest? What plans had you for them?"

"Only to cast them into the fountain in front of the Swan Park."

He removed a penny for her pocket. "One wise wish is best." Five pennies remained. "Now, you. Choose a pleasure."

She let him close her fingers over the coins. He watched as she surveyed the pier, the vendors with their trays of postcards and rock and false pearls, the penny-in-the-slot machines offering views through a spyglass or cards imprinted with riddles (*How can you make your trousers last? Make your shirt and coat first*). Farther down sounded the delighted screeches of young girls trying the Shocking Scot, the most ridiculous application of electric power John knew—a penny deposited into the Scotsman's mouth would cause his eyes to glow and provide a mild shock as you held his proffered hand. At the pier head, they'd find a fortune-teller, a chalk artist who rendered her subjects as merfolk or Greek deities, and a minstrel show.

But Betsey's interest lay closer at hand, at the booth promising ASTOUNDING, ALL-MOVING VIEWS OF LIFE.

"I've always been curious about the camera," she said. "What is it like?"

"A charm like a fairy's whistle." After the girders and struts that held the structure itself against the tides, the camera obscura was his favorite feature of the pier. "And plenty of sun, still, to make it worth your while today."

Betsey considered the coins in her hand. Then she went to her pocket for that last penny. "I have admission for two."

Nothing had changed, John told himself as the camera keeper let them in. If Betsey's manner toward him seemed different, it was the effect of place, this spontaneous holiday they'd allowed themselves. Or it was Betsey herself who had changed, and it was not his doing, because he had been careful. Whenever she was looking, he had been a careful, perfect gentleman.

He pointed out the lens in the roof, explained the physics of the image it projected into the dark booth, unable to stop himself from peacocking. He heard her delighted gasp as he used the handles above to maneuver the lens, changing the views projected onto the round, plaster-topped table: The tram loading passengers on the Esplanade, with the old part of Idensea peeking up from behind the shops and the bandstand, a colored postcard come to life. Then the foreshore, looking like a slapdash job of tiling, so many umbrellas and blankets hiding the sand. Now here came the pier where the camera stood, chockablock with tourists in cream-colored serge. Then the sea itself, bright and alive and dry on Betsey's palms.

"There, girl. All the world in your hands, just as you'd like it."

She wiggled her fingers. She had removed her gloves before putting her hands into the spill of light, a childlike action that pierced his heart.

"You are the one who wants the world."

It was so, he remembered, but just now, it felt the world went no farther than the thin walls of the camera, and held nothing but a shaft of light and the heat of summer and skin.

"You try," he said, and guided her hands up to the handles so she could control the lens. The world on the table tilted. For the first time since that clumsy dance, he touched her body and permitted his hand to rest on her back. The tiny shelter of the camera seemed to hold all the day's heat in it, turned it thick and dark and suffused it with the scent of her, of them together.

She brought the lens to rest on the pavilion at the head of the pier, then looked up from the table, eye to eye with him. The sea rolling on the tabletop shimmered in her pupils.

"Will I be the first girl you've kissed in here?"

Yes, he nearly answered. Here at the small of her back, her tweed jacket felt damp. He wanted to snake his fingers under the hem, under everything, dip his fingertips in the pool at the base of her spine.

He dropped his arm to his side. His thumb touched along each damp pad of his fingers.

"I'll not kiss you, Elisabeth." His whisper penetrated the commotion on the pier, just beyond the walls of the camera. "Kiss you back, that's what."

"Mm," she scoffed, an inch from his face.

He moved away, sitting upon the table in a wash of restless blue light. "Come with it, if you'll have it."

He counted the centuries before she moved between his knees.

She flipped his hat to the ground, ran her fingers in the sweat along his hairline. Then she put her mouth there, drew her lips lightly along that damp, salty line. His arms ached with tension of holding them down, not clutching at her when she drew back.

She put her fingertips to her lips. "Come with it," he repeated, and she came and licked the moisture above his lip, and it was enough, and his patience was spent. He caught her, finding that damp spot on her back again and pressing her close, nudging his mouth to cover hers, tasting salt, scalding his tongue: He kissed her back. Until they both were puddles of desire and the camera keeper was pounding at the door, he kissed her back.

Alphabet sentence: Pack my box with five dozen liquor jugs.
—How to Become Expert in Type-writing

*O*utside the camera, in the violence of the sunlight, he felt like something just ladled out of a boiling pot. Betsey herself appeared rather unfocused, and after a moment of gazing at him, during which her lips were parted in the most dizzying way, she made for the railing and leaned into the wind, as a seasick steamer passenger might have done.

She was not ill. She shook her head to his inquiry.

"It is only—"

The wind whipped the tendrils of hair about her face into a froth.

"Well, I won't forget it, that's all."

Then she told him to put on his hat. He supposed she thought his grin smug.

They bought lemon water ices and he made her laugh when he insisted they make proper gifts of the treat and trade with each other. One of the shelters built into the railing shielded them from the wind, and Betsey admitted the view of Idensea from the pier head was worth paying for at least once.

The ice and the bite of lemon reddened her lips. Fresh and tart, that was how she would taste now.

"You still want me to go to bed with you."

John stabbed at his ice, gulped down a mouthful that stung his teeth. "No."

"You have never lied to me before."

"I meant . . ." It confounded him, her directness in such matters. "A vow I made, not to press you."

"A vow?" Now she was confounded. "To—?"

He shrugged. "Either one of us."

"And if you didn't have to press?"

You mean if you chose me.

"You'd still want me."

He shoveled the remaining spoonfuls of ice into his mouth. He turned up the dish and drained the melted portion.

"How much?"

Bless God.

"Enough to marry me?"

Bless—

She laughed. "Don't look so worried, Mr. Jones. Both of us know that answer. Sir Alton, however, does not."

"*Sir Alton?* "

"Do you know how anxious he is to see you settled in Idensea?"

"The Kursaal finished, I'll be seeking a new position, and he knows that."

"You might be persuaded to stay, he believes, and . . . he has enlisted my aid. I seduce you well enough, you'll be quite satisfied here in Idensea with your little wife and pier company job and bit of property."

John tried to imagine the circumstances of this tactical meeting between Betsey and Sir Alton and, wildly, pictured the two of them at opposite ends of the long dining table at Iden Hall. He wondered if Sir Alton could have possibly been as blunt with Betsey as she was being right now. And Sir Alton knowing: Miss Dobson. An uneasy cushion to settle upon there.

Another detail niggled at him. "Property. Out on Hawkshaw Road?"

At last something in this conversation embarrassed her. "That's not why I was there."

"There was something to do with it."

"Only curiosity. I wanted to see the house again. I was curious why it—"

He watched her struggle with her embarrassment, recognized that rare shyness as it nearly overcame her.

"Why it wouldn't be enough for someone. For you."

She thought it should be enough. So did Sir Alton. No doubt many would, perhaps even most, even his mother, whose pride had always been tinged with sorrow for his distance from home, and his father, who tolerated his son's ambitions first as a passing phase, then from a decided, if respectful, distance.

He threw out an arm to frighten a gull perched on the railing nearby, felt grimly satisfied when it flew away.

Betsey had lifted her eyes. He met them.

"I'm only letting you know what he's about," she said.

"Kissed me, you did."

"Tell me what you think that means."

He studied the deck planks at their feet. Of course he did not believe her in league with Sir Alton.

A boy with a tray approached them. "Drink up what is left," John told her when he saw she'd let the water ice melt, little more than half-finished. She hesitated but then took her dish back from the tray and drank from it. She caught a drip on her chin with the back of her wrist. She might as well have put her hand between his thighs.

It seemed she read his dark thoughts. It seemed she kept similar ones.

"You haven't much longer in Idensea," she said. "By my reckoning, neither have I."

With alarm, he realized she was near tears. As though she were alarmed herself, she stood and hurried from the shelter, her agitation matched with her wind-tangled skirts.

She assumed Sir Alton would dismiss her once it was clear

she'd failed in her charge to keep him in Idensea. A credible assumption, John thought. Even if the board eventually decided to carry on with the excursion scheme next summer, Sir Alton could still force Tobias to hire someone else to manage it. Perhaps Tobias could put her in some other position, but still, Sir Alton had the final authority. He could dismiss Betsey from the pier company altogether.

"I ought've held on to that penny for the fountain," she said when he caught up with her, and made a point of showing her face to him: She had *not* cried, nor would she.

"Bless God, Elisabeth, this job is not your last chance."

He could have raised a hand to her and not received such an expression of disbelieving shock. He could have been Brutus with the dagger and been more fondly regarded.

He'd said nothing wrong. He felt certain she needed to hear it. "It isn't. It isn't even the best you can hope for. Of type-writing, you said that, and it wasn't true, nor is it true now."

"It seemed a good occupation until I inherit my title and fortune."

"Don't mock."

"Please do forgive me, Mr. Jones. I meant no offense, I'm sure."

She curtsied. An unholy urge to hurl her over the railing into the sea lit through him.

"Yourself, girl. I meant do not mock yourself."

She stared. He watched her turn both fierce and small, holding on while something cracked.

"I *wanted* it. You—of everyone—you should understand."

He didn't protest that he did understand, which suited Betsey. She only would have argued, despite her suspicion that she'd be wrong. Instead, as they parted ways at the photographer's studio, he said he wanted to take her someplace Saturday night—after her dinner dance had concluded, naturally.

She agreed first, asked "Where?" second. He still hadn't told her by the time they cycled away from the hotel Saturday night. They went in the direction opposite The Bows to a seaside tavern whose sign read "Sundial Public House & Pleasure Garden." Inside, he was greeted—*Jones* with and without the *Mister,* a female voice or two amongst them, a mere wary nod here and there. The place was crowded, marked by cheer rather than rowdiness.

All who spoke to John seemed to note her presence with him, and her uniform made her even more conspicuous. Too late to worry, she told herself, and relished this brief surrender, the feel of her hand swallowed up in his, her way eased by the path he cut from the entrance to a rear door that led to a garden lit by torches and oil lamps, where night-blooming flowers and damp grass thickened the scent of ale. The music she'd heard as they approached on their cycles was coming from here, a fiddler and flutist under a vine-covered pergola, dancers turning on a floor of simple flagstone.

A woman wearing a bright-striped apron and a matching cap called to John, directing him to an available place at one of the long tables in the garden, promising someone named Katie would be there soon. They shared the same rustic bench, which on another night of the week might have been for one rather than two.

Katie was a girl less than Charlie's age, and she narrowed her eyes at John after she had taken their order. "This cannot be your London lady," she accused, because even little Katie knew this was no place for a girl like Lillian Gilbey.

"You must be a regular," Betsey observed wryly upon Katie's departure.

But John shook his head. "Not so often. Some of my laborers, those men."

Which explained the wary nods, though not Katie's knowledge of his personal affairs.

"What were you thinking, bringing me here?"

"That you ought to see it."

The answer carried some gravity with it, but she didn't understand why. She rested her elbows on the table and looked about.
The name "Pleasure Garden" was perhaps more an aspiration
than actuality, for it was less than an acre in size, and aside from
the dancing area, a quoits pitch, and a bowling green, it had none
of the diversions or meandering paths one expected in a pleasure
garden. A hedge bounded the far line of the property, striking not
only for its height but also because it had been trimmed to mimic a
crenellated castle wall, casements and doorways sculpted into the
front. She spotted the namesake sundial on a pedestal nearby, in
danger of losing its prominence amongst the clutter of long tables
and benches.

In all, it was a more modest and less formal version of the dinner dance she'd just closed at the Swan's pavilion. The thought
made her smile, and she resisted the temptation to lean back into
John's chest. She felt him all along the left side of her body, and
with her chin in her hand, she turned her face to him.

He was already looking at her. "What think you, Dobs?"

"I feel like—"

Like one of my excursionists, she was about to say, but the thought
halted her. She straightened up from the table, her mind grasping
at a butterfly of an idea. Now she knew why John had brought her
here.

"I should find a new place for the excursionists," she said.

The woman in the striped apron brought their pints. Mrs.
Gomery, John said—"the Sundial's proprietor, Katie's mum, and
Ethan Noonan's sister. 'Twas Ethan what did all the hedges you
see here."

Knowing the fanciful hedge-trimming was the work of the
drunken char-à-banc driver made it all the more remarkable to
Betsey. "Ah, you know my brother," Mrs. Gomery said, as if she
understood this fact to be a stumbling block to any relationship she
and Betsey might have otherwise cultivated following this introduction.

"Miss Dobson manages the excursions scheme for the Swan Park," John explained.

"And is he doing any good for you, Miss Dobson? You can say the story blunt, now."

"He's never failed to bring the char-à-banc," she replied. "And has been sober enough to drive it on perhaps more than half the occasions."

Mrs. Gomery seemed pleased enough with this report. She ordered John to the dancing area, but both he and Betsey shook their heads at each other the moment her back turned.

Betsey took a sip of her ale. "What about the Kursaal? The ballroom there once it is finished, or is there some other space suitable for the dinner dances? Perhaps if everything was off hotel property—"

But John was shaking his head. "A part of the pier company, the Kursaal."

"But here? It looks as if Mrs. Gomery and her husband wouldn't—"

"Mrs. Gomery's the sole proprietor. A widow she's been since Katie was a babe, I think."

"Well, she has plenty of business on a Saturday. She'd have to close to the public to host excursions. Why would she want to?"

He shrugged. "She wouldn't, perhaps, unless more money could be made. But the Sundial is not the only place in Idensea." He watched her over the rim of his pint as he took a swallow. "And Idensea is not the only place in the world."

Just the only place she wanted to stay. Idensea was the first place since her mother's house that she hadn't struggled to leave, hoping for something better.

Still, John's idea merited some consideration. Did he realize it meant she would be on her own, out from under Sir Alton's thumb, to be sure, but also without the hotel's considerable resources? He must, but did he truly believe she was up to such a challenge?

"Pang in my side," he murmured as she stared at him, thinking, *He did.*

"What's that?"

"In my dad's pub I used to hear it. An old Welsh poem. *Girl who struck this pang in my side, the girl I want and wanted always—*"

He broke off to take a hasty quaff. Betsey reached up and put her hands around the glass, and he let her pull it from his mouth and set it aside.

"Why don't we . . . ?" she suggested.

He nodded. They quit the pub like its thatched roof was ablaze. As John shut the door behind him, his other arm pulled her to him, and, mouths together, they stumbled around the corner of the pub, into the shadows of shrubbery and thick curtains of ivy. The leaves tickled her ears and neck as she moved her mouth with his, following, luring, a dance of endless discovery. Every time his tongue stroked her, she felt it deep and low, and she pushed her head farther into the ivy, against the wall, opened her mouth wider, so she could have him deeper, more of him inside her.

A labored, suppressed groan escaped him. He moved his lips from hers only far enough to allow speech, half-formed words upon her skin. "The sky's clear and bright as jewels tonight."

"Mm-mm." Her tongue toyed with his bottom lip. She couldn't remember what the sky looked like. She could open her eyes right now and probably not be able to find it.

"There is magic to bathe under the moon. Have you ever?"

"I don't know." What did he mean? What was the moon? She pressed kisses under his jaw. "I don't know how to swim."

"Made for it, girl." In one slow, insistent caress, he passed his hand over her thigh, and up and up until he'd splayed the length of her arm and each finger against the wall behind them. "Mind and body." He matched the spread of her fingers with his and started a path of kisses at the bend of her elbow. "Will you come?"

Her daze took a giddy turn as she watched him, anticipating his arrival at her earlobe. Would she go swimming with him? He kissed her neck and she giggled, the delight of sensation, the delight in his effort. Creating excuses to get her out of her clothes.

He didn't know. He didn't know she'd decided, that she'd known on Hawkshaw Road.

There'd be no one like him again, not for her. He was going away, and she wouldn't try to stop him. But before that happened, she would lie down with him. She would take what was here, what was now.

Nobody wants slovenly work, smutty pages, bad spelling,
or sentences made senseless by the careless omission of
words.

—*How to Become Expert in Type-writing*

They went along a little lane Betsey had never traveled
before. John stowed their bicycles in the brush, then
led her down a path, steep and narrow, but too well-defined to be
abandoned.

"People come down this way," Betsey said, picking her way
down in the darkness, her hand in his.

"The locals know it. But this time of night, none will come."

It was a cove, lit by the moonlight, secluded and loud with the
sea's roar. Betsey paused at the bottom of the path to take it in, this
place John had chosen for them, perfect and wild this night. She
wondered how well he knew it, if he'd brought other women here.
She wondered who they might have been. Not the Miss Gilbeys
he'd sought, of course, but others?

She followed his lead, pausing to remove her boots when he
did. Then he surprised her, throwing off his cap and coat, undress-
ing with no preamble, his back to her. It was a disappointing sort
of surprise, but she unpinned her straw hat and cast it, along with
the disappointment, into John's growing pile of clothing.

He noticed it and turned to her, throwing away his shirt, then standing quite still. How beautifully the moonlight touched his shoulders. She went to him and ran a hand along the ripples of his bare arm, pressed a kiss above the neckline of his under-vest, pushed it up, and he removed it. A pause, then she turned her back to him.

Nothing for a moment, though she could hear him breathing. Not until she tilted her head over her shoulder did he touch her, helping her out of her fitted jacket. Another pause when she faced him again, but then his fingers touched the top button of her vest. She watched him work down the column, and something made her think of her nephew Francis, his quiet and solid concentration when he tried to manage his bootlaces on his own.

John kissed her mouth as he pushed her vest open and down from her shoulders. "Come to the water when you've finished," he said, and then he headed in that direction himself, still in his drawers. He waded in, launched himself over a wave, and disappeared.

Betsey rushed down, her heart tight even though she knew he would be fine. He resurfaced what seemed a far distance away, his face a spot of light in the water. He disappeared again and bobbed up closer to the shore.

"You can't come in like that," he called.

Betsey looked down at her uniform, the pleats in the skirt catching the wind like a fan. "I believed the swimming lesson to be a ruse."

"I've not got any of those. Undress and come, you. I want you to feel the sea."

She looked again at the path they'd just come down.

"No one," he said. "I'll turn my back."

And unbelievably, he did. It made her feel suddenly shy, and she rushed to remove her shirtwaist and loosen the tapes of her skirts. She was stepping out of a pillowy ring of fabric when she realized he was watching her.

"You cheat."

"Bless God, like a colt you are, those legs."

She looked down at herself and decided John intended a compliment. She held his gaze as she unbuttoned her corset cover, and then, because he was transfixed and she found that intoxicating, she drifted her fingers along the top and over the curves of her corset before she removed it.

"Your hair down, won't you?"

"You know it is cut off."

"I want to see it loose."

Her hairpins were lost to the sand, without a care for the cost to replace them. Regarding her clothing, however, she was more practical: She placed everything safely away from the surf.

"Will you come, then?" John asked. He rose, the water falling down to his waist, the skin of his arms and shoulders like polished metal as he came toward her. Betsey took the hand he extended, and for the first time since she'd been a tiny girl, she entered the sea. Her underclothes seemed to disintegrate in the chill of the water, eaten up by the waves that bewildered her body, but John wrapped his arm around her waist, cupped her head in his hand, and she felt more secure.

He would have kissed her. She touched his lips to slow him, saying, "Let's decide."

"Very well. Tell me what needs deciding."

"How many times. From tonight until you leave for your new position, how many times shall we—" She hesitated as all her usual terminology failed her. "How many times shall we lie together?"

He continued to hold her but didn't answer, either scandalized or calculating.

"Only this once?" she said, and smiled at his malcontented grunt. "Thank you for that compliment. Your suggestion, then."

Another grunt. "I haven't a job yet, even. Why must a number be put to it?"

She huddled against him, chilled standing here in the water as it beat against her thighs. "We'll know when it's done." It wouldn't become blurred, like with Avery, or blindside her, as with Thomas. Knowing the end was to let him go would hack the head off Sir

Alton's bribe; it would pierce that terrible inflation of hope she'd felt standing outside Tinfell Cottage.

"And we have to take care," she added. "I'll not look jilted when it's all done."

Suddenly, he released her and ducked into the waves. Betsey's fear was intense and instant, no matter that only a moment passed before she felt his hands take hers. He let go to push his hair off his face, then took them again and urged her farther into the sea.

"Deeper now, will you?"

She stiffened. "I want to be able to walk. Touch bottom, I mean."

"I will show you what to do in the deep water," he promised, causing another surge of fear in her as a wave crashed into her shoulder and lifted her off the seafloor. "Tread the water when you can't reach. Like on your bicycle, pedaling, firm about it. Arms, too, back and forth."

She tried it, found it worked, though not to the degree that she had any real faith in it to keep her from drowning. And the waves never stopped—what sort of defense would she have when one finally crashed on top of her?

John praised her, but her courage was failing. "Tell me more of that poem from the pub," she said, with hopes he didn't notice her fear. "The thought of being a pain in your side is so terribly romantic."

He laughed. "Can't remember, not much, so long has it been. And mostly in Welsh I heard it, you know. Take hold." He reached for her and towed her shoreward before an incoming wave hit them. "I remember he speaks to a girl, says for her to meet him on a hillside. Make a bed under the trees. By the ferns." He indicated the water with a nod. "Doesn't suit, does it?"

"No."

"Sweet things he tells her about how she looks."

"Naturally. What does he say?"

"All the Welsh songs I know praise fair girls, golden-haired, rosy-cheeked girls. Not girls like Betsey Dobson." He cocked his head as he regarded her. "I remember he says her breasts are like balls of yarn. Does that suit?"

She thought returning the smile that touched the corners of his mouth would be invitation enough, but after a moment, she guided his hand inside her chemise. His touch was almost studious, as though he searched for the proper poetic description of her breasts, which were nothing like balls of yarn, but then he pulled her close. He boosted her up, and Betsey shuddered and dug her fingers into the base of his neck as his hot tongue chased the numbing chill of the water.

He let her slip down against him. "*Dy gorph hael a'm dug o'r ffydd.*"

"Poetry? Tell me."

"*Her flesh makes me stray from God.*"

That suited too well, Betsey thought, spoke too close to the risk and the longing of this fleeting thing.

"*When she greets me, I will sing psalms of her kisses.*"

A wave nearly pitched them over, and Betsey realized with alarm they'd drifted out again. "I am with you," he promised before she could say anything. "The next one, we will go under with it. A deep breath, and under, and I am with you."

"I'm afraid."

"Still, you will try it." Not an order, that, only something in which he had confidence. He took her hand. "*I will sing psalms of her kisses, seven kisses from the maiden—*"

"I'm not a maiden," she murmured, though here, in the moonlight and relentless sea, her fingers tangled in his, their bodies close and nearly naked, there was something new and untried welling within her.

"Shh," he lulled, and began to chant, "*Seven kisses from the maiden, seven birch trees at the grave, seven prayers for evening, seven the songs from the boughs.*"

The wave hit. Betsey had tried to prepare herself, say it would be like ducking her head in the tub to wash soap from her hair, but once underneath, she knew the naïveté of that. Caught in the power of the wave, suddenly, sharply aware of the openness of the water, she wanted control again. The wave pushed her toward the seafloor and she pushed back with all her might, trying to tear loose from John so she would break the surface more quickly.

She burst to the air choking and gasping for breath, as though she'd been under for minutes rather than moments. Her hair fell in tangles over her face, stinging her eyes. Between blinks, she saw John.

"There is good, girl." He cleared the soaking net of hair from her face. "There's brave. Will you try it again?"

"Yes," she told him, and meant it, but she was trembling when he took her in his arms again, and he didn't make her prove it.

"*Seven stories for a gift, seven pearls and rings,*" he crooned beneath the water's roar.

Her teeth chattered. "Why seven?"

"Don't know. Seven's magic. Odd and even, the boy and the girl. *Seven verses writ in grass, seven times to sigh. Seven hymns for—*" He hesitated. "Her name he says here."

"Little chance it's Elisabeth."

"No matter." Her head was resting on his shoulder, and he kissed her cheek. "*Seven hymns to Elisabeth's firm flesh, seven twenty times. No longer does she lock away the payment owed—*"

Nothing else suddenly. "Owed? To whom?"

He didn't answer, and like a finger snap before her face, she realized he didn't mean to. A wave broke high against his back. He swayed, and water splashed her face. She lifted her head to get her bearing.

"Too far. Too deep," she said, not sure if she wanted to cling to him as a safety or push away again, somehow get herself closer to the shore.

"There's safe. I have you, Elisabeth."

"Please. Go back."

"I'm taking you." He caught her up in his arms and moved them closer to the shore. "Stretch out, now."

She clung more tightly to his shoulders. "What?"

"Rest on the water. I have you."

Rest on the water. Hell. Still, she tried, tried to shove down the fear, tried cautious movements toward straightening her knees. But whenever his hold loosened, she jerked up, tense and uncertain about the gathering waves.

"I have you," he said. "Look you up, the stars and moon."

His hands worked beneath her, encouraging her back and knees to relax. She felt his support, but when water lapped around her face, splashing in her ears and under her chin, she started again.

"Betsey, be easy with me. The simple part this is, nothing for you but to lie back and feel the water, see the stars. Do it, now."

Again and again she tried, each time breaking the pose he wanted her to make, aware of the rising tension in his voice but certain he was misjudging the height and strength of the waves rolling in. Finally, she shoved hard against him and broke free, only to be caught in a swell that filled her mouth with salt water.

John caught her, and she fought against him, coughing, her feet scrambling for a bit of sand, rock, anything. She heard him saying something, shouting perhaps—probably—because she felt herself panicking, and why should she not, for she was drowning now, going under for good, shore and shallows in her sight.

Then, air. She was vaulting through air, and it took her breath as surely as the water had. She hit the water, terrified and insensible, grasping and kicking for purchase until she realized her knuckles scraped the pebbly sand. Knees, too, and she crawled, gasping, to the water's edge.

"You damned idiot!" she swore to the ground. He'd *pitched* her. Still on her hands and knees, she turned back to the water, half-expecting to see him grinning, pleased with himself.

He was too far out yet for her to make out his expression by the moonlight. But he was moving closer, thrashing through the water, his stride creating a white wake.

Betsey leapt up. She bent over and filled her fists and fingernails with the coarse sand—as much pebble and tiny shells as sand—and flung it out to the water. Most of it broke apart and went wildly off course, but some of it struck him, leaving dark splotches on his shoulder and jaw. A pebble glanced off his cheek, and it halted him for a fraction of a moment as he flinched. She could see his face then, terrible and furious, and he came pounding out of the surf at a stride to match.

Betsey ran. She turned, she ran, heading for the path that led up the hill, but losing her footing on the dry ground and falling. John grabbed her ankle, tried to rake her back down toward him. She shook her foot, strained her arms in the opposite direction, but he held her ankle fast, then crawled up over her, breathing hard.

"Bless the bleeding Christ! I want you to be easy with me."

"*What?*"

"I want you to be easy with me, not forever looking at me like—like I'm handing you magic beans, or trying to keep you from getting a good breath. I want—I want you to rest with me, girl, that's all."

"You ought have thrown me a little farther, then, or into the deeper water. I'd be as easy as a corpse just now."

"I know—I frightened you—"

"Get back from me." She elbowed him, and he rolled onto his back with a sigh. Betsey sat up and drew her knees to her chest, shivering in the warm air as she brushed sandy hands across her knees in a vain attempt to remove the dirt on her drawers.

"John, my God," she said after a moment, "here I am in the middle of the night wearing nothing but my underclothes. I don't know that I could be easier."

He made a noise that advanced from sigh to wheeze to full laughter. He stirred beside her, and she felt his head, cold and wet, at her elbow. Like a contrite puppy, he nudged his way beneath her arm to nuzzle against her stomach and breasts. Well, and who could resist a contrite puppy, she thought, and leaned back again.

She closed her eyes as he pushed up her chemise, surrendering to the warm relief of his face against her damp skin. He lay there with his cheek on her belly.

"I pushed you too much."

"The water—it's so . . . big," she said, and laughed a little, for she sounded like a child.

"Not just the water you feared."

She watched the stars, as John had wanted her to do in the water, heard the waves thrashing at the shore, and liked the weight of his head on her stomach, how it grounded her, made her conscious of each breath she drew in and released.

"How many times, then? Let's decide."

His thumb, broad and crusted with sand, stroked up and down her ribs. "Seven twenty times. Seven seventy times."

She smiled, thinking they'd be horizontal for months with figures like that. Even seven times, like that poem of his, was too many. How many times could she afford to multiply her heartbreak?

"Three," she said. "Three."

A sigh crossed her skin. "Do you always negotiate like this?"

"No." She answered promptly, before she noticed how that word *always* had stung her. *Always* because of that list, that catalogue of her lovers she'd supplied him the night on the Sultan's Road, and she hated herself for doing it, hated John for being human enough to remember it.

I've never been so wise before. The comment was curling on her tongue, infused with all the cynical venom at her disposal.

But he spoke first. "Have ever you seen someone in a fever, a fever that takes them away? And they keep asking for things that can't be—people long dead they want, or places far off, no longer there, or secrets out of their dreams nobody understands. They ask and they ask, but nothing none can do for them but pray for the fever to break." He lifted his head. "Bless God, that's what it's like, Elisabeth, wanting you, how I wake up sometimes—"

"You're mad," she said, and drew down his head to her neck, sighing softly as he kissed her there, in all her hollows. "I'm not some aristocrat's daughter, you know, not any lady or heiress. I'm just a girl, and you invited her for a tryst, and she came."

He stopped kissing her and looked her full in the eye. For a long time. She grew self-conscious.

"Elisabeth Dobson you are," he said at last.

"That's right. That's all. So come on and fuck me, John."

It was that or weep, weep for what she thought she heard in his voice, the thing beyond his lust. But he didn't like it. He didn't like her saying what they'd come here to do. He continued to stare down at her, something hard in his face now. She'd never seen it before, and her hard words had put it there, which made her want to weep more.

She reached up to stroke his cheek, soften it again. He caught her hand.

She was afraid to say, *I know you care more than that.* She pushed herself up so she could kiss him, pulled him down with her, kissing his mouth and jaw, sand grating between his skin and hers.

Her kisses came back to her, magnified, hungry. His under-clothes were sopping and cold, but the fever of his body still reached her. They grappled together with her drawers, and his hand ground sand and tiny pebbles against her skin as it touched her thigh and hip. He was sorry, he said, sorry about this place, all the dirt, he hadn't thought . . .

He left off without finishing the apology, positioning himself between her legs. He leaned down and kissed her cheek. "Are you sure I cannot make a babe in you, girl?"

Lizzie, are you quite certain you're barren? That was what Avery Nash had asked her the first few times they had coupled. Perhaps he would have continued to ask if she hadn't tossed his brandy in his face the third time. As John went on in awkward, distracted half sentences, she thought of Avery's question, and was so disconcerted she could only mumble, "I'm sure." So disconcerted, she didn't realize until too late that John was shoving his drawers out of the way, that he intended to enter her right now.

"John," she said. She needed him to slow down.

He didn't seem to hear. She gasped in pain as he thrust inside her. She lifted her hips, hoping at first to signal him with a gentler rhythm, but he took no heed. She tried to match him, desperate to salvage what was going awry. She tried to see his face to confirm this was John, kind and good, but his neck was bent, his face obscured by a wet curtain of hair.

He drove against her, frantic, oblivious, and Betsey didn't have to wait until he was finished to know: She'd been well and truly fucked.

*S*he wanted to wash.

"Turn away," she told a still-panting John, and when he had, she stood and started to tie her drawers together so she wouldn't have to walk to the water half-naked. They were cold and sticky and filthy with sand, however, and in disgust, she finally stripped them off again, muttering, "Hell." She wrapped the garment around her hips as best she could, the skin on the back of her shoulders and arms burning with every movement.

The dark water felt doubly cold now, the waves seemed more violent, but she ventured to water that came to her waist and kept her back to the shore. She unfurled her drawers, trying to clean them, then removed her chemise and rinsed it out as well. Both were ruined, she feared, streaked with dirt she'd never scrub away. The loss made her furious.

Her hair was knotted and filled with grit, and though she hated the thought of being underwater again, she took a deep breath and sank, clutching her clothes in her fist. And somehow the fear was less now, the pull of the waves not so terrifying. She surfaced and slipped down again to hang in the dark muffle of peace.

No longer does she lock away the payment owed—
The payment owed to—

Love. That was the word in the poem John hadn't forgotten, only hadn't wanted to say.

The realization shot her up above the surface.

Or almost. She'd drifted, and now found she could barely scrape the seafloor with her toes. Afraid, she pumped her legs and arms the way John had taught her, pumped and pumped as air fought to get out and come in at once through her throat.

"John." The word limped out pitifully in the wrong direction, out to the wide dark sea.

Nevertheless, he heard her. He was there already, right behind her, sweeping her toward him, towing her back to safety. Her arms and legs wrapped around him, relieved for his solid strength.

"I didn't like it, you out here alone."

She slackened her hold, gritting through a sudden fall of pain on her shoulders. She must have a thousand tiny cuts from the coarse sand, every one of them filled with salt water now. "I was managing."

"Were you? Perhaps you'd best paddle out and fetch your underthings, then."

"Oh!" She twitched around in dismay, catching sight of the ghostly puddle of white that had already drifted far from them. Her best things, and the loan from her brother-in-law that had paid for them still over her head. "Hell and hell. Can't you get them?"

"Half to America they will be by the time I see you safe and then swim out again. But here—" He gripped her in one arm, while the other disappeared under the water. In a moment, he produced his own drawers and tossed them in the direction of hers.

"Wasteful," she chided, but couldn't help smiling at the sight of their underclothes floating off to America together.

·   ·   ·

John tried not to notice his disappointment when Betsey asked him to bring her clothes to her. He told himself the cold had become too much for her, and left her in the surf while he returned to their piles of clothing.

Up by the path, he quickly dried himself with his shirt and tugged on his trousers, then collected her corset and stockings and uniform and all the white garments he could find, and carried them down to the surf. She hesitated, crouched with the water up to her neck.

"Come, you," he said.

She didn't. "Turn away. Please."

He gave his back to her and held out to his side an arm draped with the rather surprising weight of her attire, but he couldn't ignore how it rankled, this shyness from her. They'd been flesh to flesh tonight. And . . .

And plenty of other men had seen her out of her clothes. That rankled, too, and not least because it made him a cur to think of it. He stood looking at the dark path to the road, unable to dismiss the ugly sensation that this modesty in Betsey was something false. She was no maiden, she'd reminded him tonight. She was already ruined, God damn him for thinking it.

He turned. She had put on all her petticoats and had her hand inside her corset, adjusting her breasts, which were nothing like balls of yarn or any other such workaday article. She felt him watching her and looked up with her brows aslant, a shy and wary hellion whose sweet loveliness would never cease taking him by surprise.

He dragged the backs of his fingers along her forehead and cheek. He wanted to say something, apologize, maybe, for slandering her in his thoughts, or ask, *Did I break my vow this night? Somehow is it still intact?*

He pulled her to him for a deep kiss. Briefly, she leaned into him but then pushed away, taking her boots from him and going to the edge of the surf again. All night, this pushing and pulling.

Her petticoats gathered in her arms, she tried to finagle washing the sand from her foot and then getting foot to stocking minus sand and water. She came close to pitching herself into the surf.

"You'll have your boots full of water." He went and scooped her up in his arms, throwing her over his shoulder.

She struggled. "I don't need—"

"Hush, you." He tapped her behind.

He carried her to the rocks near the path and set her down. He fumbled with her stocking—his fingers were full of nerves, touching the thing—and she told him to never mind, she would just have her boots, and she could put them on herself.

John lifted her leg anyway, as certain he could right things as he was they'd gone wrong somewhere along. Her petticoat slipped back past her knee, exposing a long, long length of white flesh. He swallowed and held her boot for her.

"All that cycling," he said as she wiggled her foot into it. "'Elisabeth's firm flesh' was an apt expression."

"One true thing in that poem, I suppose."

His hand drifted over the laces, making him think of her sitting on Sarah Elliot's step, making every crisscross a flat, straight X. Rather than try to imitate such precision, he bypassed the laces altogether and let his fingers graze the skin of her calf, then over her knee and to the inside of her thigh. Betsey's face turned up to the sky, eyes shut, bottom lip between her teeth. She was lithe and lovely, and he hadn't touched her nearly enough before.

"I want to take you to my bed. You in my bed, girl, the night entire."

"And in the morning?"

He felt her quiver under his touch. It turned his brain like a top, that twitch of her muscles, that hitch in her breathing. "Fine as well. Betsey in my bed, morning, noon, and night."

"You know that isn't what I mean." She moved his hand away and leaned over to lace her boots. "I suppose it oughtn't happen again, anyway."

He said nothing while she tidied each X. The task took quite a while.

"Why tonight, then?"

"I wanted it."

"But you don't now."

"No." Standing, she reached for her skirt and tossed it over her head. She adjusted it and fastened the tapes, sure and hard, like a sailor securing the mainsail. "You should be glad."

"No doubt you're right, girl. Just tell me for what I'm glad so I get it right in my thanksgiving prayers."

"You don't have to worry about me wanting too much. Falling in love and all that."

He stared as she slipped on the little waistcoat to her uniform. Her fingers sprinted down the column of buttons.

She shrugged. "That's why you stopped."

"Stopped . . ."

"*No longer does she lock away the payment owed to* love—isn't that the rest of it? You didn't answer me because you didn't want to say it."

Poetry was the undoing of it all? She wanted to throw him over because he'd stumbled over a line of *poetry*?

But no, it was because of where he'd stumbled. He couldn't think why he'd hesitated, it was so trivial, except it had surprised him, had come sneaking onto his tongue almost before he could do anything about it.

"A trifling verse is all it is."

"Yes, just a trifling verse, and you might have finished with no consequence. I'm not so far gone for you that I'd have thought you meant a promise by it."

"Thanks, there," he muttered. Not so far gone for him. *You gave yourself to me tonight.*

"John. You're kind. You meant to keep from hurting me, I know, but you didn't have to. We had it settled, didn't we? I knew what we were about. Still, I—" Her direct gaze, her direct words faltered. She toyed with the lower buttons on her vest. "I believed you'd come to care for me, in some way, and that would make it different. But it . . . it was rather . . . worse, so . . . I think we'd just best forget it, all right?"

That word—*worse*—lifted the lid on John's overboiling brain, cooled his protests and questions. *Worse*. This, he understood as perfectly as anything he'd ever understood in his life, was his cue to agree, right, just forget it, to part, quickly, and to bury this moment, this night, in a deep, anonymous, worm-riddled grave.

There was something he wanted more, however, which was for a moment like this to never happen to him again, and so in a voice nearly as low as his pride, he said, "Explain *different*."

She shrugged, as though it had cost him nothing to ask this, as though she were about to enlighten him on nothing more interesting or urgent than balls of yarn. "I don't know. Like with Thomas, I suppose is what I mean."

Thomas. Thomas Dellaforde. John almost spat, remembering the name, the only one she'd spoken with longing that night on the pleasure railway. He grabbed up his boots, the gesture so impatient that Betsey could not fail to notice his disdain.

"He loved me," she said evenly. "He showed it when—when we were together." She cleared her throat, but her voice was still husky as she added, "I want it again."

Betsey Dobson, *in tears*. For Thomas Goddamned Dellaforde. She'd told him, one of those late evenings at Sarah's, about Goddamned Dellaforde. Begun, at least. The conversation lost its way, ran over a cliff, and died an ugly death when he'd discovered she'd been a fourteen-year-old maid in the Dellaforde household and Thomas Goddamned Dellaforde the master's son, five years older than she.

"I know you—I know it isn't the same," she rushed to add, her voice clearer. "We aren't in love, but I'd believed—I'd thought it was not just to get a poke in."

"Bless the bleeding Christ!" His voice was a crushing implosion, restraining his impulse to shake the filth from her lips. "What do you think your Thomas was doing? He couldn't have loved

you! Not how you believe! Bless the bleeding Christ, Elisabeth,
you were scarce more than a child, and he—he was using you, he
took advantage. He thought it the privilege of his position and he
took advantage—don't you see it after all this time?"

"His position? Over me, you must mean."

He was *not* a hypocrite. In the pause that followed her comment, he worked on some way to articulate why not, but finally
said, "Out on the street you were put, nothing to your name, and
he let it happen!"

"Such things happen every day, don't you know it?"

"Not to you!"

He'd shouted. It startled her, and he was gratified to see that
infuriating cool of hers disturbed, how she stepped back in alarm.
Because he was mad. He could feel it; he didn't blame her for
thinking it. Standing barefoot on a midnight shore, in a rage over
events ten years past, having just coupled in the dirt with a woman
not his wife, John was well aware that somewhere along the way
he'd left his sanity behind like an umbrella or the morning paper.
He threw his boots to the ground, then dropped down beside them
to put them on.

Betsey spoke carefully, as one should to a madman. "You
understand . . . what I meant?"

It all depended on to what she referred. He supposed he'd
grasped the key point, that apparently—and it took him a few long
moments to wrestle with this, to confront it in his mind—*apparently*, he was a damn poor lover. Or at least inferior to Thomas G.
Dellaforde, and he held that complete stranger in such contempt
he could hardly bear to be second to him.

And was he even second? He searched his memory for the
names of the other men, trying to determine where exactly he
might rank. There was Nash, of course, but surely he was no competition. Surely? And the others . . .

But it didn't matter. He didn't care if he was second, third, or
thirtieth. It only mattered that he wasn't first.

And that Betsey thought him a poor lover.

What sort of woman told a man *that*?

He stood, put on his coat and cap, avoided her eyes, muttered "I do" as he moved past her and started up the path. He heard her behind him, struggling with the uneven, uphill way, and turned back to offer a begrudging hand. The one she held out to him clutched her stockings. He grabbed her wrist and pulled her over the roughest patch, up to where he stood, not bothering with a jot of the solicitude he'd employed in helping her down. They shared the same scrap of earth and air for a moment, and John wanted—suddenly and very much—to press one or two of his fingers to her lips.

The next moment, he understood why.

"And you won't hold me to two more times?" she asked.

Moral: Do not let paper scrapings get into the machine.
But if they do, brush them out carefully.

—*How to Become Expert in Type-writing*

He let loose her wrist so fast she nearly stumbled backward. She reached out for a sapling, dropping her stockings on the ground.

In his best business voice, he answered, "I assure you, Miss Dobson, you are released from your contract."

He left her to manage how she might. She was good at that, managing.

Once on his bicycle, he forced himself to pedal away at a rate that would not leave her too far behind. Still, she had to have pedaled rather madly to catch up with him as quickly as she did. She matched his speed for a long stretch of the road, a rather impressive show of strength considering she was calling to him all the way, ordering him to stop in a quashed voice that obviously longed to be riding a wave of air, screaming to rouse the residents of every cottage they passed. John kept pedaling.

"John, you stop now, or—"

And then she hushed. Because she was putting all her energy into passing him, he realized, as she began to edge ahead. And though who held the lead was only a childish difference, though it mattered only that he got her to Sarah Elliot's as quickly as possible, he sped up, too. But not for nothing was that firm flesh he'd noted tonight. She moved ahead, and just as John was preparing for another hard push, she veered in front of him.

John swerved hard to the left and thought he'd missed her, but in the next instant, his rear wheel clipped hers. He heard her go down with a grunt and the rattle of the bicycle.

He let his cycle fall to the road as he turned to see how Betsey had fared. She was crawling out from under the bicycle with all the grace of a sheep escaping its shearer, but appeared otherwise intact.

"Easy mad, you. What's in your head, to do that?"

"You—" Sitting in the road, she started to put her hands up to her eyes, then stopped suddenly, examining her left hand.

"Put out your hands, did you? I warned you not to."

"It happened too fast."

He came and crouched beside her. "You did it on purpose, you ought've been ready."

"I meant you to stop, not run me down!"

"I kept from running you down!" He held her hand, tilting it to catch the glow of her bicycle's lamp. Bright blood oozed from a small cut on her dust-covered palm. He pulled out his pocket handkerchief.

She jerked her hand away. "It is your mother's. The blood will spoil it."

He glanced up, surprised she remembered some reference he'd made to the handkerchiefs his mother had sent him every season. "Hand, now," he commanded.

She held her wrist stiffly as he tied the handkerchief. He asked if she could bend it.

She tried, tentatively at first, then with more vigor, though she grimaced at it. "Just tender, a bit."

One part of her, at least. "The other."

"It's fine."

"See it, I shall."

She shook her right hand to prove its soundness but then let him inspect it. "I've never taken a spill before," she said.

John thought what she had done more akin to murder and suicide than a simple spill. "Be careful, girl," he said with a sigh.

She looked depleted, drained, a soldier resigned to survival by way of defeat, and the sight stabbed painfully within him. He couldn't name this loss, or even say which of them had suffered it, but he stroked his thumb in the hollow of his palm with a wish for restoration.

"Be you careful," he repeated, and sandwiched her hand between his, sealing the wish.

"Iefan," Betsey said, but too low and too late; his movement to stand and help her to her feet scattered the sounds to the night. And what would have followed those bereft syllables? Afraid to know, she felt glad he apparently wanted to accomplish the ride to Sarah's as quickly as possible.

At the gate to Sarah's garden, she paused. "I need to ask . . . you wouldn't try to—"

She stopped, shame heating her as she realized she did *not* need to ask; she knew better. She knew him better.

But he said, "You're safe." His voice was stark: He'd guessed. "I'll not get you sacked for letting me get a poke in. Nor not letting me."

She wouldn't have said it like *that*. Oh, something like that, perhaps, but room remained for a denial. "I wasn't accusing—"

"Not that? Want to remind me I'm lucky to be so callous a man as to keep you from being in love? How I made so poor a job of fucking you don't care to repeat it?"

Misquoted, but in no way misunderstood, Betsey clamped down on her lip.

"See you how well I listen?" he said in that winter-stark voice. "Helps me feign kindness to snare a convenient fuck. Since I was seventeen, no convenient fuck, so I do what I must when one comes my way. Blessed you, to be so clever to see through it."

She wanted to tell him to stop saying *fuck*, that it sounded ridiculous and heartbreaking on his lips. Instead, she turned from him and wheeled her cycle through the gate, and noticed with something she would label relief that he did not follow, but pedaled away.

On the stairs to her room, she focused on avoiding squeaks and kept to the outermost parts of the treads. At her door, she reminded herself to open it slowly, silently.

Her fingers poised on the latch, she blinked.

Since I was seventeen, no convenient fuck.

Since I was seventeen . . .

No. She'd misunderstood. She hadn't heard him right. *No.* Her care for silence forgotten, she fumbled with the latch, thinking it was impossible, and she hadn't heard what she'd heard.

The open door spilled light into the corridor, redoubling her bewilderment. How could she have left a lamp burning?

Charlie, sitting in the rocker near the window.

Her relief did not last long. However much she enjoyed indulging his request to go onto the roof, she should never have let him cross the threshold to her room.

"You nearly parted me from my wits," she whispered, the accusation harsher for the other ways she'd failed to observe boundaries tonight. "What are you doing?"

Charlie stood, his thin arms at his sides, the candlelight making dark hollows of his eyes. Betsey tucked the hand holding her stockings behind her back.

"I saw John bringin' you home," he said. "I could have, I tell him every week—"

She softened. "I know. I am sorry. It is just so late, you know, and your mother . . ." She crossed to the chest of drawers to hide away her stockings, catching a glimpse of her wretched reflection in the looking glass that hung above it, her hair half wet and loose, her clothes soiled and not quite in place. "Your mum would rather have you home early." She hung her straw hat on the hook beside the looking glass and picked up her hairbrush, checking Charlie with an indirect glance in the glass. "I'm so very tired. You'd best go—we both of us need to get to sleep."

Grains of sand fell onto the sleeves and bodice of her jacket as she brushed out her hair.

"Were you glad it was him? Him and not me?"

Betsey closed her eyes, hurting for him. "I've told you, I think it's absurd, anyone seeing me home at all. For pity's sake, in London—"

"Where've you been? You look—" His face contorted suddenly. He knew. Had some idea, at least.

Ignoring his question would confirm his guess but would also, she hoped, show him the topic was not for them to discuss. She went to the door and opened it for him. "Good night, Charlie," she said, as kindly as she could and still convey her meaning.

His head lowered, he took the few steps to the door and stopped. Betsey barely heard him as he said, "Mum won't favor it."

When she didn't ask what he meant, he glanced up at her, his eyes no longer hollows but catching the lamplight with a sharp glint. "Mum won't favor it, a whore under her roof."

Betsey's hand tightened around the door latch. Withholding what—comfort? A slap across his cheek? She hardly knew, but in either case, she held her grip with all her strength and let the comment settle on them both, a dusty layer of filth. Charlie looked down again.

"Good night," she repeated, and this time, he fled.

The sounds of the usual bustle of Sunday mornings woke her, but Betsey remained in bed, and when Sarah came to check on her, she simply begged off from breakfast and church, no excuse nor lie. Sarah, with less than a quarter hour to services, an apron over her clothes and her hair still undone, had no time to press for reasons.

Betsey had been dreaming of the Sundial. With the room

growing warm, she threw the covers off, a vague idea she'd had about riding into Idensea suddenly seeming urgent.

Bathed and dressed, she retrieved her cycle. One of Sarah's boarders was reading in the back garden and asked where Betsey was off to, adding a warning about impending rain. "Just wandering," Betsey answered, but this was dishonest, or at least inaccurate, for *wandering* implied no purpose. The better word would have been *scouting*.

Because what if John's idea about her striking out on her own was not so absurd? It hadn't seemed absurd at all last night, when she'd first considered it. The logistics and cost of beginning such an endeavor were daunting, but perhaps she could begin by looking about town, discovering whether there just might be some place to serve her purpose.

In many ways, the Sundial was ideal, though she did not know if Mrs. Gomery would be agreeable to such a business arrangement. Too, something handier to the rail station and Esplanade would be preferable. She took a circuitous, less familiar route from Sarah's to the town center, considering every structure, including a barn or two, that appeared large enough to host a gathering of perhaps a hundred or so.

Somewhere in her exploration, the what-iffery firmed into a more substantial thing, and she itched to be making notes and numbering lists, getting a plan to paper. At Idensea's town hall, a new building she'd never been inside but which she knew held an assembly room of some size, she realized the brief shower she'd waited out under a garden door was not the end of the rain, and decided to go to the hotel. She could eat there, and her little desk in the empty offices would provide a quiet place to make her notes.

She was refusing the bellman's offer to take her umbrella when Mr. Seiler called her name. His voice carried the usual unruffled authority, but Betsey realized at once her mistake, using one of the main guest entrances, especially in her current state. Though she had her umbrella, the rain had begun before she had reached the bicycle shelter, no doubt leaving her somewhat bedraggled-looking in her decade-old printed skirt.

"I'm sorry," she murmured as Mr. Seiler handed off her umbrella to the bellman and offered his arm as though she'd just been delivered from a gilded carriage.

"A singular occurrence, I'm certain."

"The office entrance was locked," she explained, letting him escort her into his own office. Inside, he opened a cabinet door to reveal a washstand and small mirror, and though Betsey knew he was not *always* at the hotel, he did give one the sense he was constantly available.

He offered a towel. "Because it is Sunday, Miss Dobson."

In other words, why was she here? As she blotted the dampness from her shoulders, Betsey explained her errand, telling him in the process about John's idea.

Mr. Seiler motioned her to a chair. "There remains every chance the board will renew the excursion scheme. You have not given up or grown so unhappy here that you are eager to leave the company?"

"Just the opposite, really. Only—" She hesitated, unwilling to reveal to him the bargain Sir Alton had tried to strike with her.

"You've seen for yourself how Sir Alton regards the excursion scheme," she said. "Not to mention its manageress."

"An alternate strategy is never a poor idea, true. You considered the Black Lion, I suppose?"

"Yes." She had stood before it for some minutes today, wondering if it was too down-at-the-heels, imagining it alight with the warmth and bustle of Mrs. Gomery's public house. The large inn had been Idensea's best before the Swan Park had opened, though Betsey did not know if its shabby appearance was due to losing trade to the Swan or simply due to more than seventy years of use.

"Mr. Seiler, have you ever heard of a woman managing a hotel?"

"You aspire to take my position?" he asked, with humor, and then his blue eyes turned suddenly sharp on her. "When Mrs.

Seiler and I first came to this country, you know, we traveled, we visited any number of inns and hotels. Both our families have been hoteliers for generations, but we wished to acquaint ourselves with the British ways, to know what the British traveler expects and desires. We learned a great deal, Marta and I, from these hotel managers, and manageresses."

Betsey's lips parted at this final word.

"This interests you, Miss Dobson?"

She suppressed a shrug as doubts reared up inside her, everything from her sporadic education to the time she'd bloodied the nose of one of her fellow laundresses for claiming Betsey's basket of finished shirts. How could she, or Mr. Seiler, for that matter, imagine she could be fit for such a career?

"If so, perhaps at the end of the season, you can begin training in earnest, yes?"

Yes. Yes, though it all depended on how far past the season she lasted.

Mr. Seiler allowed her to use his private stairway to go down to the basement, where the afternoon service period in the staff dining hall was closing. The lentils were gone; she was lucky to get a pair of brown rolls and some cheese. She had no sooner squeezed into a place at the women's tables than a bell rang, prompting a commotion of scraping benches and final jollities as the staff returned to duty and left her alone at the table.

Though not in the hall. At the men's tables, deeper in the hall, sat Mr. Jones, tipping his bowl to get a few last bites into his spoon. It looked as if he had a dish of strawberries, too, which irked her, as they were a rare treat in the staff kitchen. His absorption in his meal provided her the chance to stare unstintingly, as a condemned man might suck down the scent of his last plate of chops. She recognized the suit he generally wore to services and wondered that he was here—often, he gave over his Sunday afternoons to Charlie.

She wondered if John, too, had become a target of Charlie's petulance. Perhaps he had thought best to leave the boy alone.

She fastened her gaze to her plate. No doubt he thought best to let her alone. She ripped the end off a roll and pushed a bite of cheese inside before filling her mouth with it, as though she could stuff back all of last night's disappointment, keep it from rising and choking her with the pain of it.

"Iva, let Miss Dobson have this, won't you?"

"Yes, sir."

The dish of strawberries appeared at Betsey's place, delivered by the scullery girl who'd been wiping the tables with a damp rag. Betsey tore another bite from her roll and drew her gaze in even closer, so the strawberries were excluded. *I know you,* that gift meant, but what else? She was afraid to guess.

How could he not have been with a woman since he was seventeen? Over the rows of tables, she said, "I find it hard to believe." That he would give up his strawberries, that he'd been chaste till last night. Let him make what he would of the remark.

He grunted. "A thing men lie about, that."

Amusement threaded the response, however grim his tone. Betsey swallowed, then touched her lips, remembering his kisses, her spongy knees and tunneling vision after that first one in the camera obscura.

A broom whisked over the stone floor, nearby, then moved off. John spoke again, also low. "Ignorance you've mistook for carelessness, girl."

She pinched her lip, then took a strawberry. The brown knot that had caused it to be rejected from the restaurant supply did not affect its sweetness. She heard John's bench scrape the stone and pushed the strawberry dish toward him when he paused at her table. He straddled the bench opposite hers and didn't turn in to face her, though he did pop an entire berry into his mouth.

"Why so long since you bedded a woman?"

"Bless God, your mouth. Speaks of whatever it pleases."

"That's right. So tell me."

He gave her a look: *Here?* But Iva, the little scullery girl, swept like the devil himself inhabited the crumbs; she'd not hear if they kept their voices soft. John tapped the tabletop with his thumb.

"Were you never taught God's commandments? I know you didn't have your mother and dad long, but no one else warned you how fornication would mar your soul for heaven?"

"I've been warned," she replied, so flatly that he slipped a sideways glance at her.

Then he smiled down at the bench. "My mother—there was fierce she could be, telling her sons how God had a special anger for men what used children and women ill. That to take a girl's purity from her was like robbing a beggar. That you married a girl before you had relations with her." He softened his voice even more to add, "Or if she'd had your tongue, Dobs, she'd've said a man doesn't fuck a woman."

It sounded especially ugly, spoken here and by him, and so softly. Anger licked through her. She said, "You're ashamed," and made a movement toward leaving the table.

His hand flashed out. Elsewhere, he might have latched on to her hand, but now he stopped short of that and left a fraction of space between their fingertips.

Then he moved his arm off the table completely. "I only tell you what you asked to know. I left my home early, but with certain things branded into me. And when I was seventeen, and thought I didn't need to bide them anymore, I had them put to me again, with a good, hot iron."

"Put to you? What do you mean?"

"My scars—my mouth and eye—"

She had asked about them before and had received a brief, vague story about a navvy who made a vicious drunk.

"Tokens of my first time. First and last, till last night."

"John! What happened, then? Who—who was she?"

"The navvy's wife. 'Twas like I told you, when I was at work on the Severn Tunnel. And we were caught, and I got the beating I deserved. Thought it was more than I deserved at first, bones broke, bruises like pitch, head all soft with swelling. Blind in my eye for more than half a year. But a man's wife." He bowed his head.

Betsey asked, "What did he do to her?" and regretted it immediately, hearing his sigh. "Never mind. I oughtn't ask."

"I don't know what happened to her. He didn't touch her while he had me in his grip, I know that. I stayed out of sight for a good while. There was an engineer who liked me, took me in and made me study till I was fit for work again. Never saw her again, except in my mind when I woke nights sweating fear and weeping repentance. I understood what my mam meant, then, and it wasn't just fear of hell anymore." He paused. "I hope—I hope she told some lie of me, something to save herself."

"I'm sorry." She wished she had not made him recount the story, even as she wished she had known his guilt and confusion sooner. She wished poor Iva would stop sweeping in that same place, timidly awaiting her chance to clear the last dishes and clean the missed spots under the table where Betsey and John sat.

"All wrong, this, isn't it?"

"That must be it," she agreed, though she didn't. She didn't have a jealous husband. Thomas had not made her feel like a beggar robbed. John had made a vow, he'd told her on the pleasure pier, to respect her wishes and not pursue her, and she had released him from it.

Yet here he sat, tortured, bewildered, because he'd failed in something she'd never asked of him.

It occurred to Betsey that, possibly, he loved her. Possibly, John loved her. Well, she loved him, too, and as she could think of no better way to ease his anguish than to be gone, she rose from the table and took the first way out of the hotel she came upon, though the rain still was pouring and her umbrella was at the bell stand.

She slogged across the grounds, only her straw hat for protection, and was in the bicycle shelter struggling to extract her cycle when she realized she ought to leave it overnight, take the tram.

She swiped her sleeve over her damp face and prepared to start home all over again.

John stood inside the wide doorway.

"Don't ride to Sarah's in this wet," he said.

Write every exercise as though it were to be put on
exhibition.

—*How to Become Expert in Type-writing*

I shan't."

It was so loud, the rain drumming down on the shelter, slapping the stone at the threshold. John's shoulders were
drenched, his hair sopped down to his brows. He held an umbrella,
quite closed, at his side, and she—well, she could not remember
what had driven her into the rain.

"Come into my bed with me, Elisabeth," he said. "Soft as a
whisper, those sheets, and you are the loveliest sight my eyes have
seen, and I want to make love to you."

Betsey moved out of the tangle of cycles and went to him. She
touched his face, the scrawl of his lips and the scar in the corner of
them, the bristle of his lashes as his eyelids fell shut.

"Why?" she whispered. "After so long, and—me?"

Ah, her hope. She couldn't keep it from spilling from her heart
any more than she could keep the rain in the clouds. *Because I've
fallen in love with you, Elisabeth Dobson.* It was so foolish, but out it
spilled, and she couldn't help it.

"Elisabeth," he said, "you give me a pain in my side. That is
why."

Her hand flew to her mouth, making a cup. She laughed her surprise and disappointment into it. "That is the worst poem I've ever heard." Even Keats and his *belle dame* were better.

The umbrella fell to the ground as he grabbed her arms. She gasped as he swung her round to the wall of the shelter, where the rain was like a curtain over the doorway beside her. He pinned her, one rough hand splayed over her neck and cheek, the other on the wall.

"There's plain it is. There's true. Me taken like a rabbit in a trap by you, and no will to scratch my way out, more than half-wanting you to come fast as you can to break my neck and skin me for your roasting pot."

"Oh my God," she breathed, filled with disgust, or something that made her shiver and melt.

"I know. I don't speak fair to you. But true. "

"Lust is all that is. More than ten years of it."

"Yes, it is, through me like blood poison, you think I don't know, that I've never had it before? In my eye when I look at you, on my hands, how I've touched you, you think I don't know it? But that stab—"

His grip on her gentled; he leaned into her and put his lips on her neck, pressed her hand flat to his left side, where she could feel his heart fast at work. "Here's that pain in my side, girl. How sore and tender it is with you, I wish I could finer say."

She crumpled the fabric of his suit in her hand. "You are so hard to believe."

"You think I lie."

"No, I mean like the size of the ocean, or a job that pays a woman commission with her wages. Or magic beans. That sort of hard to believe."

He squeezed her hand. He found her hat pin, and once her hat was gone, his fingers loosened her hair as he kissed all the fragile places of her face and neck. Into her ear he whispered, "Tell me how to please you—I want to," and she said, "Iefan," tears threatening because she'd made him so unsure. They kissed, and she told him it didn't matter. *No, you tell me. You tell me what he did to make you weep for him still.*

She wrapped her arms about him; she burrowed her face against his chin, into his shoulder as he held her, and she believed. She believed his affection as she believed his ambition, his instinct to compete. She believed in the impulse that had made her leave him at the table and the one that had made him come after her. All of it she would take into her hands, a complication of spun glass.

"You call me 'girl' sometimes, Iefan," she said as he held her. "I don't mind, you see. I like it. But when you touch me . . ."

She hesitated, and he guessed, "Lady." He nuzzled into her hair. "I know it. I have been too rough with you."

She smiled at his guess. It was very dear.

Part of the shelter was reserved for repair space. There she led him, her finger hooked into a buttonhole on his coat. She shut the lid on a chest of tools and bicycle parts and sat him there.

"Woman, Iefan," she said softly as she stood before him. With his gaze touching her mouth, she added, "Yours."

His lips parted in silent response. He met her eyes again, firmly fastening their gazes together. The force of his attention penetrated the gloom of the shelter and brushed every feminine part of her, from the curves of her flesh to the bends of her instincts, into peaked, expectant awareness.

Over her hips, her fingers rippled, lifting her skirts an inch at a time. "Touch me like you know that."

She gathered her skirts to a point just above her knee. Just past that boundary, he claimed her, pulling her between his thighs as his other hand caught the back of her head and brought her even closer, into a kiss. The hand on her head moved lower, down her back to join its mate beneath her skirts. As she kissed him, letting go of her skirts and wrapping her arms around him, he explored her. He pressed beneath the edge of her corset, he crumpled the fabric of her drawers, kneading her buttocks and the backs of her thighs.

He found a tear in her stocking. There, a single finger ventured onto her skin, worked itself under the cotton. Betsey broke their kiss with a gasp, shocked by a spasm of anticipation as his fingertip roughed the baby skin at the back of her knee.

"Oh God, your hands," she whispered. She closed her eyes and surrendered to the sensation. "I love them, did you know? How high the heels of your thumbs rise. Your fingers, they're wide and hard, and I . . . oh, I think about them, John, I do."

This made him laugh. Betsey took a step back, pushing his arms away. Hiking up her skirts, she put a foot up beside him on the chest, and insisted, "I do. I think about them here, doing this."

His amusement evaporated. He watched her hand disappear into the slit of her drawers. When he reached for her, she untied the tapes and guided him. He touched her, and both of them made some animal sound, wordless and telling.

She came on his palm, her knees shaking until he had to brace her from falling.

John had spoken of his bed, the soft sheets, but they didn't go to it. Down in the dust of the shelter floor, behind a curtain of rain, she rode him, her skirts billowed over him, his blunt nail bearing into the crevice of her bended knee.

Then a stillness, beyond the one stealing over them. The rain had stopped—how long ago? They'd not even shut the door. Somewhere, deep and away, this knowledge and all it meant sat, a heavy thing in a covered box.

Betsey was shuddering still; she would be raw deep into her dreams tonight, but now they had to rush. Clothes put to rights, dust pounded away, a simple plan formulated: She would leave first; he would wait until she was well clear. For they had to be cautious.

They paused before they parted. John seemed to study her, the shadow in his face the result of something more than the shelter's gloom. Perhaps he regretted coming after her, or wondered why he was willing to take this gamble. It even seemed possible he wondered on her behalf, why *she* would do it, which would be a first in her experience with men.

In the end, however, the shadow in his face remained a mystery. So before she pushed her bicycle out the door, she said, "We could consider this the first of three."

His brows crooked.

"Not count last night," she explained.

Didn't it assure him of her willingness? Didn't it offer him options, from calling it off entirely to making a grand gesture on bended knee? He could even negotiate, as bloodlessly as he no doubt believed she could.

He touched her cheek and murmured, "There's grace." Then, while she stared at him, he motioned for her to go. "Before someone comes."

"A dozen hankies for each eye your mother will need when she sees you, Charlie," John said. They stood together before a looking glass inside Reede's of London, Charlie looking taller and very smart indeed in his first man's suit.

Mr. Sommerson, the clerk, flicked a clothes brush over the garments. Charlie pretended to dislike the fuss.

"The hat department ought to be our next venture," John said. "We will find something to replace that cap."

"Nonsense, sir," said Mr. Sommerson. "It will be my pleasure to bring some samples to you—have you a particular style in mind?"

John feigned a moment of indecision. "We're to go to the American baseball exhibition this afternoon, so . . . a boater, perhaps?"

Charlie's eyes, formerly fixed on his own reflection, now darted with interest. Mr. Sommerson snapped his tape measure around Charlie's head and vanished.

"Mum won't like me in a boater much."

"I expect she won't."

"She'll say I'm too young." Charlie put his hands into his pockets and studied the effect in the mirror.

"I expect she will. Fortunate we left her in Idensea, is it?"

Mr. Sommerson returned with an armful of hats, but his first choice was perfect. He stood before the boy to make certain all was properly aligned, subtly signaled to John a bit of a hair trimming might be in order, then stepped aside to re-present Charlie to his reflection.

Charlie's mouth twisted with his effort to suppress his grin, but it finally triumphed, his first real smile all day. "Mum will most certainly hate this."

John nodded. "Best brace yourself for a smothering of kisses."

Charlie ran his fingers along the brim. "Thanks, John."

The expression of gratitude relieved John. Charlie hadn't been precisely uncivil today, but neither had the outing been the joyful thing he'd envisioned when he and Charlie had planned it months ago.

"Happy birthday, Charlie."

"A month, yet."

"Close enough."

The two of them were headed toward the underground station when Charlie asked if he could see Betsey home when they returned to Idensea. "Fine," John answered, though he wondered over the wisdom of it, whether it needlessly encouraged Charlie. But he didn't want to upset the careful, peaceful balance of the day.

For the same reason, he had dashed to the pawnbroker's while Charlie was having his fitting with the tailor rather than explain he was getting a gift for Betsey. He'd traded Lillian's ring for a necklace, and the brass birdcage, too, since it had been there still. The birdcage was to be sent, but the necklace was nestled in his pocket.

After a moment, he suggested, with some care, perhaps they both might see Betsey home.

Charlie looked much the child, despite the new boater. "Never mind. She wouldn't want me, anyway, not after—" He paused. "She went and told you, didn't she—I said some wicked things to her a while ago."

"She's told me nothing of it."

"She hates me now, I suppose. Doesn't matter." He strode ahead and clipped down the steps to the underground station.

John didn't try to continue the conversation until he'd bought their tickets and they were waiting on the platform. "Apologize, then, if it troubles you so. But whatever you said, she doesn't hate you, Charlie. You know it, same as I."

Charlie stared at the rails below the platform. John searched for a new way to tell him the truth he wasn't ready to hear, though he suspected it was a thing Charlie must sort for himself. A lonely passage for Charlie, though. Nor was waiting John's best thing. He wanted Charlie back.

The black tunnel began to roar. John touched Charlie's shoulder, reminding him to step back from the platform's edge. Charlie shrugged off the touch. "You oughtn't see her home anymore, either, you know," he said. "Everyone talks of you and her. You don't hear it, but they do."

And with the platform vibrating with the train's approach, Charlie took off his boater and tossed it down to the grimy tracks.

The desire to collar the boy out of the station and all the way to Idensea flashed down John's back, but Charlie hopped on the train ahead of him and looked so fearful and defiant when John found him that John only said, "There is ungrateful, that act just now."

Which made them both miserable. They chewed through the rest of the outing, polite guests of an incompetent cook. Eventually the game diluted the tension, and that night, when they arrived back in Idensea, John said he needed to check on the Kursaal, that Charlie should meet Betsey at the pavilion.

That demolished the fragile peace. He wasn't doing it, Charlie growled; he didn't want to ever again, and he stalked away, sure to ruin his mother's evening, too, arriving home alone and in such a foul temper. The entire day felt like a failure to John, so far from what he'd intended.

In the end, he sent word for one of the night watchmen to tend to Betsey, and he went to the Kursaal, where he ignored the fact it was too dark to inspect anything. He kept thinking of the boater, smashed beneath the train, how Charlie had said, *Everyone*; how Betsey had told him, *I'll not look jilted when it's all done.*

But Monday night found him at Sarah's front door again. When Dora Pink drew him inside with a playful scolding for his having missed supper, when she showed him into Dr. Elliot's old office and there was Elisabeth's straight and slender back to him as she stood on an ottoman, Sarah fitting her for the dress she would wear to the opening of the Kursaal—when Elisabeth looked over her shoulder to see who had come in and her face changed, lit, and glowed because she saw it was him—

Few men would not understand his helpless, shameful weakness.

They made a resolution that someone other than he would see her home on Saturday nights. He failed to stop showing up, however. She failed to ever send him away. Crossing the grounds from the pavilion to the bicycle shelter one night, she said, "Mr. Seiler mentioned the Gilbeys would be arriving soon."

John said he supposed this correct.

"I think he is very set on you marrying her."

"My friend, Tobias. Not my father."

With a laugh, she ran for the shelter, tagging the wall, and then—in a gesture that left him scarcely able to walk, let alone run—she lifted her skirts and waited.

John landed against her, greedy and famished. He knew something savage lurked in her play but could not care enough to watch his step, not even when she said, "The Kursaal is almost done. Miss Gilbey is coming. We'd best wind up our contract in a hurry, don't you think?"

Betsey Dobson and how she used sex. It was her attack, it was her resignation.

His hand beneath her skirts, he reminded her, "It doesn't matter when she comes. I gave her up."

"You gave up on her."

He would not argue over such a scrap of word as *on,* not with Betsey unfastening his trousers. "Mr. Jones," she was sighing, "Mr. Jones. So fine a gentleman, he fucks me with all his clothes on."

There. The spring of the trap, lethal and true.

Never mind he'd been wary, half-expecting it. Eagerly, the pain flared, and he seized her arm, wresting her hand from his trousers. "What if I do? Here, on this wall, what if I do—will it count second, or third? Because rather muddled you left it, didn't you?"

Then, under an airless seal of sorrow, his anger died. In all his confusion, in all the ways he was ignorant and blinded and plain garden-stupid in this business with Betsey, he was clear-eyed regarding that limit she'd imposed. It carried more blame for what was wrong between them than did Lillian, present or not. He had never liked it, but only in this moment did he understand why she had imposed it.

"Didn't you, Elisabeth?" he repeated.

Though she hadn't been fighting his grip, he felt a give, a release, an expansion of the stillness within her. With the grating whisper of drapery, her skirts fell between them. John pressed his forehead to hers and felt the wings of her pulse as he curved his hand alongside her neck.

It's no good for you, girl. Expecting nothing better, it's no good for you.

What place did he have to say it?

She told him, "I'm sorry."

The next afternoon, they rode their cycles far into the country-side and Betsey let him teach her to swim in the stiller waters of a woodland pool, where the boys who arrived for an afternoon of play were not particular regarding mixed bathing or appropriate swimming attire, though a couple of them did follow, with intense interest, Betsey's progress when she removed herself from the water, her white underclothes stained with the pink of her skin. John took it as a sign of their health.

They dried off in a mottled patch of sunlight. The boys' horse-play was so unrelentingly noisy that John and Betsey stopped noticing it. They talked. She told him a story about her niece that deepened the curls of her mouth. His speech—one good enough to deliver from the stage of the Kursaal's recital hall opening night, not the wooden thing he'd written out for Tobias to appraise—had rolled out from his brain like a shiny apple as he'd lain with his head in her lap.

If they'd been alone, he would have made love to her there in the wood, surrounded by ferns and an awning of summer-laden branches. He would have kept no tally; he would have let the afternoon drift to infinity, if the choice had been his.

Do not strike the keys as it happens, but strike them systematically, intelligently, and in such a way as to save effort.

—*How to Become Expert in Type-writing*

*N*ear dawn the day of the Kursaal opening, the last seat in the recital hall was fastened into place, ensuring the Duke of Winchester and all the other guests would not, as John had feared, be viewing tonight's performance from milking stools.

Laughter and cheers went up when Corbin Ludd plopped down in that last chair and pretended to fall fast asleep to prove the soundness of the installation. John, on the stage reviewing a final few details with some of the workers, turned to the grand piano and struck the cheeriest chords he knew, from that American tune he'd prepared for Lillian Gilbey's party.

But he'd not committed it to memory as fully as he'd thought. He stumbled through the opening, delighting the men with this opportunity to ridicule him. Laughing, he laid out the opening to "A Mighty Fortress," the only song besides "God Save the Queen" he and his schoolmates had learned from the wife of the village's preacher. Within a few measures, the hall was filled with a masculine chorus, and thus was the Kursaal christened with its first performance. The Spanish soprano entertaining the Duke tonight must settle for second.

According to John's arrangements, the paymaster arrived. For most of the men, these hours through the night had been their last with the pier company, and another round of cheers sounded when John announced wages would be paid on the spot.

But the queue that formed before the paymaster's table with such good-natured jostling turned sober as it shortened. John shook each man's hand. He would see them together again—Lady Dunning and Sir Alton hosted a picnic on the grounds of Iden Hall each September for all the summer employees—but this moment marked a passage, and he wished to acknowledge it, simply, man by man.

"You won't forget me, Mr. Jones, if it comes you need to hire?" asked Paul Higbee, who had been with John on every work site since he'd come to Idensea, as, indeed, had nearly all of the men remaining now. The ones who'd taken places in the rear of the queue, John realized, included some who'd come on as thin, green youths and now were men, former day laborers who'd become foremen—Mandy Wainwright, whose wedding John had attended, and Iesten Gwyn, who never failed to call him Mr. Iefan Rhys-Jones with a tang of a sneer but who had also turned up in March to deliver John to the rail station the day he left to attend his mother's funeral. During the drive, Gwyn had sung "Suo Gân" in a voice like an unbroken thread of yellow honey and never once turned his eyes from the horse and the road to notice John's tears.

"Sure not, Mr. Higbee," John replied, a knot of emotion threatening to choke and embarrass him. He'd been so intent on getting the building finished, he'd forgotten to put himself here, to picture this moment and anticipate how it would feel: *finished*. *Finished*, one of those words that deceived, sounding so uncomplicated and absolute.

Higbee was local, and with no new construction by Idensea Pier planned for the near future, he would have to find some other employer. But the same was true for the others, like John himself, who'd come to Idensea for the work and intended to move on when the job was concluded.

From the portico, John saw everyone off into the colorless predawn, breathing in the scent of fresh-turned earth from the flowerbeds, lately made over to include yellow rosebushes. The groundskeeper had had to have his job threatened to be convinced to move and replant a dozen fully blooming bushes, but the Duchess was known to have a partiality to yellow roses, so as long as they were there for her to see Friday, they could die Saturday, as far as Sir Alton was concerned.

Back inside, John gathered his papers, tucked the bench back under the piano. Before he pulled the lid over the keys, he tried the parlor song once more and got through the place that had hung him up without a missed note. But the sound felt overpowering in the empty hall, and he left off at the refrain.

He swiped his coat sleeve across the lid to erase the fingerprints. For sheer luxury, this piano was likely the finest thing he'd ever put his hands on. If Betsey were here, she'd touch it with a single fingertip. The mystery of his confidence in this rolled restlessly in his heart, and he stood looking out into the hall as the Spanish soprano would tonight—as he himself would, too, when he delivered his speech. The newly installed seats would not resemble rows and rows of headstones once they were put to use, filled up with ladies and gentlemen, alive with the stir of fans and flashes of jewels, ears cocking to lips to catch a whisper.

He'd be able to find her, wouldn't he, when he took the podium?

He walked the aisles of seats, found a spanner and a small dented tin of tobacco. Two pennies, some unused bolts, a pocket comb he was certain belonged to Rafe Dixon, and a red kerchief. He was nearly to the rear of the hall when he heard voices. Expecting the staff who would be doing the final cleaning and decorating, John continued with his inspection of the aisles and was thus surprised when Lady Dunning appeared, her arms full of fresh flowers, the Kursaal manager at her side identically burdened.

They both exclaimed over the transformation of the hall, seeing the seats in place and the chandeliers burning.

"Oh, darling boy," she cried when she saw John. "You've been here all night! You and my husband, no sleep, and such a day ahead." She allowed John to take the flowers from her, and though she was *tsk*-ing over him and Sir Alton, her eyes held evidence that she'd had little rest as well.

"It's the *speech* that had him in such a state," she continued. "The speech! He said he found it less vexing to direct a hundred-piece orchestra in a full symphony than to compose a little welcome speech, which! Which, months ago, from the time the Duke accepted the invitation, I tried in a most loving way to convince him to do precisely that, compose something for the occasion, conduct the performance. 'Idensea Idyll,' wouldn't that have been lovely? And if he and Noel could have collaborated in some way, even to the slightest degree, can you imagine the attention that might have attracted? But I never even suggested a title, far less a *collaboration*—the entire notion, well, he simply refuses."

They'd come to the stage steps, and Lady Dunning paused, her shrug toward John communicating more sadness than resignation. "He won't think of himself as a musician, not anymore."

She refused his offer to stay and help, ordering him to at least a few hours' sleep before the Duke arrived. He could hear her directing the manager in the stage decoration as he made his way out. Cycling toward the hotel, he threw a glance over his shoulder at the Kursaal, still waiting for the illumination of full daylight. He would have ridden past Sarah Elliot's, but he thought the luck of finding Betsey on the roof, ready for a personal tour, was not likely to strike twice.

Have you slept at all, Betsey wanted to ask John, but she couldn't, not here in the busy company offices. She might have managed it if it were only she and he at her desk, but John had dropped in with the Kursaal's architect, his daughter, and her husband. Betsey swallowed the question down as John glanced through the trials the photographer had prepared for the Duke's picture at the pleasure railway, testing distances and angles.

"We shall close to the public beforehand," she said. "No tickets sold for at least an hour, I'm afraid. The photographer insists he needs the time."

Standing at John's side, the architect's daughter pointed her approval of a particular photo. "An hour's not so long. And one never knows—one might arrive early."

Her husband plucked playfully at her earring. "One's husband knows the odds of—"

He interrupted himself to greet Mr. Seiler, arriving with a slim box in hand, which he presented to John. "From Marta and myself."

"*That* is Meyer and Mortimer wrapping," the architect's daughter announced with confident anticipation.

The box contained a simple black silk necktie. Simple, yet Betsey had seen enough gentlemen this summer to recognize its extraordinary fineness. As did John. Visibly moved, he thanked Mr. Seiler with the same spare elegance as the gift itself.

He used the convex looking glass right there in the office to change neckties. Along with everyone else, Betsey watched him, though she guessed she was the only one gripping a desk edge to restrain herself from joining him at the looking glass. She longed to straighten and pat it done, to have that moment of trusted connection.

"Dearest," the architect's daughter said to her husband as she moved to assist John, "you should consider yourself fortunate we were engaged already when I met Mr. Jones. One never knows . . ."

She straightened. She patted. The architect's daughter, whose new husband had been hired into her father's firm and featured in *The Building News*, fixed John's tie. John glanced over her head to Betsey, the same *Am I presentable?* question on his brow as she'd once seen him address to Mr. Seiler.

Betsey smiled and nodded, glad she didn't have to speak, the longing still digging into her soul. They departed, the father, the daughter, the husband, and John in his silk necktie, off to meet a duke at the rail station.

The closer the carriage drew to the station, the more festive Idensea became, people turned out in their Sunday best, storefronts and lampposts decorated with banners and swags of bunting. John spotted some of the men who'd spent the night at the Kursaal, spruced up and walking with their families or sweethearts, and he felt glad for getting their wages to them early. But it wasn't truthful, he realized with a wave of weariness, how he'd thought of himself as one of them, out of a job now that the Kursaal was complete. Sir Alton would have him as managing director.

A band played across from the station, and the massing crowd made it difficult for the carriage to find a place amongst the retinue of vehicles that would accompany the Duke and his family on the tour of Idensea. The architect directed the coachman to let them disembark and walk the rest of the way. At the station steps, John noticed a sunny yellow parasol imperiling the eyes of other spectators as it bobbed about.

Lillian Gilbey. She and her family had been due to arrive the day before yesterday, but John had not seen them until now. Lillian beamed at him; John felt as if she'd willed him to look in her direction.

She stretched out an arm as she pressed to the front of the crowd. "I knew you'd rescue me from this crush. It's all right," she added, perhaps noticing his uncertainty as she grabbed his hand. "Mama said I might go with you—see her there with Aunt Constance and the girls? Papa's in town still, but he'll be here in time for the gala. Help me over the rope, won't you?"

John glanced down at the narrow rope marking off the Duke's path. "Lils, I'm helping with the tour. I'm not free to squire you about. You'll have your introduction tonight, just as I promised."

"Oh, you needn't worry a bit about introducing me to the

Duke *now*—truly, I only need some relief from the heat and noise. I won't be a smidge of bother."

She was irrepressible. He'd been fond of that quality, he remembered, along with her smile, always at its most beguiling when she wanted something. The brilliance of it pleased him. Lillian nursed grudges, and he probably deserved a cooler greeting, leaving early after he'd tried to upset her music party.

"Take my shoulders," he said. He lifted her over the rope, and she thanked him and reached up to pat his tie and said he looked very dapper, even if he had been exceedingly naughty in not showing his face since she'd arrived, but then he'd been very busy, she was certain, and she promised again not to be a bother, but did he know, "I've never yet met Lady Dunning and Sir Alton. Perhaps, while we're waiting for the train . . . ?"

Inside the station, coming to the platform where the Duke and his party would disembark, John realized his job-seeking efforts had been lacking of late. Besides the pier company board members, the platform held at least a dozen other men he should have been speaking to. But with the Kursaal opening tumbling at him like a boulder off a mountainside, when had he last had the time to lounge in the smoking room?

Saturday nights, he chided himself. Sunday afternoons. Pearse Leland (of Leland Steel) noted John's arrival with a cordial lift of his chin, and John would have joined that circle of conversation if not for Lillian tugging at his arm and telling him she saw Lady Dunning and Sir Alton, wasn't it lucky to find them together, but where were the children, Mr. Dunning and his sister?

Surprised she didn't already know, John started to tell her Dunning was in Vienna, but glancing in the direction Lillian indicated, he caught the eye of Walbrook, Sir Alton's secretary, and knew at once something was the matter.

"Horace Gilbey's daughter? Darling, Horace Gilbey's daughter," Lady Dunning said upon the introduction. The repetition was for Sir Alton's benefit. John could see him arriving at the connection—*the carpet maker*—though whether he recalled that the carpet maker's daughter had been one of the reasons for Noel's frequent absences from Idensea, John couldn't say.

In any case, he was more concerned with what news Walbrook possessed. He left Lillian to the chitchat and turned toward Walbrook, who opened his portfolio and presented a printed paper to John.

"Mr. Jones, you'll want a copy of the new itinerary."

Only that innocuous statement. Still, even as he pulled out his spectacles, John had a fair idea of the alteration he would find.

"When was this decided?" he murmured.

"Quite recently. Or I can only assume so, as I myself had to wake the printer last night to order the copies."

Walbrook was too discreet to exchange even a knowing glance, but surely he joined John's suspicion that the new schedule had existed a good long time before making its appearance today.

John found Sir Alton watching him with an expression indicative of sympathy. "You'll be disappointed. But it was the only thing."

"I'm not disappointed. However . . ." John folded his spectacles and put them away into his pocket. Disappointment figured little to nothing in his feelings at the moment. "It just won't do, Sir Alton."

"John, dear!" Lady Dunning gasped. She had not often witnessed John directly opposing Sir Alton, but time was too short for the oblique strategies he usually employed.

"We need that photograph," John said, not to Lady Dunning.

"Good heavens," she replied nevertheless, "a photographer will be along all day. There will be ample opportunity—"

John had been intending to mind his manners and let her finish, no matter how impatient he felt, but she suddenly stopped, smiled, and drew herself and Lillian to the side, speaking of Vienna.

"We need that photograph of the Duke and his family on the Sultan's Road," John repeated.

"You're making too much of it, Jones. The schedule was tight; I provided some breathing space. We'll be glad we have it, you'll see."

"Everything is in place for it. Every party involved is expecting it. Miss Dobson is there to oversee and make it as clean a process as possible."

"Oh!" Sir Alton exclaimed. "If someone had mentioned the type-writer girl was at the helm of it all, I should have had no qualms whatever. However, as it's done . . ."

He shrugged. John rubbed his thumbs along the sides of his forefingers. Across the way, the architect's daughter was leaning into her husband, playfully poking a finger into his chest.

"You see Mr. and Mrs. Croyer there?" he asked Sir Alton. "They just returned from holiday."

"So I've heard. The French Riviera, no less."

"Right, the French Riviera. They aren't nobility. Wealthy enough, I suppose, but not extraordinarily so. And they traveled to the Continent for their seaside holiday, and in that, they are not so extraordinary, either."

"Oh, goodness . . ." Sir Alton put a finger on his bemused, indulgent smile. "You think to educate me on my own business."

"Idensea cannot depend—"

"How obliging. How—"

"—on people—"

"—*novel*. How—"

"—like the Croyers—"

"—superfluous—"

"—to make—"

But then John gave up trying to talk through Sir Alton's relentless lilt. Like everything else about his person, it was a wall. Sir Alton continued until assured John had yielded and finished: "It simply is not dignified, a duke on that garish, vulgar *entertainment* we were forced to build."

He paused, perhaps to see if John would offer further argument. John didn't.

Sir Alton patted John's elbow. "You've not forgotten I'm willing to pass over my own son to give you the opportunity to head this company? But you understand I need to know you care for Idensea's future."

John did not reassure him that he cared for Idensea. Walbrook mouthed an apology as he followed Lady Dunning and Sir Alton to join another group on the platform.

John told Lillian, "I've got to go make a bosom friend of a coach driver. And get a message to Elisabeth. Shall I deliver you to your mother, or would you like to stay here on your own?"

"I don't care."

Despite his preoccupation, John felt a mild alarm hearing Lillian Gilbey claiming apathy on . . . any subject, really, but especially one with direct bearing on her. She seemed to mean it, too, her gaze as distant as her voice had been. But then she realized he had noticed, and her face transformed, taking on that beatific smile of hers.

"Mama, if you please, and then I'll release you to enigmatic errands. These messages you're sending to ladies are not familiar ones, I trust?"

If screwed too tightly against the iron frame, [the stop-collar] may interfere with the proper working of the machine.

—*How to Become Expert in Type-writing*

That photographs carried no sound was a fact Betsey had never given any particular thought until this moment, when it seemed their finest quality. The Duke's youngest grandson was in a red rage, yowling and twisting in the arms of his nurse, but however miserable the poor babe (and his nurse), the final image would show nothing but silent cheer.

And everyone else did seem in good spirits, for the most part. John's message, warning her to have the photographer and all the other details in readiness earlier than planned, had been something of a surprise, but no great trouble. After closing the Sultan's Road to the public, she and the photographer had even been able to plan the arrangement in front of the hanging gardens in the main arch. Willing bystanders had substituted for the Duke and the others of the party, and so when the true subjects arrived, Betsey could assist rather ably in getting everyone into place. Although—

Had she truly ordered His Grace to stand rather than sit, and to make a three-quarter turn toward the camera? Despite Mr. Seiler's tutoring on addressing nobility, she feared it was true.

But the Duke had not seemed to mind. For an aristo, in fact, he seemed quite affable, his sole request in the process being to keep a particular grandchild in his arms.

The culmination of hours of preparation came suddenly in an acrid plume of smoke. One more, and then the arrangement broke like an ice floe, the babe's mama being the first to drop her pose and hurry to her son.

From her place beside the photographer, Betsey noticed some uncertainty, a hesitation amongst those remaining, and went to see if she might be of assistance. The Duke wondered whether there was to be a demonstration of the pleasure railway—why, the youngsters were counting on it.

John flashed her a grin as he took aside the brakeman who had posed for the photograph. Soon the passengers were settled in, and the cars disappeared into the first tunnel. The automatically tripped organ sent music drifting out to the platform.

Sir Alton elected not to ride, though he had taken his place for the photograph. He had departed his carriage with a curse, but since then, he'd held his mask. "As you wish, Miss Dobson," he'd answered when she had directed him into place, his smile never slipping.

He spoke now with one of the men who had arrived with the touring party. Sir Alton's side of the conversation was too low to hear, naturally, but Betsey heard the word *contractor* from the other man and soon realized they spoke of John. "I visited the Kursaal the day I arrived," the man said. "No humble endeavor, that, nor the Swan. He seems well able . . ."

Then: "And the delay?"

And: "Of course, London is a different animal altogether."

Betsey frowned, frowned more as she continued to eavesdrop. The man in the black suit was someone both Mr. Seiler and John had pointed out to her at the hotel. Pearse Leland, some man of business from London.

Mr. Walbrook, ever a convenient distance from Sir Alton, approached her. "Well done, Miss Dobson," he said in an undertone, and put out a hand, not in the way a gentleman took a lady's proffered fingers but as though he would shake her hand.

And so he did, with more vigor than she would have predicted. "Thank you, Mr. Walbrook, but your cooperation made it all much easier. I gather there was some sort of snag earlier?"

Mr. Walbrook pulled a thin stack of papers from his portfolio. "Would you mind disposing of these for me? They're rather useless since Mr. Jones apparently commandeered the Duke's coach."

The papers were copies of the tour itinerary. She read it over, and when she glanced up, Sir Alton was approaching.

"His Grace did not appear terribly put out, if I may say so, sir," Mr. Walbrook ventured as Betsey folded away the itineraries into her pocket.

"Indeed not," Sir Alton agreed cheerfully. "I daresay he'll return from the little expedition even more enthused than when he boarded. Who should have guessed a duke to have such common tastes?" His own enthusiasm had a vicious edge to it. "Our Mr. Jones, I suppose," he added, in answer to his own question. "He's clever about a number of things, and a decided expert on common ones. And how *are* you coming along with your assignment, Miss Dobson?"

Floundering in the wake of his insult, Betsey at first thought he meant the photograph. But no, the only assignment Sir Alton had entrusted to her was to keep John in Idensea. Her confusion multiplied: Less than a minute ago, he'd been listing John's shortcomings to Pearse Leland. If he thought so poorly of John, why—

But she hardly needed more than that to sort it through. Even with just half the conversation, she'd known Sir Alton had fed Leland lies, or at least exaggerations, and not because he didn't respect John. Because he wanted John here in Idensea.

As did she. Her stomach turned. She and Sir Alton, allies.

Betsey tugged at her fingers, girlish and shy. "You may find Tinfell Cottage out of your hands sooner than you expected, sir."

Because she, too, could lie outright.

•   •   •

Had she expected a Cinderella moment? Once in her gown, some of Sarah's rosewater on her neck, the anticipation of the night shining ahead like a city, had she thought to look in the mirror and feel enchanted?

She didn't. Perhaps it was the dresser-top mirror, which required a great deal of tilting and retilting, to-ing and fro-ing, to get a look at all her parts, plus the mental effort to imagine them together, in order, but, said and done, Betsey felt not at all touched by the wand of a fairy godmother.

No, if anything, she was Puss in Boots, a schemer, contriving a ball gown from a Sunday frock purchased from a secondhand stall at the market, conniving with pins and curls to make her hair appear it had a decent length wound into it. And literally, in boots: None of the women in the house had slippers to fit her, and Betsey couldn't bear to spend another penny on this impractical ensemble.

Sarah was in a fluster when Betsey stopped by her bedchamber. Betsey's completed toilette put her in a greater panic, so Betsey left her to Dora Pink's ministrations and went downstairs, expecting John at any moment.

But more than twenty minutes later, he still had not arrived. The house was atypically silent, Charlie and the rest of the household having departed already for the Esplanade and pleasure pier, where festivities associated with the Kursaal's opening gala were ongoing, and she could hear Sarah on the steps, calling to Dora to bring her forgotten wrap.

Relief cleared Sarah's expression as she realized Betsey waited alone in the parlor. "He's not come, then? I *knew* Dora had changed the clocks. It's become quite a tiresome trick of hers, especially as she seems to believe—" Sarah released a long breath and dabbed at the curls by her temple. "Am I . . . ?"

Betsey caught Sarah's anxious hand. "Splendid." She had never seen Sarah in anything but black, so it was a revelation to behold her now in pink. She looked years younger, the effect heightened by the flush her haste had brought to her cheeks.

"Well, if I'm half as lovely as you, my dear, then John has two extraordinarily fetching companions tonight."

"I've never seen his like for luck," Betsey agreed with a laugh, though the word *companions* surely overstated the circumstances. Once John had driven Sarah and herself to the Kursaal, they would part. John had responsibilities tonight, and in any case, he and Betsey could not go about like a courting couple.

Whatever Dora Pink might have done to the clocks, John was late, and Betsey wondered at it. She drew aside a window curtain, but there was no sign of him.

Sarah said, "It would make a lovely wedding gown, you know."

Betsey turned from the window, taken by surprise.

"That lace I showed you—I know you didn't want to take it—but for a wedding—a bit here, and on each sleeve?" Sarah touched each of her own sleeves, where lace already adorned the cuffs. It was Betsey's pale yellow gown she meant. "And the garden. My daughter Sophie had her wedding party there, why not do it again?" She went on, her voice tremulous with forced cheer, but details spilled from her lips readily, as though she'd been considering them a good while. "Why, everything could be arranged without the least trouble, almost as soon as you and John like."

"As . . . soon as we like."

"I'm not supposed to know yet, I realize that, but—"

"There is nothing to know. John and I aren't—"

"Charlie, that imp!" Sarah interrupted in a burst. Her smile held—held and yet changed, the way freshness depart white linens once you unfold them and put them on the table or the bed. Still clean, bright, but something departed.

Betsey's confusion departed, too, at the mention of Charlie's name.

Sarah said, "Charlie gave me the notion that you—you'd be

marrying soon," and it was time for Betsey to say just almost anything, anything to usher the moment along, see it to a more comfortable place where Betsey's knowledge of Sarah's knowledge could wait, fidget in private until Betsey knew what to do with it.

Sarah's distress drained the roses from her cheeks. A part of Betsey, aged fourteen and answering to Lizzie, rejoiced in it, felt brutally glad to have someone share her shame.

Sarah stammered, "It is . . . it's August . . . I just couldn't keep it, such happy news, to myself anymore, you know how it is."

"Yes. Charlie told me, too," Betsey agreed. "How you 'wouldn't favor it,' was how he put it. You wouldn't favor having a whore under your roof."

Sarah blinked, wobbled like someone whose step had landed on the edge of a carpet, and Betsey's shame only swelled. With her next breath, she whispered, "I'm sorry," but it did nothing to ease the pained shock in Sarah's eyes. "This is your home, your livelihood, I'm—"

She rushed for the stairs.

At the first landing, she met Dora and could do no more than mumble at the maid's exclaimed compliments.

By the second landing, she knew she was going to her room to pack, that wherever she ended up tonight, she had spent her final hours in Sarah's home.

She was crushing one of her tweed suits into her valise, wondering how she had come from London with only this bag when she realized this upper room was stifling.

And she was unlatching a window, hungry for air, when she saw why John was so late.

She heard Sarah in the corridor, calling tentatively. "Betsey?"

Sarah's eyes filled with tears the moment she noticed the valise on the bed. "Oh!" she cried softly, and paused, and the pause made Betsey think Sarah, too, had caught the scent. Betsey's nostrils were filled with it already, her throat stinging.

But perhaps that was her imagination, triggered by what she'd seen, for Sarah's concern remained with the overflowing valise. She was sorry, she hadn't meant, she hadn't thought, she—

Betsey interrupted her. "Sarah."

No, that scent was not only her imagination. It reached Sarah and stilled her as though she'd come upon a snake, sunning itself in her path.

Betsey rushed to take her hand. "Sarah, the pier is burning."

Make the head help the hands. . . . Then make the hands
help the head.

—*How to Become Expert in Type-writing*

*B*etsey stayed on Sarah's heels on her sprint down the
steps, and was tempted to follow her out the door, but
forced her better sense to overrule her fear.

Dora Pink stood in the foyer, gaping at her mistress's flight.

"The pier's burning, Dora."

She knew Dora's thoughts went the way her own had upon
seeing the billows of smoke from her window: back to this morning's breakfast, and Charlie's delight with having earned some
pocket money to spend at the night's festivities. Charlie asking his
mother's permission to join his friends in watching the fireworks
from the pier. Charlie's grin when his mother gave him a few extra
coins in addition to her permission.

Betsey had no experience with carriage-driving, but Dora
proved deft in hitching the mare to Sarah's small gig, and they
soon caught up to a breathless, perspiring Sarah.

"It's hours before the fireworks were to begin," she gasped as
she took Betsey's hand and squeezed into the carriage. "He mayn't
have gone onto the pier yet."

Betsey agreed, but the longer they drove with no view of the fire except the thick pillar of smoke scaling the sky, the more fervently she clung to that hope. Dora Pink alternated exclamations to the Lord above with reassurances that she was certain the boy was fine, just fine, likely caught up watching all the excitement with his schoolmates.

And if Dora felt free to call to the Lord, Betsey felt something like the opposite as they turned onto the Marine Road and the seafront came into view—the urge to cower, the sensation that she was shrinking to nothing, a bit of paper over a flame, curling into ash. She was simply too meager to take in the depth and breadth of the horror before them.

The blaze was concentrated at the concert pavilion near the head of the pier, but a line of flames, almost unnatural in the intensity of their orange, had begun to lick up the promenade as well. Smoke which might have looked black in the day billowed toward the shore, palely aglow against the colored threads of the summer twilight. Sparks sleeted prettily down from the pier promenade into the water like curtains of falling stars.

The Marine Road curved out in both directions where it met the Esplanade, and this broad place seemed to have become the gathering point for uninvolved spectators, sitting in their conveyances or standing in the road, shouting their conjectures and observations to one another. How casually they debated whether the buildings on the Esplanade would catch sparks and recounted how they had first noticed the smoke. One woman had her hand, *her very hand*, upon the turnstile to enter. But that was nothing. Others had been part of the panicked rush to get off the pier.

Did everyone get off, then?

Ain't possible. Why, look at it!

Betsey hated them, their indifference, their interest, how, for them, the worst was over. She hoped Sarah was too distracted to notice, though for herself, it was somehow better to let that inanity reach her ears more closely than the monstrous mumble of the fire, the terrifying sounds of things splitting into nothingness.

The bitter smell of smoke made the horses restless. Dora's bent for command proved an advantage here; their progress was slow, but her shouts and sure control of the reins kept them moving. As they crept forward, Sarah scanned the crowd for Charlie's tow-head on her side of the carriage, while Betsey did the same on hers. Above, on the cliff, the Kursaal wore her rosettes and garlands like a disappointed debutante. Reflections of the flames mottled the soft glow beneath the glass of the winter garden, and over the terraced lawn of fresh flowerbeds stood groupings of guests dressed for a night amongst nobility, one of celebratory speeches and champagne and dancing.

With a wave of sadness for John, for Idensea itself, she swept one look up to the lantern room and the silhouetted figures on the balcony. She wanted to find him. All her worry was for Charlie; John she imagined in some sort of overseeing role, well-informed and ready with answers, including that to the question of Charlie's whereabouts.

Finally, they turned onto the Esplanade, also clogged with vehicles, but the drivers here at least were driving, or trying to, and the pedestrian spectators had been forced off to the balustrade fronting the beach. Others rushed between the spectators and the traffic, shouting for someone or on some other urgent errand.

Betsey and Sarah stood in the carriage and added their voices to the din, calling Charlie's name. He could be in that mass along the balustrade; he could be one of the dark figures dotting the beach. He could be on the pier.

The sea glowed as though flames blazed beneath the waves as well as above, all manner of small craft marking the water. Rescuers. People were trapped. They were dark specks against the fire's glow, pressed against the railing at the head of the pier, or less distinct shadows, clinging to the girders below the platform. And some, surely, waited in the sea, treading or swimming to shore, fighting the water until help found them. She knew something of that fearful condition.

She knew, too, John wasn't overseeing anything. He was out there.

The Esplanade had become all but impassable, the mare increasingly uneasy. Sarah and Betsey stood in the carriage and scanned the scene. "Charlie would be here," Sarah said. "If he were not on the pier, he would be here; he wouldn't miss this sight."

Betsey followed Sarah down from the carriage, but kept her from tearing into the crowd. "Let me search the Esplanade. Dora can take you to the foreshore. Look there, and meet the boats. If Charlie is still on the pier, one of them will have to bring him ashore."

Betsey pushed her way through the crowd, pausing to climb on benches and planters, whatever could offer her a wider view. She stopped anyone she recognized and every child who appeared close to Charlie's age to ask if they'd seen him. When she caught sight of Idensea's fire engine, her hope buoyed with the conviction Charlie would want to be as near as possible to it, but he was not to be found. Firemen were spraying down the pier tollhouse, attempting to protect it from stray sparks, but they did not appear to be advancing much past that.

When she wondered aloud at this, a bystander removed the handkerchief over his mouth and nose. "Not hose enough," he said. "If they took it onto the pier, the pump would likely take up sand with the sea water and clog. That's why the brigade captain called for axes."

With his handkerchief, the man gestured farther down the pier, where more brigade members and other volunteers were tearing up the decking of the promenade. "Better that than to wait for the blaze to eat its way to the hose."

So the pier had been given up. But hadn't she known that the moment she'd looked out her window? The smoke had dwarfed everything.

Shouts, then the crowd made way for a wagon carrying Mr. Seiler. He called out, and men surrounded the vehicle immediately, taking axes and crowbars from it and heading onto the pier. Sir Alton and some of the board members, all of them dressed for the ball, approached the wagon to speak with Mr. Seiler.

No John amongst them.

With a last look about, smoke stinging her eyes and throat, Betsey turned toward the steps that would take her down to the foreshore. No idle spectators here clogging the way, just the dark, writhing confusion of activity as boats brought the rescued to shore. "Here, luv, get these out to the poor things," a voice said, and Betsey found her arms filled with a tangle of the hotel's linens.

Offering the dry wrappings, she felt a bit of relief. The people were shaken, yes, and soaked, many of them, but they were all right. As long as they'd been found by one of the boats, they were all right.

"It's going now!" came a call from the dark, and Betsey and everyone else looked out to the water in time to see the roof of the pavilion cave in, collapsing like a child's blanket fort. Bright debris sprayed the air, the water lit and hissed, and waves lifted the flaming timber.

Betsey swallowed back a surge of tears and offered the last towel in her hand to Deborah Walton, the vicar's daughter. She'd been with Judith, her sister—had anyone seen her, Deborah wanted to know, her gasping so harsh and deep Betsey could scarce make out the words. But when she did understand, Betsey was able to answer yes, to say that she remembered passing Judith as she'd come down to the surf; someone had been carrying her. Saying this, Betsey felt the same relief she saw in Deborah's face. It confirmed, again, that all would be well again soon. Deborah and Judith safe, reunited. So, too, everyone else. So, too, Charlie and his mother. Perhaps already.

But when Betsey found Sarah, she waited yet. Betsey slipped an arm around her waist, and they stood, eyes fixed on each approaching vessel. A cutter brought a handful of rescues, a rowboat two more. And then, not far from where they stood, another small fishing boat headed in.

"It's John," Betsey said as soon as she recognized the figure leaping from the boat. She hugged Sarah's waist. "He'll be able to tell us something."

She called his name, and he seemed to hear her over the roar of surf and fire. Sarah put up a hand to wave, but he was already bending back down to the boat. When he faced them again, it was with Charlie in his arms.

With a sob, Sarah broke into a run to meet John as he strode from the surf. John's coat was gone, and his white shirt clung to his shoulders, soaked. His black hair framed a stony expression. It offered Betsey no clues to the condition of Charlie, whose face was turned up to the night sky. He'd lost his shoes. John glanced down at him, then shifted the boy closer into his chest.

"Dr. Nally," she heard him say to Sarah as they met, and immediately, Sarah ran for the seawall, where the doctor was tending those who needed care.

Betsey matched John's relentless strides. "Charlie," she whispered when she saw the dark spot in the boy's light hair, how it was blurring brightly, wetly into John's sleeve. Tears in her eyes, she looked at John, searching his face again.

"I don't know," he said, and looked away, and increased his pace.

"I could be of some use here," Betsey said, though her survey of the foreshore was a doubtful one. John understood her conflict, one instinct urging her to help here on the shore, another to remain at Sarah's side.

Charlie, if you spoke loudly enough, would respond. He'd rolled unfocused eyes to his mother, said something with the word *penny* in it, but it was as though he were under the water still, sluggish and vague. Dr. Nally said the cut on his head would be best stitched, but it was minor, however frightening the bleeding had seemed. He recommended the boy be moved home to rest, and he, Dr. Nally, would see him there soon. Lady Dunning, who had ordered the hotel linens brought to the foreshore and had spoken comfort to every person rescued from the pier, had volunteered her coach so that Charlie and Sarah might be transferred more comfortably.

"Be with Sarah," John said to Betsey. Reason told him she was in no danger and would have the makeshift clinic and information point that had sprung up here organized in a flash, but something very unreasonable needed her safely home and close to Charlie.

Betsey nodded. Then, impulsively, she reached her hand to the back of his head and pulled him to her cheek. "Don't go out there again," she whispered, and he knew something more powerful than worry, fiercer than fear, had insisted on that impossible request. How desperately he wanted to honor it.

"I will take care."

He helped her into the coach. Charlie looked a giant and a babe at once, sprawling over his mother's lap, a white bandage scarring the portrait of peaceful sleep. *I had a concussion,* John reminded himself. He'd been not so much older than Charlie; it had been severe; it had taken part of his sight for a time. And now he was fine. He was fine. Charlie, too.

The coach pulled away. John turned to look at the line of raging light that had been the pier. When had the pavilion fallen? Perhaps when he'd been under the water searching for Charlie. He didn't know. His lungs burned still. He filled them up and headed out to the surf again.

Hours later, he ran fresh water from the pump at Sarah's carriage house over his arms, an effort to rid himself of salt and sand and smoke, though he knew they had dried in his clothes, just like the blood crusted on his sleeve. He put his head under the pump, then shook out his hair like a dog, and when he stilled, there was Betsey with a towel. As he sat on the pump platform, she dried his face, pressed each of his arms inside the towel, then rubbed his hair and neck.

"How is he?"

"Not conscious. He was restless in the coach—jerking his arms about—but he's not roused since."

"I didn't see Nally's carriage."

"He's been round twice. I expect him in another hour or so. Miss Everson's sitting with Sarah."

Betsey's fingers combed his hair. John pulled her closer.

"The fire's done? There's still so much smoke."

His face moved against her bodice, some sort of gesture to answer her, but he couldn't speak. The fire done? It would smolder for hours yet, but the promenade was destroyed, so there was no more danger to the Esplanade. No more people were stranded by the flames. The rescuable had been rescued.

But three bodies had been brought to shore and covered with sheets. There was a list, too long, of missing. And when John had left, black wreckage was already littering the shore, and there stood the vicar with elderly Mr. Fowler, still trying to convince him no more boats were coming.

John pulled Betsey into his lap. Holding her did not banish the terror, it didn't drown the fear or the heartbreak, but it did make bearing those things seem possible.

In Charlie's room, Miss Everson was certainly asleep, and John thought Sarah must be, too, for she lay beside Charlie on his bed, as still as her unconscious son. The door creaked as he let himself in, but several moments passed before she said, "Who is it?"

She did not respond when John answered. He came to the foot of the bed for whatever visual appraisal of Charlie's condition he could make, but the lamp was low and Sarah huddled next to him, her hand at rest on his cheek. Had he roused? Opened his eyes? What had the doctor said? None of his whispered questions were answered.

He waited.

The room wasn't silent. Miss Everson breathed gutturally, Sarah in staccato sobs. And Charlie—

Suddenly, John's heart was pounding in his ears.

He almost overturned the lamp in his haste to reach it and turn it up. Sarah braced her arm like iron against him when he tried to move her hand from Charlie's face, grunted and resisted his increasing force, and over the boy's body, a fierce and quiet war ensued. Finally, John ordered, "Let loose, Sarah, Christ, let loose," and used honest strength to push her back. She wilted into the mattress, shaking with sobs.

"Charlie!"

He shouted an inch from Charlie's face, where the warmest place was where Sarah's hand had rested. He remembered how Charlie's eyes had opened when he'd done that on the shore, so he shouted for a long time. He remembered holding Charlie in the boat, the difficulty of finding that slow, dim pulse, and so for a long time he searched. And then he shouted again.

Again. How many times?

Sarah was begging him to stop.

He sank to his knees beside the bed, Charlie's wrist circled in his hand. "Sarah." The word scratched his raw throat. He didn't understand how she had lain there. He didn't understand how Charlie had gone, his mother at his side, how there could have been no warning to make her call for help, no time to do anything.

He felt tension in Charlie's arm. His mother, pulling his body to her. John let go. He pressed his face into the bedclothes as Sarah's long, low keen twisted through the room, pulling tight as a rope around his chest. *Stop it,* he wanted to tell her, *stop it,* because the sound was killing him, it was worse than a rope, it was burrowing inside him, eating him alive.

And yet, when the sound did stop, he knew he'd been wrong. What was more fitting, more righteous, than that moan from Sarah's soul? Not the quiet that came after it, white as a frozen field, a deadness in it that belied the throbbing, twisting growth of this pain.

Sarah's voice came, flat, empty, the opposite of her cry. "Was he afraid?"

Of course. They all were. John had known nothing as sickening as that moment he'd spotted Charlie up there on the pier.

"He was brave," he answered. "Prepared to dive off that pier." John had taught him to dive the year Dr. Elliot had passed. He'd nearly upset the boat, jumping up to get Charlie's attention and wave him off the dive.

"I did not ask whether he was brave."

John made a fist. He wanted to cover Charlie's head with his hand once more, but he would have felt like a trespasser, the way Sarah held him.

"I want to know whether my child was afraid. I want to know why didn't you—" A sob plowed through her voice, crumpling her words. "You could have—no one else—I was standing there, waiting, and I saw—there was no one else hurt as he was! No one else! Why didn't you make sure?"

His head buzzed as he tried to sort out the answer to her question, reviewing flashes of memory as he realized Sarah must be right. He'd been in the water, waiting for Charlie's jump. He'd swum where Charlie landed; he'd known when it was taking too long for him to resurface. How many times had he gone under to search? Someone had speculated the boy had hit the underside of one of the craft on his way up. Why had John not anticipated that, made certain there was more clearance?

He left the room because Sarah was telling him to get out. Screaming for him to get out. He didn't know how many times she had said it.

Every member of the household huddled in the corridor outside Charlie's room. Someone brushed past him to tend to Sarah. Weeping, questions. Assurances: The doctor had been sent for; Mrs. Elliot didn't know what she was saying. He squeezed past, summoning up the responses they needed.

Betsey slipped her hand into his and did not make him stop until they came to the door.

"I'll send the wires to her daughters," he said.

"Let someone else. She will want you."

He smeared the tears on one of Betsey's cheeks as he kissed the other. "Send to me if anything's needed."

Mr. Fowler still waited on the foreshore, and the vicar with him. John joined them after he sent the telegrams, and the three men sat in the sand, passing barely a dozen words amongst them, moving only as the tide dictated.

Sunrise bleached the sky.

The pier looked like a wasp.

John saw some of his men and, on the spot, hired them to supervise clearing the washed-up wreckage from the foreshore. The act was the initial pebble of responsibility that came landsliding toward him the moment he reached his office.

He spoke with witnesses and survivors, compiling information for the Baumston & Smythe agent who would arrive soon, as well as for Sir Alton, who anticipated an inquest. All agreed on the source of the fire, a flare-up in the kitchen of the refreshment stand, decorative bunting hanging too near, easy fuel. Precious minutes were lost as the staff attempted to put it out. One man wept, describing how the flames turned from manageable to monstrous between blinks of his eyes.

Four of the missing were located, safe and sound. The body of Mrs. Fowler was recovered. Her name was added to the list of the dead, along with that of Charles Simon Elliot, who had almost reached his fourteenth birthday.

That afternoon, the Duke presided over a subdued official opening of the Kursaal. John attended because Sir Alton insisted, and found himself swaying in place as the various officials had their say, the exhaustion of three sleepless, pressure-loaded days finally collapsing over him.

No gala ball, no fireworks, no Spanish soprano. A band played a hymn, and the vicar remembered the victims and their families in his prayer. The afternoon sun bore down on the crowd, which had stretched itself rather lethargically across the lawn, more interested in shade and breezes than in being able to hear and see the program.

The Kursaal testified to the town's inspiring growth, and now it also stood for Idensea's hope and resilience; all of the Duke's remarks were appropriate. Sir Alton's followed a similar vein, but they left John cold and unsettled.

After the ribbon cutting, Sir Alton and the company architect approached him. They'd been discussing the pier. The new one.

They appeared puzzled when John could only stare. Finally, he shook his head. "I am not speaking of this now, there's no reason. I am—" He paused, saw their puzzlement grow, felt his own thoughts fray.

"Done" was all he could think to say.

Sir Alton followed him beyond the thick of the crowd. "*Done?* You mean you're not staying?"

"I do."

"For the opening?"

Sir Alton's request for clarification made John halt. "*I* am your worry?"

"A great many things worry me just now, Jones," he snapped in an uncharacteristic display of irritation, no doubt allowed by his own weariness. It was suppressed immediately. "And, yes, you are amongst them, considering your recent efforts to discover what leaving Idensea might gain you."

"I've made no secret of it."

"Nor have I blamed you, a young man making his way. Yet—" A calculated hesitation, then a smile. "Neither have I considered you too thick to recognize a bird in the hand when it lands there. Someone of your background—you ought to hold tight. And the company relies upon you." He gestured toward the Esplanade. "Idensea herself relies upon you."

Suddenly, John's depleted spirit rallied. "You'll not put that on me. That is not all mine, and you'll not put it on me."

"For God's sake—"

"Did you know every one of the confirmed dead was a local?

Our neighbors—why could you not say something to *them*?" John pointed to the podium where the speeches had been delivered. "Up there, why not speak to our neighbors? They came, and only to hear how they will *thrive*—"

"Better to expound on failure and defeat?"

"They deserve to be acknowledged, their part in this! What this company owes them deserves to be said. Why couldn't you say it, a lifeboat station, something besides a twenty-year-old manual pump for our fire brigade? Some help to the families who . . . Charlie Elliot—his father delivered your own daughter . . . bless the bleeding Christ, it needed to be said."

"It was not. The occasion." The words were heavy with warning, but then Sir Alton sighed lightly. "It will come, I daresay, and I hope you will be there, but for now—go rest, Jones. You look like hell itself, and you've done more than your duty today."

I hope you will be there. John distrusted the liberality of the statement, sensing Sir Alton was foisting everything to him, all but blackmailing him into staying if he wanted to see things done right. Or was that something he clutched all on his own?

He went to the hotel, intending to eat and wash and borrow a conveyance, because the notion of cycling out to Sarah's house brought a roaring protest from his body.

In the end, his body toppled his will. When he woke, it was dark, and someone was stealing his boots. Between slit eyelids, he registered the glint of brass buttons and was no longer alarmed.

"I'm going to The Bows."

"Sarah is sleeping. Her daughters are there. The doctor gave her something. There is nothing to do until tomorrow."

It seemed unlikely. But it sounded true, grounded in the authority of this girl who loved him.

He slept. Later, he discovered her shoulder, tender and bare, near his own. "I'm sorry," she said, because he was weeping into her neck. Things were so broken, and he still did not see the way to fix them.

"Iefan, I'm sorry. I'm so very sorry. You loved him, and I'm sorry."

Her voice broke with a sob. She took him into her arms as he covered her with his body, kissing her, thanking God she had come to him, thinking, *God, what if she had not?* Her flesh stole him from despair. Against her cheek, he could leave his tears; beneath his touch, her body quivered and her pleasure was his refuge. Such goodness here. That she should come to him, that their brokenness should make something whole, it was good, and she had brought it.

He made love to her, whispering, "I love you, Elisabeth. Bless God, I love you so."

IF THE CARRIAGE STOPS:

You may be at the end of your ribbon.

—*How to Become Expert in Type-writing*

*T*he plash of water, the press of daylight woke Betsey. The door to John's bathroom stood ajar; she could see his back, bare, braces hanging from the waistband of his trousers. She smelled his soap and let her eyes close again, permitting herself one more fleeting, indulgent dream of breakfast here in this room, she wearing John's shirt. Sitting beside him in services. A walk afterward, hands clasped.

Her lashes were wet when she opened her eyes. She and John had never sat in church without the Seilers or Sarah and Charlie between them.

Across the room, John was doing up the buttons of his shirt, his black hair lopping over his brow, his shoulders bearing the light from the windows.

He reached for his necktie draped on the back of a chair, and paused when he realized she was awake. She wished she had said it last night, or even a moment ago. *How I love you, Iefan, how I love you.* She wished she did not think it too late to say now.

He draped the tie round his neck. "A fuss it will kick up, me bringing you to the house."

"I gave up my room to the grandchildren. No one expected me home." The few things she had brought with her were stowed under her desk in the company office.

"Then where were you to be last night?"

"Here."

His jaw was damp, pinked from his shave, and the light caught a ripple of muscle. They'd needed each other last night, but this morning, her choice troubled him.

She added, "So you don't have to worry about smuggling me back in place."

"I was prepared for the fuss, Elisabeth."

Lying on her side in his bed, she gave a one-shouldered shrug, a thoughtless acceptance that the deed was done. Only a few moments later did she grasp his meaning, understand for what he was prepared. To spare her the scandal. To make the sacrifice, complete the rescue.

He was—he had been—prepared to marry her.

Beneath the pillow, she opened her hand, felt on her cheek the pressure of her fingertips through the feathers. "You keep mistaking me for some protected virgin."

"I see you." He made a point of it, fixing her with a thorough gaze. "I *see* you. You are the one mistaking it."

"I would never have demanded that of you." She sat up in the bed as her voice rose, clutching the sheet to her chest. "I never counted on it. We had the contract—"

"Never you throw up that sham contract to me again—"

"—and last night finished it."

"—do you hear? A matter of convenience it's been for you, and you'll not have it—"

"There are no obligations between us!"

Silence fell. The room seemed to breathe and blink, light fading and rising again as a cloud passed, a shift creaking somewhere in the floor. John came to the bed, and she drew up her knees to give him a place to sit.

"Well, I love you, girl. No lie nor passing fancy last night, that."

Betsey rested her forehead on her knees. She believed him. She believed she'd known even before he did. In the cocoon of her arms and legs, she saw Tinfell Cottage, blurred by her mocking lie to Sir Alton, by a cynicism all her own and perhaps uglier than Sir Alton's. Why—*what*—was she fighting? Why couldn't she take what she wanted, however it had arrived?

John found her foot beneath the bedcovers and gave it a squeeze. "Pearse Leland leaves today," he said, making her lift her head. "I am going to see him, do all I can to get him to hire me for that London job."

"Be careful." She repeated what she had overheard between Leland and Sir Alton at the pleasure railway. "I meant to tell you the night of the ball, but—"

The ball had never happened.

John did not show much surprise. "No telling what damage that man has been doing me ever since he decided I ought to be grateful to spend the rest of my life managing his company. But I have board members who will speak for me, enough to undo the slurs, perhaps."

"Of course." She did not doubt that if he wanted it, the job was his. He did want it, obviously; it was the sort of position he had been seeking, *before*. Now, *after*, the fire and Charlie . . .

It settled uncomfortably within her, that he seemed to want it still.

"So," she began, "whilst you washed up, waited for me to wake, you—" She bit her lip, afraid how the words would balloon once she spoke them, become urgent and fragile. "You decided we'd marry and go to London."

His mouth winced in apology. "You hate London."

She shook her head. "I only swore to myself I'd never live there again."

"Different, you'd find it, no longer all on your own."

Every thought of London was paired with the bleak and often frightening struggle of feeding and housing herself. To imagine herself as a wife there, she had to summon up images of her sister, and Mrs. Dellaforde in Manchester, even Lady Dunning. None of them quite took.

"Let me say the rest of it." After a quick glance at her, John studied the carpet, his thumb tracing upon the covers an outline of her toes. "I am for Wales, soon as I can get away. I want to see my family. I mean to speak to my dad, and get Owen, to have him come live with me."

Betsey straightened. "Your brother? John, you are going to raise him yourself?" She knew John thought much of the boy, but he'd seen the child only twice in his life. "And what of your father, what will he say?"

"Dad will see. I can give Owen a better life. That he will see, with this job with Leland."

"But—"

She bit down on her words. John plainly did not want to hear *but*. Despite a full night of sleep, his bath and shave, he looked—

She thought of her months as a laundress. Mountains of used-up-ness that made you despair if you thought of them all at once.

Gently: "But you're an idiot."

He smiled. He leaned toward her, and she lay back into the pillows as the deep, deep well of his palm skimmed her body, as his weight came upon her. He kissed her, and she thought, *I need him,* and also, *Isn't this my trick?*

All done up in his Sunday best, John settled beside her in the spent, tangled sheets, pulling her to his chest, stroking her hair back from her face.

"Waking up, changing everything about your life?" She spoke softly. She hardly knew whether she wanted him to hear. "Bringing a little child into all that turmoil with you? Iefan."

"No turmoil. Putting things back is what it is, I know how it needs be, it is all very clear. I had my plans before, and I have them still. I know how it needs to be."

"I wasn't what you planned."

"No, girl. In no way that."

She could take that low laugh of his for nothing but appreciation. It was his certitude that filled her with fear for him. "Tell me how you felt this morning. You decided you would save whatever scrap of honor I still have by marrying me, you'd give up your chances for money and connections, and children—"

"Owen we'd have."

"No. He isn't part of it." Somehow, it made it worse that John had broken in with that particular justification. "He isn't—"

She sat up. His collar looked like a knife-edge cutting into his flesh as he lay on the pillow. She tried to adjust it, then skated her fingertip along the starched crease of his shirtsleeve. On the bureau across the room, a black pasteboard frame barely contained John's large family, his mother in the center, Owen a babe on her lap. A stray, wild thought of Avery Nash popped into her mind, of that cozy flat he'd had when she first knew him, his type-writer and books.

"Owen isn't what you'd be giving up."

"Elisabeth." He was exasperated.

"Just tell me. How did you feel?"

"What do you think? I felt glad, I felt . . . relieved, that's what. . . . It was good, a good decision. It *is*."

He turned his face to the ceiling when she didn't agree. She couldn't. She was at a loss, taken unaware by *relieved*, unsure what she had expected or hoped for in the first place.

"Do you think this morning was the first time I'd thought of marrying you? The Kursaal was finished, Elisabeth, the end of the season was coming. I was looking for a new position. Bless God, Pearse Leland had all but offered outright. Had I set to it, he would have, whatever Sir Alton was rigging behind my back. But—" He propped up on an elbow. "I was dragging my feet."

He waited for her to draw the conclusion. *Because of you.*

"Couldn't think how to do it," he added.

Leaving you.

"Too hard it felt, but this morning . . ."

Again, he waited.

She said: "You believed your choice had been taken away, and you felt relieved."

Wrong conclusion. A shot of dismay, then a stone wall of challenge. Betsey turned her back on it, removing herself from the bed.

"That was not my meaning, don't say it that way."

Her clothes were waiting in the neat stack she'd folded last night. She began to dress, her hands trembling. "I know, it isn't very nice. It isn't anything you'd find in a poem. But neither of us is much for fine poetry, John."

"God damn it, you're twisting it, you're making it—" In frustration, he bolted from the bed and came to her, putting his hand over the remaining garments in her stack of clothing. "Why are you making it into this?"

"Because it's *you*! You, John, the one who trusts his instincts, who makes decisions without a backward glance, at least when it's not to do with me. You were *glad* to have the decision taken away from you."

"You don't understand."

"I can't—it doesn't make sense. Nothing you're about now makes sense. I don't understand how you can leave Idensea, and Sarah, just now. Someone else could, not you."

"Look at this room, Elisabeth!" His hand dropped off her stack of clothes, and he repeated more calmly, "Look at this room."

She did, though she was perfectly familiar with it, for its furnishings matched those of the other guest rooms of the hotel. She took in the shambles of the vacated bed, the photographer's pasteboard frame surrounding John's family, one of her own brass buttons sitting enigmatically on the mantelshelf, and her survey was complete.

"Does any part of it tell you I ever meant to make my home here?"

"Please only think—"

"Idensea isn't mine!" He tore back to the bed to rummage through the bedclothes, searching for something, but so desperately Betsey could only watch in fear. "I wasn't meant to stay. I had—I *have* plans, and they aren't to settle for Tinfell Cottage and use my days to tend business for a man I can't even trust."

Amongst the white linens, a black necktie appeared. John snatched it up. "It will all go to the devil if it's waiting on my care."

Her heart was breaking for him. She didn't know whether it was right or wrong, but she pushed: "Even Sarah?"

He shook his head madly and hooked the tie around his neck. "She will want you. She will need you to forgive her."

"Whatever Sarah needs from me, she has, even if it's to hate me."

He struggled with the tie. After a few moments, Betsey went to help him, though her fingers were hardly steadier. This was not the fine silk thing Mr. Seiler had given him. She wondered if that had gone the way of his coat, whatever way that was, last night. When she had finished the knot and smoothed down the ends, John clutched her arms.

"Come, you. Just come with me."

He released her before she responded. He knew she would refuse. Still, she answered, "I can't. You are asking me to trust you, and I don't."

The words created a long, dark tunnel between them. It stretched and it stretched, and across the distance, she whispered, "Not as you are now. I don't believe you know what you are doing."

For Betsey, watching him in the days that followed was like seeing the pier blaze again—an overwhelming sense of smallness, help-lessness. If she believed he'd somehow taken leave of his senses, did she also believe he would come back to them? She saw he did not allow for the opportunity; she saw his bruised-looking eyes, how the circles beneath them never faded. Correspondence and telephone calls flooded the office, meetings were held at all hours, a trembling old man appeared and insisted on confronting who-ever was responsible, and John was in the thick of it all; John was the one who steered the old man to his office. And though Sarah refused to see him and most everyone else, Sarah's daughters relied on him for any number of deeds and words of advice. The day of Charlie's funeral, he was never more than an arm's distance away, and in the quiet of the graveside prayer, Betsey recognized the sound of his thumb rubbing alongside his forefinger and felt surprised it was the grating of calluses she heard rather than the wet smack of blood.

Nights, crippling pangs reduced her to a ball; she shrank into the bedclothes aching for Charlie, for Sarah, for herself. For John, for John, for John, wondering, *What will become of him?*

How brightly, how terrifyingly he burned. And so swiftly, too. Little more than a week past the pier fire, Betsey entered an office sinuous with the vines of hearsay and speculation.

Mr. Jones had submitted his resignation. He was taking a position in London.

Exact rules cannot be given for every emergency in life.

—*How to Become Expert in Type-writing*

*L*illian understood that the unfortunate fire had left John with rather a lot to do, but she could not imagine him committing so abominable an act as standing her up. He was—well, he was not quite a gentleman, but he was decent, and he was neither forgetful nor hateful. He could be counted upon. She was counting on that. To go hunting for him felt indecent on a number of levels, but Lillian saw no other option left her.

Besides, she was running out of time. She'd promised Aunt Constance: By the time the rest of the family returned from their tide pool walk with the naturalist, she, Lillian, would be engaged.

Thus, she found herself pretending to an office of dumbstruck clerks that *certainly* she had known Mr. Jones was traveling today; she had only mistaken the time, and now she was not quite sure what day he'd given her for his return, if someone could be so kind as to refresh her memory . . . ?

Every fellow in the office had come to his feet upon her appearance in the doorway, but thus far, only a young man had spoken for the group. He shrugged now. "Couldn't say, miss. That is, he didn't say, leastways that I know of."

"I see."

Another, his face as white and round as a clock's, put up a finger to attract her notice. "Miss Dobson can tell you something of that, I should think. Miss Dobson, when might we expect our Mr. Jones back with us again?"

A shuffle rippled across the office, and then no one was looking at Lillian anymore. A few gazes dropped to the desktops; most slipped right past Lillian to a spot behind her. Turning, Lillian found at the door a young woman of alarming height, dressed in dun-colored tweed. She did not spare a glance for Lillian nor anyone else as she brushed by to one of the desks, replying, "You are mistaken, Mr. Hamble. I do not know."

"Ah," the clock-face said. "There you have it, then, miss. I was mistaken. Miss Dobson says she knows nothing, and we can only believe her, I suppose."

From a place deeper in the office, sniggering. And Lillian understood it. She could not have said how, but she did.

"Thank you. That will be all," she said in the same tone she used for the household servants, and made a firm step toward Office Girl's desk.

But Office Girl met her with a gaze so unnervingly steady that Lillian faltered and glanced about the office, where there seemed to be a sudden rush to return to chairs and desks and tasks. Oh, what did they imagine was about to happen? That she, Lillian Gilbey, was about to tussle with an office girl? Over a man?

She plucked back her poise and smiled down at Office Girl, sitting at the desk. "Miss . . . Dobson? My father will be arriving from London to spend the coming weekend with my family, as he generally does, but it is his birthday this week, you see, and I'd hoped to arrange a private dinner party for him here at the hotel. Would you be so kind as to help me make the arrangements?"

"No, Miss Gilbey."

"No?" Despite her resolve, Lillian found herself cowed by the direct and unapologetic refusal, not to mention the fact Office Girl knew her name. "I—I don't see why not."

Office Girl smiled. Her cheekbones were worthy of some envy.

"If that's true, then I can only assume you ignorant of certain arrangements here at the hotel. I suppose the one relevant at this moment is that my duties do not regularly include service for hotel guests. I'd direct you to Mr. Seiler, the hotel manager, instead."

"I see." The reply was frail. Office Girl looked back down to her work, apparently finished with the conversation. But she'd forgotten that she'd inked her pen already, and so a great black blob began eating up her paper, and she cursed. Only Lillian could hear it, and only just, but the vehemence with which it was whispered was as shocking as the expression itself. Lillian drew back. She couldn't speak with a creature such as this.

"I see," she repeated, and turned to leave, except—

She was desperate. She must have something to tell Aunt Constance, or Aunt Constance would—

She turned back and leaned over the desk in a most unladylike posture. "Please, Miss Dobson," she said, her plea as low and earnest as Miss Dobson's curse. "I should like—I need to speak with you, and I cannot do it here with all these fellows looking on. Please, won't you walk out with me, only for a moment?"

Well, Miss Dobson was a very hard sort, that was plain, but somehow Lillian had managed to move her. She relented with a soft nod, then led Lillian from the office to the veranda on the side of the hotel, moving out of earshot of the guests sitting with their afternoon papers. When Lillian failed to speak, Miss Dobson asked what she wanted.

"I must know when John—Mr. Jones—is due to return, and I am persuaded you know something of the matter."

"He's resigned, Miss Gilbey, didn't you know?"

Every response at hand would have disclosed the extent of her ignorance. Lillian could only nod, inscrutably, she hoped.

"He will return to tie off some things, but he's only just left for London, then Wales, and his business may take a few days, or a few weeks. I'm afraid I don't have the information you require."

This she said as she dabbed at her ink-smudged fingers with one of those horrible homemade handkerchiefs John always carried. It weakened the credibility of her claim, to say the least. Lillian pressed her lips against the rising anxiety she felt and mentally rehearsed her next question. She must strive toward indifference.

"Miss Dobson, are you in love with Mr. Jones?" *Not at all bad.* If only Miss Dobson were not so excessively tall, the entire effect might have come off more successfully. Lillian kept up her brows (one brow would have been so much better, if only she could do that) as she awaited a response.

"That isn't really what you need to know, now is it?"

"It—it isn't?"

"I should think what must concern you is whether or not John loves me."

Lillian gave up her pose, looking away to blink back tears. Ah, God, what should she do if that were so, if John were in love with this girl? For all the improbability of it, Lillian suddenly felt it could be no other way.

"I don't know why I am crying," she lied. Miss Dobson held out John's inky handkerchief to her, which only made Lillian lose control of an ugly sob as she shook her head and dug into her little handbag. "It is just—just that I need him. I need him!" Unable to find her own pocket handkerchief, she brought the entire handbag up to her face and crushed it against her eyes.

"You *need* him? Rather say 'want,' Miss Gilbey. It will be far more truthful, and you'll find it easier than pretending to understand need."

Lillian pulled her handbag from her eyes. It was Indian silk, embroidered and beaded and suitable to carry with nothing she owned but the afternoon frock she wore now. Miss Dobson, in her drab tweed, holding nothing but an unrefined and borrowed handkerchief, thought Lillian Gilbey could not understand need. Thought Lillian Gilbey would take what she wanted, even if it left the other party empty-handed.

"I do need him, though," she whispered. "I need—I need to marry, right away."

Miss Dobson yanked her by the elbow so hard and fast that Lillian dropped her parasol. She was steered off the veranda, across the carriage drive, to the fountain with its noisy cascade of water.

"Whatever else that damn idiot has done, he's *not* rutted you and got you pregnant!"

It wasn't the rough handling nor the rougher language that made Lillian's jaw drop. It was the word *pregnant*. The doctor Aunt Constance had smuggled her to one afternoon hadn't said it, and even Aunt Constance, much given to bluntness, had euphemized her way toward the topic. She'd narrowed her eyes when Lillian, dispirited since that episode at the rail station, had let it slip she was almost glad the fire had ruined the gala ball, for she was quite ready to go to bed. And after Lillian donned the same walking costume two of three afternoons, her aunt had taken her aside in concern.

But it required many false starts before Lillian began to understand what her aunt meant, inquiring after her health and whether or not she was *just as she always had been*. And then to discover why her aunt was curious about her cycles—

It had amounted to a very confusing and shocking sort of conversation, and Lillian had the feeling it would have gone more smoothly had Miss Dobson been there to mediate. She was somehow grateful for Miss Dobson's directness, however vulgar.

"Not John," she confirmed. "Another."

She hadn't realized how tightly Miss Dobson had been holding her until she let go. The flesh above Lillian's elbow echoed with pain even though she rubbed it.

"Why the devil don't you marry that one, then? And do hush your crying—you will attract attention."

She held out the handkerchief again; this time, Lillian took it and folded the inky part inside so she could dry her eyes and nose. "He has given me up," she said, which prompted another eruption of tears. "I'm in such terrible, terrible trouble. I know I deserve it, but I did not understand—"

"Stop crying, Miss Gilbey. You must stop."

But the office girl's voice carried something steady in it now, steady and almost warm. And wasn't Lillian grateful for it, ready to grasp it like a Christmas orphan? Aunt Constance, for all she wanted to help, could not conceal the depth of her disappointment, and Lillian knew it would be much worse if her parents discovered the truth.

Miss Dobson held no expectations, though, only seemed to know it was possible for a girl to get herself in trouble, and that it was sorrowful when it happened. Such sympathy seemed the most extravagant gift she'd ever received, a string of pearls a mile long.

Benches surrounding the fountain offered places to rest with a view of the sea. They claimed one, and Lillian worked to control her tears. Looking out at the water helped, as did the distraction of remembering some Tennyson: *With blackest moss the flower-plots were thickly crusted, one and all.*

"A six- or seven-month baby—did you think John would believe that?" Miss Dobson asked after a moment.

"I don't know. . . . Do men notice that sort of thing?" Thanks to Aunt Constance, Lillian herself had only recently noted the problematic arithmetic of certain couples in her acquaintance, but Miss Dobson's incredulous expression now made this seem atypical. "I don't know what I thought, except that of all the eligible gentlemen I know, John seemed the one—"

"Most willing to raise another man's child. To save you. Save the child."

"He is good." And he was here. At least, he had been. "He would not be unhappy with me, I think. I think he meant to ask me, once. Before . . ."

Miss Dobson gave her a frightening smile. The woman leaned toward her, and Lillian could not help shrinking back.

"That's right," Miss Dobson said. "Before *me*. Don't know what to make of that, now, do you?"

Lillian shook her head, intimidated into agreeing. Lying. On the contrary, she had a very good idea what to make of it. Tears welled afresh; John was lost to her, and with him, any hope. She pressed the handkerchief to her lips, but the awful press of emotion escaped in an embarrassing, snorting sob.

"Cry, then, I don't blame you," Miss Dobson said. "It's a wretched shame what you're going through. But hear me well, Miss Gilbey."

With that, she touched her fingertips to Lillian's chin and, with no physical force whatsoever, compelled Lillian to look her in the eye.

"I didn't let John go so he'd be handy for the likes of you to use up however it suits."

The *likes* of her? Lillian's tears were shocked into abeyance. She was not the *likes* of anything, or at least she never had been before. But now she was fallen, so perhaps . . .

But Miss Dobson wasn't finished. "And if you dare take this selfish, desperate request to him—"

Thoughtfully, she surveyed the milliner's landscape atop Lillian's head; leisurely, she withdrew the hat pin and held it pointed end up between them, all while confining Lillian with the lightest touch to her chin.

"You had best beware your neck."

It was the most shocking liberty ever taken with Lillian's person, excepting, of course, *that* one. Rather as with *that* one, it was done before she realized she'd submitted to it.

And now, with Miss Dobson striding away with her favorite hat pin, Lillian was all alone again, in full view of the veranda. Her parasol was up there; retrieving it was bound to be awkward.

She remained on the bench, holding her hat against the breeze, delaying the lonely, humiliating walk into the hotel.

Well, she'd gained two useful tidbits of information for Aunt Constance. John was in London. And Miss Dobson had given him up.

She touched her neck.

A long shadow fell over the bench.

"And I want my handkerchief back," Miss Dobson said.

For every change of a subject there must be a new
paragraph.

—*How to Become Expert in Type-writing*

*M*r. Seiler intercepted Betsey's dash into the hotel,
speaking her name so firmly that she was certain she had missed a subtler signal to conduct herself more
decorously.

She couldn't speak. It was all there, an apology, an assurance
she was returning to her desk, but her throat would not allow passage.

"My office, if you please?" he murmured, and she feared she
was in for some of that demented coffee he preferred or, worse, a
sympathetic ear.

Instead, he gave her a stack of correspondence to answer. It was
thick; it would require hours to complete. Betsey would spend the
remainder of the afternoon at the type-writing machine, too busy
to think or even to make eye contact, too close to the rhythmic din
of the keys to hear the whispers that had followed her ever since
Mr. Jones had announced his resignation.

"Thank you," she said to Mr. Seiler.

His lips pursed thoughtfully. "Congratulations once more upon
your success at Bradford. The board will be pleased, I am certain."

"I hope so." She had traveled to Bradford yesterday to meet a mill owner who had tried to cancel his employee outing after the fire—an effort well worth her time since it would increase her profit report to the board.

She appreciated Mr. Seiler's attempts to turn her thoughts, but whether the excursion scheme would continue past this summer was a separate question from her personal employment and whether Sir Alton would allow *that* to continue. If he had ever truly believed he needed her, the reason for it had vanished the moment John submitted his resignation.

Betsey turned to the door, having Mr. Seiler's implied permission to leave, letters clutched to her bosom.

"He may marry her," she said quietly to the doorframe.

"*Ma chérie*, he may."

Her throat shut again. She thought she might die with the agonizing pressure of it.

Mr. Seiler said, "We had expected so, before—"

He hesitated, the way Miss Gilbey had done. Everyone understood Betsey Dobson as an intermission in John Jones's life. Everyone, even Betsey, and except for John.

Very well, damn it, *damn it*. But she had been attempting to protect John from his own foolish, fevered self, not deliver him to Miss Gilbey.

She made a brisk trip of the walk to the company offices, trying to outpace her worry, remembering Charlie's funeral, haunted by the sound of John's thumb rubbing alongside his finger.

She wished she had slipped her fingers between his to hush that anguished rasp. She wished she had said yes to any mad plan he made, any upheaval he needed to create, just so he would know he was not alone.

All eyes noted her return to the office. She sat down at the type-writing machine and discovered John's pocket handkerchief inside her hand, wound and crumpled around Miss Gilbey's hat pin. She tucked the handkerchief inside her cuff, the pin into her hair, and prepared the machine with sure, familiar actions. Then she skimmed the letter on the top of the pile and proceeded to smash onto the page the heading and the salutation to one Mr. Jerome Worth. She began the response.

Thank you

Her fingers held over the keys, immobilized. She could not see the words—the machine was a model that required the operator to lift the carriage in order to view the work. Such a detail mattered only to insecure type-writers, not someone with Betsey's experience, but suddenly those words hidden inside the carriage filled her with sorrow.

Was her strength for his sake, or hers? Why hadn't she taken his hand? Said, *I can't come with you, but I love you . . .* ?

Or, *You've taken leave of your senses, and I love you . . .* ?

Or simply . . .

Miss Slott would not have approved. Mr. Wofford would have accused her of stealing. But when Betsey's hands stirred again, the letter was hers and hers alone.

When he comes back, I will tell him "Thank you."
Regarding the following:

1, Idensea.

2, Sarah, Charlie. My chair at their table.

3, A needless vow. As though you were some saint
and I was too.

4, Rail fare.

5, The widest sky I've ever seen and that type-
writing is not the best job a girl can hope for
afterall. Mr. Seiler, bicycle, how to ride it, how to
swim, every thing I try because I thik you might
thinkI could do it.

I will tell you my thanks, and by the by thankyou
also means I lvoe you..

I love you.

John had told Betsey, *I know how it needs to be*, and yet here he
stood in an empty parlor, stalled, unable to imagine such an extravagance of space furnished. Wouldn't he like to see the other rooms,
the house agent suggested, and John said yes, and then he said no.
The place was fine, perfect, he would come round the agent's office
this afternoon to arrange the lease.

Well, why not? The agent had obviously heeded John's stated
requirements, and John had things to do. See Pearse Leland, hire
a nurse for Owen, acquire furniture, catch a train to Wales. He'd
made plans.

Outside, in the little square park across the lane, a Salvation
Army band in full uniform played, and John stood watching the
musicians and the singers, two women with good strong voices
singing "A Mighty Fortress." Feeling in his coat for some coins, he
started to cross the street when he heard his name.

He looked about, then spied the elegant curve of a hat brim
poking out from a hansom cab waiting just down the street. Lillian Gilbey?

"How are you, John?" she said, smiling, when he came to the
cab.

"I am surprised," he admitted. "Back in London already?"

"Oh, we—Aunt Constance and I—decided to return early.
You remember my aunt, Mrs. Middleton."

John nodded at the woman as she leaned forward to look out
at him.

"Aunt Constance has a visit to pay nearby here. She says I may
sit in the square with you whilst she goes there."

With no chaperone? Thoroughly bemused now, John opened

the half door of the hansom and helped Lillian out. The cab moved on, and he offered his arm.

"How did you find me?"

"Oh—" She waved her hand as though it had been no great task. "Your hotel, and then the house agent's office."

He tried to imagine Lillian Gilbey inquiring after a man at a hotel. Could not. He stopped and turned her around to get a good look under the hat brim. "You are mystifying me, Miss Gilbey."

She tolerated his scrutiny briefly, then glanced away with a scowl, holding her hands up to her ears. "Oh, that racket!" she said of the Salvation Army band a few feet away. "Can't we come away from it? It's too horrible—I can't think over it!"

John started to lead her to the other side of the square, handing some coins to one of the uniformed singers as they passed. The singer broke off from her verses of "Onward, Christian Soldiers" to say "God bless ye, sir" to him, and John hesitated there in front of her before he felt Lillian urging him on. He swiped a few dead leaves from a bench for her, then sat watching the band.

"You have taken a house?" Lillian finally said.

"Just rooms."

"It's not terribly smart here."

"Safe and respectable will have to do till I have more cash."

"Oh, certainly. I didn't mean to offend you."

John frowned. When the world had been normal, Lillian always scolded him if he mentioned money in any specific way. "You didn't offend me, Miss Gilbey."

She took a moment to draw off her gloves, fold them, unfold them, then pull them back on. A tense laugh. "My dear papa—do you know what he has promised each of his daughters?"

"Everything from a mockingbird to another day?"

He feared, with no little shock, the gentle jest would send her to tears, but she manufactured more laughter instead. "You think me spoilt. I shall never dissuade you of the notion if I tell you Papa's promise. A house, you see. One for each daughter, isn't it funny?" Her eyes darted to his. "A house as a wedding present?"

If he'd been walking, he would have stumbled; eating, he would have choked. Sitting here, John found he could not hold her gaze, pretty and blue and entirely too hopeful. He glanced back to the band in the middle of the square.

Bless God, had Lillian Gilbey truly tracked him down in order to propose to him?

"You have, I am fairly certain, thought of marrying me before."

She had.

It was as topsy-turvy a scene as ever imagined in Wonderland, but here it was in this perfectly rational square in staid old London on an ordinary Wednesday afternoon. With a Salvation Army band booming "Onward, Christian Soldiers," no less.

"Lillian, I don't—"

"I know you have changed your mind, John. I know. But if you could see any way to . . . that is, if you still had any inclination toward it . . . I'd like you to think of it again, and know I'd accept."

So she was asking *him* to propose. This made a touch more sense, he supposed.

"There is the house," she went on, "but I have a dowry, too, naturally. And my father would find a place for you in his company, or you could stay on with this new position of yours if you prefer. Or study architecture. You mentioned that once, didn't you? You could do it, now. And I would be a good wife for you. I shall be better than I have been, more pliable, and pleasant—"

She had wrenched off her gloves again; John caught one of her hands to hush her. "Lils. You never considered yourself a parcel in a shipment of goods before, not so I could tell. So what is this?"

"I want you to understand—there would be benefits, should you choose me. Enough benefits, perhaps, to make it worthwhile."

"Lillian Gilbey, I know you've read too much poetry to believe you must settle for a man who marries your fortune."

Well, and that made her cry. John handed over his handkerchief like an automaton. He was so damn exhausted, every emotion he'd kept at bay these past weeks pressing upon him—his grief for Charlie, yes, and Betsey, too, for he had no other name for

how he missed her, what that cold panic was when he remembered
he was without her. The disaster of the fire; Sarah's accusations,
which she didn't mean but were somehow true; leaving Idensea
and all the uncertainty of starting this new life in London—the
only thing that felt right and true was that soon, he would be in
Wales to bring back Owen and give the boy a new life, one with
promise and goodness.

"It—my fortune—is all I have," she said. John started to scoff,
but she shook her head vehemently. "It is. I'm ruined, John. I am
ruined, and . . . and with . . . and with child, and I . . ."

John stood, not hearing the rest. John stood, not to walk away,
but because his body seemed to demand some confirmation that it
was awake and in the world, the real one, not one conjured from
dreams.

It was something he would remember the rest of his life, this
moment when he realized that, for all his instincts, he really didn't
know a damn thing.

Oh, there was one thing of which he was fairly certain right
now. "Noel Dunning," he said.

Lillian looked up, surprise suspending the flood of tears. But
then all John could see was the top of her hat, which seemed to be
outfitted with enough netting to capture every cod in the North Sea.
A long, fluid feather waved to the rhythm of her heaving shoulders.

He let her weep. A hansom cab made a pass around the square,
then exited to a side street for another slow tour of the neighborhood. It would return twice more before John managed to extract
all the necessary details from Lillian, whose discomfort with plain
speech about the topic hampered communication as much as her
fear and embarrassment. But it seemed Dunning had stopped calling on her after *it*—"*it* " being the closest she came to naming the
act of intercourse—except for once, a few weeks before her family
had left for Idensea.

"Lillian, did he know about the babe?" John asked.

"Of course he knew!" Fresh sobs welled up from her. A bright
berry fell loose from her hat and rolled into the swaths of netting.

"But he only told me he was so sorry for *it*, for everything, and I was cold to him—I hadn't any choice about that—but I—"

"Why not?" John interrupted.

"Why not?" His ignorance apparently bewildered her. "How would it look for me to forgive him, just like that? Didn't you hear me say he didn't call for weeks after—after *it*?"

"Bless the bleeding Christ! You meant to punish him."

"Only that day! Only until I came to Idensea. Except I went, and—and he wasn't there! He wasn't there at all!"

Because he is bloody in Vienna, John thought. He wondered if Dunning had paid that last call before or after he'd known his father was sending him away. In any case, he'd left a pregnant Lillian for his many months of piano lessons. A dark monster dug into John's gut as he watched Lillian's feather wave, there to reside until he next set his eyes on Noel Dunning.

He sat back down beside Lillian and allowed her to cry over what she called her foolish, evil choices, the self-evident fact that she was unlovable and easily forgotten, the general faithlessness of all men, and a great many other things he couldn't quite make out. The brim of her hat swiped his eye as she lifted her face to his to ask him again to consider marriage to her.

"Lillian . . ." The hansom cab was entering the square again. "It is a great thing you ask, a secret like that. To have it with us all the rest of our lives."

It was one misgiving amongst many. He bowed his head to his fist as Lillian's tearful noises started up again. "Please stop that," he said, failing to quash the impatient note in his voice. He heard her gulp, trying to regain control of herself. Trying to be tractable, do just as he asked.

His life was on fire, and here he scrambled on his hands and knees, trying to brush back together the grains of his admiration for Lillian Gilbey, collect them all and see what they amounted to, burning walls all around. He could remember sitting with Tobias and Marta the night after Lillian's Whitsun visit to Idensea, laying out all the reasons Lillian would make a good wife for him, seeing if they agreed, having met her. They had, and all those reasons, all those grains, were they not still there?

Plus, now, this: "If we marry," he said, "you will be a mother even earlier than you imagine."

Halfway through his explanation of Owen, she began nodding as though her head were on a spring. Of course they should take him in, she would love him as her own, it would be perfect, and oh, wouldn't she welcome the chance to show how grateful she felt?

A pliable, grateful little wife, his for the taking.

His hand lifted, a gesture of refusal, not taking. It was involuntary, something from his animal brain, and as soon as he noticed it, he distrusted it and folded it away. He had to close his eyes and force himself to remember where he was, how he had come here.

London, his job, forward, upward. There was a path, and it was marked, and it seemed possible he would sleep again after a few irreversible steps.

And Elisabeth.

She had refused him. His life on fire, him knowing what to do, how it needed to be, and she refused him.

"Please," Lillian begged in a whisper that seemed the echo of his own misery. For all he knew, parallel miseries made a fine enough marital bond.

"If you intend to say no, do it now."

He didn't say no. Lillian didn't cry again, not until she was out of sight and almost out of earshot inside the hansom cab with her aunt. He gave her credit for the effort; it was nearly as much as he himself was able to manage.

The curtains were gone.

The absence of the snow-blue fabric John had sent his mother so long ago, along with the general stillness inside the cottage, disoriented him briefly, made him wonder if he'd ducked into the wrong house. And at the oak table dominating the space that was kitchen, dining room, and parlor together sat a stranger, peeling potatoes with a dull knife.

His dad's new wife since June, three months after the first one had passed.

Dilys, his sister of fifteen, apologized for no one having written him. Nearly everything John knew of his family since he'd left home had come from his mother's twice-monthly letters. He'd made excuses for no one else taking up the practice yet since her death, but this . . .

"I know it is quick," Dilys whispered to him later while his stepmother—not a stranger, quite, but a girl he'd known in school—tended the pot in the hearth, and John cleaned and sharpened all the knives of the household. He drew blades over the steel in resolute strokes and listened to Dilys explain it was for the best, as she would be marrying Emrys Morgan as soon as she passed her sixteenth birthday in October. There were still three young ones at home; someone had to see to the housekeeping and child rearing she herself had been doing since their mother had fallen ill. As for the new Mrs. Rhys-Jones, she was the daughter of Gavin Pritchard, explanation enough for why she'd be happy to leave home to be second wife to a man more than twice her years.

The degree of her happiness seemed to John a difficult reckoning. He apologized as he distributed the gifts he'd brought, telling her he would have brought a wedding gift had he known. She shrank back, a picture of herself in school days long past, Mared Pritchard, a year or so behind him, venturing a tap on his brother Davey's shoulder, then looking like a washed-out sheet when Davey turned round to her. "Generous you've been already," she said, and John supposed she meant the portion of his wages he sent each month.

Dilys and she seemed to get on rather the way Mrs. Seiler got on with the new girls on her staff at the hotel. The three little ones—eleven-year-old Janny; Briallen, seven; and little Owen—tended to appeal to Dilys for their needs, even though Dilys told them, "Ask your mam."

"Mam" always glanced over their heads to Dilys before making any answer.

Not long before she would be bearing her own children, John guessed. Better for her to have Owen out of the way. He'd send for the little girls within a year, he decided during this first evening home, until he remembered there was Lillian to consult on the matter. Miss Gilbey, his fiancée.

Let go of the lever and the pointer will slip back to zero.
—*How to Become Expert in Type-writing*

*W*ith time before his father was due home from the quarry, John headed for the churchyard, discovering along the way Briallen and Owen trailing after him, both of them licking the sticks of rock he had brought from Idensea. For a moment, he didn't know he wanted the company, but Briallen, with Owen in tow, looked as sturdy and determined as her mother used to, and John let them come along.

"Who sees to the grave?" John asked her, in Welsh, when they arrived. The gravestone, of the purple slate mined from the quarry, hadn't been in place when he'd been here for the funeral. Beside it, a heliotrope still had a fresh-planted look to it, and the trimmed grass seemed tender despite the growth of a spring and summer. A bouquet of meadowsweet tied with string lay before the stone. "*Anwyliaid,*" read the inscription below the name and dates. *Beloved.*

Kneeling, Briallen picked up the bouquet and began to pinch off the wilting blooms. "Everyone," she answered.

A fullness in John's throat tripped up his smile. Briallen's encompassing response was probably not so great an exaggeration, considering how the village had loved his mother. Briallen tucked back one corner of her mouth, studying him.

"You're not used to missing her?"

"I am not, little one. Are you?"

She shook her head and replaced the bunch of meadowsweet. "But you've been far off a great long time."

"One sort of missing that is, being far off. Another sort to have her in heaven."

"Mam is with the brothers," Owen said suddenly. He was lining pebbles atop the footstone that marked both brothers' graves: Davey, gone at age thirteen, and Gildas, the babe John had never seen.

"Do you think it's so?" Briallen asked John.

"I do. And look at you." He sat back on his heels and bade her stand before him so they could look each other full on. He held her little waist. "A good deal of herself she's left behind in you, Briallen-my-girl, and glad it makes my heart to see it." He rocked her lightly, laughing at her pleased smile. "What think you, Owen-my-boy?" he said, noticing Owen watching them.

"Her arms are little. She can't hold me strong in her lap."

Briallen's smile slipped. John clutched her to him. His other arm invited Owen. Owen hesitated, and once more, John grieved his decision last March to leave without saying good-bye to the boy. He'd been hoping to save Owen some tears, but what if he'd only created distrust between them?

"Come, you," he said, his voice a rasp, and Owen did and let John rough his hair and fold him in next to his sister. "Bri's arms will grow strong, you know. They will grow strong."

And his own were strong already.

The cottage needed attention before winter came upon it. After Mared timidly showed him a small area where the thatch had begun to rot, John ordered enough slate from the quarry to replace the entire roof. He borrowed an Irish-car and a horse to pull it, gathered up the children, and crossed the bridge to Cardigan to buy a new pane of glass. The children he charged with an errand to buy the widest variety of sweets they could with the coins he gave them, and then he went alone to order wedding gifts, a tea service for Dilys, a pair of chairs for his father's house. They would be a surprise, delivered weeks after he had left.

He'd never spent so much money in a single day. He signed bills of sale and did not know if his scruples were for his prodigality with his savings, or that it felt mean to have such savings in the first place.

Climbing a ladder the following morning, he reminded himself, either way, it little mattered. He was going back to a good position and a wealthy wife and a fine house her father would pay for. Every damn thing he wanted was waiting for him back in London, so what difference if he spent every shilling he had?

Roofing was hazardous work. It put you above, it put you alone. He was glad when the children were out of doors, playing and calling up to him, helping him sort tiles and watching him drill holes in the slate. Passing neighbors provided occasional relief. When there was no one, he fitted tiles with ardent care. He pounded pegs with vehement concentration. The task, as John performed it, did not permit introspection.

In the evenings, his father joined him when he was done at the quarry, not taking the usual time to wash away the slate dust. One night they spent half an hour pretending it was not too dark to work, and then Mared picked her way up the ladder with two tankards of cider for them.

"Will I keep supper?" she asked her husband as he sidled down to take a tankard and pass it back to John. He took a long swallow from the other before he shook his head and told her to feed the children, he and Iefan would be in later.

He took another drink. "There is good, Mared."

Exchanges like these were all John had witnessed of their relationship—Mared, careful and eager to please; his father a host, trying to make her welcome.

"As well to go in now, is it?" John asked. "Not much for us to do, and it dark."

"Thought you'd like to come to it."

John paused with the cup at his mouth, the liquid tickling his lip.

"Or wait another night or two, you could," said his father, his tone dry, "if you are thinking still on how to say it."

"No," John answered, but in truth, he wasn't ready. He had yet to speak a word of his purpose to his dad, to anyone here, save a silent prayer at his mother's grave.

He edged down the roof so he could sit beside his father. The rear of the cottage looked to the Preseli Hills, and their scrubbed black peaks barely ruffled the horizon, still lit with the last blush of the faded day. One massive cloud, as smooth and purple as the roof slates, bore down on the light. He could hear dishes and the children's voices clattering together, the sounds rising up with the scents of warm food and damp earth.

Deeply, he breathed it all in.

"Dad, I want Owen. Janny and Briallen, too. Take them back to live with me."

The words hung in the air, like blasphemy from a pulpit. They sounded too stark. In his imagination, this conversation had been direct, rational, but spoken aloud, to his father, his request seemed threaded with something obscene.

His father said, "I suppose I can see to them what I brought into the world."

"Dad—"

"Just like this roof. I'd've been seeing to it soon enough. It didn't call for your notice, and sure didn't call for such extravagance as what all this slate is."

"I meant to help. I want to help the little ones. I can do fine things for them with this new position—"

"Already heard of your new position." His father edged toward the ladder and climbed down, going to the water pump. John scrambled after and stood by as his father stripped off his waistcoat and shirt and stuck his head into the stream of water.

"I think Mared—"

Water sprayed the air as his father jerked up his sopping head. "Respect for your stepmother, if you please."

John's jaw locked. He could not refer to that girl he'd gone to school with as *mother*. She came rushing from the house with a towel, a corner of it in each hand to have it at the ready. She backed away uncertainly when her husband took it and bade her go back inside.

"You think she's put under by the little ones," he said to John when she was gone, "but she knew what it was when she took my offer. She's learning, is all. Takes time."

"I meant no ill to her. I only want Owen and—"

"He's my son. The only son God gave me to raise."

John started.

"See to a man, is what I mean," his father added. "Your poor brothers, rest their souls, never came close, and you—you raised yourself, Iefan. John. Ran off and took care of yourself, soon as you could. You ran off, your brother Daffyd taken from us hardly a month."

He pulled on the pump handle and put his head back into the water, scrubbing his face and hair. Watching, John remembered a letter his mother had written him, years after he'd left home, in which she'd confided that her heart, in those first months of John's absence, little knew the difference in her griefs for him and for Davey. Her heart had known two lost sons, and that was all.

John hadn't thought of that when he'd left. At twelve, he had only known he'd woken from a fever to find Davey already in the ground, and it felt like those hills that ruffled up against the horizon were in his chest and throat, and the need to get out and *live* had come after him, a derailing train demanding either his flight or his surrender.

Standing here, John now knew his mother's confusion, the old grief and panic for Davey snarling up with the freshness of Charlie's death.

His father's face disappeared into the towel, and it seemed like that moment at Charlie's bedside again, when it snapped in his brain that possibly, Sarah lay beside a dead child, but no, such a thing couldn't be. If he could just get to Charlie soon enough, it would not be.

"Dad, you listen to me," he said, groping for the thing spinning out of his reach. "You have to hear me."

His father took down the towel and turned to pull on the shirt Mared had left for him. "Your mother's last babe, Owen is, and his father I am, and will be. Same for the girls."

"You're not even thinking! Just tossing it all aside, before you even give it a look. Have some time, won't you, to think on it—and ask the little ones, before—"

"Iefan! The little ones hardly know you."

"They do! They know me—written, I have, sent gifts and money—come here, visited each time I could. They know me, and know I love them."

"The kind stranger you are, and hardly more."

"I'm their brother, damn you."

John stumbled suddenly, jerked forward by his father grabbing a handful of his clothes.

"And I their *dad*, please you to remember."

After so many years, there remained a familiarity in the shock of being yanked by the shirtfront, notwithstanding the fact that now he looked down on his father's face rather than up at it, as he had as a boy. John's father had whipped him but once, for saying a lie to his mother, but he'd demanded his son's notice in this way often enough for it not to be forgotten.

Always, John had hated it. But this evening was the first time he tried to get free of that hold, twisting away as he gave his father a shove that was perhaps unwarranted and certainly too emphatic. His father staggered, tilted, and missed falling utterly to the ground only by one hand that planted itself in the mud surrounding the water pump. He leapt up again, almost with no betrayal of his age, almost before John realized what he'd done.

"And *your* father, too," he said. "And into my house you'll not come again until you've remembered, now."

He pulled his fingers into a muddy fist and went into the house, ignoring John's demand that he listen, just think and listen. John felt the hills, ragged and black, in his chest. He felt his feet turning cold, the puddle his father had yanked him into seeping into his shoes. He thought of Elisabeth at the shore, treading into the waves alone.

"Dad!" he called once more, loud enough to drive the image away. The door finished closing, and when it didn't open again, John charged for it and burst inside.

It had been clawing for freedom, this thing in him, bold and alien and hostile, but in the face of his family, blinking up from their supper, it cowered and abandoned him. His father, not yet seated, stilled in the act of cleaning his hand, Mared close by. Dilys and Janny's spoonfuls of *bwdram* hung in the air, and the corner of Briallen's mouth remained tucked back as she considered him. Owen said, "*Shw mae,* Iefan!" and held out a crust. Bread crumbs dotted his black hair.

John revoked his entrance, his invasion. A duck of his head, a backward step, and he was over the threshold again, and then he was striding into the sunless chill of the moors. At an ancient congregation of stones, he went to his knees and put his face into the earth, his entire being a prayer unarticulated, a need unnamed.

The dampness of the ground infused his clothing as he knelt there. After a while, he felt it reach his skin, and he heard his father calling for him—*John*, once or twice, then *Iefan*—and he sat up, answered, "Here."

The ground hissed slightly under his dad's steps. He held a bowl down to John. "Have it."

He sat down at the cromlech with John, and John ate, the first bites a duty. Then his hunger overtook. The dish, of oats and salted herring, was wholly familiar, as though his mother still lived. Dilys's work, he supposed. Bread there was, too, buttered and topped with blackberry conserve normally put up for wintertime.

"You wanted something different," his father said as John was scraping the last tastes from the bowl. "So may your brother and sisters someday, but till then, I'll spare them the heartache of being sent from everything they know."

"You are their dad."

"Your own little ones you will have."

John wanted to lick the bowl. It was dark and he sat upon the ground, so he licked. And even though he was ashamed to tell his father the fraud he was doing, though he knew he would choke if he had to speak Lillian's name, he said, "I am to marry. Before the summer is done."

"Bless God! And nothing you've said of it!"

"I've not."

"Well, and who is she? English?"

"So she is. She is—"

The calamity of my life if I leave here without those children. And even if I don't. A promise I have made, but she is a lie to my heart, no matter what.

"She is—"

Without warning, his gut seized, and he rolled over onto an elbow and vomited every mouthful he'd just consumed.

His father said, "Wedding day, no more than toast to eat, hear?" and flagged his pocket handkerchief.

John swiped his mouth and sweaty forehead, dimly noting the texture of the fabric and feeling certain better light would reveal it the blue in fresh morning snow. He pressed his forehead to one support stone of the cromlech, and the coolness from its depth took the sweat from his brow. Owen would play here, just as his older brothers and sisters had.

John said, "She is a good girl."

"She is, sure. What name has she?"

Around them, the uplands rustled with matters of the night, the digging in, the preparation of the hunt, the mild bow to the mist. John whispered, "Elisabeth," and the sound was like one of those furtive creatures in the night, one of the cautious prey, and it was all wrong, spoken like that, and it demanded correction.

"Elisabeth Dobson," he repeated, louder, and the release and comfort of it made him laugh. He rubbed his hands over his wretched face, laughing, and he stood, laughing, and he shouted into the night.

"Elisabeth!"

How he needed her.

"I am in love with her," he added softly. "And I mean it when I say she's good. Like a tune you must sing each time you think of it."

His father snorted. But then added, "Sure, I know."

"And Dad—well, but I do not feel good with her. Good, you know, by the way of the straight and narrow."

Heat struck his cheeks, and he could all but hear his father blushing, as though that cottage where he'd raised his children was not made of close rooms and slight walls.

"As it should be," his father said after a moment.

"She would have given Owen and the girls her whole heart."

"And so she will your own little ones."

"I know it." He couldn't be certain of children, but he was certain of Betsey's heart. And what had he done to it, that fierce, raw—true—heart of hers?

"She is not—not what I expected to need."

His father did not answer this time, except for a sound in his throat.

"Foolishness I have to undo," John said. "The nearest telephone is in England still?"

"It is."

"Then I will send wires," he said, and started across the moor.

```
. . . brush the type with a dry tooth or type brush, being
careful all the time not to let any strain come upon the
type bar.
```
—How to Become Expert at Type-writing

*A*side from the funeral, Betsey had seen Sarah nowhere except within her own bedroom, where the tidiness was so absolute that it chilled Betsey. Dora Pink had had her way in there as Sarah sat, indifferent and possibly oblivious, sometimes acknowledging her visitors, sometimes not.

Thus, as she waited under her umbrella for her excursion group to arrive, Betsey felt stunned by the sight of Sarah driving up to the rail station alone. The softness of Dr. Nally's medicine was absent, making her I'm-doing-fine casing brittle as shale, but since she seemed so determined to maintain it, Betsey did what she could to help.

This was the day Baumston & Smythe came for its outing, Sarah remembered, and asked whether Betsey were uneasy about it. Yet her attention drifted as Betsey responded, and soon she interrupted, "When are you coming home?

Betsey had stayed with the Seilers while Sarah's family was in Idensea, unsure if she would ever return to The Bows as a tenant. So much had changed since that quiet row between them, before the night of the ball had become the night of the fire. But hearing Sarah's expectation removed her uncertainty. What a comfort it would be to restore that portion of her life.

"I'm going with Sophie when she leaves," Sarah added, referring to her older daughter. Betsey nodded, glad. The only times she'd seen Sarah somewhat at peace since Charlie's passing were when she was with Sophie's children, an infant and a plump toddler.

"Perhaps I won't come back."

"Oh, Sarah," Betsey sighed, aching for her.

She asked if Betsey would oversee the management of the house until she decided what she would do. None of the servants could do the account books, and Dora Pink, well, Sarah would not say a word against her, but Betsey understood Sarah's reluctance to give Dora official authority over the house and the rest of the servants—she claimed enough as it was.

"And Charlie's room . . ." she began, but got no further. Betsey closed her umbrella and climbed into the carriage, circling her hand over Sarah's back as she promised again and again that of course Charlie's room should not have boarders, of course it was his room, his room alone.

Eventually, Sarah calmed. With the whistle of the London train sounding in the distance, she refused to allow Betsey to see her home but did accept the company of the hotel page Betsey had along to assist her.

After the page and Betsey had changed places, Sarah pursed her lips at the depot. "I hope he returns before I—in time for me to—"

"Sarah," Betsey said firmly. "If John believed you were spending a moment of worry over how he cares for you or whether he forgives you, it would kill him."

But she understood Sarah's anxiety, her desire to speak the truth, not let it exist in implication only. Since Miss Gilbey's sudden departure, Betsey feared John might not come back at all, that she would never again have the chance she had squandered before.

It felt lonely, frightening, to see Sarah drive away. She'd promised to take care of the lodging house, but what would it be, deprived of Charlie and Sarah? What would Idensea be to her if Sir Alton forced her dismissal from the hotel? And if John—

Not now. Not until Baumston & Smythe had concluded its most pleasant outing ever and was headed back to London. So resolved, she hoisted her sign welcoming Baumston & Smythe, Insurers to Idensea and drilled her attention to the rail station.

And there was her sister. Betsey caught her breath, seeing Caroline on the top step of the entrance, so far ahead of the other passengers in disembarking that it seemed she might have been the only one aboard. Caroline saw her, too, and cried out and came dashing down the steps, heedless of the rain.

"You wrote me Richard would not hear of coming!" Betsey exclaimed as they embraced.

"I made him hear it!" Caroline stepped back to look at her. "I wanted to surprise you, and oh, don't you look splendid, all your brass buttons! But are you well? Your eyes—"

They hugged again, and Betsey felt she could stay in that embrace for ages. But Baumston & Smythe employees were fast gathering round them, Richard leading the way.

"For pity's sake, Caroline!" He stooped to collect Betsey's discarded umbrella and shielded his wife with his own. "Will you please remember what company we are in?"

"Look at Elisabeth, Richard!" Caroline sang. "Look how well she's done for herself!"

Whatever this long-dreaded day held for her, Betsey experienced a moment of victory now, meeting Richard's eyes, his expectation that she would come running to him and Caroline for help defied. She thanked him for bringing Caroline and realized she would be able to pay the last of her debt to him, this very day and in person. Happily, and with a touch of mischief, she kissed his cheek as his coworkers gathered near.

She circulated the printed schedules amongst the crowd, then climbed up on Ethan Noonan's char-à-banc to offer an official welcome. In their curiosity to discover what had happened to the scandalous type-writer girl who'd fled the premises back in May, they were the most attentive group she'd addressed all summer.

She concluded by reminding them the Kursaal offered plenty of indoor diversions while the rain held.

"Don't you mean to warn us against the unsavory sorts that frequent watering places?" someone in the group called. "Thieves? Confidence men? Women of dubious morals?"

There was a gasp at the last suggestion, probably from one of the wives. As for the question itself, Betsey knew exactly from whom it had come and precisely where the inquiring bastard stood. She didn't look at him in the beat of silence which followed. She avoided looking at Caroline and Richard, too, dreading the sight of her sister's face, bound to be fraught with fury and sympathy. No, she glanced once more at the rail station entrance, and then, from beneath her umbrella, she gazed down at them all with a Sunday school smile.

"I'm afraid Mr. Wofford is correct," she said. "Pickpockets down on the Esplanade aren't unheard of. But do inform me if you come across some fellow who puts his fingers in the wrong place. I shall tell you how to make short work of him."

She let the laughter ripple for only an instant before she wished them all a pleasant visit. The island of umbrellas began to break apart. Betsey let her gaze rest on one unmoving spot: Mr. Wofford's scraggly-bearded face, pink with his seething.

Whatever had caused Lillian to throw the book, John had missed it. He'd been staring out the rain-splashed window, lost to anything occurring within the train carriage, until Lillian's sharp cry had roused him and he'd turned in time to see Noel Dunning get clouted in the shoulder by a volume of sermons. At the very next stop, Lillian's aunt threw protective arms about her niece, and the two women left the first-class coupé—Dunning's money, that—for the dining car.

"What did you do to her?" John asked.

"Offered to read her book aloud," Dunning confessed.

John returned to the window, willing the passengers outside to alight or to board more quickly so the train might resume its journey *now-bless-God*. He could have advised Dunning to expect all his groveling to be met with rejection—sermons flying at his head, gazes from the depths of January—for some time yet, at least until Dunning and his new fiancée were forced to present a united front to their parents, and probably for a good while after.

He didn't, though. He had little interest in alleviating Dunning's personal hell just now. He was only glad Dunning had obeyed John's wired demands to depart Vienna for London without delay.

Now, at last, they were bringing the good tidings of Lillian and Dunning's great joy to their parents. The train, should it ever happen to *move-again-damn-it*, was bound for Idensea, where Lillian's parents were finishing their summer holiday.

Where Betsey was facing the Baumston & Smythe excursion alone.

Finally, the conductor gave his all-clear, and the train resumed its journey. For a while, at least. This was a stopping train, stacking stones of time in his way back to Idensea, back to Betsey.

"She despises me."

Dunning looked like something you'd find in a ditch and leave there. He'd been traveling the better of three days, John supposed, sleeping but little. The greeting he'd received from John upon his arrival in London showed redly below his left eye.

"She's stopped weeping, at least," John offered as comfort.

"She's been crying?"

"Not since you came."

"Too busy despising me."

"I don't know." He didn't think so.

"My father will despise me."

"Not forever." John closed his eyes. As ever, he saw Elisabeth, this time as she had been that Sunday dawn, on her stomach,

sprawled in sleep, her slight, strong hand at rest on his arm. He
had leaned over her and kissed the small of her back, something
in him moved to lay some protection on that vulnerable shallow
of flesh.

Dunning broke the momentary quiet. "But *she. She* thoroughly
despises me, enough to last forever."

He spoke of Lillian, of course. But John's heart tightened anyway. A rise of fear, the squeeze of uncertainty.

"If I could just have her alone for a minute or so—Jones, I
swear to you she never told me about the child."

"She said you knew."

"I didn't. I didn't! She is lying, for some reason, or—or else
perhaps—"

John opened his eyes. Dunning's ears colored.

"What?" John said.

"She was so awfully innocent . . . that is, of course she was . . .
but I mean of *everything,* Jones! I didn't realize . . . I don't believe
she even understood . . . where things were going, you might say,
not until . . . you know . . . it was happening. That is, *happening*,
you see. Lord, but it was wretched. Not quite *all* of it, because of
course, we'd been getting on swimmingly right before—"

John wished he hadn't asked. He wished Dunning would
shut up.

"But then we came to the *act*, and, oh, *God*, what a mess—she
just turned hysterical, began weeping, for God's sake, and her parents just in—"

"*Dunning.*"

With a gulp, Dunning shut up. "Right. Sorry, old chap," he
whispered, and sat fidgeting with Lillian's book as the rails rattled
beneath them. "It is only that I need a smoke. So frightfully bad."

"Forty shillings, you can have it," John said unsympathetically,
speaking of the fine Dunning would have to pay if he were caught
smoking on the train.

Dunning shook his head. "It makes her sneeze."

"Ah." John had not known this. He closed his eyes again.

"The thing of it. What I meant to say, that is . . ."

Dunning paused, perhaps for encouragement to continue, which John didn't offer. As it turned out, he didn't need it.

"I meant only to say that perhaps she told you I knew about the child because, in her innocence, or what have you, she is under the assumption that to . . . to *engage* in . . . in the *act* is to . . . to *conceive*. Inevitably, as you might say."

John felt inclined to believe this. Dunning had, after all, proved cooperative in every respect since getting John's wire—departing Vienna immediately, accepting John's fist in his eye as a reasonable greeting, protesting his sudden engagement not even a little.

"Let us not speak for a while, Dunning."

"Very well."

And Dunning was very quiet for nearly a full minute before he pleaded with John to find some way to distract Aunt Constance so he might speak privately to Miss Gilbey before they faced their parents.

For he loved her, it seemed, and wanted her to know.

On the pavilion, Betsey chafed her hands over her arms as she stole a moment from the dinner dance to look toward the hotel. She could make out lights on the upper floors only; a white mist had all but swallowed the grounds tonight, and fine points of moisture blew into the pavilion. Soon it would be too chilly altogether to have entertainments here; soon the board would decide the fate of the excursion scheme.

Someone touched her arm, and she turned to accept the compliments of one of the type-writer girls, Julia Vane, who wanted to say again what a lovely outing they'd had, never mind the dratted weather. Betsey thanked her, and Julia was swept again into the dancers as a staffer came to murmur in her ear, "Sir Alton wishes to speak with you, Miss Dobson."

Sir Alton, putting in an appearance tonight for the sake of the business between the pier company and Baumston & Smythe, was already looking her way.

Earlier, she had entertained a fancy that tonight, Sir Alton would note how well things were going, how capably she managed this job. Now she knew she would have been luckier if he'd continued to overlook her, for there existed the very unlikable likelihood someone had by now told him about her last day at Baumston & Smythe. Forgery. Wofford's broken fingers. Flight.

Sir Alton greeted her with a bow and a lilting good evening. "You have heard from our Mr. Jones," he stated. "A telephone call! Rather urgent of him, true?"

Betsey, in town for Mr. Seiler, had missed the call, but it had created a stir in the office. The switchboard operator had personally delivered the message that there was no message and attempted to engage Betsey in guessing what the message might have been, had one actually been left.

"Something regarding Mrs. Elliot's house," Betsey had offered to end the game.

The past two days, she'd spent more time than she would ever admit making up words for John to say from miles away, but Sir Alton's interest in the call was limited to one aspect.

"You surely would have informed me had his plans changed," he said. "He still will move on to London, and you . . . you will remain here."

It was a sideways confirmation that John had thrown her over, wasn't taking her with him. Considerate of him.

Betsey waited with her hands clasped behind her, watching the dancers twirl through a polka. Old Mr. Baumston and Lady Dunning, Julia Vane and the type-writers, the clerks and the underwriters—heavens, even Richard with Caroline—they were all turning, smiling as they skipped, pale flames against the wet night beyond the pavilion.

She wished Sir Alton would see it, how beautiful, how *worthy* it all was.

She took a breath, about to be as open as she dared with him, to tell him she wanted to stay in Idensea, that she had done fine work this summer and knew she could do even better with more time. But the breath caught at the sight of Mr. Wofford across the way, making no secret of the fact he was watching her with Sir Alton. He nodded at her, his mouth smug.

"So many, many prospects as you must have, Miss Dobson," Sir Alton went on, "and you wish to stay on here? My gratitude for your loyalty. Still, I would have thought—if you'd wanted to keep your position—you would have made yourself more . . . valuable. Particularly in matters close to me."

Such as keeping John in Idensea. Betsey turned her gaze from Wofford to find Sir Alton appraising her as he might a worn garment: Burn? Or cast off to the beggar outside the gate?

"I expected too much, of course" was his bland conclusion, and Betsey crushed her lip between her teeth, for she had, too. In all sorts of ways, she had expected too much.

How young Caroline looked! She beamed at Betsey as she and Richard spun by, and Betsey knew Caroline's pleasure in the dance was exceeded only by her pride in her sister, standing in her smart blue uniform beside Sir Alton Dunning. Even Richard regarded her with warmth; he had accepted Betsey's final payment to him with more grace than she might have expected, and nodded with apparent sincerity when Caroline hoped Betsey would make a visit to London soon.

"Curious, how hope will insinuate itself," Sir Alton murmured as Caroline waved to her, as Wofford lurked like a jackal waiting his turn at the carcass. "Even in the bedrock of logic. I hadn't realized I was such an optimist."

Betsey tightened the clasp of her hands behind her back. Very well, damn it. She had expected too much. But of him. She'd expected too much of him, while of herself . . .

Not nearly enough.

She bent her head for a moment, long enough to glimpse her buttons, long enough to make a vow: Whatever happened this night, at the end of it, she would be proud of everything she'd said and done. She concentrated on her remaining duties for the night, ordering a mental list of dances, refreshments, speeches, and, oh, the favors, the paper frames and tobacco. She had left them on her desk at the hotel. She would have to fetch them, or send someone—

"You did, I presume, permit him to fuck you with sufficient frequency?"

The folding of a letter is a matter of no little importance.

—*How to Become Expert in Type-writing*

The timing, the pleasant, offhand notes of Sir Alton's voice—the vulgarity—it was all calculated to take her breath away. His reckonings were true, and Betsey reeled. Without warning, the pavilion lights dipped and swirled like eddying currents. She blinked hard, looked up and swallowed, and the tears subsided and the lights stilled.

And her voice was clear. "You presume too much, if you imagine I did anything to help you except to make money for your company and show it to advantage. If you imagine you've any right to ask for more than that, you presume far too much, Sir Alton."

A light, fine interest dusted Sir Alton's features, as though he found the sound of her voice a mild oddity. Apprehension brushed along her spine. Sir Alton reached inside his coat and produced a letter, which he offered. Expecting to see her own foolish work, the forgery she'd made at Baumston & Smythe, she opened it.

It was indeed a typed letter, but John's scrawling signature drew her eye first. She frowned, skimming back up to the salutation. John had written Wofford? So it seemed, though Betsey recognized the fluffed-up language of the company secretary as she read:

We appreciate the apparent concern prompting you
to contact Idensea Pier regarding Miss Dobson.
Pray be assured your warning will be remembered
should future circumstance warrant. As for your
monetary claims, you will please understand a
letter from your physician is necessary to verify
any sum Miss Dobson may owe.

John, her ally from the start. Far more than the implications of the
letter in Sir Alton's possession, the ache rushed out to her—she
missed John. Where would she find such extravagant trust and
kindness again?

She returned the letter to Sir Alton, who wished her a pleasant
evening as he slipped it into his coat, his needs regarding her met.
What else had they to discuss? He would no doubt present the letter and Wofford's version of the story when she gave her report to
the board, and even if the report persuaded them to continue the
excursions scheme, the letter would do little to convince them that
she should continue to manage it.

Caroline, rosy and breathless, came to her with arms extended.

"I'll be back in a bit," Betsey said into her sister's ear, hoping
the unsteadiness she felt in her hands would go unnoticed. They
tingled, her hands, as though they'd been deprived of blood.

"Are you all right?"

"Yes, yes. I only have to go back to the hotel and fetch the party
favors."

"I shall come with you, then!"

"No, stay. I'll manage, and look—I think Richard could be
cajoled into another dance. Stay and enjoy yourself."

The path from the pavilion to the hotel was more mud than pebbles and crushed shells, and belatedly, Betsey realized the mist had
turned to rain again, her umbrella left behind on the pavilion. She
turned to go back to get it, only to find Wofford nearly on her heels.

"God damn you," she hissed, as startled as she was furious.
"You've done your worst, haven't you? Now let me alone."

She reverted to her original direction, deciding to forgo the umbrella.

"Come back here," Wofford ordered, quite as if he had the right, and not at all as if he meant to offer the use of the umbrella he carried. Betsey kept walking, wriggling out of the fitted jacket of her uniform as she tried to dodge the worst of the puddles, not easily visible in the night. She heard a plunking splash and realized he was following her.

Holding her jacket over her head, she kept going and trusted the length of her legs to outpace him. Still, she could hear him behind her, each footfall an irritation when all she wanted was the refuge of the empty office at the hotel, just for a few moments, to breathe and to gather her grit for the rest of this night.

"You will return to the pavilion with me, Miss Dobson! Stop where you are."

Not stopping, she snatched a glance over her shoulder, prepared to mock him, but felt a small bell of alarm instead, seeing the determination with which he was bearing down on her, realizing she was being chased. She didn't like it; she hadn't meant to be running away.

She stopped and turned on him so quickly he fell back a step in surprise.

"I've said for you to let me alone. And you are even more of a sodding fool than I knew if you think you can compel me to go anywhere with you."

"You owe it!"

"I owe—? I owe you nothing, nothing you'd want, at least. I owe Mr. Jones, perhaps—he paid your doctor, didn't he? Likely too much—Julia Vane told me there's been some doubt as to whether your fingers were, after all, broken. Perhaps Sir Alton owes you— what a shame for you he isn't more given to spectacular scenes— but I assure you, you've reaped your revenge all the same."

Wofford advanced. "That's not the end of it. You disgraced me before everyone, and you will go up to that pavilion and beg my pardon before everyone—"

"Hush!" Betsey threw her fingers in front of her lips, ignoring Wofford's outrageous demand in order to listen to the path. She let her jacket slip down from her head and shushed Wofford once more as she turned from him, listening.

Then, two words, escaping the mist from far down the path, over the splatter of raindrops, reaching her plainly, piercing her.

"Bless God!"

Someone else was with him, a man. She lifted her jacket again, blocking the rain and whatever Wofford was trying to say. A staffer, or Mr. Seiler, perhaps? She couldn't catch enough of the words or the voice to be certain, and they were still too far inside the mist for her to see them.

Then came a feminine wail of distress she instantly recognized. Miss Gilbey.

Stumbling, Betsey left the path, intent on little more than seeking invisibility in the mist and darkness of the grounds, but when Wofford followed, she thought better of going too far from the path. She stopped beneath a tree, too slender to really shield her but enough cover for this night.

She lowered her jacket again; Wofford's voice hit her ear. "Have you considered what it's been like for me, working there after such humiliation?"

"Not even once," Betsey assured him in a ruthless whisper. "Have you considered what it will be like for you, if you are discovered in the dark, sharing your umbrella with Miss Dobson?"

He jerked the umbrella away but did keep his mouth shut. Betsey touched her forehead to the tree trunk, pressed a thumbnail into the damp, spongy bark, and listened as the gritty noise of footsteps grew closer. Miss Gilbey was talking about her shoes—to herself, it seemed—for John and the other man weren't answering. When they had passed without noticing her and Wofford a few feet away, she indulged—punished—herself by watching John's back disappear into the mist.

And so much for her vow. She was too much a coward to face Miss Gilbey and her fiancé.

"Now then," Wofford began.

"Are you still here?" she said dully, dullness spreading like spilled ink inside her, a thick and thorough soaking into her spirit.

"You can't just ignore me." One syllable was touched by a whinging, almost childish note. "You owe me an apology, in front of everyone."

"What I owe you would keep your beard from growing."

She started for the path, but Wofford yanked at her arm to make her face him, the force of it suggesting he'd expected more resistance. And yet, she hardly felt it. When she said, "You had best let me go," it was with a coldness unattached to anything she felt for him.

Briefly, his expression flickered, let slip a trace of something like uncertainty or discomfort, but he didn't let her go. "You ruined everything for me at Baumston and never paid for it—just swept off here, didn't you? And now you believe you may look down on us all, as if you matter, you in your . . . your . . . uniform."

His eyes dipped, and he seemed to run out of words.

"Like my buttons, do you?" Betsey asked softly, prompting another look from Wofford. "Well, they're nothing but tin, but I worked for them, and they're mine, and they're much too good for the likes of you to breathe upon."

She didn't tell him again to turn her loose. She wrenched away but didn't quite free herself, and a tree root put off her balance as she tried to get her knee to the crucial locality. Another hard wrench, and she was staggering backward, Wofford coming along with her.

Business letters should consist of short, clear, terse sentences.
—*How to Become Expert in Type-writing*

Fuck!"

The word soared from the mist, stopping John dead on the path. He smiled and said, "Elisabeth, that will be," and broke off from Lillian and Dunning to go after her.

He found her in the grass, crawling out from beneath a groaning fellow she was cursing far past the devil's good taste. Amongst John's reactions, surprise did not particularly register.

What did register was the groaning fellow's efforts to sit up, his arm stretching toward Betsey, his fingers about to grasp the hem of her skirts as she scrambled on hands and knees away from him.

The man's groans burst into a shout as John launched into him, but after that, he went still, submitting to John's weight pinning him to the ground, his eyes saucered.

John didn't ease up his force as he glanced over his shoulder. Dunning had followed him, and John saw with an unreasonable irritation and sense of loss that Dunning was taking Betsey's hand, helping her to her feet. He took it out on the man under him, his fists bearing down on his chest just enough to provoke a squeak.

"Did he—" John began, but the question triggered a snap of self-consciousness. He couldn't ask if this coward had hurt her, not before he'd had a chance to ask her forgiveness himself. "Are you all right, Elisabeth?" he amended, and with Lillian proffering her pocket handkerchief with shy concern, Betsey assured him she was fine. It might have relieved him but for the ragged edge in her voice, where her anger was fraying into something else.

John looked down at his wide-eyed captive. "Good evening, lad. And who in hell might you be?"

"Just—just Wofford, sir."

"That supervisor at Baumston and Smythe," Betsey said, and John knew instantly whom she meant.

Wofford seemed to realize the identification did him no favors. He lifted his head from the ground defensively. "She—"

John pushed him back down. "Don't trouble yourself, lad. Miss Dobson will tell me everything I need to know."

"Just take him away," Betsey said. "He doesn't matter, only keep him away from the pavilion. I don't want the dance spoiled, so please just take him somewhere."

She started away down the hill, toward the hotel, and only said, "Please, Mr. Jones," when John called for her to wait for him.

"Shall I go after her?" Dunning asked.

Should Dunning go after her—*Dunning*, go after her? John knew Dunning meant well, but John wanted to get him under his knee, too, because John ought be the one going after Betsey, and he oughtn't have to do that because she oughtn't've gone anywhere in the first place. She ought have stayed and said thank you or fuck you or what have you. She oughtn't just leave as though there was nothing to say. And she oughtn't've called him Mr. Jones, either.

"You'll not," he answered. "I want you to go up to the pavilion—"

"The pavilion?" Dunning interrupted weakly.

"There should be a staffer there—great broad fellow, red hair. Name of Frederick. You've surely noticed him. Tell him to bring along another staffer and meet me down here. And don't make a show of it. Quick and quiet, is it?"

"But Jones—" Dunning stepped a little closer and spoke softly to keep Lillian from hearing. "My *father* is on the pavilion." He squatted down beside John and Wofford and whispered, "You said you'd be along, you know, when the time came. You know, to face the old boy."

"Come you here, Noel," John said, and Dunning leaned in, and John clutched his necktie and pulled.

"Oof," said Dunning.

"Send Frederick. Get you your father and Lady Dunning down to the hotel to meet with the Gilbeys, and the next time I see you, 'twould be best for your health if an invitation to your wedding you were delivering to me."

"Redheaded fellow, you said?"

John released Dunning's necktie. Lillian rushed to his side to keep him from falling completely on his arse. When the two of them had gone, Wofford mentioned it would be quite safe for John to get off him now, and John explained the ground was rather wet for sitting and stayed where he was until Frederick and another staffer found them. He put Wofford into their custody, to be escorted to the rail station and seen aboard his train. And then—

And then he ran after the thing he wanted.

The office was empty, dark, and Elisabeth's still figure cut a silhouette against the window, as slim and solitary as a churchyard angel, dissolving John's haste and frustration. He touched a hand to the pain in his side and whispered her name. "Elisabeth."

She roused, just a lift of her head. Overcome by a sensation of having run upon the edge of the earth, suddenly and without a single warning sign, John hesitated.

Within that instant, Betsey shook off the last of her reverie, and said, "Yes, I know," as though responding to something he'd said. "I need to hurry back. I only—I—"

Her knuckles came to rest against her mouth, and she cast her glance about the shadows for a moment before settling it on the desk that held the type-writing machine. There she headed and readied the machine as she said, "I need a character. You won't mind? I can type as you dictate, it oughtn't take long."

"You . . . need a reference letter . . . tonight?"

"Soon. Wofford, he brought that letter, you see, the one you sent him? All the way back in June!" She fumbled the slightest bit with the machine's carriage. "It was kind of you, by the way, so unbelievably kind. . . . Only Wofford's brought it and given it to Sir Alton, you see, and has likely told him an even worse account of what happened, so I don't imagine there's much hope for me anymore."

She sat down. John stared.

"Here, I mean. Hope for me here. But I've spoken with Mrs. Gomery whilst you were away. About the Sundial, remember? And whoever owns the Black Lion, I'd wager they've given up hope of competing with the Swan Park, but I've thought of some ways they might revive their trade."

"I don't doubt it."

"Please—" Tension snagged her voice, and he heard her breathe in before she continued, "Just a reasonable character. I'm ready." A flurry of snaps issued from the type-writing machine. "*To whom it may concern.* Go on, then."

"Bless God!" He wanted to propose marriage, not dictate a letter.

"*To . . . whom . . . it . . . may . . .*"

"Very well! *To whom it may concern.* Allow me a moment."

He crossed to where she sat. She was nearly soaked, he realized, her little blue jacket gone and the sleeves of her blouse clinging limply to her arms. He took off his coat, which was damp enough itself but better than nothing, and she wordlessly permitted him to help her into it, shuddering hard, once, after she had it on.

"Well, then," he said when she had her fingers over the keys again. "*The Idensea Pier and Seaside Pleasure Building Company has been blessed to have the skills and intelligence of Miss Elisabeth Dobson at its service for these past—*"

The type-writing machine snaps stalled only a moment after John did, struck by the realization that what felt the whole of his existence had been but three and one-half months.

"*Three months,*" Betsey said and typed, a trifle viciously.

"Another fortnight since I met you in London. The first time I saw you, Elisabeth, I thought, 'That's what I need.' Did I ever tell you that?" *That's what I need,* and his instinct had never been either more true or more faulty. Quite misguided in what he needed her *for*, his instinct.

"You didn't." She curled her fingers into her fists, then stretched them out over the keys again. "But I don't think that sort of thing is necessary. Go on. *Fortunate to have the skills and intelligence of Miss Elisabeth Dobson at its service these past three months.*"

"I didn't say 'fortunate.'"

"You needn't worry, I know how to spell it. Go on."

"*These past three months.* Mmm. So, at our service the past three or so months. *In fact, we consider her departure from our employ a tragedy*—"

"For God's sake! It is business correspondence, not a sermon."

"*A . . . tra-ge-dy.* T-r-a . . . j—"

"I've got it. *Tragedy.* L-o-s-s."

"*Of the greatest*—ahhh—*magnitude.* Magnitude. *In fact, we at Idensea Pier and Seaside Pleasure Building Company consider ourselves the most foolish of all asses for letting her go.*"

Betsey stopped typing. "I'll ask Mr. Seiler to do it." She folded her hands in her lap and bent her head down.

John whipped a chair next to hers, sat, and reached over to stroke her cheek. Her stillness did not seem an acceptance of the gesture.

She said, "How is Miss Gilbey?"

Careful.

"Likely in tears by now, if her future father-in-law has been informed of the engagement. But she will come along all right, I think. She and Dunning."

"Mr. Dunning?"

"That's right. You were kind to her, she told me—said you . . . She said you gave me over to her."

This last part was not precisely how Lillian had phrased it, but it so thoroughly banished the frightening blankness from Betsey's expression that he couldn't regret the fabrication. He laughed gently, because the pitch of her demonic brows gave him hope, and Betsey looked down again, obviously feeling tricked.

"I thought it sounded rum," he said. "Just giving me away, not a shilling for your trouble. You had best not ever try it again." He caught her chin between his thumb and forefinger. "It would never work, in any case."

She gave him the magic-beans look, forcing him to remember that he had, in fact, been engaged to Lillian for a few days. He remembered it as a suicidal man, rescued, might recall the window ledge, but he had done it.

"Even if I had married her," he added, "it wouldn't have worked. You'd still have me. All the way through. That is what I have found out, Elisabeth."

He had more to say.

The rain had pasted her fringe of hair to her forehead, and he combed it aside, thinking of the night she had let him trim her hair. He had expected a flat refusal, coming at her with the scissors, but Betsey had shut her eyes, leaned toward him, let him do it. He had been so careful, so wary of taking too much.

His throat shut suddenly, clogged with grief for that broken trust, and he watched Betsey's dark eyes open and turn wet.

"Forgive me, girl."

He'd wanted the words to sound forthright, strong; he'd meant to list every promise; he had a speech in his best English. But holding her face, her eyes glistening with answering grief, he was reduced to a few broken, husky syllables.

As was she. "I did. You?"

"I did."

She pulled his hand from her face and kissed his fingertips, then turned and skimmed her own fingertips along the letters of the type-writing machine, tracing the round edge of each black key. "I believed I knew what you wanted," she said softly. "I was trying to manage without you. But I made a wreck of it all, didn't I? Just as Richard said."

"I don't know that. If the board heard your report, who knows what they would say? And not run off half-cocked, have you, and fought your dad and spent your savings and made you some sham engagement?"

She shook her head, the curl at the corner of her mouth rising. "I suppose I wanted to do something to prove myself, on my own. Something by myself."

He smoothed his hand along the side of her head. "Do you still, girl? All by yourself?"

And suddenly, his girl was crying, and he was reaching for her, gathering her into his lap, smearing her tears with his cheek.

"There is good, then," he whispered as he held her. "Because neither do I. Neither do I."

He'd meant to be on his knee. He had a ring he was unwilling to reach for just now. He'd plotted for the sea and the starlight, not the cold glint of a type-writing machine.

"Marry me, Elisabeth," he said anyway, and it felt perfect. "I love you so, and no telling there is of what will become of me without you. Marry me, girl."

Her body shook in his arms. Through her tears, into his shoulder, she spoke, but nearly every word was unintelligible to him. He caught one, *Owen*, and pressed her to him harder, trying to stop her shaking, banish her doubts.

"Owen would be lucky," he said. "The fiercest protector he would have, and he'd belong to the sweetest, purest heart, and stand by him always, she would. And bless God, some unfit language he would learn, and likely never win a cycling race, but a mother he would have, and he would be lucky, and there's sorry I am I could not bring him to you."

Her hand on his cheek. Her hand, saying, *I'm sorry,* acknowledging his disappointment for that loss while tears held her voice captive.

She tried to speak. He couldn't understand her. What made even less sense was how she bolted from his lap, snatched a pair of baskets from her desk, and ran from the office.

Remember the machine will not work well unless the
carriage tension and the finger key tension correspond.
They must be equally weak or equally strong.

—*How to Become Expert in Type-writing*

*T*hank you, she had said, and *I have to pass out the favors,*
but Betsey knew she sounded like a bawling calf. She
knew she couldn't turn up at the pavilion in such a state, every
breath collapsing into a sloppy sob, but she kept going, aware of
the stares as she rushed through the hotel, aware when the rain hit
her face that it would spoil the packets of tobacco and the paper
frames, aware that John had come after her, that he was at her side,
taking one of the baskets, putting his hand to the small of her back
as they walked—ran, almost. She could do nothing about any of it.
Her body had quit itself of any submission to her mind.

The band was playing "Now and Then," which meant the
speeches were done already, the final galop in progress. And
though the party favors mattered not a jot just now—after all, she
was falling to pieces, drowning in a sea beyond her control, and
anyway, she was probably going to resign or get the sack no matter what she did with the damn favors, and most of all, John—oh,
God, John had asked her to marry him!—no, the favors didn't
matter at all, but she cut off the path to tramp through the grass

and the mud just the same so she could reach the pavilion before the music stopped.

John came after her. He was with her, carrying the basket of ruined tobacco, not telling her to stop her foolishness, just with her and carrying the basket, the damn basket. When her ankle turned and she fell, he was with her, there in the grass and the mud. He propped himself over her and kept the rain from falling on her face.

"Boys and dogs," she gasped.

"Bless God, what are you speaking of, girl?"

"You said you wanted them, and little girls to feed sweets at tea."

"I have a ring for you." He fumbled in his coat, which she still wore. "No stone to it yet—you would not believe such a lot of slate as what I spent my money on whilst I was away—but no other woman has worn it, and it has this box, you see, because a proper jeweler it came from."

He held up the box. She didn't reach for it.

"An inscription, too."

"Poetry?" she guessed.

"A four-letter word, girl."

She wondered which one.

"So this ring I have. And money enough to see us a start in California—"

"America!"

"Do you like it? Rolly Brues has property to develop—he promised a place should I come. Or there is Pearse Leland and London still, or I will sell my pier company shares and invest in this young manageress I know. There is anything we can dream up, Elisabeth. And boys and dogs and girls and teas in the middle of Wednesday with six kinds of sandwiches—those things will come if we are meant to have them. But you are what I cannot do without."

He tucked the ring box between his teeth, swiped the backs of his fingers over her cheeks, then pulled the box away from his mouth.

"You had best to answer me yes, so you will quit these tears."

"I have never said that I love you." This admission produced another swell of tears.

He started to contradict her. Then he frowned. "Have you not? I'm certain you do."

Laughter, both of them. She closed her eyes, smiling, tilting back her head to catch the rain dripping off his hair.

He said, "We've been caught, you know."

Yes. She'd been aware of it, the music closing, the voices from the pavilion growing closer. Footsteps on the path, *almost* passing them by. She and John had an audience.

"All our caution, wasted."

"It is. Wasted. As if we'd not even tried."

She remembered her vow to herself. *At the end of this night, she would be proud of herself.* She lay on the sodden ground, bedraggled and muddy. The paper frames and tobacco had spilled out of their baskets and were turning to mush. Also, she had a man on top of her.

She touched his chest, and he rose, putting out a hand to help her. Thinking of her vow, she stood, a spectacle with plenty of spectators.

She kissed him. John kissed her back. She took his ring; she said, *I love you, Iefan*. The spectators eventually dispersed, except for Caroline, who stayed to embrace her sister. And not long after, Betsey Dobson was dismissed from the employ of Idensea Pier & Seaside Pleasure Building Company.

Or did she resign?

So many years later, when the story was told during supper, at a table that was not fit for a king but which did always have plenty to hold; which sat in a room that looked to a great ocean where two lovers were known to swim in the moonlight; which was filled with faces that resembled the table's owners not at all, faces that smiled far more than they didn't—

At that table, so many years later, neither John nor Betsey quite remembered *that* part of their story.

Historical Note

"The Sultan's Road" is a fictional version of the scenic railways LaMarcus Thompson was building in the United States starting in 1887. They didn't appear in Britain until the early 1900s, so I've taken some liberties in placing one in Idensea a few years prior to that. Their novelty and adventurous qualities were just too much for John to resist.

Acknowledgments

One night over dinner, a fellow novelist sighed, "It's about the hardest, messiest thing a person can take on, writing a book." At the time I agreed, but I find now I've mostly forgotten the hard and messy parts, thanks to the following people:

Generous writers. Simon Adamson answered my questions and provided wonderful resources regarding pier building and firefighting. Eloisa James encouraged me early on and gave me advice so astute that I wish I'd listened immediately. Jenny Crusie told me about these things called turning points and helped me figure out what Betsey's were. My fellow writers at LRW never fail to make me feel supported and understood.

The dedicated team at Gallery Books, including Parisa Zolfaghari, Jaime Putorti, Regina Starace, copy editor Mary Beth Constant (I'll refrain from hyphenating your name, Mary Beth), and Abby Zidle, my editor. Abby, the moment you retold a scene from *The Typewriter Girl* with pitch-perfect attitude and inflection pretty much made my life as a writer. Your faith, talent, and perception grace the story, and I am grateful.

My agent, Emmanuelle Morgen. *The Typewriter Girl* would be a slush manuscript with a very bad title if not for you. You had a vision for Betsey; thank you for your dedicated efforts as we saw it through.

The Typewriter Girl

Alison Atlee

Introduction

Betsey Dobson is a typewriter girl, bound and determined to earn her own living in Victorian London, even if one can barely call it a living. When she's offered a job as excursions manager at a seaside resort, Betsey seizes the chance for a better position and a different life. In order to succeed and realize her dreams of independence, Betsey must prove not only the worth of the project, but of herself. When Betsey's friendship with John Jones, her boss, turns to something more, she must decide whether romance and ambition can coexist, and whether her fiercely sought independence is worth sacrificing.

Topics and Questions for Discussion

1. What does the first scene of the novel reveal about Betsey's character? How do her actions and attitude set her apart from the other typewriter girls? In what ways is she unconventional for a woman in the 1890s?

2. During her last night with Avery, Betsey wonders if "she wanted the wrong thing, this job that could end with the turn of a season, this life in a place she'd never seen" (page 23). Why is she eager to leave London and take the position as excursions manager in Idensea? If she hadn't accepted the position, what might her future have held?

3. What does John Jones see in Betsey that inspires his confidence in her? What does his interest in Betsey reveal about his own character? Why does he continue to support her after her inauspicious arrival?

4. Lillian believes that she has her suitors in hand and that she's on schedule to be married. What makes her so confident? How does she mishandle her relationships with John and Noel Dunning? What proves to be her undoing?

5. What does John mean when he says that Betsey is not for him? What do Betsey and Lillian each represent to him? What are John's ambitions and what does he see as the steps to realize them?

6. What do John's reminiscences of his family reveal about him? Why is he keen to bring his brother, Owen, to live with him?

7. Each chapter opens with a quote from *How to Become Expert in Type-writing*. How did these quotes shape your reading?

8. Why does John take Betsey to the Sultan's Road the night of Lillian's musicale? How does Betsey feel when she realizes what he wants from her? Why doesn't she yield to him?

9. Betsey's sexual freedom is unusual for her time, a time when "in all the ways a man could meet ruin, there was one way in which he could not, one especial way reserved only for woman" (page 184). What motivates Betsey to live as freely as she does? Why is it so essential that she "choose"? Why is she intent on remaining unmarried?

10. How would you describe Betsey's general attitude toward men? What events have shaped it? In what instances does her independent streak inspire admiration or condemnation from the men she works with?

11. What natural talents does Betsey use to her advantage to make the excursions scheme successful and to win the respect of her employers? What does she learn from John and Mr. Seiler about business and managing the board of directors?

12. What sort of man is Sir Alton? What does his treatment of Betsey reveal about his prejudices? In what ways does he undermine John, despite admiring and relying upon him?

13. When Betsey says she "wanted only to be safe and not owe anyone anything" (page 192), do you believe she's being honest with herself? How do her plans for the excursion scheme prove otherwise?

14. The night after the fire, when John tells Betsey he wants to marry her, why does she refuse? Why does she tell him that she doesn't trust him?

15. Discuss the ramifications of class in the novel. In what instances does it stand in John and Betsey's ways and to what lengths do they go to overcome it? What part does it play in their romance? How does it affect the development of Idensea and the Swan Park Hotel?

16. At times, Betsey speaks bluntly and her language is coarse. Did this surprise you? Is there a pattern in the circumstances in which she speaks this way? Why do you think she expresses herself as she does?

Enhance Your Book Club

1. Has your book group read other historical or romance novels? How did *The Typewriter Girl* compare? Discuss with your book club members.

2. Betsey resents the indignities and lack of opportunity at her office job. Have members of your group held office jobs? Were they similar to Betsey's? Discuss how entry-level jobs for women today are similar or different from Betsey's.

3. Put your typewriting skills to the test! Have each member in you group type out a favorite passage from the novel. Time each member and see if you can adhere to the instructions from *How to Become Expert in Type-writing*. If you don't have a typewriter, use a computer instead. Do you think you could make it as a typewriter girl?

4. Wish you could go to Idensea? Bring in vacation photos, postcards, or brochures from local tourist attractions. Discuss anything that reminds you of Idensea, as well as how tourist spots and seaside vacations have changed in the past century or so.

A Conversation with Alison Atlee

What inspired you to write the novel? How long did it take you to write?

A year or so for the basic story, but then the novel underwent so many revisions that I'd question my sanity if I counted them up. The initial seed of inspiration was an old postcard of the switchback ride on Folkestone's seashore. I came across it during research for a different book, but when I saw it, I knew I had a setting for my next story.

Did you do background research? What about this time period interested you?

The clothes! Elegant lawn parties! Telegrams! To my childhood self, this period seemed like the perfect blend of the modern and the old-fashioned, a place where I could have lived very happily. As long as I had plenty of money, of course. Like the clothes, what's underneath all that beauty is often restrictive and complicated, but that interests me, too, and it means I do lots of research.

Betsey seems a very unconventional woman for her time. Did many women in this period have the ambitions she did? How did her character take shape?

A good part of Betsey's character comes from how difficult it was for women to achieve nontraditional ambitions, especially education. Schools for working-class women like the one Betsey attends did exist, but, as *The Typewriter Girl* suggests, the courses could be watered-down versions of what men were offered. Plus, with the lower wages women earned and the need to be at work six or more days a week, you really had to sacrifice for it. I connected Betsey's situation to the single parents I know, trying to get a degree in the midst of holding down another job or two and caring for their families. It can be done, but it takes grit, and plenty of it.

Betsey's sexual history also makes her somewhat unconventional. What inspired this portrayal? Was it important that she not be your typical romantic heroine?

The first time I wrote about Betsey's London flat, I recall being surprised that she lived with a man. Other than that, I'm not sure what inspired this part of her character. But Betsey's sexual values make her even more of an outsider in this upper-middle-class world she enters—I'd say emphasizing that contrast was more in my mind than creating an atypical heroine.

For Betsey, career and the means for independence are more important than love or marriage. Do you think the two were mutually exclusive at the time?

Not necesarily, but it's always a tough balance, isn't it? Tougher then, no doubt.

Could you tell us a little more about the setting? Was there a particular seaside resort after which you modeled Idensea and the Swan Park Hotel?

References in the novel put Idensea near Bournemouth, but it's definitely fictional, created from research and my travels on Britain's coasts. One of my favorite places is Abbotsbury, and the name for Sir Alton's hotel came from the swannery there.

You interview authors for a romance novel website; what attracts you to this genre? What do you look for in a good romance? What is your favorite love story?

Personally, I often feel most creative when I'm working "with one hand tied behind my back"—meaning I'm restricted in some way, without endless possibilities or resources, and still have to figure it out. So that aspect of romance or any genre fiction appeals to me. I love for authors to surprise me, to do something unexpected within the parameters of the genre.

I also want the "indelible moment" in a love story, the one that sticks after you finish the book, the one that reveals what's at stake, all the hope and all the potential for heart-crushing failure (see chapter 24 of Laura Kinsale's *The Shadow and the Star*).

I'm terrible at narrowing down favorites, but the first time I recall being intensely invested in the outcome of a love story was at age eleven or twelve, when I read L. M. Montgomery's Emily of New Moon series.

When was the last time you typed on a typewriter?
Recently! I have my grandmother's manual Remington, and play on it once in a while. I also used it to type the letter Betsey composes in chapter 35, going as fast as possible to see what mistakes occurred (far more than Betsey would make on her worst day, which is kind of what's happening in chapter 35).

Do you enjoy reading historical fiction as well as writing it? If so, what are some of your favorite books or authors?
Taking a quick glance at the bookshelf in front of me right now: *Year of Wonders* by Geraldine Brooks, *The March* by E. L. Doctorow, *Alias Grace* by Margaret Atwood, *The Illuminator* by Brenda Rickman Vantrease, *Agincourt* by Bernard Cornwell, *Octavian Nothing* by M. T. Anderson . . .

More shelves, more favorites, but I'll stop there.

What should readers know about you? If you were interviewing a favorite author, what would you want to know about them?
I'm always curious about writers' routines or rituals. Me, I like to have something nearby to keep my hands busy when I stop to think or daydream or just feel stuck. I make a lot of sticky note collages and tiny sculptures from foil candy wrappers.

What are you working on next?
A couple of historicals are in the works, one in a timeline similar to *The Typewriter Girl,* another much removed.

rance and I would sidle up to her and whisper into her ear, "He's still my husband. Keep your filthy paws off him." Then I'd say, "You can have what's left of him . . . after the divorce."

But that was about as far as I could get with the divorce fantasies, because once I got beyond handing Jenna the comeuppance she so richly deserved, there wasn't much else to look forward to, and there was a lot to dread. Of course, all our friends would side with Joe. He was the one who could get anybody house seats to anything. Who could, if you were with him, get you whisked past security lines in airports and invited aboard yachts and onto private jets. I'd have to date and eventually reveal my body to another man. The breasts that had shrunken after nursing Joe's babies, the loose skin on the belly that had expanded to accommodate Joe's offspring—what kind of offerings were these to a man who had no claim on the children who marked me, forever, as the former estate of another?

When Sammy and I arrived home, Ruby and Catalina were sitting together on the living-room couch watching MTV. Over the years, Ruby had gotten Catalina hooked on all her shows and favorite bands, and Catalina, as a result, was the hippest sixty-year-old on the Upper West Side. She watched *TRL* and *The Real World*. She hated Eminem, but loved Shakira, of course, and also Muse, Kanye West, and the Arctic Monkeys, and would drop anything if a Gorillaz video came on TV. Now they were watching *Cribs* and knitting. Catalina had taught Ruby to knit when she was quite young, so Ruby knit compulsively, whenever she watched TV.

"Hi, guys!" I said. Sammy ran across the room and leaped onto Ruby's lap.

"Sammy, watch it!" said Ruby.

"Hi, Julia!" said Catalina. I smiled but Ruby looked straight ahead at the TV, her knitting needles clacking angrily against each other.

"How was school, Ruby?" I asked.

Silence.

"Ruby?" said Catalina.

"Ella abusa niños," Ruby said to Catalina.

"Ella no abusa niños," Catalina scolded. *"Hablas con su madre."*

Because my spoken Spanish is so bad, Ruby and Catalina think I can't understand what they're saying. I understand enough.

"¡Abusa niños!" Catalina said again, rising now and laughing. "Americans! In my country, if a child hit his mother and she no hit him back . . . *that* is child abuse! Because he might grow up and think nobody ever care enough about me to teach me anything about what is right and wrong."

Then she said, "I'll finish the dinner," and she kissed Ruby on the top of her head.

"Thanks, Catalina," I said, and she looked like she was going to give me a little hug, but I must have given her some kind of nonverbal indication that her touching me would cause me to dissolve into a sodden pile of tears, because she just touched my arm and went into the kitchen.

"I guess she knows where her bread is buttered," Ruby muttered.

"RUBY!" I shouted. "THAT'S ENOUGH!"

The decibel of my shouting caught Ruby and me both by surprise and Ruby looked at me, startled. Then she started to cry. I wanted to keep shouting. I wanted to tell her to give me a fucking break. That I was obviously in over my head when it came to parenting. That what little I knew about being a mother I had learned from Catalina—a woman who went to Mass every morning and mysteriously crossed herself whenever she heard a siren. That Ruby's whole life, the best I could do was act as if I knew what I was doing. But I didn't keep shouting. Instead, I sat next to Ruby and put my arms around her, and she didn't pull away. She hugged me back and sobbed. Sammy patted her and said, "No crying, Ruby! No crying!"

"Everybody at school is asking me if Daddy's gay!" Ruby sobbed.

"What?"

"It's what all the kids at my school are talking about. Daddy picks up guys at nightclubs and is secretly gay."

"Ruby, you know that's not true," I said.

"How am I supposed to know it's not true?"

"You'd know if your father was gay!"

"There are gay men whose *wives* don't even know they're gay."

"Okay, I've told Catalina again and again, I don't like you kids watching *Oprah*."

"Why all the gay rumors, then, if Daddy's not gay?" Ruby sniffed.

"People are sometimes jealous and resentful of celebrities and they make up things out of spite. A miserable, miserable, pathetic person made up those stories about Daddy. Everybody'll forget them soon, don't worry."

"Also . . . I want a chin implant. I know that's adding to my insecurity about Daddy. . . ."

Ruby was playing on my sympathy here. She is a beautiful girl, but she had decided almost a year earlier that she had a weak chin. "I have *no* chin," is what she said, and she'd been angling for a chin implant ever since.

"How does a thirteen-year-old even know about chin implants?" Joe had asked after she first broached the subject. I guess Joe doesn't get to see a lot of daytime television in that trailer of his. I had told Ruby again and again that she was too young for cosmetic surgery, but now I felt my resolve weakening. I felt like one of the world's worst mothers. It would be so easy to ingratiate myself with Ruby again by giving in on this issue. I couldn't take back the ridiculous rumors I'd started about Joe, or the fact that I had slapped Sammy, but I *could* make her an appointment with a surgeon and buy her a new chin!

Then I came to my senses.

"No," I said.

"Why not?! You obviously spent a fortune on your hair extensions, and everybody can tell you've had your lips injected—I don't know who you're trying to fool! You can do anything you want to try to improve your looks, but I'm not allowed to fix my facial deformity?"

"That's right," I said coolly.

"It's my face!"

"It'll be your face when you're eighteen. Legally, it's my face now and it's not finished growing. And you're right about my lips and hair. If I had it to do over, I wouldn't have done all this—"

Ruby stood up and started to leave the room.

"—*but* I'm a grown-up, and when you're grown-up, you can do anything you want to your face!"

"Uggggh!" Ruby shouted from the back hall before she slammed her door.

I went into the kitchen, where Catalina was tending to a roast pork tenderloin. A pot of potatoes was simmering on the stove. Joe was due home any minute and I suddenly wanted the kitchen to myself. I felt full of wifely goodness. Goodwife Ferraro, I was. In a few short hours, I had advocated for one child at his school and set limits with another. This was the best mothering I had done in weeks. Now I wanted my kitchen back.

"You don't have to stay, Catalina," I said with a smile.

"Oh . . ." she replied, confused.

"Just show me what to do and I'll finish making dinner. You can have the rest of the night off."

"Okay. Is almost ready. The roast needs to stay in the oven for another twenty minutes. Then it'll be finished. The potatoes are almost ready to be mashed. You're sure you no want me to stay and do that?"

"No, I remember how to mash potatoes."

"There is salad in the fridge, and a tofu stir-fry for Ruby. Just put it in the microwave for about a minute."

"That sounds good."

"And those green beans with garlic that Joe likes. They're on the stove. They're all done."

"Great," I said. "Thanks."

I said good-bye to Catalina and dumped the boiled potatoes into a bowl. I poured cream over the potatoes and dropped some butter in as well. "Plenty of salt," my mother used to tell me when I helped her make potatoes. Mashing potatoes was one of only a handful of things I clearly remembered doing with my mother. I'll have to show Ruby how to make mashed potatoes, I thought, and I'll say, "My mom always told me that the secret to her mashed potatoes was plenty of salt."

Ruby has a bit of a biased perspective on my mother. She thinks she was careless—even more careless than me. "Things were different then—we had more freedom," I had told her the day, two summers ago, when we visited my old neighborhood. Joe was shooting a film in D.C., so Ruby and I had taken a day trip to Annapolis, and after we went on a tour of the Naval Academy, we went to my old block. We gazed at the house—it had been a two-family home when we lived there but now it was a grander single-family home. I led her down to the old railroad tracks—now overgrown with weeds—and I told her about how Neil and I used to play down at the tracks in the late-summer afternoons, looking for snakes and bottles and treasure. I told her about the Confederate money that local kids believed had been buried in the woods behind the tracks. And about the house on the corner that was supposed to be haunted by a wife-murderer. It was hard to explain to literal-minded Ruby how the ghosts of murderers and witches and Confederate soldiers swam in our little minds. We didn't go to preschool, and we didn't need the constant supervision of our parents, the way kids do today. We were never expected to sit quietly in groups or develop sequencing skills. Our teachers were the six- and seven-year-olds in the neighborhood who told us that in elevators in skyscrapers there is no gravity, that dogs' mouths are cleaner than people's, and that cats can fall safely from a five-story building by landing on their feet.

"You were only five when you lived here, but you could run around the neighborhood without any grown-ups?" Ruby had asked.

"We weren't allowed past the railroad bridge," I told her, pointing to the stone structure ahead of us. It had seemed like the end of the world to us back then. "I can't believe it's really such a short distance from our house!"

The bridge looms large in my memories of that neighborhood because we were forbidden to cross it, but we had done so late one night, according to my father. He and my mother had left us alone in the house, Neil and me, because we were sound asleep. "You kids never woke up once you were asleep. Never!" my father said.

"Sometimes, not often, we'd sneak out after you puppies were asleep, just to run up the road to the neighbors for a beer," and the term *sneak* used here always amused me. The idea that my father—young, handsome, and strong—and my free-spirited mom had to "sneak" behind our backs to do anything was astonishing. Anyway, one night they returned from their drinks at the neighbors' and found Neil and me, frantic and hysterical, running across the railroad bridge in our pajamas in the dark. "Where were you two pups running off to?" my father used to laugh when he recounted the story, but I have no idea, because I think my only recollection of that night left for me is of his telling it.

I never share this story with Ruby—she wouldn't get it, just like she doesn't get the fun of "rounds." I had tried to get her and Joe, and later Sammy, to sing rounds in the car with me, but they all thought it was too tedious and kept muddling their parts. "You sing it yourself," Ruby said the last time we tried, and I had sung one verse, but it's no fun singing "Merrily, merrily, merrily, merrily, life is but a dream" when nobody's following you. When it ends, when you're alone—it's all at once. It's like hitting a wall.

When Joe arrived home half an hour later, the table was set. Ruby was in her room instant-messaging her friends, Sammy was watching Nick Jr. in our room, and I was in the kitchen opening a bottle of Chardonnay.

"Dinner smells good," said Joe. He walked up behind me and kissed the back of my neck. "And you do, too!"

I turned and kissed him on the lips.

"I know about Jenna," I whispered. I thought I'd take back my husband, while I was at it.

Joe stiffened, then pulled back a little. "Who?"

I grabbed the front of his shirt and remembered fighting with my brother as a child and the mistake of the shirt grab. Neil used to wriggle out of his shirt while I tugged on it, cursing and crying, trying to smack him on the head. He would squirm free of the shirt in the blink of an eye and then start shoving me, or worse.

I released Joe's shirt and he backed up a few steps.

"Jenna who?"

"Jenna! Your girlfriend. I've heard all her messages on your voice mail over the past two weeks. And, by the way, change your code. I can't get anything done because I'm wasting all my time listening to your simpering whore moaning about how horny she is. . . . Kids! Time to eat!"

The call to the children was issued in a singsong voice, but the preceding words had been said in the same quiet, controlled, but somehow ultra-menacing tone that my father used when he was really, really angry. His extensive military training always kicked in when he was emotional about something, and we knew that he was raging, fighting mad when his voice lowered to almost a whisper and he had to get real close to our faces so we could hear.

I lifted the platter of roast tenderloin from the counter and carried it into the dining room.

"What the fuck are you talking about? Wait a minute," Joe said, following me, but Sammy was running into the room and Joe picked him up for his hug.

"Wait," said Joe, "I think I know what this is about. . . ."

"We'll have to talk about it after dinner, won't we, honey?" I said, smiling and motioning toward Sammy.

Needless to say, Joe didn't eat a lot during dinner, but I finally had my appetite back.

"I've said it before, but I'll say it again: Catalina can really cook. This is delicious," I said, beaming. I took a small sip of my wine. I had to watch myself and not drink too much, but I wanted to drain the glass down my gullet and pour another. (I thought of my dad, in his current home at the VA hospital, cursing at nurses, his hands shaking and his mind sodden, and I left the rest of the wine in my glass.)

Ruby stared sullenly at her plate. Joe was in full spaniel mode, looking up at me imploringly and then looking away.

I don't know why I felt so good. Like I was in full charge, for the first time in weeks. Ruby brought up the chin surgery again and I thought Joe was going to break down and weep as he told her that she was perfect the way she was.

"You look like your mother. Like your beautiful mother, when we first met," he said, and I smiled as I cut into my meat.

After dinner, Ruby helped me with the dishes while Joe put Sammy to bed.

"I'm sorry about what happened last night. With Sammy," I said. "I've already told Sammy I'm sorry, but now I'm telling you."

Ruby moved about the kitchen quietly. She covered up the vegetables and placed them in the fridge, steering a wide path around the platter of meat.

"You're so . . . psycho lately."

"I know," I said. "I'm a little stressed."

"What do you have to be stressed about?" Ruby asked with a little laugh. "I'm the one who's taking too many honors classes. Daddy's the one who has to support us. You don't really have to do anything."

"I know. You have no idea how stressful that is," I said.

Eventually, Ruby went to bed and Joe and I were alone in our room. I was in bed, pretending to read, when he came in and shut the door quietly behind him.

"Jenna doesn't exist," he said.

I put my book down.

"It's Susanna."

"What?"

"Susanna has been cast in a film where she has to play an American. She's trying out this Southern accent—you know how British and Australian actors who can't really do American accents always do Southern accents?"

It's true about the Southern accent, I thought. *For some reason it's easy for foreigners.*

"She was just being silly and playful. You know she has no interest in me . . . and vice versa! I told her she could try out the accent on me, so she calls me sometimes after her sessions with her voice coach and she can never think of anything to say, so she just leaves those dirty messages."

I was looking right at him. He was looking right back.

"Call her," he said.

"What's the name of the film?" I asked.

Joe thought for a moment. "I don't know," he said.

I gave a short little laugh.

"Spike Jonze is directing it!" he announced.

Joe's laptop was next to the bed and I lifted it up, my eyes still fixed on his.

"Go ahead," he said. "Look it up."

I Googled Susanna. There were ten million Susanna Mercer links. Then I Googled Susanna Mercer and Spike Jonze and found a link to *Variety.* I clicked on the link.

Susanna Mercer is set to costar with Owen Wilson in You Rang?, *a new Spike Jonze film, DreamWorks producer Jeremy Winston announced today. . . .*

"I'm gonna have Susanna call you," Joe said. "She's going to feel horrible when she finds this out. I'm actually going to be a little embarrassed to tell her that my wife secretly listens to my voice-mail messages. . . ."

"It was an accident," I said. "We have the same code." And I told him the story of how I managed to get his voice mail instead of my own that night at Pastis.

"It was an *accident*," I said.

[f i f t e e n]

So you believe him?" Alison asked. We were in the Beverly Hills
Vera Wang showroom. It was the following Friday, just two days
before the Golden Globes. The dress I had chosen the week before
had been flown to L.A. that morning, Joe and I had flown in that afternoon, and now I stood on a raised, carpeted pedestal while a
seamstress carefully pinned my hem. Alison sat on a stool with her
legs crossed and her ankle jiggling madly.

"Yes," I said. "I really do, Alison." I indicated with my eyes that
I couldn't say more in front of the seamstress but Alison was determined.

"And how did he explain the . . . dirty talk?"

"The same as everything else. She was just working on the accent. Couldn't think of anything to say. Trying to be funny!"

"I see," said Alison, in a tone that implied she saw something I
didn't.

"Turn, please," the seamstress said. I turned away from Alison and
faced the three-way mirror, and there I was. My long, wavy blond

hair was parted in the middle, looking, I thought, very seventies-
chic. My skin glowed with yesterday's spray-on tan. My forehead
was as smooth as a baby's, and when I smiled, no smile lines! The
gown was simple but elegant, a satiny, steel-blue column that
matched the color of my eyes and made me look tall and willowy.
Behind me, through the floor-to-ceiling windows, clouds drifted
by and palms swayed in the afternoon sun, and I thought, *I love
California.*

We had thought of moving to L.A. when Ruby was younger.
We looked at houses in Venice one winter, when Joe was shooting
a film there. There were still some ramshackle bungalows right near
the beach then, and Joe and I dreamed of buying one and fixing it
up. A house was a very romantic notion in those days, when we
were still renting and paying off debts. Now, when we go to L.A.
and look at real-estate prices, Joe often says, "Why the hell didn't
we scoop up one of those shitholes in Venice when we had the
chance? Those places start at five million now." But what's the use
of thinking like that? How could we have known then what we
know today? It's like asking why we didn't look at ourselves then
and see how precious everything about our marriage was. We
should have poured ourselves into each other instead of miserly begrudging our time and energy, fighting over whose turn it was to
get up with the baby and who got less sleep than the other. Everything appreciates over time. A long-term marriage is a rare and valuable thing, but fourteen years ago we weren't looking to nourish
something that would someday be rare and valuable. We were just
trying to claw Joe's way to the top. Now, standing proudly erect for
the silent Filipino seamstress who crawled around my feet, I viewed
myself as the steadfast guardian of our marriage. A weathered but
still somehow beautiful figurehead proudly thrusting my protective

bosom before the rising bow of a bountiful ship. My duty was to protect our marriage, not to dash it onto the rocks! I saw that now. That morning before we left for the airport, when I had guiltily tried Joe's voice mail one more time (just to be sure), I was met with a recording that informed me that his code had been changed. *Good!* I had thought. *I'm finished with all that witchery.*

"I'm sure she's going to the show on Sunday. Are you going to ask her about it?" asked Alison.

"Who?"

"You know," she said, and when I glanced at her, she mouthed the word, "Susanna."

"I doubt it."

"Julia! You have to!"

"It's too embarrassing! I'd have to admit to listening to . . . you know what, and she'd think I'm some hopelessly insecure shrew. . . ."

"No, she'd think you have her number, which you do."

"I'm just going to mind my own business. Joe and I are getting along great! It's like we're on a second honeymoon."

I hadn't told Alison or Beth about my Gawker postings. I couldn't. I could trust my two best friends with my life, but not with such a great bit of celebrity gossip as that. It would be too tempting at a party, after a few drinks, when the conversation switched over to celebrities, or the Internet, or to who's gay—there were many, many possible segues to the shameful "My friend is married to Joe Ferraro and she once, in a fit of anger, posted on the Internet that he's gay" story. Nothing had happened with the fake postings, anyway. Joe never followed up with his lawyers and there were no more blind items.

"So are you coming with us tomorrow night, or what?" I asked, changing the subject.

"Oh yeah, what is it again?"

"The *Entertainment Weekly* party." Alison knew that. And I knew she wouldn't miss it for the world, but she needed to pretend it was all too boring for her. Alison's career had sort of passed her by. Actually, in Alison's mind, it had not passed her by but had jumped ship and attached itself to Debra Messing when she barely beat out Alison for the part of Grace on *Will and Grace*. "Three callbacks," Alison still sometimes lamented when she'd had a few too many drinks. "And that bitch isn't even funny!"

"Okay, I guess I'll come." She sighed. "Maybe I'll buy something to wear. Can Joe get me on the list?"

"Yeah, I'll call his agent."

"Because I don't need him to. I'm sure I was already on the list, and when my assistant asked me about it, I said no, like I do to almost everything, but since you two are going, it might be fun."

"I'll make sure you're on the list," I said.

When the fitting was over, I made arrangements to have the gown sent to our suite at the Four Seasons. Alison gave me a kiss and dropped a small pill bottle into my purse.

"What's that?" I asked.

"Xanax. For the red carpet Sunday, in case I forget tomorrow. Just take half if you want. Me? I'd take two. Most people double their red-carpet dosage for the major awards shows."

"Well, thanks," I said.

Outside, I handed my parking stub to the young valet and he sprinted off, returning promptly with the black BMW Z4 rental convertible that Joe had surprised me with that afternoon. Joe had a meeting with his agent, but while I was unpacking, he left the keys to the car with a note that said, "In case you want to go to the beach. I've heard this is quicker than the bus! Love, J."

The first time Joe and I ever came to Los Angeles—for his first paying film job—we took a Metro bus from the Roosevelt Hotel in Hollywood to Santa Monica. It had looked like such an easy trip on the bus map. One bus would take us to Beverly Hills (Beverly Hills!) and we would switch to another that would take us to Santa Monica. To the beach!

My earliest impressions of Los Angeles had been largely formed by a handful of *I Love Lucy* reruns that I adored as a kid. The episodes where Ricky goes to Hollywood to sign a motion-picture deal and Ethel and Lucy go sightseeing in Beverly Hills. I felt, on that first L.A. trip, that Joe and I were a little like Ricky and Lucy, *sans* the Mertzes, but *avec* the wide-eyed, look-who's-hit-the-big-time attitude. It was pilot season and Joe's agent had arranged some meetings and auditions for him during the week we were in town, and when we flew into LAX, we felt as if we were being deposited on the very threshold of a bright, golden destiny.

We arrived on a Sunday and Joe wasn't scheduled to start shooting until that Tuesday. On Monday morning we woke up early, owing to the time change (this was before Ruby), and we decided to walk around the neighborhood. We strolled along the "Walk of Fame," and we studied the names on the stars with delight. Across the street was Grauman's Chinese Theatre and we meandered across Hollywood Boulevard, hand in hand, and just as we stepped onto the curb on the opposite side, a police officer on a moped pulled up next to us. The officer asked if we had a good reason for choosing not to cross at the light. We offered the lack of approaching automobiles as a good enough reason and were surprised to see the officer whip a citation pad from his breast pocket. He explained that there was a forty-dollar fine for jaywalking in the city of Los Angeles, and we honestly thought he was joking. Joe tried to explain that we had just arrived from New York City, where people are allowed to cross the street at will, but the cop would have none of it.

Anyway, that afternoon I wanted to go to the beach. Joe didn't particularly want to go, but he was willing, because I wanted so desperately to walk along a California beach. Somehow a rental car had not been part of Joe's deal (a teamster drove him and another actor to and from the set each day) and we couldn't really afford to rent a car, so we decided to take the bus. (I've told this story at a few Los Angeles cocktail parties and this is where people laugh uproariously.) Why bore you with the details of that epic journey? Short version: Long. Hot. Dehydrated and jet-lagged. Menacing Mexican gang behind us. Obvious TB victim catching sputum in hand, one row ahead. Otherwise empty bus that stops every few minutes even though there is nobody to discharge. Eyeing drivers in other cars, also stuck in traffic, we learn that even homeless people, even the blind, the limbless, the lepers, apparently even the children, DRIVE CARS in Los Angeles. Hours pass and finally it is time to switch buses in Beverly Hills! Hours later we arrive at the Santa Monica Pier and I have just enough time to sprint down to the surf and get my toes wet before we have to rush to make the last "express" bus back to Hollywood.

We had more or less wasted Joe's one free day in L.A., but he never blamed me or complained. That's one of Joe's pluses. He's really not a complainer. The first time my father went to a rehab for his drinking, my senior year in high school, he went to a good place—a real rehab with counselors and group sessions. When Neil and I went up for a family therapy weekend, one of our exercises was to list five positive things about each family member. It's hard to hold on to ill will and resentment toward somebody who has five good things about them, our counselor told us. And it turns out, we learned in that session, everybody has at least five things. One of Joe's is not being a complainer. Other things? He's generous. He has never begrudged me a thing—rather, he has told me that he wishes I would splurge on myself more. If I had driven straight over to Fred Segal that afternoon of the Golden Globe weekend and run up a ten-thousand-dollar bill, he would have been pleased for me. He's smart and intuitive. He can look at a situation and deconstruct it in a minute—for example, the time Sammy had the meltdown at his school interview—and know what to do next, while I'm more the type to panic and make things worse. *He's funny and loving and patient and . . . loyal,* I told myself that sunny Friday afternoon. *He's loyal.*

The valet pulled up with the black roadster and I tucked a twenty-dollar bill into his palm. I climbed inside and decided to put the top down. Why drive a convertible in Southern California with the top up? The valet saw me fumbling around with the roof latches and he leaned into the car.

"Like this," he said, reaching across me to unlatch one side, then the other. His arms were tanned and he smelled like shampoo and sweat and something else, some kind of musky aftershave, and this, combined with his youthful exuberance, made me smile.

"You have to put your foot on the brake. . . . That's it," he said, and he pushed a button on the center console. The roof retracted obediently and the young man stood back up and gave me a big grin.

"Thanks," I said, smiling back. I can't describe how long and blond I felt as I pulled away from the curb.

The car was equipped with a Global Positioning System that greeted me with a loud "Welcome!" and, to my surprise, announced that my destination was the Four Seasons hotel. Somebody at the rental agency must have programmed in the address of the hotel for us.

I started down Rodeo Drive. As always, I marveled at how immaculate the streets of Beverly Hills are. Joe says it's from the lack of snow and road salt and sand, but where is the detritus of man? The beer cans and chicken wings and pigeon shit and last night's vomit and spat-out gum that bejewel the sidewalks and streets of New York, London, Rome? Driving through Beverly Hills always makes me feel complicit in some kind of brilliant, but evil, urban-planning scheme. The garbage and dirt has to be *somewhere*. Now, though, driving a shiny black roadster down the pristine boulevard, I felt as if I was one of the chosen. The deserving. The breeze blew my hair extensions around my face and I flipped my head back like a teenager.

"In fifty feet, turn left," instructed my GPS guide.

Okay!

"At the next intersection, stay to the right."

Will do!

I followed the instructions of my electronic guide through several intersections and within minutes I was pulling up in front of the Four Seasons hotel.

"You have arrived!" announced the GPS.

You bet your ass I have!

I handed the car over to yet another valet and was welcomed into the lobby of the hotel by the doorman.

"Welcome back, Mrs. Ferraro. There's a FedEx package waiting for you."

"Thank you," I said, and I walked over to the desk to receive the package in all my blond loveliness.

"Mr. Ferraro left a message for you. He won't be back until six-thirty," said the concierge, handing me the package. We had decided to skip the various pre–Golden Globe parties that evening, to instead have a romantic dinner served to us in our suite. Now I had some extra time before Joe returned to the hotel. I would call the kids and then maybe take a nap.

As I headed for the elevators, I passed a door with a large Frédéric Fekkai sign above a photograph of a beautifully coiffed model. Two women were walking out of the door with bags full of hair products, and when they looked up, I saw that one was Teri Hatcher.

A hair salon. Perfect. I would get my hair extensions blown out while I was waiting for Joe. That way I wouldn't have to have it done before the *Entertainment Weekly* party tomorrow.

I smiled at Teri Hatcher, who smiled blankly back, and I pushed open the door of the salon. Inside, I waited behind two women who were checking in at the reception desk. When it was my turn, the perky young receptionist glanced down at a long list and asked, "Your name please?"

"I don't have an appointment, but is there any chance I can get a blow-dry?"

"Excuse me?" she said. The two women who had just checked in turned and stared at me.

"Just a shampoo and blow-dry," I said, smiling.

"Um, this isn't . . . a salon," said the receptionist.

I looked at her and then I looked around the salon, which, indeed, turned out not to be a salon at all. It was a conference room that had been turned into some kind of Frédéric Fekkai–sponsored, women-only cocktail party. Instead of hairstyling stations and blow-dryers and sinks, there were tables with white cloths and beautiful floral centerpieces, handsome waiters walking around with glasses of

wine and trays of delicate hors d'oeuvres. There was Patricia
Arquette and Claire Danes and . . . was it? Yes! It was Jessica Lange!

"What is this?" I asked the receptionist. I was whispering.

"It's a private party honoring Golden Globe nominees. I'm
going to have to ask you to leave." She was braying.

My face turned crimson. "Oh," I said.

The two women were quietly cracking up next to me.

"Maybe I'm on the list. My husband . . . he's a nominee."

I had no interest in staying, but I knew that Joe and I were on a
few party lists, and for some reason it was very important to me that
the receptionist and the other two women knew this as well.

The receptionist looked me over and then said, "Your name?"

"Julia *Ferraro*. I'm *Joe Ferraro*'s wife."

She floated her pencil tip down the list of names. "No . . . no
Ferraro."

"Oh," I said. "Okay."

I turned to leave and a woman handing out gift bags to departing guests absentmindedly started to hand one to me. When I
reached for it, I heard the receptionist screech, "Tracy! She's not a
guest!" and Tracy snatched back the bag and clutched it to her chest
like a baby.

Later, as I was telling Joe about it, both of us weak with laughter, I described the way I then felt compelled to back out of the
room, as if, had I turned my back on her, even for a moment, Tracy
would have planted her boot in my ass and literally kicked me back
out into the hotel lobby.

We ordered up grilled shrimp, haricot vert salad, and roasted
rack of lamb that night, Joe and me, and we dined on our terrace,
and the city of Los Angeles spread out below us like a sparkling
kingdom. We sipped our champagne and we even smoked a little

pot that Joe's driver had given him, and when I went inside to put on a CD, I saw that, in addition to the multitude of gift baskets that had been sent to Joe by various network executives, agents, and magazine editors, there was a new vase of large pink peonies that somebody had placed on the coffee table in our suite while we dined. Peonies are my favorite flowers, and when I pulled the card out from amid the blooms, I saw that it read: "To Julia, the love of my life, J." I carried the flowers back to the terrace and placed them on the table. The warm night air and the plaintive chorus of car horns and distant sirens reminded me of the summer nights of my youth, and I straddled Joe's lap like a showgirl and covered him with kisses.

[s i x t e e n]

Nobody carries their own children anymore," Karen whispered.

We were lounging by the Four Seasons pool, Karen Metzger and I, trying to get a little sun while Joe was in the gym. Karen was stirring her iced tea and peering over her sunglasses at a pair of twin babies being pushed past us in a double stroller.

"What do you mean?" I asked, blinking at the passing stroller. "What's wrong with carrying babies in a stroller? They're sleeping."

"No, I mean *carry to term*. Nobody carries her own babies anymore. Those babies had a surrogate mother."

I tried to catch another glimpse of the infants before they disappeared from view, but all I could see was the mother's back. The straps of her black bikini top and the back of her thong trisected her perfectly toned body.

"How can you tell they had a surrogate mother?"

"You can't tell! That was Brian Herriman's wife. You know, Brian Herriman from Paramount?"

"Oh, yeah!" I had met Brian Herriman and his wife (Jennifer? Gillian?) at a party once.

Karen was shoulder deep in her Marni tote. When she withdrew her phone, she said, "Gillian Herriman is in my friend Rita's book group. She tells everybody that she couldn't conceive and that's why she used a surrogate, but I think it was just to preserve that body."

She flipped open the phone. "I have to check my messages. I'm waiting for a call from Shane's play therapist." Karen touched the number 1 on her phone and that's how it dawned on me.

I didn't need Joe's code if I checked his messages using *his* phone.

Karen touched the number 1 just like I did when I checked my messages on my own phone. Apparently, 1 is the universal speed dial for voice messages. I hadn't known that. I could hear the staccato rhythm and varying tones of the different callers on Karen's voice mail as I pondered this new reality. It was still possible for me to check Joe's messages.

Why would I want to do that?

Karen snapped her phone shut.

"Yeah, so anyway, they were her eggs. She made sure everybody knew that, so I'm pretty sure she could have carried them herself. Katie Winston was the opposite . . ."

"Mmm-hmm," I said. *It's not okay. It's snooping.*

"They were somebody else's eggs, but she carried them herself so everybody would think they were hers. As if they could be at her age!"

I nodded. *He was telling me the truth.*

"That's why it kills me whenever I hear people say it's possible to get pregnant in your mid-forties. 'Look at Katie Winston!' people always say, and I say, 'Hello! Egg donor!' Katie Winston's eggs expired during the Clinton administration."

Joe's phone was attached to the charger in our room. I had nearly tripped over it on the way out. And he was in the gym.

No! Do not do it!

"Of course, who am I to talk? Everybody knows the twins were in vitro. But at least I had the decency to carry them!"

"I have to go to the bathroom," I said. "I'm just going to run up to the room."

"There's a bathroom down here!"

"I know, but I need to go up to the room. I'll be right back."

"Okay. Good, I'll call Shanie's therapist, then."

I pulled my jersey cover-up over my head, hastily pushed my feet into my flip-flops, and stumbled into the dark, cavernous hotel hallway, sun-blind and shaking. It was cool in the deserted corridor and I just stood there a moment, breathing in and out, heart racing. A long mirror ran along the wall opposite me, and when I glanced up at myself, I saw not the long-tressed beauty I had admired in our bathroom mirror just a few hours earlier, but an exhausted hag with near-jowls and dark circles under her eyes. The hair extensions seemed to actually age me in this shadowy light, and I was reminded of the "kitchen witches" sold in folksy New England shops in the 1980s with their dried-up, wrinkly apple heads and long, witch hair.

I'm just tired.

I had woken up the night before, actually in the very early morning hours, and had watched Joe sleeping and thought, *He's telling the truth. He's telling the truth.*

And yet . . .

The visit to the brownstone on a night I thought he was working. The sightings that were posted on Gawker. He had been seen making out at a bar with a blonde. Perhaps the reason he hadn't followed up with a suit against Gawker was because there were postings about him being in places he shouldn't have been, and he would be forced to prove he wasn't there.

It's easy to make up stuff and post it on those sites. Who would know that better than me?

She had said, "I love you, Joe." On his voice mail. Why would Susanna say that?

I brushed my hair away from my face and started down the long hallway to the gym. I pushed open the heavy glass door and discovered that the gym was the life of the hotel. While the pool area had been relatively empty, the gym was teeming with runners, elliptical climbers, ball squatters, and weight-machine crunchers. I scanned the robust, vigorously handsome crowd looking for Joe, and there he was, one of a long row of treadmill runners, neck and neck with the others. Joe wore headphones and was looking up at a bank of televisions—the electronic carrot that hung above all the runners, and toward which they all seemed to be pushing themselves, some sprinting madly, others slogging along at the end of a stationary marathon. I walked across the springy gym floor, and the relative quiet of the space seemed to belie the tremendous amount of human effort and energy that was being put forth. In another time and place, this amount of collective human sweat would be accompanied by the crack of a whip and the groan of oars or the resounding clang of metal upon stone. Here the only sounds were the quiet humming of the machines and the rhythmic breathing of Hollywood's glistening movers and shakers.

I padded over to Joe's treadmill, and when he saw me, he smiled and pulled off his headphones, still running, his shoulders rolling forward and back, his fists rising and falling.

"Hey," he said. His T-shirt was drenched.

"Hey," I said. "I have to go up to the room. Karen and I were going to order lunch in a little while. Do you want us to wait for you?"

Joe wiped his face with a towel that was draped around his neck and grimaced.

"I've . . . got . . . another ten minutes of cardio," he panted. "Then I want to steam."

"Okay . . ."

"Just order me a salad and . . . a banana."

"All rightie!"

I turned to leave and then looked back with a flirtatious smile. *Last night,* I thought, remembering, and I looked to see if he was remembering, too, turned to catch the old spaniel gaze, but he had his fingertips pressed to his jugular vein and his eye on his watch.

I unlocked the door to our room and saw that the housekeepers had already worked their magic. The carpet had rows of fresh vacuum-cleaner tracks, all the damp towels and dirty breakfast dishes were gone, and the gift baskets had been attractively arranged on the coffee table and bar. I had already pulled from the baskets the few items that I thought the kids would like—an iPod, some movie paraphernalia, lots of body products for Ruby—and I had meant to leave a note for the housekeepers telling them to help themselves to the rest.

The phone was on the floor where Joe had left it. He had plugged the charger into a wall outlet in the little entrance hall and left it there. It seemed like blasphemy the way he so carelessly left the phone lying there.

I picked it up and cradled it in my palm.

I would not listen to the messages, I had decided on my way up in the elevator. I would just have a peek at Joe's call log. I assured myself that the call log was basically public information. If I had come into the room and decided to use Joe's phone instead of my own—something I had done dozens of times—I might have just scanned down his call log to dial home. In fact, I was sure I had done exactly this many times. In fact, I *did* need to call the kids! I snapped open the phone and was greeted by a photo of Ruby and Sammy that Joe had stored as wallpaper. It was a close-up of the two of them, their cheeks pressed together, Sammy grinning a big cheesy grin and Ruby giving a funny little fake model smile. I slammed the phone shut and when I placed it back on the floor I felt exalted. Divine. It was what Goody Proctor would have done. It was a cold, conniving witch of a wife that spied on her husband, who had cast a wicked spell on the Internet. I wasn't that wretch anymore. I would call the kids on my own phone.

We had planned to go to the *Entertainment Weekly* party with the Metzgers that night, so Joe and I decided to drive to their house in Bel-Air and then ride with them to the party. There were a lot of paparazzi around the hotel, due to all the celebrities booked there for the awards show, and they caught us as we climbed into the tiny convertible roadster, my short skirt riding up on my thighs, my ridiculous long locks blowing wildly. A small crowd gathered around us and a woman pulled a beautiful silk scarf from around her neck and handed it to me. "Tie it around your hair," she said in some kind of elegant European accent. "I'm staying here at the hotel—you can just leave it at the front desk later." I tied the scarf around my head, and with my black sunglasses and all the makeup I had put on, I felt a little like Grace Kelly or Audrey Hepburn, so I gave the crowd a very dramatic wave. Joe also waved to the crowd. He put the car in gear, revved the engine, the crowd cheered . . . and then he popped the clutch and we stalled out violently, our upper bodies rocketing forward like a couple of test-drive dummies.

"*Ease* your foot off the clutch," I mumbled through my aching grin.

"I know, I know," Joe sputtered, starting the car again with a series of growling curses, and then we were off. The crowd cheered us on again, and as we pulled away from the curb, Joe reached for my hand and squeezed it tenderly. The afternoon sun cast a blaze of gold on the buildings around us, and we sailed down those gleaming, palm-lined avenues, Joe and me, smiling merrily, merrily, merrily. . . .

There was a red carpet and a long press line outside the *Entertainment Weekly* party. When we pulled up to the curb in the Metzgers' Town Car, we saw that a huge battalion of photographers had been stationed on one side of the roped-off red carpet, and on the other side were hordes of fans being carefully watched by large men wearing earpieces.

"You guys get out first," said Karen.

I was on the side of the car closest to the red carpet, which was unfortunate. It's better if the star gets out first. It always is.

The driver hopped out of his seat and opened my door. The fans pushed and shoved and craned their heads and cheered. The photographers cocked their cameras.

I placed one Jimmy Choo out on the sidewalk. Then the other.

The crowd roared with applause. Somebody yelled "Angelina!" and the whole street went berserk.

I stood up and turned toward the crowd. The screaming stopped and the clapping petered out like the sudden end to a much-needed summer rainstorm. The photographers lowered their cameras and resumed their conversations with one another, and then Joe stepped out of his side of the car and all hell broke loose. The crowd erupted in applause and cries of "Joe! Joey Ferraro!" rang out into the evening air.

The photographers were in full cry: "Joe, over here!" "Right here!" "Can you and the wife stand here?" "Here! Joe!" "Joey, over here!" "How about one alone, Joe?" "Without the wife!"

The first time I heard a photographer call Joe's name, I thought he must have been an old friend of his—perhaps somebody Joe knew from school. This was at the first L.A. film premier we ever attended. It was for *Siren Song,* the film Joe had done when we took the fateful bus ride across L.A. Joe only had a small part in the movie, but it turned out to be a breakthrough performance, with all the critics singling him out.

When the film came out, we were in L.A. again. Joe was working on his second mob film. He had a new agent by that time, a man named Scott Lendel, and we also had Ruby then, so Joe had told Scott that we wanted a car big enough to accommodate Ruby and her car seat. When we arrived in Los Angeles and were transported to the house that had been rented for us in Santa Monica, we were thrilled to find a gleaming black Lincoln Town Car parked in the driveway. When I told my dad that we were driving around L.A. in a Town Car, I think I heard him weep with joy for us. He drove a rusty pickup truck. Always had. We strapped Ruby's car seat into the back and we spent an entire weekend exploring Los Angeles in our luxurious chariot.

Soon after we arrived in L.A., we had dinner with the film's director, Jason Cummings, and his girlfriend the supermodel. They happened to arrive at the restaurant just as we did, and when we got out of the car to greet them, Jason burst out laughing. "That's too much," he said. "That's perfect."

We smiled stiffly. "What?" said Joe.

"The car," Jason said, and he laughed uproariously as he followed us into the restaurant.

We found that everyone we met in L.A. had one of two reactions to the car. Some, like Jason, would laugh conspiratorially as if they got the joke. Others would ask in all seriousness if we were driving my parents' car. One night we had dinner with Joe's agent, who, upon seeing the car, flew into a rage and started madly dialing numbers on his cell phone. "Don't worry," he said, "we'll sort this out."

We told Scott not to worry, that we loved the car. And then we drove it to the premier of *Siren Song*. When we pulled up to the red carpet that night, we were just following all the other Town Cars, not really cognizant of the fact that the passengers in the cars ahead of us were all being dropped off. When we arrived at the entrance, a uniformed man bent down and opened the door to the backseat of the car, which he found to be empty. He quickly recovered from the shock of seeing Joe and me in the front seat, all dressed up.

"What'd you do, rub out your driver?" he asked, laughing loudly. Then he directed us to a nearby parking lot. We parked the car and it was on the shameful walk back to the red carpet that a photographer stepped in front of us on the sidewalk and said, "Mind if I take a quick photo, Joe?" and started shooting away. We finally stepped onto the red carpet to flashes of lightbulbs and cries of "Joe! Joe!" from all directions.

"How do all these people know your name?" I asked. I still thought everyone knew him as "that guy."

This annoyed Joe. "I've told you again and again," he hissed, "I'm fucking famous, Julia!," which made me giggle, and Joe started laughing, too, at himself, at his *fucking famous* self, and we clasped hands and walked, blinking and dazzled, right into those blinding lights.

[s e v e n t e e n]

It was on the red carpet in front of the *Entertainment Weekly* party that Joe's cover was blown. People wonder why actors are always hitting photographers. Here's why: As we walked along that red carpet, posing and smiling, a rogue photographer, somebody from the street who hadn't been allowed into the approved, cordoned-off press area, pushed himself into the crowd and yelled, "Joe, where's Jenna McIntyre tonight?"

Joe's head swiveled around and he glared at the photographer, who was rapidly snapping off shots. I saw Joe glance at me, saw him out of the corner of my eye, but I pretended I hadn't heard the guy. I just held Joe's hand and posed, waving gaily, blinking at all the flashing lights. They make your eyes tear after a while, those lights.

When we got inside, Alison was already there. She was with Richard, her husband, and Isaac Mizrahi, an old friend of hers from New York. We all sat at a table in a corner of the vast outdoor party space, and everybody gossiped about all the celebrities who walked by. I tried to join in the merriment but mostly I just sat there quietly.

I was thinking. I was calm. I realized that I had already known, that I had never believed Joe, really. We sat on one side of the table, on a bench covered with cushions, and several times I heard Joe's phone ringing in his jacket pocket. He didn't answer it. The third time it rang, he looked at the caller ID, then shut off the phone.

"Who was it?" I asked. Casually.

"Hmm?" Joe said. He was gazing off into the crowd. "Hey, isn't that Cloris Leachman over there?"

"Can I use your phone, honey?" I asked. So casually. I was squinting out at the crowd, acting as if I was trying to see Cloris Leachman. "I want to check on the kids."

"Sure," Joe said. He handed me the phone.

I touched the 1 key. Hers was the first message. And the second. *"Hi, baby. I miss you. Call me,"* was the first. The second said, *"When are you coming back? I just got a job in L.A. and might fly in on Tuesday! I know you said we shouldn't see each other for a while. I'm only going to be out there for a couple of days. . . ."*

"What's up? Nobody home?" Joe asked.

"No," I said, slamming shut his phone.

"C'mon. Let's get out of here," Joe said.

Outside, he put his hands into his pants pockets and his phone rang and made him jump.

"Maybe it's the driver," he said. "I just called him a minute ago to say we were on our way out."

"Well, answer it," I said.

Joe pretended he didn't hear me.

"Here's the driver," he said, and he opened the back door of the Town Car so that I could climb in.

———

I didn't sleep that night but Joe did, which is another of his pluses. He doesn't let anybody rain on his parade. You'd have thought he might feel a little guilty about the messages. Instead, he seemed almost jubilant on the ride home, and when we walked into the room, he leaned against the little bar in the living room and said, "C'mere."

I pretended I didn't hear him.

"Julia," he said, and then he stepped up behind me and pulled me close.

I turned and planted a brief kiss on his lips.

"Can you believe we're here?" he said, smiling. "Did you ever think, back when we were living in that dive in Alphabet City, that someday we'd be in a suite at the Four Seasons waiting to find out whether I would win a Golden Globe award?"

"No."

"Oh, thanks a lot," he laughed. He opened the mini-fridge and grabbed a beer. "You want anything, hon?" he asked.

"No thanks."

"So, you never thought I could do it?" he said, taking a swig off the beer.

"No, it's not that I doubted you'd succeed. . . . It's just that I don't remember this being the dream."

"It was mine, baby," Joe said, and he walked out onto the terrace and lit a cigarette. He leaned his back against the balcony rail and smiled at me. It was the old spaniel smile—and yet it wasn't. The old, heart-melting spaniel look had been replaced, over the years, by something more confident. More take-it-or-leave-it. His old expression said, *I can't bear to look at you for another second, I want you so badly,* and it was just for me. The new one was his "Yes, it's me" look. Joe shared it, generously, with everybody.

"My battery's dead. I want to see if Ruby or Catalina called," I said. "Can I use your phone?"

"Sure." He pulled it out of his jacket pocket and tossed it to me. Then he turned around and gazed across the city. I opened his phone and pressed the number 1.

Hours later as he slept, naked, curled up on his side, I marveled at the vulnerability of the human body. Devoid of fur, shell, claws, and quills, when our brains are at rest we are really as vulnerable as new-born babies. I was sitting on a chair next to the bed, smoking one of Joe's cigarettes, and I watched his eyebrows raise and lower and his lips quiver slightly in some kind of a dreamy soliloquy. Perhaps he was dreaming of his acceptance speech, or a scene he had been read-ing earlier for next week's show. Maybe he was having a conversa-tion with a buddy or perhaps he was professing his love for Jenna. Maybe he loves her, I thought and watched, exhaling slowly, as Joe rolled from his side onto his back. His fingers were curled in toward his palms and his legs were splayed. I thought about a nature docu-mentary that I had watched recently with Ruby, and how I learned that a wolf goes belly up when confronted by a more threatening member of the pack, exposing his throat, his soft belly, and his gen-itals to the menacing wolf. The narrator of the documentary com-mented on the effect this show of submission has on an aggressive wolf, who will sink his teeth into the throat of an upright, fangs-baring challenger, but will simply ignore the wolf who offers his gut, his balls, his soul. I stubbed out my cigarette and lit another. Joe sighed contentedly in his sleep. I watched him for some time. I sat in that chair, watching and smoking, until the silvery light of dawn crept over the City of Angels, under our drapes and into our suite, marking the dawn of Joe's big day. Then I pulled on a pair of jeans and a T-shirt and called down for the car.

I drove down La Cienega and took the 10 West toward the Pacific, my bare foot pushing the gas pedal to the floor at one point, just to see how fast I could really go on an almost deserted highway. I exited the freeway and drove west until I found the beach, and then I drove out onto the Santa Monica Pier and parked the car. Gulls dive-bombed the pier, snatching up stray french fries and pieces of hot-dog rolls, and as I walked along the splintery planks, I thought that it must be close to six in the morning. The sun was behind me, rising over the Malibu hills, and I walked down the stairs of the pier and onto the beach heading south. It was slow, heavy going in the deep sand, but when I got down below the tidemark, the footing was so delightfully firm and fast that I broke into a little jog. I followed the coastline, traveling just at the frothy hem of the surf, and when a rogue little wave suddenly wrapped itself around my knees, I found myself giggling helplessly. I remembered a game that Neil and I used to play in the surf and I made my way along the beach, running away from each wave and then following it as far back into the sea as I could without getting wet.

The early-morning crew was out, the beachcombing tractors making their way around me. Up on the wide-paved walkway there were garbage collectors and cops on bikes and fitness buffs getting in an early-morning run. I kept following the beach, in and out of the surf, past playgrounds and volleyball nets and homeless sleepers and dog walkers.

I walked and walked until I arrived at Venice Beach, and the sight of the boarded-up, surfer-inspired souvenir shops and tattoo parlors somehow eased this sense of doom that I had felt welling up inside me all night. I had seen these shops many times during the

day, and the tattooed vendors and freaky locals and smell of mari-
juana and sounds of bongos and reggae music had all given it an au-
thentically exotic air then, but now that the walkway was deserted,
it seemed as if it had all been staged. As if nothing was real. I felt as
if I was walking past an abandoned movie set. Even the hazy morning light seemed filtered and artificial and temporary.

I sat down on a bench. A woman wandered past me pulling a
shopping cart that appeared to hold all her worldly possessions, and
she stopped for a moment to search through its contents for something. She appeared to be in her sixties, and when she glanced up at
me, I could see that her face had been cured to the color of an old
paper bag, and was deeply creased and wrinkled from decades in the
sun. The dark brown tones of her skin made her eyes appear to be
an unnaturally pale shade of green. Her hair was caught up in a long
braid, and while it was mostly gray now, there still remained a few
yellowy blond streaks. She had the handsome bone structure of a
Daughter of the Revolution, and I imagined her arriving here
sometime in the 1960s from someplace like Boston or Greenwich
and being absorbed into one long, wild night upon her arrival in
California, only to find herself, one morning, living out of a cart. I
wondered if her family missed her or whether she had children who
spoke about her resignedly in crowded Al-Anon meetings. When I
was a teenager, I sometimes tried to imagine that my mother wasn't
really dead but that she had just run away. If she had, I could see her
coming to a place like this and finding her tribe and never leaving.

I was tired. The bench was hard on my back and I decided to go
rest on the sand for a few moments. I would just lie there for a little
while and then drive back to the hotel to get dressed. I wasn't ready
to make my morning call to the kids. It was Sunday, so I couldn't
call Beth's lawyer to see about having separation papers drawn up. I

had decided, while watching Joe sleep, that I would (a) let him live and (b) kick him out. But I decided to wait to tell him after the awards show. Maybe on the flight home. I had Googled Jenna McIntyre while he slept and learned that she was a young actress who had had small parts in a couple of television pilots, and a film here and there. Now I just wanted to rest. I stretched out on my side on the sand. My feet were cold and I grabbed a half-buried T-shirt that somebody had tossed on the beach. It was a large ripped yellow shirt with a faded portrait of Jimi Hendrix silk-screened on the front, and I wrapped it around my feet and placed my head back against the sand. The breeze was cool but I could feel the first rays of the morning sun on my face. The skin on my cheeks and forehead grew warm and then, gradually, hot and tight. I heard the sound of the waves slapping the shore. I heard the gentle chatter of a little girl playing on the sand nearby, and the lonely call of a gull. A plane droned overhead. The girl, the gull, the engine of the plane, and the foamy wash of the surf all began a staggered descent with me. I was falling asleep, leaving the waking world for just a little while, and the singsong voice of the little girl and the cry of the gull and the sound of the waves on the beach washed over me.

[e i g h t e e n]

The drone of airplane engines and the whisper of the distant surf were interrupted every few moments by the clear, earnest words spoken by a young man.

"Did you know that you have unlimited capabilities," he was saying, "and that your dreams and aspirations *can* be realized?"

There was a pause and I heard the clacking of skateboard wheels and the far-off pounding of some kind of drum-dominated world music. Then a girl's voice said, tentatively, "No?" as if she was afraid of getting the answer wrong.

"It's true. I'm only maybe one one-hundredth of the way to re-alizing all my capabilities, but the discoveries I've made so far about myself are fucking mind-blowing."

"Shit!" said the girl. "But what were you saying about a test? Do I have to take the test?"

"It's not like a test you take in school. It's a personality test. It's fun!"

"Oh. So it improves your personality?"

"The test itself won't improve it. But if you want to improve your personality, taking this test is the first step."

I sat up and blinked at the gawky, pimpled red-haired man—a boy, really—who stood over the teenaged girl sprawled out on the sand just a few feet away from me. *The girl is an easy mark,* I thought. It didn't take a Scientologist to see that her life could use a little changing. She was underweight and dirty. She looked like she had been "rode hard and put up wet," as my father had said once, much to Neil's and my great amusement, about a floozy in a bar.

"Where do I go?" she asked, and the boy kneeled down next to her and handed her a brochure.

The air smelled beautifully of the sea and of Coppertone, and every few moments the smoke from somebody's cigarette wafted past me in pungent, languid gusts. I just sat for a moment, blinking at the bright stillness of the sand all around me, and I breathed in the dissipating smoke, sucking it in through my parched nostrils. All that smoking last night had sparked up the old urge. My father is a smoker, so is Joe, and now the smell of tobacco filled me with a nostalgic sense of longing for men I have loved, and for my youth. The sun was high and I knew I shouldn't still be on the beach, but I sat there for another few minutes. Then I rose to my feet and kicked the soiled T-shirt onto the sand and began walking, sleepy and sluggish, back along the now-crowded beach to the Santa Monica Pier.

I arrived at the hotel almost an hour later, dizzy with hunger, and realized I had forgotten my key card. When I rang the doorbell to the room, I braced myself for Joe's enraged greeting. It was almost two o'clock and our car was picking us up at three-thirty. *He must be in a complete panic,* I thought, but when the door opened, it wasn't Joe but his agent, Scott Lendel, who greeted me.

"Hey! Julia!" he said exuberantly, and he pulled me into his arms for a rough hug. "It's the big day, huh? Where were you, at the pool?"

"Uh, no . . . Where's Joe?"

"He's in the shower, Julia," said a loud woman's voice. It was Joe's publicist, Laney, who was now pushing Scott aside to give me a hug. "Where have you been? Listen, I'm going to do the red carpet with you and Joe, hon. I've done the Golden Globes every year for the last ten years and it'll be a breeze."

"Okay."

I looked around the suite and saw that it was crowded with people: Joe's agent, business manager, publicist, network producer, and various wives and girlfriends. They were all dressed up already, and when I stepped into the room, they seemed to spontaneously form a sort of receiving line.

"Hi, Julia! Justin Fairlawn from NBC. You remember my wife, Helena? Just dropped by to wish you all luck!"

"Julia, so great to see you again. Love the hair! Love it!"

"I know Joe is going to win, Julia!"

"You must be so proud!"

Several room-service tables had been wheeled in, and a buffet of bagels, pastries, and salads had been set up and picked over.

"The groomers just got here," Laney said. "They were hoping to start on you, but since you weren't here, they're going to start on Joe first. Do you need to shower? You should jump in right after Joe."

I didn't have too many occasions where I had to interact with Laney, but I recalled now that all of her conversations were like this. More like monologues in which she rambled on and asked multiple questions and had no interest in the answers.

"I need coffee," I said, and Laney screamed, "Where's that girl that works for Joe? Kathleen! Julia needs a coffee!"

"Her name's Catherine," I said, wincing, as everybody in the room dove for the coffee table at once.

All the stares and smiles made me feel like a self-conscious bride, and I bit my lip and glanced at the closed bedroom door, and then down at the floor.

Laney clasped my wrist. "Uh, Julia, honey, you look a little burned."

"Yeah, I can feel it on my face," I said. "I fell asleep on the beach."

"You went to the beach? Today?"

"Yeah."

"Okay, well, you should have used a little sunscreen. Half of your face is really burned."

Somebody handed me a cup of watery-looking coffee, and I made my way through the crowd and into the bedroom, where I found Joe seated on the bed with a towel wrapped around his waist. Catherine was using a hand steamer on his tux and he was watching ESPN.

"Hey," he said, glancing up at me. Then something on the television screen caused him to cry out as if he had been stabbed.

"No! That's it!" he said. "I've had it with the fucking Knicks! Let's see some fucking defense, guys!"

"I'm gonna take a shower."

"Okay, hon. Where were you? Getting your nails done?"

"I went to the beach."

"No, no, no, NO!" Joe hollered at the television, leaping to his feet and almost losing his towel.

"Joe, do you know that there's a roomful of people out there?"

"Yeah."

"Oh," I said, and I went in to the bathroom to take my shower. When I came out, Joe and Catherine had left the room and there was a petite "groomer" named Annette seated on our bed. She wore black jeans and her blond hair was pulled loosely back into a ponytail. "I'm doing your makeup," she said, standing up, and she studied my face carefully. She pointed to a stool that she had set up next to the window, and when I sat down, she pulled the heavy bedroom drapes open as far as they would go, allowing the midday sun into the dark room.

"Laney warned me about the burn. You're swelling up already," she said with a sympathetic pout. "Let's put something on that. . . ."

Annette applied creams and then a foundation to my face. I closed my eyes and felt the light, upward stroke of her delicate fingers against my tired, sun-ravaged skin, and I breathed deeply, relaxing for the first time since I left the beach.

"I shouldn't have taken the 10," she said, and I thought that I had never heard anyone speak with a voice so sweet and whimsical. "The local roads would have been the faster way." My eyes were shut tight. I heard the clean sound of a lid joining a porcelain jar. I had a sudden memory of my mother's nightly cold-cream ritual—her long fingers sweeping rapid white circles all over her face as she glanced at herself in the mirror, first from the outer corner of her left eye, then from the right. She smoothed the cream into her forehead and cheeks and down her throat before she plucked a tissue from a box next to the sink and wiped her face clean with quick swiping motions, her lips pursed, her eyes open wide. Sometimes, without taking her eyes off herself in the mirror, she managed to dip one of her fingers into the tub of cool, slippery cream and plop a dollop right onto the tip of my nose to my delighted squeals.

Did it happen once? Every night? Ever?

Once, when I was pregnant with Ruby, I opened a jar of cold cream in a Duane Reade. I had to smell it. I intended to buy it and start using it, but when I found that there was no smell, I slid it back onto the shelf next to the other cold-cream jars. I had thought there would be a fragrance, that I'd remember my mother clearly when I inhaled it, but there was nothing.

When I left Dr. James's office—was it just a week ago? It felt like years since I had slapped poor Sammy—he had shaken my hand as usual on my way out.

"I wish I could kiss you," I said, and then I had blushed and bit my lip, because I had really meant to say *hug*. Really. I meant to ask him for a hug.

He loosened his grip on my hand. "That's probably not a good idea," he said.

"I know, I know, it's not you I want. It's my father . . . blah, blah, blah."

"No, it's because it's me," he had said. Then: "Did it ever occur to you that you've created this idealized persona and assigned it to me?"

I squinted at him through my puffy eyes.

"And that these traits—honesty, reliability, genuine caring— might be what you're looking for in a partner and that you might find them someday, either in Joe or in somebody else?"

"I don't think genuine honesty will ever be one of Joe's pluses."

"People change. Act as if you believe he's capable of changing. He might surprise you."

Act as if. Two hundred dollars an hour and that's what I get.

————

I opened my eyes. Annette was removing compacts and brushes from a makeup box and I realized that I was starving. I hadn't eaten all day.

"Can I get up for a minute?" I asked.

"Sure!"

I walked to the door, but when I opened it, I saw all of Joe's people again. They were still there and Joe was with them now, in his tuxedo trousers and a wife beater, smoking a cigarette and taking a sip of coffee. Somebody had turned some music on, so I couldn't hear what Joe was saying, but I didn't need to. I could see by the glimmer in his eye and by his smirk that he was trying to be amusing, and he had a great audience—most of them were on commission and the laughs came easily, the adoration already bought and paid for. I returned to Annette's stool.

"How do you feel about eyelashes?" she said.

"Hmm," I said. I supposed that I liked eyelashes.

"I think we should do eyelashes. Definitely," she said, and I watched her remove a delicate curving wisp of black lashes from a case.

She smiled and slowly lowered her eyelids for me, then opened them. "Close," she said, and I closed my eyes, just as she had shown me. I felt the lovely tickle of lashes against my eyelid and I thought of butterfly kisses and the tender touch of my children.

"What the hell is all this grit in your hair? Is that . . . sand?"

My blowsy hairstylist's name was Lana. Annette was packing up her case and I had just nodded off for a moment.

"Yeah," I said, stretching my cramped legs out in front of my stool. "I fell asleep on the beach."

"You went all the way to the beach? This morning?"

I didn't answer. I just looked at my reflection—at the thick matte complexion, the smoky eyes with the heavy cow lashes, the bronzed cheeks and the glossed lips.

Who?

"It seems like the bonding agent on your extensions kind of melted and then hardened again with sand attached. It's like your head is covered with . . . spackle."

"Oh," I said. "Oops!" It was like I was drugged. I was almost giddy with exhaustion.

I dozed off once or twice while Lana chiseled away at my hair. At some point I dreamed that I was a Persian princess being attended by beautiful handmaids. Their faces were veiled with brilliantly colored scarves, and all I could see were their dark, almond-shaped eyes, heavily lashed. I lay on my back and they rubbed scented oils into my scalp, and instead of dressing me, they placed delicate silk panels across my body, one on top of the other. The silk swatches formed a paper-thin gown that accented my breasts and youthful, tanned skin and made my lower body look long and lean, but if I moved, the swatches would drift off to the side, revealing a lumpy, shaggy, wrinkled body underneath. I asked my handmaids to help me sew the panels together, but they couldn't understand me. They just continued laying the silk panels across my skin.

The phone rang. Lana answered it and said, "Just a minute, sweetie!" Then she handed me the phone. "It's a little one!"

"Sammy?" I said, my voice hoarse. I had to hold the phone away from my just hair-sprayed coif.

"Hi, Mommy!" he said, and I could see his sparkly face.

"Hi, baby," I said.

"Come home, Mommy," Sammy said.

"I will, baby. Tomorrow."

"Is Daddy coming home tomorrow?" he asked.

"No," I said. Almost cheerfully. "I love you, baby! Now can I speak with Ruby?"

I could hear Sammy drop the phone, and then, after a lot of calling back and forth between the two kids, I heard Ruby pick up.

"Hi, Rubes!"

"Hi, Mommy!" She missed me. She only called me Mommy when she really needed me.

"What're you up to?"

"We're watching the pre-preshow. I can't wait to see you and Daddy."

"I'll tell Daddy to say hello to you when he's on camera."

"No! Mom! Do not!"

"Okay." I laughed. "Let me speak with Catalina."

"I miss you, Mommy."

"I miss you, too, sweetness. See you tomorrow."

There was a pause, then some mumbling in Spanish and then Catalina said, "Hello, Julia!"

We spoke about Sammy and Ruby for a few moments and then Catalina said, "You sound tired, Julia."

"I am a little tired."

"Eat," she said.

"Okay."

"No, really. Eat, Julia. *Barriga llena* . . .

"*Corazón contento,*" I finished with her. "I know. Thanks, Catalina."

"We'll be watching you and Joe!"

Annette and Lana had gone. Back in New York, I'd bought a

padded bra to wear with my strapless gown, but now, wandering aimlessly around our room in a pair of Spanx (it's a sort of . . . girdle) and heels, I couldn't find it anywhere. It wasn't in my bag or in any of our drawers or in with the dirty laundry. I could go braless, of course, but the dress had been fitted with me wearing that padded, strapless bra. Without it, it was possible that my deflated breasts wouldn't even keep my dress up. And those Spanx! I couldn't breathe. I pulled them off.

Laney stuck her head into the bedroom.

"Oh, sorry, hon. I thought you'd be dressed. The car's here!"

"Okay," I said, "I'll be ready in a minute."

She left.

Then I forgot what I was looking for, so when Joe walked in a minute later, I was just staring at the ceiling.

"Why aren't you dressed? We're supposed to be on our way there now," he said, and then I remembered and explained to him about the bra. He went into the closet and threw a few things around. Then he reemerged with the bra in his hand and I smiled gratefully up at him from where I lay across the foot of the bed.

"Julia, what're you doing?"

"I'm hungry," I said. "And I'm tired."

"Well, grab some candy out of the minibar. We're late. Here, put these on," Joe said.

He helped me put on the bra and then he started examining the Spanx.

"What the . . ."

"Give me those," I said. I peeled them on.

"Okay, for some reason, the sight of you in these . . . granny pants . . . now I've got a fuckin' hard-on. Shit," Joe said. Then he said, "Didja ever do it on the way to the Golden Globes?"

"Joe . . ."

"C'mon," he said, and started kissing me, and before I knew it, we were all sprawled out across the bed.

"Wait," I said. "I think we should stop." But I was getting a little turned on, too. What would it hurt? Once more for old times' sake?

"Hmm?" Joe whispered, kissing my neck. Then I thought about Jenna.

"You know what?" I said.

"What, baby?"

"I think I'm gonna stay here."

"When?" he murmured in my ear.

"Tonight. The awards. I don't feel like going."

Joe sat up. "WHAT?"

"Actually, I might see if I can get on the red-eye. I miss the kids. And I want to see my dad."

Joe stared at me. "You're joking, right?"

"No, I really don't want to go."

"Why?"

"Why do you think?" I said.

"Listen, Julia . . ."

I stood up and reached for the gown, which was draped across the bed. I wanted to be sure that it went back in the same condition it came in. I didn't want to have to pay for it. Then I wondered if the Vera Wang people would make me buy it since I had reneged on our agreement that I'd wear it on national TV.

"Julia . . . listen. Listen to me," Joe said.

I started to gather up the fabric.

"Look, I was going to tell you. I . . . just wanted to figure out how we could discuss this. We need to talk . . . about things. I haven't been as honest as I could have been and I hate myself for it. . . ."

I folded the silk panels into one another.

Joe whispered, "Please, Julia. Look at me."

After a moment I peered through my heavy lashes into those puppy-dog eyes. Ugh, he was tearing up. Crying is like yawning, easily faked by some but also hopelessly contagious, so I grabbed a tissue from the bedside table and dabbed like crazy. Any moisture on those lashes would be a disaster—I imagined a tar-black tsunami crashing down my cheeks and over the gown, false-eyelash flotsam everywhere. So in order not to cry, I thought of one of my favorite memories: a video we have of baby Ruby running down a hill in Ireland. It begins with her at the top, the tall grasses tickling her chubby thighs. She performs her adorable new wave for the camera, her fat hand flopping back and forth on the end of her wrist, and then she starts to gambol down the hill toward us.

"Careful, Ruby. Careful," is my off-camera warning, but on she comes, running now, and as she gains momentum with the steep decline of the hill and her little legs start to pump faster and faster, we realize that she's wide-eyed and panicked. She can't stop. The video becomes shaky and blurry here because Joe, who is working the camera, is panicking, too. "Whoa, slow down, Ruby, Jesus Christ . . . SLOW DOWN!" he says, but she has no choice but to ride those runaway legs all the way to the bottom of the hill, where she finally tumbles over, pausing for a moment to assess the damage, then bursting into tears.

She was fine, just scared. Now whenever we watch the video, Ruby laughs until she cries every time. We all do.

"You're the one I love. You're the first woman I ever really loved and you'll be the last, Julia. I swear. She was an extra. She was always hanging around the set. Always paying all this attention to me. One night we got drunk . . . it was after the wrap party . . ."

I didn't go to the wrap party at the end of last season. Those parties are like a company picnic—only fun for the employees, really. And Ruby had something going on that night, somebody's bat mitzvah, and I had wanted to stay home to help her get ready. Joe went alone. I forced myself to think again about Ruby running down that hill. It really is impossible not to laugh when you see that video, because in its brief course lie all the elements of a great drama. The expectant joy on her face as she begins her spirited descent, then the dawning realization that she doesn't yet have the skills necessary to control the situation. The moments of unbridled panic—little white shoes a bionic blur—Joe bellowing, me screaming, and then . . . it's over. The child is in one piece.

"Change is difficult but not impossible," Dr. James said to me once. It's probably what he would say to me now, if he were here.

"Don't be a crybaby," is what my father would have said.

"Where's Mom?" I imagined Ruby asking Catalina when they saw Joe on TV later, and I thought of Catalina crossing herself, imagining the worst.

"Okay, Joe," I said. "I'll go. Let's just go to the show. But let's not talk about the rest of it tonight."

"The rest of what?"

"The details."

"Details? What— Are you thinking of leaving? We have to talk about this, I want to explain. . . ."

"Explain, then."

"Julia. We need time. To talk. Stay tomorrow, let's talk in the morning. . . ."

"How much time does it take to tell the truth?" I asked. "It's quick. I'm the one who planted those gay rumors about you on the Internet! See? See how quick that is?"

Joe laughed nervously. "Right," he said. Then he said, "You just made that up, right?"

"Let's just go to the show so the kids don't think something happened. Then I'm taking the first flight to New York in the morning. I'm gonna pick up the kids and drive to Bedford. Today's my dad's birthday. I want to go see him."

There was a loud knock on the door. "It's getting really late, kids. You do *not* want to be walking down the red carpet behind Brad and Angelina!"

"Okay! Okay!" Joe shouted. Then he said, "Julia, let's not fuck everything up over this. . . ."

"I'm not talking to you about it now," I said quietly. "Should I put the dress on or not?"

"Yes," Joe said. Then he said, "Please tell me you were joking about the Internet thing. . . ."

"No. C'mon, let's go, it's late."

"Okay . . . so no, you won't tell me you were joking, or no you weren't joking?"

"Believe whatever you want," I said. "Let's go."

And so we went to the Golden Globes, Joe and me. We really were late, and the line of limos and Town Cars leading to the Beverly Hilton seemed to stretch for miles. We were in the backseat of the Town Car this time. We knew not to drive it to an event like this ourselves. We had a driver and a publicist sitting next to him, madly barking at some assistant on her BlackBerry. We had two kids, two cars, a Manhattan apartment, and a beach house in Amagansett. We had stocks and mutual funds, hard cash, liquid assets, and various trusts. We rode in silence. When we arrived at the Beverly Hilton, Joe was on the right side. He knew to get out first, and the crowd showed its appreciation with a triumphant roar. If you saw us on one of the preshows, you might have thought, *There's Joe Ferraro. That must be his wife. Look how she holds his arm so lovingly, how she gazes up at him. . . .*

Because I did hold on to Joe's arm that night on the red carpet. I actually clung to it during the long series of interviews, the California sun scorching into me, melting me beneath my borrowed finery. Cameras were flashing and people were nudging us from all directions. I feared that if I let go, I would lose him forever to the crowd and I would be forced to make my way back, upstream, through the pressing throngs to where our empty car awaited. I clutched his tuxedoed arm—the same strong arm that had held me so tight when we made love, that I had seized like a vise during childbirth, that had cradled our babies so tenderly, their plump bodies fitting perfectly into its crook. We followed Laney through the thick, antsy flock of celebrities, stepping over the long trains of flighty young starlets and bumping up against the gentle giants— great legends of television and film who smiled patiently and waited their turn to be interviewed. We stopped and smiled and posed for photographers and later, after Joe won, we had to go to the outdoor press area, where Joe posed again and again with his gleaming Golden Globe award held triumphantly above his head. Somebody asked us to kiss. For the cameras. And of course we did. Joe pulled me into his arms and we kissed giddily, and the cameras shot us just like that.

Joe and me kissing, the trophy pressed into my back.

The photo ended up in *People*. It looked like we were madly in love again, like we were starting anew.

"What's it like being married to Mitch Hollister?" a reporter called out to us.

I never know what to say in situations like that, so I mumbled, blushing and stammering like an idiot, "He's just . . . Joe to me . . . I guess."

"Yup, he's a Joe, all right," my dad would have said if he was there.

The next award recipient, a shaken and hysterical best actress, was led onto the platform and Joe's moment was over. We stepped out of the bright gaze of the hundreds of cameras and into the blackness of the night. I was still holding Joe's arm and he pulled me close, and we walked tentatively together like that, like two uncertain children, taking one little step and then the next.

"Watch it," Joe said, helping me lift the train of my dress. "Watch your step."

"Okay," I said, holding his arm tight. "Okay."

And we walked on like that a little longer. We were being careful. It was so dark. Phantom auras of flashing lights still swam before us, so we went along slowly, helping each other find the way, one step . . . and then the next . . . until our eyes grew accustomed to the dark.

Acknowledgments

Many thanks to Sally Kim, my gifted editor; to all the great people at Shaye Areheart Books; and to the smart Davids: Black and Larabelle at the David Black Literary Agency. Also to my friends Dani Shapiro and Heather King for their generous advice, wisdom, and support. Thank you to my beloved sister, Meg Seminara, and my sainted mother, Judy Howe, who read the book and said only nice things about it. Warmest thanks to another smart David, who suggested I write something, and finally, my deepest love and gratitude to Denis, Jack, and Devin for bearing with me while I did.